SAPHYRE SNOW

MARCIA LYNN McCLURE

Copyright ©2012
Saphyre Snow by Marcia Lynn McClure
www.marcialynnmcclure.com

Published by Distractions Ink
P.O. Box 15971
Rio Rancho, NM 87174

Published by Distractions Ink
©Copyright 2006, 2009, 2012 by M. Meyers
A.K.A. Marcia Lynn McClure
Cover Photography by
©Konradbak and ©Danielkrol | Dreamstime.com
Cover Design and Interior Graphics by
Sheri Brady | MightyPhoenixDesignStudio.com

2nd Printed Edition: February 2012

All character names and personalities in this work of fiction are entirely fictional,
created solely in the imagination of the author.
Any resemblance to any person living or dead is coincidental.

McClure, Marcia Lynn, 1965—
Saphyre Snow: a novel/by Marcia Lynn McClure.

ISBN: 978-0-9852740-7-8

Library of Congress Control Number: 2012931785

Printed in the United States of America

To Dewey and Peggy,

My beloved mother-in-law
and cherished father-in-law…
What adventures we had with Saphyre Snow, did we not?
Thank you for the gift of your love and support
and most especially for bringing such an astonishingly wonderful
man into the world…

for he has been the pure making of my happiness!

PROLOGUE—
SAPHYRE SNOW

The cool frosted moonlight of early winter lent a beautiful and blue shimmer to the falling snow. There were those who had witnessed the rare and miraculous event before—the soft and quiet splendor of indigo-laced frost drifting from a clear sky, as if the diamonded stars in the heavens sprinkled small, lustrous sapphires from their fingers to bejewel all the still earth. Indeed it seemed the soft blue moonlight and indigo frost whispered to the woods and meadows—breathed of a secret—a secret something of extraordinary worth. All who beheld this pageant of nature's artistry believed it to be a herald of benevolence from above—a remembrance that moments of peaceful respite were of far more merit than wealth. All who lingered in the blue moonlight, all who felt the cool radiance of the sapphire frost sweet upon their faces, knew respite and hope. Thus, this quiet, beautiful rarity of occurrence—the serenity borne of the blue light and frost—became known among the people of the Kingdom of Graces as the sapphire snow.

Indeed, the sapphire snow was uncommon. No man could call down from the heavens a cool blue moonlight and downy flakes of frost. Even the king of the kingdom could not summon the mystical sapphire snow. Thus, as is often the way with rare events, it was on one of these uncommon evenings—an evening of beauty and peaceful wonder, of blue moonlight and indigo frost—that a young mother gave birth to an uncommon child. On this evening of serene enchantment—of blue frost and indigo moonlight mingling to blanket the earth with beauty—the princess Saphyre Snow was birthed.

All those living in the Kingdom of Graces wept with happiness; each subject, common or noble, rejoiced when King Jordan announced the birth of his granddaughter. A good king, beloved of his people, King Jordan was resplendent with merriment himself at the birth. The lovely Queen Penelope was at the king's side when he himself heralded the coming of the princess Saphyre Snow. The babe's father, Prince Michael—only son of King Jordan and Queen Penelope—stood at the casement with his king father and queen mother as the king offered proclamation to the people of the Kingdom of Graces of the birth of a new royal. Prince Michael's graceful and beauteous young wife, the Princess Felice, listened as all the kingdom cheered their joy at her daughter's coming. Yes, the birth of Saphyre Snow was the most blessed event in the kingdom—a kingdom beloved by her king and queen, who were loved their subjects in return.

The father of Saphyre Snow, Prince Michael, was sole heir to the throne of the kingdom. A good and handsome prince beloved by all his father's subjects, Prince Michael owned much honor. He had commanded legions, warriored well in battled, and owned titles for doing so. Still, perhaps most wondrous of all, Michael had won the heart and hand of the Princess Felice of Avaron.

Hair as dark as midnight and eyes as violet as the velvet curtains of twilight, Felice of Avaron was an exquisite beauty, both of body and of spirit. The daughter of a king and queen in a far-off land, Princess Felice had been greatly sought after. Many men had battled for a mere chance at gaining her favour. Yet Felice of Avaron was bred of a long lineage of honor—and of true love. Descended from a mighty line of a great kings and noble queens, Felice of Avaron did not give token of favour in light manner. Nevertheless, upon first sight of Prince Michael of the Kingdom of Graces, the Princess Felice of Avaron had known at once where her heart would ever remain.

Thus, Prince Michael of the Kingdom of Graces gave full his heart to she who filled it, and a betrothal followed forthwith.

On their wedding day, the Princess Felice gifted her young husband a token—a favour of such profound worth that all who witnessed the giving of the gift knew the heart of the beautiful Princess Felice would never waver. The favored gift was a sword, forged long ago, generations before, by a master craftsman. The sword was named the Crimson Frost and had been forged in honor of a great knight who had once lived and walked the earth in such glory and honor as to birth eternal legend—a knight who had risen to king, a king who had sired progeny, progeny from whence descended Princess Felice and the babe princess, Saphyre Snow.

Thus, though Prince Michael was handsome, it was every subject of the Kingdom of Graces hoped that the babe, Princess Saphyre, might grow to be as beautiful as her mother—that the strength and honor of the royal family might mingle with the legendary power and beauty of the Princess Felice's ancestors to craft as rare a princess as was rare the miracle of nature's artistry for which she had been named. It was not long before the king and queen, Prince Michael and Princess Felice, and all the subjects of the Kingdom of Graces began to see that the wee princess would indeed inherit her mother's beauty. As Saphyre grew, it was certain to all who looked upon her that she mirrored her mother's beautiful image and countenance. Hair as black as silken ebony, skin as soft and as fair as porcelain, and lips as sweet and as red as any ripe cherry or fragrant rose were those of Saphyre Snow—an immeasurable and truly ethereal beauty. Yet perhaps the most striking feature of the Princess Saphyre was the color of her eyes—as deep and as bright a blue as any sapphire on earth, with such a spark of life in them as to enchant any who might own the blessing of her gaze.

Further, it was certain to all who knew her that her mother's strong ancestry had fared well in her blood. The child Saphyre Snow owned a rare gift of empathy and compassion. An obedient child, she was yet strong of will and did not linger in despair. All who looked upon her admired her, all who spoke with her felt joy, and all who were privy to her company in any manner loved her.

Thus the young princess grew in love and happiness, cherished by all her family and every soul in the Kingdom of Graces. Beautiful and happy and safe lived the princess Saphyre Snow—for a time.

Seven Souls

Saphyre paused, leaning against a strong pine for support. The crisp, spiced scent of the forest—of tree bark and leaf litter blanketing the ground—did little to soothe her. Brushing a strand of ebony hair from her tear-stained face, the princess attempted to catch her breath before pressing on. Her bosom ached from breathing the cold night air. She looked to her arm—to the wound there administered by a mean-spirited holly branch she had intruded upon while running through the wood. The lesion, though not profound in size and no longer bleeding in profusion, yet stung painfully. Saphyre winced and determined to ignore the discomfort. She was cold and frightened and alone, without any conception of how she should proceed. No time had been allowed her—no time to consider or plan. She had known only the necessity of escape, and she had fled. And she must yet elude—run—keep far from what lay behind her—pray it was not yet following.

Crumpling to her knees, full careless of the moist pine needles, leaves, and other forest spoils littering the wooded ground, Saphyre buried her face in her hands and bitterly wept. How could such things be? How could it all have come to such a dreadful spectacle? She thought of her mother and wished with all her heart she had not died. The queen had passed from earthly life the year previous, and oh, how Saphyre missed her! How she missed her mother's loving embrace, her wise counsel, her beautiful smile. Saphyre shook her head, brushing the tears of pain and fear and frustration from her cheeks and chin. Her mother had died, and her father had altered entirely. He was so thoroughly changed—so very altered in countenance. Her father's wits had been complete about him before her mother's death. Everything and everyone—the whole of the kingdom—had been happy and safe. It seemed to Saphyre the Kingdom of Graces and all its subjects had begun to weaken as a whole. Upon the death of the beloved Queen Felice, the kingdom began to transform, taking upon itself a dark countenance—a countenance in similitude to the one it had begun to exhibit shortly after the death of Saphyre's grandmother years previous. In this, even King Michael had changed. Gone was the tender, loving father Saphyre had known. In his place there lingered a stranger—one who frightened Saphyre, struck her with feelings of uncertainty and vulnerability. Thus, how desperately Saphyre missed her mother now. How desperately she longed for the sense of safety and hope her mother had ever exuded.

Saphyre raised her head, closed her eyes, and listened. Sometimes, if she endeavored with great determination, she imagined she could almost hear her mother's voice on the evening breeze—nearly feel the soothing touch of her gentle hand. Yet the caution-call of a black crow in a nearby tree startled Saphyre. There was not time to linger in recollection or regret, for an ominous evil yet pursued the princess Saphyre Snow—fairly nipped at her heels.

Leaping to her feet, Saphyre ran—fled further into the depths of the forest—for darkness was fast falling. Saphyre knew she could not endure another night in the frigid forest uncovered and unprotected from the elements—and anything else choosing to prey upon her. Autumn threatened to come early to the Kingdom of Graces and all the forest surrounding. Saphyre knew this night would be colder and crueler even than the night before. Near frantic, she looked about for a cave, a tree with a drooping branch, anything that might provide her shelter for the night. Yet there was nothing, and so she pushed onward—onward until she thought her feet could carry her no further—onward until she could see nothing through the dense forest now blocking the moon's light. The night was cold—near frigid. Saphyre's arms and legs burned with weariness borne of unfamiliar striving. Such a weariness was upon her as to cause her to wonder if she might not simply drop in her own footsteps.

Then, of a sudden, a large and weathered structure—veiled in night's shadows—loomed before her. It seemed a ruin of some sort—still, a ruin with remnant walls. And even remnant walls would provide some shelter. She wondered for a moment what other creatures had considered the same—perhaps taken up residence within. The ruin broke the canopy of tall trees, and by the moonlight, Saphyre could see it looked to be the vestige of an old castle keep. Saphyre then remembered. As a child, she had heard tales of a once great castle of the Kingdom of Graces. It was said the castle was lost—destroyed by an ancient war battled generations before. She wondered whether this ruined keep was perhaps all that remained of the place—the legendary castle of which stories were now rarely told. Saphyre frowned as she gazed at the moss-covered stones and a weathered, yet quite solid, oaken door. She fancied the keep must once have been a great stronghold indeed, for anything that could cling so long to pure existence must surely have known strength beyond understanding. Reaching out, Saphyre placed a hand against its mossy outer wall. She was assured then—it was indeed real. She had not fallen asleep, exhausted from two days of running aimlessly, to find herself dreaming. The musty velvet moss grew thick on the outer wall, further testament of a vastly aged edifice.

Through an opening in one damaged stone wall, Saphyre tentatively entered the ancient keep. Without the forest of trees to impair, blessed moonlight beamed in through the near vanishing ceiling and roof. A ceiling there was, yet once massive beams were now rotted, and moonlight streamed through great holes and cracks. Saphyre closed her eyes, thankful for the full moon, for it gave her enough light to look about. Several doves startled as she stepped further into the keep. Saphyre gasped as they took flight, escaping through the damaged roof. She stood quite still as her gaze fell to a fire pit in the center of the room. Dying embers there breathed more warmth than Saphyre had felt in two days, and though the prickle of the hair at her neck, the whispered warning in her heart, admonished caution, she could not resist moving nearer, dropping to her knees and rubbing her hands over the still-glowing cinders.

Saphyre glanced about her once more, wondering who had built the fire, knowing it must have burned hot and bright only hours before. Still, her overwhelming weariness and need for warmth numbed her sense of caution, and she remained kneeling before the fire, warming herself as best she could. She mused that whoever had built the fire had long since taken his leave. Surely it was safe to linger for a few moments more, to perhaps lie down on one of the nearby logs and rest a moment—only a moment. It was all she was in need of—only a few moments of respite. Would not it be safe to merely close her eyes—for just a moment?

No sooner had Saphyre closed her eyes, however, than she began to dream—to dream of the nightmare her life had become. Her dreams were disordered—lovely visions of her mother, followed closely by ghastly ones of her mother's death—moments spent in the safety of her father's arms, mingled with visions of her father, the king, battling perplexity, struggling to maintain the strength of his mind. Visions of her grandfather King Jordan were in her dreams—of the great man he had once been—of the love she had once known for him. Vile visions of her step-grandmother intruded—her step-grandmother, Queen Carmen—of her great beauty coupled with obsessive vanity. Even visions of Kornelius were somehow provoked—of handsome Prince Kornelius, the subject of every young woman's dreams.

Every young woman in the kingdom would faint away with the bliss at having caught Kornelius's eye. Yet not Saphyre. Kornelius was vastly handsome, strong, and perfect in manner—a bit too perfect in Saphyre's opinion. There was nothing unique about his perfectly pressed, perfectly flawless attire, nothing overly masculine in his perfect posture and perfect behavior. Yes, he was perfectly comely—tall, broad-shouldered, square-jawed, with the lightest fair hair and darkest green eyes. Still, he did not appeal to Saphyre's heart, and she was sickened as she wandered through her discomfited dreams that Kornelius should be the suitor her father had chosen for her.

Saphyre next dreamt she was standing in a forest, sunlight radiating warm and happy. Kornelius stood before her, beckoning her to come to him. But Saphyre did not wish to go to him and instead turned to find herself staring into the gaunt, angular face of the huntsman! He stood before her dressed in the green of a huntsman's cloak, his eyes narrowed and his appearance being overall that of a roughened man to meddle not with. Oh, the expression he wore spoke of concern—guilt, fear, and self-loathing. But the knife in his hand—the knife stained and dripping with blood—told of his true intent. The fact he had released Saphyre—shouted at her to run, to run for her life and never to return to the kingdom and father she loved so—his freeing her did not atone for his initial intention.

In her dreams, Saphyre turned back toward Kornelius, but he was gone. In his place was only the darkness of the forest. The trees themselves seemed to threaten harm. Yet there was no choice given the princess Saphyre Snow—no choice but to run—to enfold herself in the uncaring embrace of wooded darkness.

In her dreams, the huntsman continued to shout at her as she ran—shout at her as he truly had. "Run, Princess! Run away!" he called. "Never to return! For returning will find you slaughtered like an unsuspecting deer, your heart cut out, and the beasts of the forests feasting on your flesh! Run!"

Saphyre gasped, her heart pounding with remembered fear. She sat up, screaming at the first sight her waking eyes beheld! At first, she thought she was yet dreaming, still lost in the nightmare with the huntsman. Quickly, however, she realized she was full awake—though another nightmare was upon her then. There, crouching before her, was a man—at least a thing that had once been a man. The beast before her glared at her through blue eyes—chilling blue eyes. Yet it was not his eyes that held captive Saphyre's attention. It was not his eyes that caused her to cry out in terror. Rather it was the immense deformity on his face. The blue-eyed man glaring at her owned only hollows where his nose should have been—two large, gaping hollows surrounded by remnants of flesh! She noted the man must once have owned a nose, for the majority of the bridge of it indeed remained. Still, the flesh around his nostrils was gone, leaving the two open hollows. It was pure terrifying—to awaken from a nightmare to behold such a dreadful face.

Saphyre covered her mouth with one hand to keep from screaming once more.

"Hush, child," a voice said—but not the noseless man's, for his lips did not move as he continued to stare at her.

Saphyre gasped as, of a sudden, another face joined the one in front of her. This man was not so terrifying in his appearance, yet there was something different about him as well. "Hush, child. No-Nose would not harm a flea."

Weakened and frightened as she was, Saphyre managed to rise to her feet, stumbling backward. The man without a nose rose also, and Saphyre was further frightened, for his height was so great as to only further intimidate. It was only then she noticed the other man stood his full height already—but several inches shorter than herself. She looked from one man to the other, unable to fathom what nightmare she had awakened from desperate dreams to find.

"I-I...I..." she stammered, near petrified with fear.

"What finds you here, miss?" another man said, coming to stand next to the shorter man—obviously his brother. This man was also smaller than most and looked the image of the first small man.

Saphyre began to tremble most wildly, uncertain as to what she must say, what she must do. Instinct led her to take one step backward—away from the man with the maimed face—away from the two unusually small men.

"Do not be afraid, miss," the first small man said. "We will not harm you."

Yet Saphyre was not so simple convinced—for the past two days had taught her the truth of treachery and ill-intention. She knew now there was no wisdom in trusting some she knew, let alone strangers—in particular strangers who were men.

Her heart whispered: the time had come to flee once more, and she turned to run. But a fourth man, now standing directly before her, took hold her arms and stayed her. It was then the princess Saphyre Snow owned great humility, for of a sudden she knew she had not escaped the huntsman. The huntsman had freed her; he had willed her to run—to escape. She sensed this man now holding her arms in such brutal grip did not own the same mercy of the huntsman.

"What do you want here?" the man growled.

Fear rendered Saphyre breathless as she looked up into his fiery eyes. They seemed violet—red or brown. She could not tell which, but in their glaring there was anger—fury. Strong determination set his jaw, and by the vise grip of his hands, Saphyre knew she was, once again, as helpless as a fox in the huntsman's snare.

"Why are you here?" the man growled again.

Saphyre shook her head and stammered, "I-I want nothing. I only entered here to find shelter from the night. I..."

"Rogan!" a new voice from the darkness growled. "With ease, Rogan. With ease."

Saphyre began to weep when the man's eyes narrowed as he looked at her. He was loath to find her in the keep—loath to look at her. This she knew from the fire in his eyes, from the tight set of his clenched jaw.

"What do you want here, girl?" he asked again, though Saphyre felt his grip lessen at her arms.

"I...have told the truth of it," she said. "I was seeking shelter from...from the forest." Saphyre was certain the brutal man did not hold her word as truth. Still, for whatever reason, he released her, slight pushing her backward as he unhanded her.

"How came you to be this far in the woods?" the man called Rogan asked. "This ruin is deep in the forest...half a day's ride from the edge of it."

"Two days' walk," Saphyre whispered.

"Then how came you here? Are you lost?" The man quick glanced over his shoulder. "Are you alone?"

Saphyre trembled with trepidation. How should she answer? Should she confess—answer him full truthfully—that she was alone?

11

Should he know no guard was with her, no protection, she would be entirely at his mercy and that of his counterparts. Yet should she deceive—say she was in company of others—his vexation may be kindled to rage. Then might he plunge a dagger into her bosom rather than wait for her comrades to arrive and strike battle against him and his comrades?

"He has asked you a question, wench!" Another man stepped from the shadows. This man was not as immense as the man before her, nor as tall as the noseless man behind her, neither was he small as the two men now standing at either side of her. His hair was fair, and the fire flaming in his eyes spoke of his intense anger—anger at her intrusion.

Her decision in answering made—to speak the truth and hope for a venue of escape—she answered, "I am...alone, and...and I am lost."

"Well, you have stumbled into the wrong keep this night, girl!" shouted yet another man. Dark-haired and large, this man stepped from the shadows.

Saphyre wondered how many more lurked unseen.

"It is back into the forest with you!" he growled. Taking hold of her arm, he began pulling her toward the opening in the old stone wall.

"Leave her be, Edmund," another man ordered, stepping from one dark corner and into the moonlight.

Saphyre's trembling was so powerful as to cause her pain! Fearful of another attacker, she watched as the man limped toward her. He appeared older than the others—older and less capable of causing harm. She soon saw he too bore physical ailment. A large hump to one side of his back caused him to appear stooped—to move with less comfort than other men would. "Cannot you see she is frightened of you...of us all?"

"Heed not Belmiro, Edmund! Throw her to the wolves!" the fair-haired man shouted.

"You would not have her thrown to the wolves any more than the rest of us, Salomonè!" one of the small men said.

12

Saphyre did not draw breath as the small man took hold her hand. He did not move to harm her, however. Rather he smiled at her, pressing her hand between his own, offering comfort. Saphyre felt fresh tears on her cheeks—tears of fear, yes, but also tears of hope. Weeping for the small man's kindness, she attempted to return his smile.

"I am Marcellus," the man said to her. "And that," he continued, pointing to the other small man, "is my brother, Thaddeus."

"I-I am honored," Saphyre stammered.

"Marcellus and I are twin brothers, miss," Thaddeus said as he came toward her. "Each of us may be somewhat ill-matched for this world…but well-matched as brothers."

"Except for our eyes," Marcellus said. "For I've one blue eye—the right one—and one green."

"And I've one green eye and one blue…the left," Thaddeus interrupted.

"I am pleased to meet you both," Saphyre said, brushing tears from her cheeks.

"Do not offer to us such pretense of allegiance, miss," the fair-haired man said. "You're no more pleased to meet us than we are to find you here!"

"That is Salomonè," Marcellus said. "He is the ill-tempered one."

"Edmund is the one who wanted to throw you out of the keep," Thaddeus explained, smiling.

Saphyre was astonished by the accepting natures of Marcellus and Thaddeus. She was likewise soothed somewhat, for her soul spoke to her concerning them. Neither of the small men meant to harm her.

"And Belmiro is the one who saved you. Though Rogan is our leader and would never have let them throw you to the wolves…no matter what he would prefer you to think," Marcellus said.

Saphyre glanced up at the brutal man—the leader—the one called Rogan. He continued to stare at her, fiery eyes narrowed, his frown thick with distrust.

"And No-Nose is the one who frightened you most, I think," Marcellus said.

"A pleasant change for Marcellus and me," Thaddeus added. "It is usually we who cause strangers the most discomfort."

The thought lingered in Saphyre's mind—that these two small men were the only two of the seven men who had attempted to soothe her, however in the least effective the soothing was.

"I am sorry I frightened you, miss," the noseless man said. "I am afraid I am a frightful beast to look upon."

Saphyre's weeping lessened as she looked to him. Something in this man's voice comforted her—gave her a feeling of familiarity and warmth. In truth, save his lack of nose, his countenance in whole put her much in mind of her father.

"I was enduring a nightmare when you woke me, sir," Saphyre told him. "It was that which frightened me."

The noseless man scratched the long whiskers at his chin and smiled. "I am fond of this one already. She is a liar."

"A beautiful liar," the crooked man said, smiling at her.

"Beauty is often the mask worn of harm," Rogan said, striding toward Saphyre and taking her chin in hand. He turned her face toward the moonlight, studying her for a moment, a deep frown creasing his brow. Then he took hold of her shoulders and turned her away from him. Saphyre gasped as she felt his hands at her waist, her ribs, her back, and her hips. Slowly, his hands traveled over her hips—down the outside of her legs. Her fearful trembling increased, for she could only guess at the vile intent of his measures.

"She hides no weapon I can find," Rogan grumbled.

"Or *feel*…for that matter," the noseless man chuckled.

"Quit fawning over the girl like a newborn kitten," Rogan ordered. "She is not yet to be trusted." Frowning, he growled, "Build us a new fire, Edmund. The girl is yet chilled."

Saphyre noted the manner in which Edmund glared at Rogan. Still, Edmund nodded and went about the task.

"You will sit by the fire and warm yourself for a time," Rogan told Saphyre. "We will feed you, and once you are warm and fed… you will tell us why you are here. Then we will decide what is to be done with you."

"I mean no harm to you, sir," Saphyre said.

Rogan's eyes narrowed. "Do you believe me—a roughened man you have never before set eyes on—do you believe me when I say that I mean no harm to you?"

Saphyre glanced away, discomfited by the truth of his implication.

"Then do not expect that I should believe you...one whom I have never before laid eyes upon."

"Of course," Saphyre quietly responded, still trembling.

"I will see to her meal," Marcellus offered.

"Very well," Rogan agreed. "But do not let her sleep until I have returned."

Saphyre near laughed aloud. Sleep? In such circumstances?

Still, after she had sat before the warm fire and enjoyed a simple meal of roast pheasant and broth, Saphyre indeed began to feel weary once more. Her eyes were heavy, her tortured mind tired.

Yet once Rogan had returned, she sat again near petrified with renewed apprehension. Surely if he, or any one of the men, meant her harm, harm would have come already. Oddly—for the rough and frightening look of them all and even for her knowledge of what these types of men usually did to unsuspecting women—Saphyre's fear began to soften as she watched the group of disheveled vagabonds. Sitting around the fire pit, they conversed in low voices.

Saphyre studied them—each one—as they sat in conversation. Indisputably, the one called No-Nose was the most disturbing to look upon. He was of an unusual height, broad-shouldered, his beard the least groomed of any in the group. Yet Saphyre determined that if one could look beyond the morbidly distorted area where an ordinary nose might once have been—if one could perhaps ignore the large, gaping hollows serving as nostrils—the man's eyes were comely. The brightest of blues, the eyes of the man known as No-Nose, shaded by thick, dark lashes, were in truth quite striking. Still the unkempt beard and mangled flesh where his nose would have been were quite disturbing, and Saphyre turned her attention to the next man.

This man, Salomonè, was shorter than No-Nose. His fair hair and darker beard were well groomed. Saphyre wondered at what sort of pride or vanity would motivate a man in such dismal circumstance to own such care in his appearance. His hair was combed and clean looking, his teeth quite a set of white pearls. He displayed no obvious ailments of body or mind, and Saphyre wondered—with such a comely appearance, what reasons had Salomonè for lingering in such feral company?

To the left of Salomonè sat the two little dark-haired men. She had heard men of such unusual appearance dubbed dwarves—men much smaller in stature than most, with an ethereal sort of appearance about them, as if they were a kind of magical being, above mere humanity. Saphyre felt a slight smile tug at the corners of her mouth as she watched these two near indistinguishable fellows, for they were smiling and whispering to one another as if they shared the most delightful secret. Marcellus and Thaddeus were they. Saphyre had felt drawn to them near instantly. She frowned a moment, trying to remember which had told her of their different colored eyes—which man had a blue right eye and which a blue left.

"Blue right eye," the man sitting directly next to Salomonè mouthed to her, "Marcellus." He nodded, and she blushed, embarrassed at having been caught staring. She feared Marcellus thought she stared because of his unique stature and appearance, when in fact she had merely been trying to determine what his name was. Still, perhaps he did know—for had he not offered his name to her? In the depths of her soul, Saphyre felt that Thaddeus and Marcellus could be trusted.

Turning her attention to the man seated next to Thaddeus, she frowned. Edmund. This man did not appear honorable. Had not he nearly put her out of the keep? Had not he made it plain he owned no sympathy for her? Nearly the most disheveled of them all, this Edmund did not seem to be sharing conversation in like manner as the others. Rather he seemed angry—absorbed in his own thoughts. He sat frowning, hatefully staring into the fire, only grumbling a response when Thaddeus smiled at him, prodding him to involvement a bit with one elbow. Thaddeus shrugged his shoulders and returned his attention to his brother. *No,* Saphyre thought. The man called Edmund was not to be trusted.

The poor soul with the hump and crooked back was next. Saphyre was saddened as she gazed upon his pitiful rags. His breeches fit well enough, but it looked as if he had taken three or four different tunics and somehow awkwardly sewn them together in attempt at making a covering for his upper body. She frowned, and her heart ached as she noted the spare sleeve hanging at the back of the garment. It could be neither warm nor comfortable, and she felt miserable imagining the hardship this man must have endured throughout his undoubtedly unhappy life. Further, he had championed her in a manner. She felt grateful to him for it.

Yet unable to endure the distressing feelings washing over her as she studied Belmiro, Saphyre turned her attention at last to he who was the leader of the band of vagabond peasants—Rogan. It was a rather noble-sounding name for a vagrant. Further, he was the only one of the men not hiding behind a heavy growth of face hair. He was by no means clean-shaven, but she reasoned it had not been more than a week since he had last shed himself of whiskers. This man was as disturbingly handsome as he was intimidating. Obviously the most unsettled at her presence, she sensed he was somehow likewise the most protective. Was it merely because men will emulate the actions of their leader that he had shielded her? Or was there hiding in him some spark of chivalry—some residue of good manners dormant beneath his gloomy, angry exterior?

As she studied him, she found Rogan intrigued her much more, and in a far different manner, than did any of the others. His hair and whisker stubble were black as night, his eyes a strange color—violet and crimson swirled together in some sort of brown to create an extraordinary, unearthly hue. His gaze, through such mesmerizing eyes, captured its prey, holding it unmoving and fearful. The memory of it caused Saphyre to fear him even when he was not looking full at her. His jaw was square, a princely cleft in a noble chin, and he was tall, broad-shouldered, exuding strength of body and mind. Saphyre marveled at his comely features and powerful form. *No doubt a criminal,* Saphyre thought, *but a handsome one all the same.* Still, Saphyre knew there would be wisdom in staying from Rogan's path. He was a man to be wary of. As he himself had said, beauty was often the mask of harm. No. Perhaps Rogan was the leader—Saphyre's defender in a manner—yet she would not assume his character were as pretty as his face.

Thus, the princess Saphyre Snow sat amongst seven men who were strange to her—strange to all the world, by the look of them. Seven men who could have as easy beaten, violated, and killed her as to have shared their shelter, fire, and sustenance. These were seven souls—seven souls visibly weathered and plagued. Of a sudden, Saphyre sensed a kinship to the strangers before her—for had she not been driven from familiar life? Was she not now also adrift in a world ruled by fear and uncertainty?

ℐNNOCENCE ℒOST

The fire burned hot and red in the pit, and Saphyre's eyes again began to long for the sweet respite of slumber. Still, she dared not close them for a moment in the presence of these seven strangers, and so it was she continued to study the men—wonder of their lives before the keep—and their secrets. It was certain they owned secrets, for did not she? All human beings owned secrets—some more than others perhaps, but all owned them. Thus, she sat in contemplation. What secrets would drive men to such solitude?

"Have you sorted us all out then?" Rogan unexpected asked. His gaze bore down upon her like the red heat of the sun. "Have you sorted the gentlemen from the miscreants? Determined who will serve as your lover and who will be your footman?"

Saphyre gasped, astonished at his insinuation of her choosing one of them for a lover. All the men chuckled—though Rogan only slightly grinned.

Saphyre silently scolded herself as the thought traveled through her tired mind—*You, Rogan, would most certainly be sorted in as my lover*. She shook her head, attempting to dispel the notion of such a man as Rogan being her lover. Yet as she considered him in contrast of Kornelius's perfect manner—the perfumed scent about him—she dared to steal another glance at the disturbingly handsome

19

vagabond. Strangely, her fear subsided for a moment as she looked at him. Even more extraordinary was the manner in which her heart's beat increased of a sudden—and not from fright.

"Oh, leave her be, Rogan," No-Nose said, though still smiling. "You will drop her dead with fear…and then what will we do with her?"

"We will do with her what we did with the last one," Rogan said, his smile fading, his gaze returning to the fire before him. "We shall eat her."

Saphyre's eyes widened, and she leapt to her feet. The men burst into laughter, obviously amused by Saphyre's response to their leader's taunting. Saphyre felt her hand go to her throat and took several steps back as anxiety and fear began to win over her calm once more.

"He is not in earnest, miss," Thaddeus said, hopping to his own feet. He walked to her, his brother close at his heels. Taking one of her hands, he looked up to her, smiling. His hand was warm and friendly, and though it seemed odd to be looking down at a man instead of up, his smile warmed and calmed her. Marcellus took her other hand, and he too smiled up at her.

"Do not mind Rogan," Marcellus said. "He has a jesting manner at times."

"Come," Thaddeus said, tugging on Saphyre's hand. "Come and sit next to us 'round the fire."

"Yes, miss. Come with *us*," Marcellus added. "We will not let Rogan have even the smallest nibble of you."

Saphyre smiled and began to follow the two men as they led her toward the others. Upon passing Rogan, however, Saphyre gasped as, of a sudden, he reached out, taking hold of her wrist, causing that both Marcellus and Thaddeus dropped their hold of her hands. The sense of Rogan's vice grip encircling her wrist did, at once, both terrify and please her somehow. Looking down into the fierceness of his gaze, she realized she had never known such a man as this. She had never known any man akin to any of these men, and for some reason she could not fathom, she was oddly as thrilled as she was fearful.

"You have not spoken since we sat to the fire…and now you will give me a name before you sit again," Rogan growled. "We here know we can trust one another. I will trust no man—or woman—who will withhold a name."

Saphyre opened her mouth to speak, but his touch and nearness so disturbed and worried her, she could make no sound.

"A name, girl!" he growled again. "Or I put you out to the elements this night myself."

"Go on, pretty miss," Marcellus whispered. "I promise…he will not eat you."

"Especially if he knows your name," Thaddeus added.

"True," Marcellus said, looking to his brother and nodding. "I have never known Rogan to eat *anyone* once he owned their name."

"That is true!" Thaddeus exclaimed. "He never eats them after they have named themselves."

"As long as it proves to be their true and given name," Marcellus added, wagging a finger in his brother's direction.

"True. It must be their true and given name," Thaddeus confirmed. "Give him your true and given name, miss," Thaddeus instructed. "Then he will of a certain not eat you…and you can join us at the fire once more."

Saphyre looked down into the angry yet alluring eyes of Rogan. Even the attempts of Marcellus and Thaddeus to lighten Saphyre's heart did nothing to lessen Rogan's threatening countenance. His frown was severe, and she thought he truly meant to put her out if she did not give him her name. She wondered for a moment if he already knew her—simply wanted to test her measure for honesty. She dared not lie to him, for if he did know her and she were not truthful with him, he would surely put her out. Would he not?

At that very moment, as if he read her very thoughts, he said, "You have my word. I will not put you out this night if you tell me who you are."

"Rogan is always true to his word, miss," Marcellus whispered. "If he says he will not put you out…then he will not."

But would he ransom her? Once her name was given him—if he

knew she was the princess of the kingdom—would he endeavor to ransom her? Would the temptation of easily acquired wealth be too great for him or any of the men to resist? Surely it would be. Still, Saphyre saw no other choice before her.

"I-I...I am Saphyre Snow," Saphyre stammered in a whisper. She watched as Rogan's frown deepened—flinched as he pulled on her arm, causing her to crumple to her knees next to him—her face so close to his, she could feel the warmth of his breath on her cheek.

"Lie to me again, and I will slit your pretty throat!" Rogan growled.

"Rogan," No-Nose scolded. His reprimand seemed to have a quantity of effect, for Rogan indeed drew a deep breath and released Saphyre's wrist. He took her chin in one hand—more gently than he had held her arm—and turned her face to his.

"Dare to tell me again that you are Saphyre Snow, the king's daughter," he challenged her.

Tears sprang from Saphyre's eyes, trailing freely over her cheeks. Fear clutched her heart. "I...I am Saphyre Snow...the king's daughter," she whispered, melting into a sobbing heap next to him. She did not struggle nor was she surprised when she felt Rogan take hold of the shoulder of her frock, ripping her dress to expose her tender flesh. Her birthmark was legendary. She knew Rogan would seek after it—for it could not be discounted.

"Rogan!" No-Nose shouted again. "Stop! At once!"

"A half-moon...the birthmark," Rogan breathed.

Saphyre's arms broke into goose flesh when she felt the callused tips of his fingers travel over her shoulder. "Faint...but still perfectly discernable. Even her frock is the sapphire blue...the color of the royal family of the Kingdom of Graces."

"We are all dead men," No-Nose mumbled.

"What say you?" Salomonè asked. "You do not mean she is the daughter of *this* king? Of the king of *this* kingdom?"

"The very one," Rogan mumbled, taking hold of Saphyre's wrist once more. "You have sentenced us all to death!" he growled at her.

"The king will have us executed for our mistreatment of you...for not hastening you home at first setting eyes upon you!"

"No! No, he will not!" Saphyre argued through her tears as Rogan stood, pulling her to her feet as well. "He will not...and...and you must not return me to my father. It may as well be you kill me here and eat me yourselves as to deliver me there!"

Rogan took Saphyre's face between his powerful hands. So tightly did he hold her as to cause her cheeks to ache.

"Never have I seen you treat a woman in such rough manner, Rogan!" No-Nose growled. "Do not begin...and with such a woman as this."

But Rogan was heedless and growled, "Saphyre Snow...the great beauty of the Kingdom of Graces. Hair as black as ebony, they say... lips as red as the blood-red rose...eyes as brilliant a blue as the priceless sapphires adorning the crown." His eyes narrowed as he studied her.

Saphyre could only tremble in his grasp as he ran one thumb over her lips.

"I see none but a frightened child who has brought death to our doorstep." He released her, pushing her backward. She would have stumbled had it not been for No-Nose there to catch her—to help her stand.

"Rogan," No-Nose said, "you must calm yourself. King Jordan is long since dead. Surely Michael will listen to reason where our part in this is concerned."

"Ha!" Rogan shouted. "You know as well as I...the old king's son—the king now sitting on the throne—has fallen under the same wicked spell his father did! You have heard the talk in the villages, No-Nose. You know as well as I that—"

"Then what finds the girl here?" No-Nose interrupted. "What finds the king's daughter in our hands, asking we *not* return her to her father's house?"

"She is thinking we are fools!" Edmund said, standing. "She was doubtless riding on her pony, lost her way, and does not want to admit to her father her folly. We will surely hang for giving her sanctuary here one hour already!"

"No! No! My father would not…he would believe me!" Saphyre cried. "If I were able to return, he would believe me!"

"She will see us hanged!" Edmund shouted.

"She tells the truth!" Marcellus shouted in return.

"What would you know about it?" Salomonè argued, standing next to Edmund.

"He knows more than you do about anything!" Thaddeus said in defense of his brother.

"Silence!" Rogan shouted. "Silence," he repeated, lowering his voice. "You said," he began, calming himself, "you said we may as well eat you ourselves as deliver you there. What do you mean to say, girl?"

"Princess," Marcellus whispered, in an effort to correct his leader.

Rogan closed his eyes and put out a hand toward Marcellus to quiet him. "Are you saying that you do not want us to return you to the castle?" Rogan asked.

Saphyre nodded, wiping tears from her cheeks. "I am…I am meant to be harmed…killed," she stammered. "Someone means to kill me."

"Nonsense!" Salomonè grumbled.

"But it is true! I swear it to you," Saphyre sobbed.

"Who?" No-Nose asked.

"I…I know not," Saphyre told him. "I know only that the queen's huntsman took me into the woods…raised his knife…but bid me run away instead of striking me down."

"The queen is dead," Rogan said. His frown was deep, but he was paying heed to the tale Saphyre told.

In desperation she reached out, clutching the fabric of his tattered tunic in her fists as she begged, "Not my mother's huntsman, but the huntsman of the old queen…Carmen. My step-grandmother's huntsman," Saphyre managed.

"Then it was the old queen who ordered you killed?" Rogan asked.

"Of course not!" Saphyre exclaimed. "It…it was merely her huntsman who—"

"Who else would order the huntsman to kill you then?" No-Nose interrupted. "If not Queen Carmen…then your father?"

"No!" Saphyre sobbed. "Father would never see me harmed!"

"The old queen meant to see you dead," Belmiro said, moving closer to Saphyre.

"No, no," Saphyre said, shaking her head. She fought to believe it. Yet in the darkest corners of her mind, her own suspicions had already marked her step-grandmother.

"Let us pretend, for only a moment, that we believe you," Salomonè said, also coming to stand near to her. "Why would the old queen want you dead?"

"She would not. Of course, she would not!" Saphyre sobbed. "I have done nothing! Nothing to wrong her! Ever in my life!"

"That is not true," Belmiro said. Saphyre looked to Belmiro, as did the others—all but Rogan—as Belmiro said, "You were born."

"What?" Thaddeus asked. "What cause for murder is that?"

"It is as the story goes. Always it has been with Carmen, second wife to King Jordan and one-time queen of the Kingdom of Graces," No-Nose said. Saphyre's hands still clutched Rogan's tunic, and he placed his hands over her own, causing her to release him as No-Nose continued, "Lady Carmen—so beautiful that no other woman in this kingdom or three beyond could compare—married King Jordan shortly after his queen, Penelope, died of a sudden and insoluble illness some six years past."

"Her beauty of face was exact enough," Rogan explained, "or so the story goes…that it was matched only by her vanity. And her vanity was exact enough that it was rumored she would do anything to ensure no other woman's beauty was ever greater than her own… at least ever greater known."

Saphyre felt all eyes in the room resting on her, and she understood—inwardly admitted what her fears had been whispering to her for months.

The silence as the men studied her from head to toe was near unbearable, and so she said, "All princesses…in every kingdom in the world…are said to be beautiful. It does not mean that they are."

"It is true enough," Marcellus said, eyes wide with excitement. "Thaddeus and I once performed for the Princess Arianna of Derkendom. Ugly as an old crone's hound," he said, shaking his head.

"And a snout just as large," Thaddeus added.

"But that is not the condition here. Is it, Princess?" Rogan asked.

Saphyre did not mistake the disdain in his voice, the contempt of the title.

"You are Saphyre Snow, and your beauty has been told upon the wind since the day of your birth. Queen Carmen has tired of the wind whispering of it, has she not?"

"Please," Saphyre begged in a whisper. "Please take pity on me. Do not force me to the mercy of the elements...or Queen Carmen. Please...a little respite...a measure of time is all, I beg of you." Saphyre looked away, lowering her head. She thought herself no great beauty. When she gazed into the looking glass in her bower, she saw only Saphyre Snow—a young woman with dark hair and blue eyes— not so unlike many young women of the Graces.

"Time? Time for what reason?" Edmund shouted. "Your father will send men to search for you."

"They will not venture here!" Saphyre said, her expression pleading with him. "They will not find me, and he will think me dead...and then...then perhaps his grief will cause him to gather his wits once more. Perhaps—"

"His wits have not been about him since your mother's death. Your death would only further plague his mind," Rogan told her.

She looked to him, somewhat astonished at his softened manner.

"And what of the old queen? She will not be satisfied your beauty is mingled with the dust without certain evidence."

"The huntsman said he...he would kill a deer...and take its heart as proof of my death. She will know me to be dead. She will have no reason to doubt it," Saphyre explained. Once again all eyes were upon her, and she was compelled to continue. "I cannot abandon my kingdom," she whispered. "I cannot. I will not. But neither can I combat my step-grandmother's hatred of me...or my father's grief at my mother's death by returning now, weak and bewildered as I am. I must have time to…to…"

"Your father will become the king his father became," Rogan growled, "a once great king, stricken with a sickness of mind until he is a miserable, tyrannical lunatic caring nothing for his subjects or—"

"No!" Saphyre exclaimed. "He will recover. He will! Something has happened in him…as it was with my grandfather, I confess. But the conclusion will not be the same. I am determined to make certain it is not."

"And how will you heal a man's sickness of mind?" Rogan asked. "You, who was nearly murdered for your beauty? How do you intend to—"

"To die for the sake of supposed beauty is, I admit to you, a thing of no measure," Saphyre interrupted. "But to die in defense of a beloved kingdom…if I return and am killed in defense of my father and his kingdom…there is something in that."

"There is nothing supposed concerning your beauty, Princess," No-Nose said. "There is nothing supposed in the old queen's envy of it. But a mind-sick king will not be so easily explained…nor healed. All who were once subject to your grandfather witnessed the truth of it."

Of a sudden, Saphyre felt as if her shoulders had been weighted. Humbly she lowered her head and whispered, "Please…please do not put me out this night. Please let me have this night to gather myself…my thoughts…to determine what I must do."

Rogan exhaled a heavy, defeated sigh before saying, "You may stay one night. Only but one."

"Rogan…you put us in certain danger," Edmund growled.

"Then I will face whatever danger may come while any coward among us runs when it appears," Rogan growled. "Come," he said then, taking hold of Saphyre's arm. "You will sleep with me."

"What?" Saphyre exclaimed. "I cannot possibly!"

Rogan turned to her, inhaled a calming breath, and then spoke. "You have intruded on seven men who have been kept from any women for weeks, girl."

Saphyre began to tremble, tears springing to her eyes as she whispered, "You mean to make me pay the price for sheltering here one night?" Did he mean to have her then? Would he dare—even such a man as this—would he dare to violate the king's daughter?

"I mean to make certain you do *not* 'pay the price' for sheltering here one night. Further, to make certain you do not flee, thus bringing the king's vindication swift upon us," Rogan growled.

"Rogan will keep you safe," Marcellus said and then, looking to Edmund, added, "from anything that might intend to prey upon you."

Saphyre looked from Marcellus to Rogan. Rogan's eyes pierced her soul as an invisible dagger. How could she possibly trust such a man as this? How could she be expected to find respite and sleep in such circumstance? Rogan tugged on her arm, but she did not follow him.

"Had I any desire for you, Princess…I would have satisfied it well by now," he growled.

"You may trust him, Princess," No-Nose said, nodding assurance. "He will not harm you."

Saphyre looked to Thaddeus, who smiled and nodded—looked to Marcellus, who smiled and nodded as well.

"Come then," Rogan said. "Have your night of rest and haven, for tomorrow you must leave this place."

With one last glance and an encouraging nod from Marcellus, Saphyre followed Rogan into the shadowy depths of the keep. She wondered as they went how he navigated the stone ruin so well, for it was indeed dark and cold, even for the moonlight peering through small windows scattered here and there. She followed him up a small flight of stairs, where he paused to light a torch on the wall, removed it, and carried it with him.

Soon he led her into a diminutive chamber, touching the torch to a mound of logs and leaves resting in the hearth nearby. Quickly a fire began to burn, warm and bright, lighting the room and revealing a bed in the furthest corner.

"Sit here," Rogan commanded, pulling a footstool near to the fire.

Still uncertain as to whether she were about to be violated, Saphyre did as she was told—yet ready to bolt if need be. The fire was hot on her face, but it felt good, comforting. "A sip of water before you retire, Princess?" he asked, retrieving a cup from the mantel and filling it with liquid from its companion pitcher. He held the cup out to her, but Saphyre paused, afraid to take the drink. Rogan simply breathed an irritated huff and put the cup to his own lips, sipping the liquid before offering it to her again.

Saphyre accepted the cup this time, whispering, "Thank you," before sipping the cool water. It did serve to soothe her dry throat, and she was glad of it, nodding in gratitude.

He returned the cup to its place on the mantel and then retrieved several branches of some purple dried plant hanging from a hook on the wall. He tossed them into the fire, and a sweet, somewhat familiar fragrance began to soothe Saphyre's senses. Almost immediately she felt dizzy—overcome with weariness and the need to close her eyes. The dizziness continued to grow, and she stood, trying to recover herself. Yet no sooner had she stood than the room began to spin, and she felt greatly weakened. She was vaguely aware of her knees giving way—of being lifted—of strong arms cradling her.

"You…you've killed me," she mumbled as she felt herself being carried.

In the next instant there was no more moonlight—no more feeling, no more thought. There were only dreams—disordered and perplexing. Dreams of a beautiful, loving mother and of two small smiling men—dreams of a man with no nose—of a huntsman and his blood-soaked knife. Dreams of a mind-sickened father—a hateful grandmother. Dreams of a handsome vagabond, who told her she was beautiful—told her of those who would kill her for the truth of it. Dreams—so many dreams—whispering to Saphyre Snow—whispering to her of her innocence lost.

"But there is no speak of it, Rogan."

The voices drifted into Saphyre's mind, and she began to awaken—but slowly.

"A princess fair vanishes and there is no talk of it? No speculation?" Rogan was asking.

"None, Rogan," No-Nose answered. "Not a word of it. No word of her gone missing…no word of her father sending out men to search for her…nothing."

"Perhaps with the onset of his father's madness, the king has already forgotten he has a daughter," she heard Rogan say.

Saphyre decided to feign unconsciousness awhile longer, the exchanging conversation being of great interest to her.

"Perhaps," No-Nose mumbled. "Yet there is something of interest still. The old queen has been seen about in her open carriages these past two days."

"The old queen? In open carriages with the chill in the air?" Rogan asked.

"Yes. And more than once a day," No-Nose affirmed.

"Her vanity is restored," Rogan mumbled. "The old queen is, what…but thirty? She is, no doubt, a great beauty still…and loath not to show it."

"Still, until two days past…she had taken to the castle and was rarely seen," No-Nose said.

"The princess…Saphyre Snow's beauty is no longer an enemy, so she thinks," Rogan said.

"I am to believe the girl, Rogan. And you and I…we are right to suspect from whence came the harm intended her…the old queen."

"How will I ever to return? How can I possibly return with no ally, with no…" Saphyre said, raising herself from the bed to sit and look to them. Her head felt light—still a bit dizzy.

"Assassinate the old queen and restore your father's mind," Rogan stated.

Of a sudden, Saphyre felt as if some greater burden had been heaped upon her shoulders. "I find your mockery neither helpful nor humorous," she said, standing for a moment before stumbling forward. It was Rogan's powerful body that kept her from falling—

Rogan's strong arms that steadied her. "And…and you tried to kill me last evening. Did you not?" she asked, looking up at him. Instantly, she was full astonished by his appearance in the clear light of day. He who had appeared so handsome cloaked in the shadows of night was even more so midst the radiance of the sun streaming through the small window nearby.

"I did not," he said. "Your fears and worries would not have allowed you a sound night's sleep…in particular with one such as I in the room with you. It was only sleeping-lavender," he explained.

Saphyre had heard of sleeping-lavender—a combination of lavender and other rare plants that, when burned and the smoke inhaled, caused an immeasurable weariness to overtake a person. Still, she realized how completely powerless and vulnerable the concoction had left her during the long night.

"You were not violated in any way, Princess," No-Nose assured her, having obviously guessed at her thoughts.

"Your father has not sent anyone in search of you," Rogan said, yawning. He looked tired, as if he had not closed his eyes all through the long night. "And your grandmamma is out about the kingdom… in her open carriage. This leaves you in quite a quandary, I would imagine."

"Do not assume to imagine who I am, what I feel, or where and how I find myself," Saphyre told him, with rather too much determination.

"Ah," Rogan said, grinning. "You see, No-Nose. Did I not tell you the arrogance would appear soon enough?"

"Why do you hold such loathing for me, sir?" Saphyre asked him. "Have I offended you? Have I wronged you in some way? Perhaps your share of the pheasant last evening was lessened on my account. Is that the reason for your disdain?"

"My harsh conduct toward you has no more to do with portions of pheasant than snow does to summer," he told her, frowning. "I simply do not trust the royal line to keep their sanity intact. Would you that I should be less suspicious and find a dagger in my heart at your hand?"

31

"You think me capable of…of murdering you?" Saphyre could not fathom why his suspicion caused more hurt in her bosom than anger—but it did. How could he think such things of her?

"I think your grandfather was King Jordan of the Kingdom of Graces," he growled, taking her chin in one hand. "Therefore, give me reason to trust you."

Saphyre felt tears welling in her eyes. She did not want this harsh man to think badly of her.

"Then I will go," she told him. "You have given me shelter for a night…as you said you would. I will go in search of another now." Pushing his hand from her face, she stepped past him and toward the door. Yet No-Nose barred her way—his stance pure that of a soldier on guard.

"You will go when I say you will go," Rogan growled, "and not before."

"You do not want me here. I dare you deny it," Saphyre said.

"I do not want you wandering about, telling others of us or this place we inhabit," he told her. "Therefore, you will stay…until such time as we can decide what is to be done."

"I refuse to be anyone's prisoner," Saphyre said, straightening her posture in an effort to appear confident.

"Better a prisoner than the huntsman's game. Eh?" he said.

Saphyre was immediately humbled and once again worrisome.

"Do not forget, Saphyre Snow," Rogan continued, "you intruded upon us. Further, you are as good as one of us now…for you dare not return to the castle in haste, not with the state of things."

"We may be monsters to look upon, Princess," No-Nose said.

Saphyre looked up at him, trying not to stare at the hollows where his nose should be.

"But we will not throw the lamb to the lions. It is not safe for you to return to the castle…and well I think you know it."

"But I cannot possibly stay here…with you men," Saphyre countered. Still, she knew no other place of refuge. She had stayed one night in the company of seven tortured men and awakened unscathed. It was a miracle of sorts. Thus, how could she risk another night—and another?

"You will not be harmed," Rogan told her. "You will return, when the time comes, to your father as pure as you arrived. Still, you will have to earn your place. Not as we do, by cutting wood and stone… but there is plenty to keep you occupied."

"But you are seven men, and I am—" she began.

"Did not your father ever place you in the care of men before?" No-Nose asked. "Was there never a time when a threat hovered? A time when you were sent with soldiers or knights to a safe haven?"

"Yes, of course," Saphyre admitted. There had been several times she had been placed under the protection of men. Still, this was different. Was it not?

"Then it is no different here," Rogan growled. "You will stay until such time as it is safe for you to return." He moved past both Saphyre and No-Nose, storming down the staircase into the lower part of the keep.

"I am afraid of him," Saphyre said, fearfully wringing her hands.

"He is afraid of you," No-Nose chuckled.

"Afraid of me?" Saphyre asked, perplexed. She looked up at the man and thought he did not look as alarming as he had a moment before.

"Rogan is a powerful man…a determined man…a leader. He leads this rabble well, and with wisdom," No-Nose explained. "But you are a woman…a woman in peril at that…and that, Princess, frightens him."

"He does not want me here, and it is ridiculous for me to even consider staying," Saphyre said.

"What choice have you, Princess?" he asked her. "Return now and you are marked for death. And death cannot help your suffering father or his suffering kingdom."

"Would you have me stay, sir?" Saphyre ventured. She felt that if No-Nose approved, then perhaps somehow it would serve.

"I would, Princess," he answered, "for you are more safe with us than you can begin to imagine."

Saphyre smiled, for she believed him. Somehow she believed him. "Very well," she said. "But…but what am I to do now?"

No-Nose offered his elbow to her and said, "Come to breakfast. A new life must begin somewhere…and why not at breakfast?"

Marcellus, Thaddeus, Belmiro, Salomonè, and even Edmund nodded a greeting as Saphyre entered the ruined kitchen of the keep. Rogan was nowhere to be seen. Saphyre wondered for a moment if he had abandoned his friends and hiding place for the sake of her having plagued it.

"Good morrow to you, Princess," Marcellus said, offering a plate heaped with sliced meat and boiled eggs to her.

"Good morrow to you, Marcellus," she said in return.

"Did Rogan molest you in any manner during the night?" Thaddeus asked.

Saphyre felt her eyes widen at the brazen inquiry. "Wh-why no," she stammered.

Thaddeus smiled and nodded to his brother in approval. "Then all is well, is it not, my brothers of the keep?" Thaddeus said, nodding in turn to every man at the table.

"Here, here! All is well!" Belmiro said, raising his cup.

"For Rogan has neither eaten nor molested the princess," Marcellus said, winking at Saphyre. The other men chuckled, amused by Marcellus's humor. Saphyre could not help but smile at him—for his character was undoubtedly charming.

Saphyre looked about the room at the six men sitting with her. They seemed far less frightening in the morning light—more honorable. Still, to stay in their company for any further length of time—would it be wisdom or folly? Yet, in truth, what other choice was before her?

THE SECRETS OF THE KEEP

Deep crimson, burnt orange, and warm golden leaves began to replace the green of summer in the leaf trees. The pines remained evergreen, yet even their needles changed in slight, turning yellow where each one sprouted from its limb—a sign of a harsh winter to come. Still, autumn was breathing cool mornings, bright sunlit days, and crisp, starry nights, as the princess Saphyre Snow lingered in the company of the seven men of the keep.

One week she had lingered as the men of the keep listened to the gossip of nearby villages. One week more she lingered. Each evening the men of the keep and Saphyre gathered around the fire discussing what the men had gleaned in the villages—what they had heard of the vanished princess, Saphyre Snow—what they had heard of the old queen.

There was still no talk of anything unusual concerning the princess of the kingdom. On occasion, it would be mentioned that the princess had not been seen out as often of late. Still, the people did not find anything odd in this. In fact, it seemed most villagers assumed that her father, the king, had sent her to the Kingdom of Alvar. It was thick rumored among the people of the Kingdom of Graces that their king meant to see his daughter wed to Alvar's prince, Kornelius. Thus, did it not seem quite likely the king would send her to Prince Kornelius's kingdom to visit? In truth, the men of the keep discovered King Michael's subjects were far more concerned with the goings-about of his stepmother—the old queen, Carmen.

As Saphyre Snow was not to be seen, so Queen Carmen was in opposite seen everywhere. Even in the cool of autumn mornings, she had been seen in her open carriage. Though she was often titled the "old queen" among the subjects of the Kingdom of Graces, Queen Carmen was far from old. In truth she was younger than Saphyre's own mother had been—golden-haired, green-eyed, slender, and graceful. All who gazed upon Queen Carmen could not resist in gazing upon her great beauty. Yet she was not beloved of the people, for she was neither kind nor compassionate. Still, her beauty could not be denied, and she was greatly admired for it—and she savored being seen. Thus, the men of the keep were ever more certain than before that it was indeed Queen Carmen had meant to see Saphyre murdered—for the sake of smiting a beauty greater than her own.

Yet with all their certainty—with all Saphyre understood—she could not simply return to her father and his castle. There seemed no ease in solution of what was to be done. Certainly Saphyre knew the impropriety of one young woman living in the company of seven men, but with no other path set immediate before her, it seemed no choice was offered her but to linger. Thus, she had determined in the silent musings of her mind and heart to think of the men of the keep as guards in a manner, like unto the castle guards who were ever posted here and there to protect the royal family. It was true Saphyre's fears concerning her father and the state of the kingdom—concerning her step-grandmother's wishes to harm her—lingered in her bosom, haunting her constantly. Yet the seven men of the keep began to give her hope somehow, for as she grew to know them better, she saw not seven distrustful and secretive vagabonds. Rather, she saw seven wounded, tattered souls—men who had, for one reason or the other, found peace in solitude. In this, she began to wonder if her lot might be the same. Would she never know a return to her father? Would she too find solitude her only course? And if solitude were to be her fate, would she find peace and contentment in it, as it seemed the seven men of the keep had found a measure of contentment?

A fortnight she had dwelt with them in their space, cooked with them, lingered around the fire at night, and listened to their conversation. In this, Saphyre Snow learned much about the men of the keep. Indeed, there was much she did not learn. Nevertheless, the information she did gather from what they each told of themselves—and of one another—was not only astonishing at times but helpful in enabling Saphyre to full see past their ragged and battered or angry appearances. In knowing more of them, Saphyre was often awed at their very existence—at their strength and endurance of hardship. It was frequent Saphyre was absolute humbled at hearing of the past lives of the men of the keep. She began to think herself quite pitifully weak of mind, body, and spirit when measured against such men.

Marcellus and Thaddeus were beloved of Saphyre. Almost at once she had taken them into her heart, for they were both kind and amusing. Often they caused such a laughter to rise in her as she had never known. It seemed she was ever wiping tears from her cheeks—tears borne of thick, delightful mirth. Ever they were chiming an amusing repartee, ever smiling, ever friendly. Such men Saphyre had never known, and she blessed the day she did know them.

Marcellus and Thaddeus had once served as jesters to a mighty court in a kingdom far away. Fame had been theirs—and a good wage. Still, they had grown weary of using their natural wit and talents simply for the light amusement of others. Thus, after many years, they left their kingdom and forsook fame. Sadly, they found many who thought two such small men could not perform the tasks of regular men of a larger variety. Work had been scarce for them, and they had gone hungry many a night—till one storm-cast day. While traveling from one village to another in search of tasks by which they might earn wages, the wildest of storms—bringing thunder, lightning, and heavy rains—bore down upon them. Cold and overcome with the great weariness of traveling, Marcellus and Thaddeus had come upon the keep. Seeking shelter from the raging elements, they had entered. There they found No-Nose and Rogan, also sheltering within. Of an instant, No-Nose and Rogan were approving with Marcellus and Thaddeus. Thaddeus and Marcellus were likewise taken with No-Nose and Rogan, and an alliance followed. From what she had been told, Saphyre gathered the four men traveled together among the villages—No-Nose and Rogan acquiring tasks as wood- or stonecutters, Marcellus and Thaddeus working with them to earn the wages of necessity. She further understood the men had been abiding at the ruined keep for several years.

Marcellus and Thaddeus's story greatly intrigued Saphyre. To leave fame and security for such a life as they now led was not weak in Saphyre's mind but independent—and brave. She admired them for finding happiness in such a simple life—in particular after having known the comforts of another. Marcellus and Thaddeus were men to be admired, men of honor and strength of character. She mused that the other men of the keep favored them for their wit and character— as did she.

Belmiro's story saddened Saphyre—caused her heart to ache with the pain of empathy. She found herself too easily dwelling upon Belmiro's trials—found tears filling her eyes often when she looked upon him. No-Nose had told Belmiro's tale to Saphyre, one night when she had lingered longer around the fire than the others. No-Nose had been out in the night. For what reason, she knew not.

The glowing embers were dying, yet Saphyre lingered—not wanting to leave the comfort of their warmth. No-Nose had entered, smiled, and taken seat next to her. It was on this night that No-Nose told to her, in secret, the story of Belmiro. It was not a happy tale, and it haunted Saphyre as a painful wound in her mind.

Born to a wealthy family, Belmiro had been shut away—hidden from the world at a young age—for the large hump that caused his crooked back was not a pretty sight to a nobleman and his wife. Raised for most of his young life in a dark turret room, Belmiro's only joy had come from his music—in particular the viol. Nevertheless, he was only allowed to play when no guests were present on his parents' estate.

One bright day, however, he could not keep himself from

playing. A mighty and noble guest was visiting Belmiro's father. The nobleman heard the music and inquired of Belmiro's father as to who the gifted musician was. Humiliated and furious, Belmiro's father cast out his son—banishing the young man from his home forever. The only possession given him was his cherished viol. At least the villainous man had allowed him that—one possession to take with him into a cruel, hateful world.

Saphyre had wept at No-Nose's telling of the tale of Belmiro. Her heart had ached so fierce in the moment of hearing it, she quite wondered if the pain of the knowledge of the mistreatment of Belmiro would ever ease. She had determined it would not. No-Nose had offered apology when first he saw Saphyre weeping for Belmiro. He had not meant to cause her misery. Yet Saphyre assured him she was grateful of the knowledge—no matter the pain it caused her. She was grateful even for the pain, for it meant her heart was tender—as her mother's had been—and ever she wanted to own a tender heart.

On the next evening, No-Nose had asked Belmiro to play his viol for Saphyre. Belmiro, humbled before a princess, was loath to perform.

"I am no musician worthy of the ear of the princess," Belmiro had said.

Saphyre had taken his hand in hers, begging him to play for her, and Belmiro smiled, unable to deny her further. Belmiro's playing was of the heavenly sort, playing angels would have lingered to listen to. He owned a rare and beautiful gift of music, awkward as it was for him to play for sake of his crooked back. Yet his music often saddened Saphyre, as did watching him play, for he never played any lively tune. From his viol, Belmiro drew slow, cheerless melodies— melodies that seemed to cast everyone into a silent disheartening.

Belmiro's story was indeed a sad one. Thus, Saphyre ached to see him bathed in some sort of delight. Still, he seemed to find moments of happiness, however, in the company of his brothers of the keep—in particular Marcellus and, strange though it was, in Rogan. It was many a night Rogan and Belmiro would sit together in quiet conversation, often smiling or lowly chuckling. These moments always seeped joy into Saphyre's heart—caused a smile to don her face—for she cherished the sight of Belmiro owning gladness.

It was perhaps miraculous that Salomonè began to warm to Saphyre as well. Ill-tempered, lacking patience, his stern brow ever wrinkled with a frown, Salomonè seemed a fortress of fury formed in flesh.

"I am not to be trusted." These words Salomonè spoke to Saphyre as she approached one midday. He was sitting without the keep, carving a piece of wood with the blade of a large knife. Saphyre had been to the stream for water. As she returned to the keep, the early autumn breezes whispering through the trees, Salomonè had been waiting—and he spoke to her.

"And why are you not to be trusted?" Saphyre had asked. It was true she was trembling—frightened at being alone in his presence. It was not that she feared he would harm her; it was simply that she feared.

"I am a thief," he answered plain. "I once stole anything I could to sell for food…to survive."

Thaddeus had previous spoken to Saphyre of Salomonè's having been orphaned at a tender age. Unable to gain waged labor of any kind, unable to find a compassionate person to help him, he thus attended to thievery as his means of survival.

It was without the keep that Salomonè spoke to Saphyre of his skill at thieving, yet in no manner of boasting or pride. He confessed to her he had remained a thief the whole of his life—that was, until he stumbled upon the keep and the men therein some two years previous.

"I confess I am not—by nature—trusting myself," he said. "If I am not to be trusted…why then should I trust?"

"But your brothers here at the keep own trust in you," Saphyre had said. "Then…if such as they trust you…why should you not be trusted by others?"

Salomonè's dark eyes narrowed as he studied Saphyre for a long moment. "Would you trust me?" he asked. "You? The princess of the kingdom?"

Saphyre smiled. "Am not I here, sir Salomonè?" she said. "Does not that alone prove my trust in you?"

"Ah, but there are six others here who would protect you from such as I," he offered.

"I have trusted you with my life," she said. "Is that not itself the greatest trust you could own of me?"

Salomonè had smiled at Saphyre then, and the sight of his smile pure awed her, for she had not before seen it. She thought he was quite comely in that moment. His fair hair and copper-streaked beard seemed to hold the sunlight, his dark eyes appearing as two spheres of obsidian in contrast.

Salomonè nodded—a nod of believing her words. It was thus Saphyre won the favor of Salomonè.

Edmund, however, was not so easily softened. Marcellus had explained to Saphyre—in a very hushed voice one evening when Edmund had retired early—what caused Edmund to so hate everyone and everything.

"He was a great knight...Sir Edmund...first knight of the king's table of the kingdom across the two rivers," Marcellus whispered.

"Of Rothbain?" Saphyre asked. It was well she knew the Kingdom of Rothbain—for it had been a kingdom steeped in great legend by her mother's family.

"The very one," he said. "Sir Edmund was a great knight...a knight in love with a beautiful peasant girl. One dark night," Marcellus continued, "Edmund was to rendezvous in secret with his lover... Arabeth was her name. But upon arriving at their meeting place, he found her not. The great knight, Edmund, waited. Long he waited... then longer still...until he began to worry over his lover...over her safety...for her father was a terrible man, a farmer who often beat and abused his daughter, the beautiful Arabeth. So worrisome did Edmund become in fear for her that he rode to the very place of her dwelling. There he found her badly beaten...bruised and bloodied."

Saphyre grimaced, unable to imagine living in such circumstances. "And it served the girl well...having a knight as her lover. Did it not?" Saphyre asked.

Marcellus's eyes widened, and he lowered his voice further, saying, "It served the girl, perhaps...but not the knight, for Edmund became enraged, shouting at the girl's father, threatening his life. The girl's father—having heavy consumed strong spirits—drew a dagger and plunged it into Edmund's leg...then into the girl's shoulder. As the villain raised the dagger over his own daughter, intent on plunging the weapon into her heart, Edmund drew his sword and slew him... slew him as a monster deserves to be slain...by cutting off his head in one swift stroke."

Saphyre wrinkled her nose and swallowed the gruesome lump in her throat. "And so...the girl was saved?" she asked.

"The girl was saved," Marcellus told her, "and angry with Edmund for having slain her father."

"What?" Saphyre exclaimed in a whisper. "He meant to murder her! That alone is enough, but consider the other...other treatment of her."

"I know. It is beyond understanding to you and I...and to Edmund," Marcellus continued. "For not only did she loathe Edmund for slaying her beast of a father, she went to the king's court and embellished the story till it seemed as pure murder. She saw Edmund imprisoned in the king's own dungeon. Rothbain's first knight sentenced to execution...and all for saving his lover's life."

"No!" Saphyre breathed.

"Indeed," Marcellus confirmed.

"But...but he was not executed?"

Marcellus shook his head. "He escaped the dungeons...assisted by the guards themselves, who would not see their first knight lose his head for the lies of a peasant girl."

"At least he lives," Saphyre whispered.

"Lives...yes. But hates and distrusts all women, Princess. It is why he loathes you."

"But I would never betray him! I would never betray any of you!"

"Perhaps not," Marcellus interrupted. "It is even once I heard him tell Rogan a woman assisted the guards in his escape from the dungeons of Rothbain...a princess of the royal family. Still, he is loath even to look at a woman…in particular a beautiful one such as you."

"I cannot fathom such a truth!" Saphyre said.

"Yet it is true…a wretched truth."

"To think a woman could fault her lover for such a heroic act…to cause him imprisonment…his life taken…or in the least destroyed," Saphyre mused.

"Edmund has been with us but one year," Marcellus explained. "And he has made some progress toward rehumanizing himself…but only with us. He never ventures to the villages on the other side of the woods. Never. Simply asks us to bring back his needful things."

It was a tragedy—a ghastly story of betrayal and wrongdoing. It was no wonder Edmund's eyes seemed so filled with hatred whenever he looked to Saphyre. She would not press him for acceptance, for she understood it would not serve.

Still, loathing of her or not, and surprising though it was, it was from Edmund that Saphyre gleaned a paltry sum of information concerning No-Nose.

"He lost his nose, that one," Edmund had grumbled one day upon seeing Saphyre studying No-Nose from a distance.

"So…he *did* have an…an entire nose before?" she ventured carefully. Certainly she was astonished that Edmund should even speak to her—in particular concerning No-Nose. Yet she had been curious—ever so curious over No-Nose from first she had set sight on him.

Edmund shrugged broad shoulders, saying, "It is what Rogan once told me. It seems No-Nose was a handsome man, strong, able…a soldier in some king's army. But in facing one particular foe, he lost a considerable portion of his nose to the blade of the enemy's sword."

"It is somewhat…disturbing," Saphyre whispered. She was fair awed to silence at hearing Edmund chuckle lowly, at seeing a smile spread across his face. She studied him a moment—his dark hair, broad shoulders. His eyes were gray—a smoldering sort of stormy gray. Saphyre could well imagine Edmund in the armor of a knight, jousting in tournament or battling at war.

"It is," he said. "And it is why he is here…with us. For each of us is hideous in some regard, Princess." He looked to her then, his eyes narrowing, once again filled with loathing. "Even you."

Saphyre glanced away and began wringing her hands where they lay in her lap. "Because I am a coward in your eyes…weak and foolish?" she asked.

"No," he growled. "But for the sake you own such beauty as to tempt a man to rash action…to tempt a queen to murder for vanity's sake."

It was all Edmund was willing to say. He rose, striding from her—leaving her quite discomfited.

Still, he had spoken to her, and not all too harshly. It was a beginning. Furthermore, she had guessed No-Nose's story to be something of the character of which Edmund spoke. There was something regal about No-Nose—something wise—something quite uncommon.

Of all the men of the keep, of all the pasts they secreted, it was Rogan's that was most secret. It was Rogan also labored longer than the other men—often several hours longer. He seldom rested, even at night. There seemed no peace about him. The man of the keep called Rogan seemed void of respite. Yet he, above all the others, fascinated Saphyre Snow. His handsome countenance indeed lingered in her mind, yet there was more—something unseen holding Saphyre's attention captive where Rogan was concerned. Still, though all the other men seemed willing enough to tell tales of themselves or their brothers of the keep, Rogan spoke of none, and none spoke of Rogan—none but No-Nose.

One occasion, while Rogan was gone to the villages for supplies, Saphyre sought out No-Nose. Her curiosity had grown near insatiable in regard to Rogan, and she hoped No-Nose would gift her some knowledge of the mysterious leader of the men of the keep.

No-Nose had paused in his woodcutting, smiling at Saphyre—

amused at her curiosity of Rogan. "He is a handsome devil, is he not?" No-Nose had asked her.

"He is an angry one, in the least," Saphyre said.

"Angry, perhaps…but still able to capture your attentions, eh?" he chuckled.

Saphyre knew she should be wary—that it was dangerous to continue along the same path of conversation. Though she had already accepted the existence of her powerful attraction to Rogan, still, she was near certain he was a scoundrel. What princess should ever care for a scoundrel, no matter how handsome?

"From whence does his passionate anger spring?" she inquired of No-Nose. "In particular toward me?"

No-Nose did not answer forthwith.

Thus, Saphyre mused aloud, "He is rarely at rest…yet perhaps this is the reason for his wearied temperament. Still, I think it is I vex him somehow."

"No," No-Nose said. "As you find him handsome…so he finds you beautiful, Princess." His response was plain-spoken—forward.

Saphyre felt her cheeks growing crimson with a blush, for she felt No-Nose spoke the truth—that he was not simply attempting to flatter her. She wondered—had Rogan told No-Nose he thought her beautiful, or had No-Nose simply grown so aware of his friend's character as to guess at it?

"Then what is it that keeps him so stirred in anger toward me?" she asked. "Has he…perhaps has he in his past…does he own an experience somewhat akin to Edmund's? Was he betrayed by a woman…a lover?" she prodded.

"He does not own the same pain as Edmund," No-Nose told her plain. "Though betrayal is the meat of it."

A small spark of hope flickered in Saphyre's mind. Hope toward what she knew not, but it was hope.

"Who then betrayed him?" Saphyre asked with pure innocence. "If not a lover, who then? And what betrayal would cause such a fury in him?"

"Your grandfather's," No-Nose answered. "King Jordan's."

Saphyre had already been made well aware of Rogan's disdain toward her grandfather. This was not novel information. She knew he held contempt for her grandfather—for his misruling of the kingdom when first his mind had begun to abandon him. Yet betrayal? How could her king grandfather have betrayed Rogan of the keep?

"I know of his loathing of my grandfather," she told No-Nose. "And I have often wondered if perhaps Rogan was once a loyal subject of the Kingdom of Graces. Was he once loyal to my grandfather before illness overcame him? Did he feel betrayed by my grandfather's madness?"

"Yes…yes, he did," No-Nose told her. "But there was far more."

Saphyre looked to him, expectant.

He exhaled a heavy sigh, and she feared he would not continue. Yet with his next breath he did.

"Rogan's father was a great knight…one of the greatest ever to sit at the king's round table of conferring…one of the greatest ever known…favored by King Jordan and the entire court."

Saphyre's eyes widened. Rogan? Begat by a knight of the Kingdom of Graces?

"And his name? This great knight…Rogan's father…did I know him?" Saphyre asked.

"Perhaps," No-Nose said. "But it is not for me to reveal such particulars. I will tell you only that when the king's mind failed him, Rogan's father tried in vain to lead him back to sanity. And can you guess his reward, Princess? Can you guess the great knight's reward for such a valiant effort…a valiant effort given out of love for king and kingdom?"

Saphyre felt the hair at the back of her neck begin to prickle. No-Nose's eyes narrowed; a dark, foreboding chill seemed to cool the air.

"No," she breathed.

"Beheading at the hands of assassins," he said.

"What?" Saphyre gasped. "Surely no!"

"The great knight was assassinated…beheaded for treason in trying to reason with the ill-minded king," No-Nose told her. "After all his loyal service, more than twenty years of it, his end reward for loyalty when all others had abandoned devotion…was death at the hand of he to whom the knight was loyal."

Tears spilled over Saphyre's cheeks. She was aghast—sickened at the tale. Long had she been ashamed of her grandfather's illness of mind, of his greed and treachery—but she realized in that moment how much of it had been kept from her.

Indeed she had heard whisperings of the beheaded knight. Lady Augustynia—her mother's favorite lady-in-waiting and Saphyre's greatest friend since her mother's death—had spoken of it but once to her—only once—and in fact had ceased in the full telling of it before revealing such details as No-Nose. The court had whispered of the deed among themselves as well, and Saphyre had understood the knight to have been a traitor—having revealed secrets to the then enemy of the Kingdom of Graces. Still, in her heart she knew No-Nose's and Lady Augustynia's retellings to be the truth of it—and it sickened her.

"It is no wonder he owns such hatred of me," she said.

Saphyre watched as he picked up his ax, returning to his work—an indication he had spoken all he was willing to speak concerning Rogan.

Saphyre turned to leave him to his work, yet No-Nose spoke once more, and she paused.

"He does not own hate of you, Princess," No-Nose said.

Saphyre frowned as she looked at the great, tall, broad-shouldered man.

His gaze captured her own, the deep blue of his eyes narrowing as he looked at her. "It is that you weaken him…and that is what Rogan hates…his own weakness. It is why he labors with such great determination and why rest does not easily come to him."

No-Nose often spoke in a manner akin to riddles, a manner leaving new questions in the wake of old ones still lingering in seeming unanswered. As No-Nose raised his ax, his powerful arms swinging it to meet the trunk of the tree before him, Saphyre knew there was nothing to be gained in pressing him further. He had told her what he would—and he would tell her no more. Thus, she left him to his work—and his secrets.

Rogan himself told Saphyre nothing of the others, offered no information. She sensed he was the guardian of their secrets as he was guardian of his own. She dared not inquire of him concerning his brothers of the keep. This she somehow understood, even for never having inquired of him.

Rogan had become, however, quite helpful in another regard—in delivering tasks into her hands, whether it was cooking, gathering wood and stacking it in the wagon to be taken to the villages and sold, or acknowledging the need to cease in labor and take to her bed. Ever Rogan found means for her to feel useful—to think she was perhaps earning her stay. It was clear he recognized her need to feel as more than a mere burden or parasite.

Rogan likewise was a fine teacher. He instructed Saphyre in the art of whittling wood for amusement's sake, as well as in skinning rabbits, deer, and other game in preparation for meals. None of these tasks appealed to Saphyre, yet she found herself glad to know them—proud to be able to perform them. Further, she reveled in the smile that would spread across his handsome face when she succeeded in learning a new task. He seemed pleased in her then—when she was willing to learn something new and perhaps difficult to perform.

And yet the manner in which her heart leapt at the sight of him—the way her eyes longed to linger on him—troubled her deeply. Whenever she thought of retuning to her father, of her father announcing her betrothal to Kornelius, she felt sickened—afraid—desperate to never leave the keep—and Rogan. Saphyre knew her feelings—her musings where he was concerned—were dangerous as well as irrational. Thus, Saphyre attempted to bury them deep in the secret-most parts of her heart—to ignore them as best she could.

Till one night—during her third week at the keep—one night proved her undoing. One night full weakened her resolve. All the strength Saphyre Snow had gathered, all the courage to eventually leave the keep and face her father and grandmother, was washed

away—washed away as a sudden cloudburst washed the dust from
a traveler's shoes.

THE EXECUTIONER'S KISS

It was a dark night. Thick clouds choked the silver light of the moon—dulled the bright twinkle of the stars. As was habit, the men of the keep sat around the fire talking, telling tales. Saphyre Snow sat with them, listening. It was she had never heard such interesting conversation as she was privy to in the keep. She glanced about the circle of men—awed at their weathered souls, marveling at their good fellowship. Such secrets they kept; such wounds they bore. Yet they sat at the fire enjoying light, merry conversation and company—as if living a life of solitude there in a ruined keep were no different than any other life led.

"I was fourteen," Salomonè said, "and the daughter of a nobleman had seen me in the street."

Saphyre's heart warmed as Salomonè smiled.

"She offered me a loaf of bread she had taken from the pantry of her father's great house. I told her I could not pay…and she told me she knew I could not. She had been watching me for days…knew I was thieving. She offered me a loaf of bread, as well as a lovely ring she wore…that I might sell it and have more to eat." Salomonè's eyes narrowed. "But the ring reminded me so of her kindness…that I kept it. I still do keep it…her ring."

Saphyre noted the manner in which Salomonè glanced to the ring he wore at the smallest of his right hand.

"And her name?" Marcellus asked.

Salomonè's smile broadened; his eyes narrowed. Saphyre knew the memory was tender in his heart. She could see it in her mind—a young man with no home or family, living in the shadows and stealing what he could to purchase food. She understood the feelings of the nobleman's daughter, for Saphyre knew sympathy for Salomonè even then, though he was no longer a child or a thief.

"Diana. Her name was Diana," Salomonè said.

"And was she beautiful?" Marcellus asked.

Saphyre smiled. How Marcellus did enjoy hearing tales of the past!

"Yes," Salomonè near whispered. "Hair as dark as obsidian—eyes at once golden and next brown."

"And how did you earn her kiss?" Marcellus asked.

"Perhaps I stole it?" Salomonè chuckled.

"Did you?" Thaddeus inquired.

Salomonè shook his head and answered, "No. She gifted me her kiss...the first I had ever known from a girl. She offered me first the bread from the pantry of her father's great house. The day following, she brought meat to me...and a sweet pastry. It was I asked her what task I might perform...what service I might lend her as payment. She told me then...she wanted nothing...nothing save a kiss. I thought sure she was in jest, that she mocked me. Yet her eyes spoke the truth, and I kissed her. It was pure the sweetest moment I had ever known...and I think now...it is still."

Saphyre sighed, delighted by Salomonè's tale. The men of the keep had been enjoying tales of their first kisses. Saphyre thought it tender and endearing that they would hold such conversation. No-Nose had told a sweet tale of a girl he had known as a child. Even it was Edmund did admit to kissing a servant girl when he was merely a squire. Saphyre wondered if poor Belmiro had ever known the soft kiss of a woman's lips. Furthermore, she wondered if Rogan would reveal—though she thought he would not.

Of a sudden, Belmiro asked, "And what of you, Princess?"

"Me?" Saphyre rather squeaked. She had not expected any of the men would inquire of her concerning the matter, for she assumed all in the keep knew she would never have known a kiss—and why.

"Of course," Belmiro said. His smile was warm—comforting. "Surely one so beautiful as you should own a tale of a first kiss."

"Well, I-I…in truth, I…have never…I have never…" Saphyre stammered. She felt the hot blush of crimson at her cheeks—hoped the men could not discern it for the low light.

"Do you mean to say you have never been kissed?" Thaddeus exclaimed. "Ever?"

Saphyre blushed and shook her head, wondering why she should feel ashamed of the truth of it. After all, kisses were *meant* to be out of the ordinary, special, and infrequent—not careless and constant. Were they not? Further, there was the royal mandate.

"Never," she admitted, straightening her posture in a gesture of defiant pride.

"Not even once?" Marcellus asked.

"No," Saphyre confirmed.

Thaddeus and Marcellus looked to one another, mouths gaping open in astonishment.

"Well, why ever not?" Marcellus asked.

Saphyre was silent—bashful—uncertain as to what response she should offer. Should she simply tell them that no man had ever desired to kiss her? Or should she tell them no man had ever been brave enough to kiss her had he desired to do so?

Before she could answer, No-Nose cleared his throat. "'Tis death to kiss the princess of the Kingdom of Graces without permission," he said.

Saphyre cast her gaze to the fire for a moment.

"Death?" Thaddeus exclaimed. "Simply to kiss her without first begging permission? Death? Truly?"

"It is not the lack of begging permission that brings the sentence of death," Rogan said. "It is the act itself." His fiery eyes glared at Saphyre as she looked up to him, startled by his response. "An ax through your throat…or a hangman's noose around it and air beneath your feet—that is where a fool would find himself if he were to kiss the princess of this kingdom. It is a royal mandated decree known as 'The Executioner's Kiss.' It is simple: kiss the princess and you are beheaded…or hanged."

"Axed or hanged?" Marcellus gasped. "For a kiss?"

"Is it true?" Salomonè asked Saphyre. "One kiss from you and a man dies?"

"Well," Edmund growled, "I have heard tales of witches and all manner of wicked women who want to see a man hanged. But, Princess, I must say this…you are the first I have ever known who owned the true and everlasting 'kiss of death.'"

"It is not my will at all!" Saphyre exclaimed. "It…you…you do not understand. It…it…"

"It is meant to lift her above other women…as if she is of greater worth," Rogan said.

"But surely, if she were to grant a man her permission—" Marcellus began.

"It matters not," No-Nose said. "To kiss the princess brings a sentence of death…unless, of course, the king himself consents. And it would seem the king would bestow consent only upon whatever prince is fortunate enough to win betrothal to the princess."

Saphyre felt tears welling in her eyes. She wanted to scream—tell them how miserable being a princess could be—how cold it kept her—how utterly alone.

"And how do you two know so much about it?" Salomonè asked.

No-Nose and Rogan looked to one another briefly. Saphyre did not miss the understanding that passed between them.

"All subjects of the Kingdom of Graces know this," No-Nose answered.

"And what feelings have you in this…this executioner's kiss, Princess?" Edmund asked. "To know a man could be put to death for touching you…for one innocent kiss?"

Saphyre did not miss the hurt, the depth of pain in Edmund's eyes, and she knew he was thinking of the woman who had betrayed him. No doubt her kiss had promised loyalty and love—not hatred and betrayal.

"Kisses are rarely innocent, in my experience," Marcellus mumbled.

"And what would you know about kisses?" Thaddeus asked him. "What vast experience have you?"

"Plenty!" Marcellus exclaimed. "Meredith Black, for one."

"Meredith Black?" Thaddeus laughed. "You cannot reckon Meredith Black!"

"Why not?" Marcellus asked.

"Because…because…Meredith Black was our relation, that is why!"

"Our relation?" Marcellus laughed. "Her widowed mother married our distant cousin!"

"Relations are relations," Thaddeus pouted, obviously disenchanted with being bested.

"And this is what we have come to, I see," Rogan mumbled. "Sitting about the fire discussing the penalties of displayed affection?"

"Well, the penalty here *is* harsh…even by your standards, Rogan," Salomonè said. "To think of our poor princess…never owning a kiss. At least without the king's consent, that is."

"And what kind of good kiss would that be anyway?" Belmiro asked. "What kind of a kiss would that be, Princess?"

"Saphyre," Saphyre mumbled. "I beg you would name me Saphyre…rather than Princess."

"Very well," Belmiro said. "What good kind of kiss would one be sanctioned only by the king…Saphyre?"

Saphyre fidgeted, uncomfortable under the gaze of seven sets of curious and accusing eyes. She smoothed the folds of her worn frock—shrugged her shoulders. "I am…I am most certain it would be acceptable…and…and…" She felt tears in her eyes and prayed for the strength to restrain them. She had no desire to reveal the tender dreams of her heart to seven roughened men. No matter how friendly they had become, no matter how accepting they seemed to be of her, she knew they would not understand the pain tearing her heart each time she thought of Kornelius—thought of his touching her—of his kissing her. She knew they would only laugh if they suspected she dreamt of love—of one true love—of passionate kisses shared with a man who loved her for herself and not her title.

"It would not be acceptable," Edmund said. "And you are doomed to never know it…for what man would risk death for such a thing? No woman is worth such risk of life."

Saphyre swallowed the misery in her throat—willed her tears to keep from leaving her eyes.

"That is only your estimation, Edmund," No-Nose mumbled. "And I will leave it to you…nor will I judge you for it…for I well recognize that you have known no such woman as is worth your life."

"Do you know such a woman?" Edmund growled. "Where is she then? Bring her out," he demanded. Edmund looked about as if searching for something. He looked to No-Nose, saying, "There is no such man as to find any woman worth kissing when the penalty is forfeit of his life." His bitterness was telling.

Silence owned the group for a moment.

Then Saphyre could no longer restrain her tears—for Thaddeus placed his small, calloused hand on her sleeve and quietly said, "No such man there may be…no such brave soul of my knowing, Saphyre." Then looking to Edmund, he added, "But I know you to be such a woman as No-Nose has spoken of."

Saphyre wept quietly, overcome with his sweet compassion. She placed a hand to his cheek and smiled at him through her tears.

"She will be the end of us, this girl!" Rogan growled, rising to his feet. "And I fear no hangman at the end of a rope woven of such preposterous conventions."

Saphyre gasped as Rogan then strode to where she sat, took her throat in one hand, and glared at her.

"Who is here to witness it? Who is here to hang me then, Princess?"

"Rogan!" Thaddeus scolded. "Behave yourself. You'll frighten our princess."

"One kiss and I am dead. Is that it?" Rogan asked her.

His voice was deep, alluring somehow, and she could only shake her head—her body tingling with the elation his touch invoked in her.

"Fear is weak. It destroys…and I fear no man and no punishment," he told her.

A moment later Saphyre was stricken to stillness—unable to draw breath as she felt the hard, angry pressure of Rogan's lips against her own.

It was not a loving kiss the like Saphyre had always dreamed of. Nor was it passionate in any positive form. Passionate only in anger it was—and coldly applied. Yet Saphyre felt her heart swell within her—a sort of satisfied delight in the knowledge Rogan had defied the king and kissed her. However brief—however heartlessly given—the feel of Rogan's lips pressed against her own pure delighted her.

Ending the kiss, Rogan continued to hold Saphyre's throat with one hand as his eyes narrowed, searching her own. His frown deepened as tears spilled from her eyes, and he released her, standing straight once more.

Stretching his arms out to his sides, he angrily asked, "And where is the hangman with his noose? Where is he? The executioner and his ax?" When no one uttered a word, he simply dropped his arms, shrugging his shoulders. "What is there to fear? She is only a girl… not unlike any other. Then let us be about our rest and leave this foolish talk to the careless musings of children."

No one uttered a word for long moments. When someone did speak, it was No-Nose. "Rogan," he growled, "the heart of a snake beats in your breast…cold, careless, and callous."

"Yes, Rogan," Thaddeus added. "You have lost sight of the reason for the conversation in the first of it…that sweet Saphyre has…*had* never known a man's kiss."

"And what a manner to first know of it," Marcellus added, shaking his head with marked disapproval.

"Pardon me, please," Saphyre whispered, rising to her feet. She fled from the room through the door.

So intent was she on escape, she did not see No-Nose take hold of the front of Rogan's shirt, angrily crushing the fabric in his fists. She did not hear No-Nose growl, "Did I not know you so well, Rogan… did I not know what truly you were feeling…what it is keeping you so angry toward the girl…I would beat you to within an inch of your life for your treatment of her in this!"

Saphyre did not hear Rogan breathe a heavy sigh—did not see his head drop forward with defeat. Nor did she hear him mumble, "You are right, my friend. You are right." She did not see No-Nose shove Rogan backward and move in the direction by which she had taken her leave.

She did not hear Rogan say, "No," put a hand to his friend's chest to stall him—then whisper, "I must go. It is for me to make amends. Not any of you."

Saphyre stood, her back against the outer wall of the ruined keep. She closed her eyes and let the tears flow freely down her cheeks. The painful ache within her was brutal, and she clutched at the space over her heart, attempting to soothe the emotion.

She wondered at how such resplendent joy could so entwine with such brutal pain. Rogan had kissed her, and it had been at once the most wonderful and most miserable moment of her life! How could it be so? And why did he hold such disdain for her over her grandfather's treachery—such obvious distrust and loathing? Yet deep within in her she knew the reason—such mad tyranny and murder could not be so easily set aside.

She thought of her step-grandmother then. Of a sudden, an additional fear began to cause her to tremble. In her soul she knew the woman to be wicked—wicked enough to order a huntsman to murder her own step-granddaughter. Saphyre knew she could not stay with the keep men forever. One day she would have to return— return to face the wicked queen, Carmen. Return and attempt to save her father and his kingdom—somehow. Still, she felt only a great weariness in those moments, and any bravery she may have owned prior to Rogan's mocking her was vanquished.

"Saphyre?"

Saphyre startled at the sound of his voice—yet warmed at his speaking her name. Instantly her heart began to hammer with intermingling bliss and fear.

"Saphyre, I...I..." Rogan stammered.

"You have said enough," she told him, brushing the tears from her cheeks. "It is a ridiculous decree...and no one understands the fact of it more thoroughly than I."

"No. I...I should not have—" he began.

"Please," she interrupted, shaking her head, "do not subject me to any further humiliation by attempting to deliver an apology or to—"

"Shh," Rogan whispered, his hand encircling Saphyre's throat and astonishing her into silence. "Allow me to say what I am compelled to."

"V-very well," Saphyre stammered.

Of a sudden, her attention was arrested by the movement of his lips as he spoke to her. He was so thoroughly alluring—from the perfect lines of his face and chin to the deep resonating tone of his voice. She tried to discern the colors of his eyes—violet, crimson, brown—but could not. She tried to will away the excess moisture gathering in her mouth as her gaze lingered on his lips, but it was futile, and she only longed for his lips to press hers once more. She marveled how this coarse man—this recluse—had captured her so completely, mind, body, spirit—and heart. With his roughened hands, strong body—his brutal beauty—he had somehow gained power over every thread of her being.

"I loathed your grandfather when he died," Rogan mumbled.

Saphyre held her breath as she felt his hand caress her throat as it moved to one side of her. She could feel his fingers firm at the back of her neck, his thumb resting along her jaw.

"It is well I know it," she said. "You have...you have kept me ever mindful of it since I first—"

"Shh," he whispered, frowning and closing his eyes for a moment, his hand moving from her. He placed his palms on the keep wall against which she was leaning—one hand on either side of her head—pushing himself back for a moment as his own head bowed before her. "Allow me to finish…please," he mumbled.

"I am sorry," Saphyre said, swallowing the lump in her throat.

Rogan stood silent before her for several long moments. Then, dropping his arms to his sides, he straightened his posture. "I loathed your grandfather, Saphyre Snow…yet I admired and loved him as well as any of his subjects…before…before…"

"Before he went mad," Saphyre finished. She would not reveal to him her knowledge of his own father's murder at her grandfather's hand. He would tell her of it if he wished. New tears trickled over Saphyre's lovely cheeks—tears of empathy, not tears of fear or humiliation. "He…he did not mean to go mad," Saphyre whispered.

Rogan sighed, the slightest of smiles donning his lips. Saphyre knew the smile to be forced. Still, she further knew it was meant as a kind gesture.

"I know he did not mean to allow madness into his mind, Saphyre," Rogan said. "I know it…now."

"I was not the one who wronged you," she ventured.

"And I was wrong to…in there…a moment ago…" he stammered.

Instantly Saphyre's heart began to pound wildly within her bosom. The thought of his kiss—no matter how unwillingly applied—gave her cause to be pure breathless.

"Was I not?" he asked.

Saphyre closed her eyes, feeling the palm of his hand on her flesh once more, as the tips of his fingers slipped beneath the hair at the back of her neck.

"No woman deserves such a miserable first kiss," he said. His voice was low—quiet—alluring. The sound of it washed over her like a fine mist of some sweet, desirable substance. "Especially a princess," he breathed. "It should have been a prince who first kissed you."

Saphyre winced as a vision of Kornelius entered her mind. She imagined a kiss from Kornelius would be as unpalatable an experience as would a kiss from a toad be.

"Instead, I have stolen the moment from you, have I not?" he said, pressing the palm of his other hand to the other side of her neck. "Me…a pitiful, worthless coward…who kissed you in anger." His eyes narrowed, and he stood before her, simply staring at her—his hands resting at her neck.

Saphyre shook her head, unable to speak—unable to tell him she would not trade the moment for any other in all the world.

She frowned, puzzled as she heard him chuckle. "It amuses you?" she asked, somewhat perplexed.

"It amuses me that I should hang for stealing your first kiss…having done such a miserable job of it," he explained. He smiled, and Saphyre felt the odd, delightful tingle of gooseflesh breaking over her body as he tipped his head to one side. He seemed to be considering her, one of his thumbs light traveling over her lips.

"I suppose," he continued, "if I am bound to hang for it…or to lose my head…I may as well attempt to make amends for performing the first so miserably."

Saphyre felt the rhythm of her breathing hasten, for his gaze now lingered on her mouth. Her own gaze was drawn to his—to the perfect shape and curve of his lips—to his tongue as he moistened them.

"It…it is the most ridiculous of laws," Saphyre whispered. "You know I would not let them hang you for it."

He smiled once more and whispered, "I *will* hang for it, Saphyre Snow…in one manner or another."

Saphyre watched, breathless as his head descended toward hers—watched until his face was so close she was forced to close her eyes for the nearness of it. She tried to draw breath as she felt his hand move to her shoulder—rest on the bareness of it where her frock had once been torn by his own hands. She tried to breathe as his cheek caressed her own a long moment before she felt the moisture of his kiss on her neck just below her ear.

Silently she begged, *Kiss me! Kiss me! Oh, kiss me, please!*

So strongly did her mind will it, she feared she might actually utter the very words aloud—but she did not. Even as his hands slid beneath her arms—pressing her ribs as they traveled to her back, pulling her body flush with his—her mind begged for the sense of his lips pressed to hers.

Saphyre shivered with heavenly sensation, her body weakening. Her head fell back as Rogan placed soft and lingering kisses to the hollow of her throat. She pushed at his shoulders—clutched at the strong leather bands at his forearms in a weak attempt to free herself from his bewitching attentions—but her strength was taken from her. She melted against him as he kissed the corner of her mouth— melted into the same arms she had so feebly tried to escape a moment before. At last, she felt his lips press to her own.

This kiss of the vagabond scoundrel Rogan was much dissimilar to the first Saphyre had known. This caused a breathlessness—a weakness in her from which she feared she would not recover. Of a sudden, her legs were numb—frail. In an attempt to steady herself, she clutched at his arms, just above his elbows. In that same moment Rogan kissed her again, and this time, the meeting of their lips was firm, moist—and Saphyre could not deny her hands the desire to travel up his arms, to slip beneath the torn sleeves of his tunic. His skin was warm and smooth—warm beneath her palms. Firm and powerful were the curves of his muscles, and he pulled her more tightly against him as her hands came to rest on the breadth of his shoulders.

He kissed her quickly again, his virile prowess coaxing her lips to parting in slight. With each ensuing kiss, Rogan seemed to tutor her further, till she sensed the moisture of his mouth mingling with her own—the passion of his kiss—of their kiss—mounting swift.

Saphyre's mind was awakened, more alive than ever it had been! Visions of the man whose arms held her—of the man whose mouth worked to enchant her—filled her mind and emotions. Sensations and feelings she had never imagined bathed her body! She was rendered breathless for long moments—yet could somehow breathe more deeply than ever before. Her entire being trembled with exhilaration, fascination, and pleasure. In those moments, Saphyre wanted only to kiss Rogan forever!

Slowly, however, Rogan began to lessen the depth of the kisses they shared. Leading her to a calmer place of mind and body, he broke from her altogether.

Stepping back and dropping his hands to his sides in releasing her, he let the massive expanse of his chest rise and fall with several heavy breaths before saying, "A second kiss...more worthy of what the first should have been, Princess." He seemed to study her, and she glanced away—ashamed of the heated blush she knew must appear fiery upon her cheeks. "What say you then?"

Saphyre was silent for a moment as she tried to stiffen her weakened knees and find her voice. "I-I am sure, sir...I shall never recover," she whispered.

He seemed pleased with her flattering answer, for she heard him chuckle and say, "I should hope not," in a low, quiet voice before turning to leave her alone without the keep.

The princess, Saphyre Snow, knew there could be no recovery from such an experience. With his bewitching kiss, Rogan had captured her—heart, mind, body, and soul. She knew he would never relinquish them—however unknowing he may have been.

Burying her face in her hands, she wept. How would she ever leave him? How would she find the strength and loyalty to return to her kingdom for her father's sake when her heart would forever be a prisoner of the keep?

Saphyre placed her fingers to her lips still tingling with the residual and blissful sensation of Rogan's attentions. She would treasure the memory of his kiss, his hands caressing her flesh, his arms about her. Such a memory would serve her for the rest of her life—prove her escape when she found herself so miserably bound to Kornelius. Saphyre realized then—she too had a secret of the keep, and she wept for want of reliving it.

THE SWORD OF THE THRONE

Several days waned—several days during which Saphyre found facing Rogan increasingly difficult. It seemed each time their eyes met, a crimson blush would rise to her cheeks—her lips tingling with the memory of his kiss. Yet he seemed entirely unaffected, treating her exactly as he had before, going about his daily labors as if nothing at all had changed.

Saphyre began to understand that for Rogan, indeed nothing had changed. He was still driven to hard labor—still unable to find restful sleep. Distraction did not seem to plague his mind as it did Saphyre's. For herself, however, everything had changed—everything! She was perpetually unsettled and found a smile would spread across her face at the mere thought of the man, while thoughts of Kornelius—thoughts of Kornelius full sickened her, even more than they had previous to Rogan's kiss.

Still, Saphyre carried on—carried on in her duties of the keep—carried on in lingering uncertainty as to what her fate would be. Often, in the quiet dark of night—as she lay in her small bed in one of the upper rooms of the keep—she would wonder if she should perhaps simply remain. The seven men of the keep had found lasting fellowship and haven in the keep—would she? Oh, she well knew she could not live out her life in the company of seven men. Yet this did not impede her thoughts from considering the idea was in some regard conceivable. Her kingdom did not seem harmed by her vanishing. Nay, it seemed she had not even been missed. Certainly the men of the keep thought this was for the fact the kingdom did not know she was gone. The men, No-Nose in particular, felt her vanishing had been kept secret—that the people had not been told of it. This did little to comfort Saphyre, however—for what of her father? Did not her father, the king, miss her? Had he not taken note of her absence? Still, Saphyre did own a knowledge of her father's increasingly strange behavior. For the weeks prior to Saphyre's escape from the huntsman, King Michael had begun to display certain behaviors similar to what his father had shown before going mad. This frightened Saphyre, but she would not believe her father was following his into madness. Still, the men of the keep had found nothing—gleaned no information to prove Saphyre's father was searching for her. In this, the cold, hard grip of terror often threatened to overwhelm Saphyre. It was in moments of near despair and terror brought by musing on her father's possible slip into madness that Saphyre most considered remaining at the keep forever. Yet in the depths of her heart she knew she could not. She could not abandon her people to another mad king, nor could she linger in living in the company of seven men. This she knew—yet the memory of Rogan's kiss would cause her dreams to whisper otherwise.

Saphyre startled as she heard the beating of strong hooves. The men of the keep kept horses in another part of the keep. However, rarely did they ride them so brazen when approaching the keep. Thus, Saphyre dropped the bucket of water she had drawn from the stream—slight gasping as she turned to see Salomonè astride a dark horse and approaching at a gallop.

"Saphyre!" he called as he reined the large beast to a halt. "I have news! Quick, come to the keep with me!"

Yet startled, Saphyre glanced to the bucket spilling water onto the ground.

"Leave it," Salomonè said. He offered her a hand, and she took it, gasping as his strength pulled her to sit in the saddle behind him.

"What is it, Salomonè?" she asked as he slapped the reins at the horse's neck, urging the beast toward the keep.

"I have been to the village south," he said as they rode. "And I bring news of the princess, Saphyre Snow!"

Saphyre's heart began to race near as brutal as hooves beat the ground beneath her. Had her father missed her at last? Did the people of the Kingdom of Graces know their princess was in some peril?

"What means this, Salomonè?" Rogan asked, stepping from the keep as Salomonè lifted Saphyre down from the mount.

"There is talk of the princess in one of the villages," Salomonè explained.

"Stable the beast, and I will gather the others," Rogan said.

Salomonè nodded, and Saphyre gasped with delight as Rogan took hold her hand and led her into the keep. His hand was warm and strong as it gripped her own, and she followed without question.

Edmund was already in the fire room.

"Where are the others?" Rogan asked as they entered.

"Two in the kitchen," Edmund said, nodding toward the kitchen. "Belmiro and No-Nose are cutting wood."

Rogan looked to Saphyre, his violet red-brown eyes smoldering with the dominance of leadership. "Remain here till we are all gathered," Rogan ordered.

Saphyre nodded—watched him quick stride to the kitchen.

"What is it?" Edmund asked.

Saphyre shook her head, saying, "I do not know. Salomonè has only just returned, and he brings news of the princess."

"News of the princess? News of you?" Edmund asked. His eyes narrowed as he looked at her.

"Yes," she managed.

"What news does Salomonè bring?" Marcellus asked, scurrying from the kitchen like a squirrel.

Thaddeus was at his heels and likewise asked, "Yes…what news?"

"I know not," Saphyre said, "only that he said he has gained information concerning the princess, Saphyre Snow."

"Marvelous!" Marcellus exclaimed.

No-Nose and Belmiro entered then with Rogan, and all the men took seat around the fire pit.

"Will you not sit with us, Saphyre?" Thaddeus asked.

Saphyre shook her head, for she was too unsettled to sit.

It seemed an eternity before Salomonè returned. Saphyre's heart beat fierce in her bosom as he joined the others.

"She is ill," he said. "The princess of the Kingdom of Graces lies ill in her bed in the castle."

Saphyre looked at once to Rogan. A deep frown furrowed his handsome brow.

"Ill?" Rogan asked. "She cannot lie ill in her bed in the castle when she lies here with us."

Salomonè shook his head. "It is what the people are being told."

"But I am not ill...nor at the castle," Saphyre said. "Surely my father knows I am not there. Why does he not proclaim the truth of it?"

"The king did not proclaim your illness," Salomonè said. "It was the old queen who told the people. She has said you are too ill to see your father...that for fear of the king taking upon himself whatever illness you endure...his counselors have determined he shall not witness you in your bed."

"The king's mind is abandoning him...just as his father's did," Rogan growled. "For what father would allow illness to keep him from his only daughter...king or not?"

"There is, no doubt, more that we do not know," No-Nose said. "Is there nothing else, Salomonè?"

Salomonè shook his head. "No. Only that the princess is ill. Though the people speculate that the illness of the princess..." Salomonè paused—glanced to Saphyre a moment.

"Salomonè," Rogan urged.

Salomonè drew a long breath, as if he did not wish to speak the rest in Saphyre's presence. "The people in the village wonder if the illness of the princess is like unto that which took her mother," he said at last.

At once, Saphyre felt hot, sickened, and near to fainting. Though she well knew she was not stricken with the same cruel illness that had taken her mother, the thought of it pure terrified her.

"You are well, Saphyre," Thaddeus said, smiling at Saphyre. It was as if the small man owned a knowledge of her dark thoughts in that moment. "You are here with us...and well."

Saphyre nodded, drawing a little strength from his kind encouragement.

"And you are certain there is not other talk that would merit consideration?" Rogan asked.

Salomonè shook his head, yet paused in the next moment, his eyes narrowing. "Unless...there was one curiosity...but I do not know if it is important...or even why the people would be speaking of it."

"Let it be told to us," No-Nose said. "I have lingered long in this kingdom. Something that you may not recognize as valuable... perhaps I may."

"It is something concerning a sword of great worth," Salomonè began, "something the king has done. The king, some weeks ago, decreed that possession of a sword should fall to his daughter...to the princess, Saphyre Snow. The mention of the princess's name is the sole reason for my even heeding the gossip of the sword. The people in the village seem to think that the king's proclamation that this certain sword would pass to the princess was ominous. They term it the sword of the throne."

"The Crimson Frost?" Saphyre asked. "Did my father proclaim the great sword of my mother's family, the Crimson Frost, should pass to me...now?"

Salomonè nodded as he looked to Saphyre. "Yes. The Crimson Frost...that was it. Your father has proclaimed it has come to you."

Saphyre felt her knees weaken, her breath still a moment. All seven of the men of the keep rose. Marcellus and Thaddeus, being nearest to Saphyre, hastened to her, helping her to her feet and leading her to sit next to No-Nose.

"What is it, Saphyre?" Marcellus asked.

"The Crimson Frost," Saphyre breathed. "My father...it must be my father fears for his life."

"A sword?" Belmiro said. "A sword passing to your possession leads you think your father fears for his life?"

"His life...or the wellness of his mind," Rogan said.

"It is well I know the story of the Crimson Frost, for it is legend in my kingdom...in my once kingdom, Rothbain," Edmund said. "Of the great Crimson Knight that rose to sit a throne...and of the Scarlet Princess who ruled with him. But I do not understand how this sword came to be here in this kingdom...nor how it is foretelling of a king's death or madness."

"A story?" Marcellus said. "Tell it, Edmund!"

Edmund's eyes narrowed. He did not respond to Marcellus, yet he studied Saphyre with seeming renewed interest. "Saphyre Snow," Edmund said, "named for King Channing of Rothbain? Are you indeed descended of the Crimson King and Scarlet Queen of Karvana?"

"Karvana?" Thaddeus asked.

"Rothbain knew a king," Edmund continued, "not so long ago. King Channing Snow...another once knight risen to king... through his wife, the Sapphire Princess of Karvana. Are you thus named, Saphyre Snow, for this lineage? Is this how the mighty sword of Karvana, the Crimson Frost...is this how your father comes to wield it?"

"I-I am named for the sapphire snow of the Kingdom of Graces," Saphyre stammered.

"The blue moonlight and indigo frost that falls rare in the winter?" Belmiro asked.

"Yes," Saphyre said. She closed her eyes, for the memory of her mother's last words to her was thick in her mind.

"You are Saphyre Snow," her mother had whispered as they lingered in the grand flower garden of the castle, "named for nature's blessing to the kingdom of blue moonlight and indigo frost that I so love to see. Yet know this. You are also so named for my grandfather... the great king Channing Snow, who rose from pageboy to squire and knight…he who loved a princess, the Sapphire Princess Afton of Karvana, daughter of the Crimson King and Scarlet Queen…who granted my grandfather the hand of their daughter and set him on the throne of the conquered kingdom of Rothbain."

It was her mother's voice echoed in her mind as a sweet summer breeze, and Saphyre said, "And I am also thus named for my mother's people…my great-grandfather, King Channing Snow of Rothbain, and his queen…the Sapphire Princess of Karvana."

Edmund fair leapt to his feet. "You are descended of such legend and greatness as is not known in our day!" he exclaimed. "Do you know the tales of the Crimson Knight and the Scarlet Princess? Of the pageboy Channing Snow and the Sapphire Princess Afton?"

"Yes," Saphyre said. "And I know that my mother gifted my father the legend sword, the Crimson Frost, on their wedding day… and that he vowed, in that moment, that he would not forfeit it till death, or worse, was upon him."

Edmund sat down once more, shaking his head in disbelief. "The Crimson Frost," he whispered. "Here?"

No-Nose looked to Saphyre. "If the king has proclaimed the sword as yours…he must know madness or death is upon him."

Saphyre leapt to her feet. "I must return!" she cried. "This day! This very moment! If my father has proclaimed the sword has come to me…then he is in danger! Perhaps the old queen means him harm as well. I cannot linger whilst my father's life is threatened!"

Rogan stood, taking hold of Saphyre's shoulders.

"You cannot return now," he said. "Your return would only find the heir to the throne surely dead."

"But I cannot forsake my father…nor my kingdom!" she cried. Tears spilled from her eyes and streamed over her cheeks. Fear was thick in her—fear for her father's life, for her kingdom's fate should he die and leave the old queen, Carmen, as ruler.

"You cannot serve them with your own death," No-Nose said. "The king has merely passed the sword from his possession to yours. I think this is not proof he is dying…rather proof his mind had not yet left him."

"I agree," Rogan said. "The king must know his daughter has not taken to her bed for illness."

"Why then would he not proclaim her absence...send out searchers for her?" Salomonè asked.

"Perhaps he has...but in secret," Rogan said.

"The great sword, the Crimson Frost...it marks the ruling monarch," No-Nose said.

"But it is of Karvana...and Rothbain," Edmund said.

"Yes," No-Nose said. "But when Felice of Avaron wed Michael of Graces, when she presented the sword to her husband, Michael of Graces proclaimed the Crimson Frost would ever lie in the hands of the king or queen who sat the throne...or in the hands of the heir to the throne of Graces. When the princess Saphyre Snow was born, Prince Michael—for he was not yet king at her birth—Prince Michael proclaimed the great sword, the Crimson Frost, would one day pass to his daughter...the firstborn of his house. He termed the Crimson Frost 'The Sword of the Throne'...that whoever possessed the great sword...would own claim to the throne of the Kingdom of Graces. Thus, all of the Kingdom of Graces knows whoever possesses the legendary sword, the Crimson Frost, rules...or will rule the kingdom."

"By the sword, the king has proclaimed Saphyre will one day rule," Rogan said. "In this he gives the people hope."

Edmund nodded. "In this he believes Saphyre is not ill...nor dead."

"In the least he believed it when last his mind was clear," Salomonè said. "For there is much talk in the village of his mind slipping slowly...as did his father's."

"I can linger here no longer," Saphyre said. "I have proven myself a coward by not returning to my father and my people!"

"The old queen is powerful, Saphyre," No-Nose said. "She gained great influence after King Jordan's death. Perhaps her reason for wanting to see you dead—to hold in her hand the very heart cut from your breast—perhaps her reason is mere vanity. Yet she means to murder you…and your death will not serve your father or your people."

Saphyre brushed tears from her eyes. "Then what am I to do? I must act! I cannot simply wait until my father is mad…until the kingdom loathes him as they did my grandfather…until hope is lost. What am I to do?"

"Find strength of endurance," Rogan said, "for to act in haste may bring destruction to you and the kingdom."

"But I—" Saphyre began.

"Would you see your royal bloodline vanquished, Saphyre?" No-Nose said. "Would you see the kingdom fall to the unworthy or wicked?"

"Would you see the Crimson Frost—the sword of your mother's great family—in the hands of one who would wield it for vanity and evil?" Edmund said.

"Edmund is right," Rogan said, "and No-Nose. Queen Carmen would take the throne if your father is mad or dies…if you are likewise dead. We must battle wise…glean information before you can be returned."

Of a sudden, Saphyre wished to throw herself against Rogan's strong body—to feel his powerful arms about her. She wished he would brave the Executioner's Kiss once more and press her lips— warm her mouth with the flavor of his.

"And we must protect you, Saphyre," No-Nose said, pulling Saphyre's thoughts from Rogan's kiss. "All of us."

"You have protected me," Saphyre said. "But I do not see how lingering will serve. My father slips into madness…and the people of my kingdom fear."

"Returning now will not save your father, Saphyre," Edmund said. "Nor can you save your people if the old queen succeeds in vanquishing your beauty from the earth. As a once knight—a knight who loved his own kingdom and would have sacrificed his own life to save it—I counsel you to linger. Let us be watchful, listen, and discern allies…or enemies…for no doubt, there are those who are loyal to the old queen. If your father is indeed slipping into madness, then there will be those who may be swayed to the old queen's ways… those who fear madness more than evil."

"I fear madness more than evil," Thaddeus whispered.

"As do I," Marcellus agreed.

"Edmund is wise, Saphyre," Belmiro said. "And No-Nose and Rogan as well. It is I have learned to trust their ways."

"As have I," Salomonè said.

"It is the strange laughter that gives me cause to tremble," Thaddeus said to his brother. "Mad folk always laugh so strangely."

"Agreed," Marcellus said. He looked to Saphyre then. "Stay, Saphyre," he said, "for we are seven who can protect you."

"Perhaps one of us could assassinate the old queen," Thaddeus said.

"And risk hanging for the murder of a monarch?" Marcellus asked. "Even murdering a vain and evil monarch is cause for hanging."

Thaddeus looked to Rogan. "Rogan could do it…for he has kissed Saphyre and is already marked for death," he said.

"True," Marcellus said. Then, lowering his voice, he added, "You are right about the laughter, Thaddeus. The strange laughter of madness causes me the utmost discomfort."

For all the terror in her, for all the hopelessness, for all that Saphyre knew that, for her concern for her father, she should not find amusement in their talk of madness, Saphyre near smiled as she saw Rogan inhale a deep breath in attempt to calm his temper where the two jesters were concerned.

Rogan's hands moved from Saphyre's shoulders, traveling slowly down her arms, till he released her completely.

"You will remain here," he said. "We here—we men of the keep—we may be cowards and thieves, jesters and condemned murderers…but we are also of no consequence to anyone. We can move near unseen among the people of the villages surrounding the forest. We will watchful bide the day and nights…continue to listen for information as we have done these past weeks."

"In likeness we counsel you to live the life of a knight, Saphyre,"

Edmund said, "to prepare for battle...that you may be ready for battle whenever it comes...and whatever it brings to your gate."

"Prepare for battle, Saphyre," Belmiro said. "You are only preparing for battle...a battle to save your kingdom. You are not forsaking it."

"Kiss her once more, Rogan!" Thaddeus exclaimed. "I have seen the manner in which the women in the villages gaze at you. You are handsome enough. Thus, kiss Saphyre once more...and perhaps she will not be so willing to leave us."

"Yes, Rogan," Marcellus said. "After all, you can only lose your head once."

"He can only hang once, as well," Thaddeus added.

"True," Marcellus said, nodding.

"Unless you two wish Rogan to hang you himself for your insolence..." Edmund growled.

"Let us speak no more of it this day," No-Nose said, laying a strong hand on Rogan's shoulder. "Marcellus and Thaddeus are right to attempt to lighten hearts. There is enough pain lingering in our weathered hearts...even yours, Saphyre," he said. "Let us take sup and take respite."

"Rogan will sup...but he will take no respite," Salomonè said. "You are a fool, No-Nose...if you think Rogan will ease his mind or body for one moment."

"Perhaps if Edmund were to tell us the story of the Crimson Frost," Marcellus suggested. "I want to hear of this Crimson Knight and Scarlet Princess."

"Please, Saphyre," Thaddeus said, taking Saphyre's hand. "Let us ease our minds and hearts for a time. We will all of us help and protect you. This you know...for have we not proven ourselves?"

"How can your father gift you this great sword...when you are not present to accept it?" Marcellus asked.

"He will leave it for me, in a secret place he once told me of," Saphyre said.

"Enough, Marcellus!" Thaddeus said. "Rogan? Respite? For those of us who seek it, in the least?"

Saphyre watched Rogan—watched his brow furrow, his jaw tighten.

"Tell them the tale of this sword, Edmund," he said, "before I put them on the spit and roast them over the fire."

"You would not want to see us roasted, Edmund. Would you?" Marcellus asked.

As Rogan turned to leave, Saphyre nearly caught hold of his arm to stay him.

"You will not linger with us, Rogan?" No-Nose asked.

"You know I cannot," Rogan grumbled as he left the keep.

As Saphyre watched him go, she wondered why it was her heart seemed so fixed to him. She had known him so little time; he was ever so thoughtful, so seeming troubled. Yet she felt as if her very soul could not exist without him. Was it simply for the sake he had kissed her? Still, Saphyre knew her attachment to Rogan—her feelings— began the mere moment she first saw him. His kiss had only served to flame the passion she had not before understood.

"There is no peace in him," No-Nose said. "Of all us, with all our secret pain, he is yet the one who finds not one moment of peace."

"Come, Saphyre," Marcellus said. "Edmund will tell us a tale, and we will be distracted from our dismal and hopeless thoughts for a time."

"Fear not, pretty princess," Thaddeus whispered as Saphyre took seat beside him. "Rogan does not often wander far. He will, no doubt, enjoy the tale…only from a distance."

"Then tell us, Edmund," Marcellus prodded. "Tell us of this great sword of legend."

"I too am curious of the tale, Edmund," Belmiro said.

Saphyre glanced at each face sitting in the circle around the low-burning fire. No-Nose—who she knew bore thoughts of concern for their leader—yet settled himself in readiness. Belmiro wore an encouraging smile, as did Salomonè. It was not often that Edmund told tales, and Marcellus and Thaddeus bore wide eyes of delighted anticipation.

Edmund paused, however, and Saphyre's thoughts again returned to her father—to her people—to Rogan. Her heart weighed so heavy in her bosom she felt as if she might needs lie down and never rise again. Fear—worry—love. All were in her mind—and heart.

"By the hand of a skilled craftsman, the Crimson Frost was forged in memory of the bloody Battle of Ballist…and the great Crimson Knight of Karvana," Edmund began.

Saphyre looked to him, willing herself to listen, allowing her weary mind a measure of respite.

"It was as Arthur and Excalibur?" Marcellus inquired.

Edmund chuckled, and Saphyre found his mirth caused her to smile.

"Yes, Marcellus," Edmund said. "The Crimson Frost and its gallant, brave Crimson Knight…as Arthur and Excalibur of old."

Saphyre listened as Edmund wove a magnificent tale of battle and conquering love. Yet her mind often wandered without the keep to Rogan. Was he near? Was he in earnest in his desire to protect the progeny of a monarch who had so betrayed him—murdered his father? If he were near—if he were hearing the tale of a great knight, told by his once-knight brother of the keep—then would not this bring fresh to his mind memories of his father—of his father's murder? Would he then still be so certain the princess Saphyre Snow should continue to find sanctuary in his keep?

Saphyre did not find sleep easy that night. Her tortured mind persisted in a lingering vision of Rogan coming into her bower, taking her from her bed, and banishing her from the keep. Yet he did not come; he did not throw her out into the elements to find her own way back to the castle and peril at the hand of her vain step-grandmother.

Instead she awoke to find she yet remained in the keep—to find Marcellus and Thaddeus juggling apples in the kitchen as she entered.

"The others have gone to the villages," Marcellus said. "Thaddeus and I are your guardians today."

"We are thick in making pastry this morning," Thaddeus said, smiling. "Apple pastry. Would you assist us, Saphyre?"

Saphyre smiled. "Of course," Saphyre said.

The bright light of day brought with it hope—dispelled the deep despair she had known during the night.

Perhaps her father was not going mad; perhaps her step-grandmother did not own the influence and power the men of the keep surmised. Perhaps Saphyre would find herself bound in Rogan's strong arms once more—taste of his kiss another night under the stars.

It was ever daylight brought with it hope—and Saphyre did hope. As Marcellus tossed an apple to her, she smiled—and hoped.

A TALE FOR MARCELLUS

Still, though hope found Saphyre by day, a new trepidation had begun to creep into her mind as darkness veiled the keep each night. Fear—fear of growing weakness and cowardice in her heart—a fear that she would never find the will to leave the keep, even for the sake of her father and kingdom—fear that her feelings for Rogan would cause her to follow a path that was pure selfish.

Further, as the days continued to wane, Saphyre began to know more and more tenderness and empathy for the other men of the keep. As she did continue to linger with them—whether for the purpose of safety, her own cowardice, or want of Rogan's company— she began to full know why they all lingered there in the deep forest keep. She began to feel and understand their contentment in their solitude with one another. Certainly she began to realize how much easier it would be to simply remain with them—to ignore who she was, what responsibility she owned to her kingdom. Likewise, she had accepted—as the men of the keep had asked of her—that, for a time, it was safer to remain in hiding with them. Yes, it was more and more clear to Saphyre why the seven men of the old keep remained in their seemingly perpetual state of avoidance and seclusion.

Something else was pricking at her thoughts as well. The seven men of the keep had taken her in and had provided everything for her—shelter, food, and even fellowship. They had not mistreated her in any regard, and Saphyre began to feel all too thankless. In truth, what had she gifted them in return for all their protection, companionship, and provisions? Nothing. Certainly, she had nothing to give—surely no possessions in hand of worth. Yet she owned no other thing as well. She had no skill in humor the like Marcellus and Thaddeus owned—always they were giving of smiles and laughter to their brothers. She had no talent, such as the viol, as Belmiro did. She had neither strong hands nor back to labor hard as Salomonè and Edmund. And where Rogan and No-Nose were concerned—it was obvious their contributions were thoroughly encompassing—hard work, leadership, protection of the keep, friendship. What had Saphyre Snow to give? Nothing.

The guilt and humiliation of giving nothing in return for all the men gifted her began to weigh heavy on Saphyre's heart and mind. Quietly, in her own thoughts, she began to title herself "The Parasite Princess," for it was how she considered of herself—as a leech drawing blood and strength from its host, leaving only an uncomfortable irritation as compensation.

Yet during one of the cool evenings spent around the fire pit, something occurred to give Saphyre hope of offering small recompense to the men of the keep. It happened quite unexpected, and yet it happened—and rained inspiration over her.

Marcellus had been full begging No-Nose for the telling of a tale. It was no secret Marcellus enjoyed a good yarn more than near anything else. Certainly, Edmund had lit Marcellus's mind with a wondrous flame in the telling of the legend of the Crimson Frost. Still, it seemed since hearing Edmund's tale, Marcellus's thirst for stories had only increased. Among the men of the keep, there was no doubt No-Nose was the best at spinning tales. Saphyre had heard No-Nose weave the same tales twice or thrice since she had arrived at the keep, and on this evening it was apparent No-Nose was weary, tired of repeating the same stories to his enthusiastic little friend.

"Please, No-Nose," Marcellus begged. "You have such a way of stirring my mind. I do not care which tale you choose or how many times I have heard it. Just give us a story this night. Any will suffice."

"I am weary, Marcellus," No-Nose said, yawning, leaning back against the inner wall of the keep. "My back is aching…and my mind aches with it. I have not the vigor to tell you a tale this night. Forgive me."

Saphyre whole felt Marcellus's disenchantment as she watched the light of his face fade with his smile. He so enjoyed stories in the evenings. Yet she understood No-Nose's weariness as well. Still, as every soul around the fire sat in silence, she could not linger in seeing Marcellus so disappointed.

"Years ago," Saphyre began, "a kingdom and its king came under attack." The fire in the hearth crackled as it burned, its warm orange light casting dark shadows on the ancient stone ceiling and walls. The scent of burning cedar hung heavy in the room. Saphyre smiled as she saw Marcellus wiggle down in his seat, the delight of an expectant child flashing in his eyes.

"You have a tale to tell us, Saphyre?" he asked, eyes wide with anticipation.

"Perhaps," Saphyre said, "though…not as good a one as No-Nose would tell."

"Go on, Saphyre. Go on," Marcellus urged.

Saphyre glanced to No-Nose. He was grinning at her—nodded encouragement—and she cleared her throat to begin again.

"Years ago," Saphyre repeated, "a kingdom and its king came under attack."

"This is going to be good," Marcellus mumbled. A broad smile curled his lips, and he rubbed his hands together with eagerness. "I can tell already."

"You see, the greedy king of a neighboring kingdom coveted the beautiful Kingdom of Graces," Saphyre continued.

"This is a story about *your* kingdom!" Marcellus exclaimed. "Even better!"

"Hush, Marcellus," Thaddeus scolded. "She will never be able to tell the story with you interrupting at every turn."

Marcellus nudged Thaddeus with his elbow, and Thaddeus

nudged back, but both men sat in rapt attention, staring at Saphyre.

"Go on then," Marcellus said.

Saphyre smiled and nodded. She glanced at Rogan to find him staring at her rather indifferently—an all too familiar weariness about him. Then, lowering her voice for a more dramatic effect, she continued, "King Gregory of the Kingdom of Gregoria sinfully coveted the Kingdom of Graces, ruled by King Jordan."

Saphyre dared another quick glance at Rogan but found no expression of disapproval; rather the same expression of indifference bore yet in his countenance. She was relieved he did not seem overly vexed at the mention of her grandfather.

"King Jordan was a good and fair ruler...at that time," she added when she saw a frown pucker Rogan's brow. "The people loved him and he them, and all of the Kingdom of Graces were well, and the land was peaceful and brimming with beauty."

"No wonder King Gregory wanted it," Marcellus said aloud.

"Shhh!" Thaddeus scolded.

"One day," Saphyre continued, "King Gregory became too covetous, too desirous in his wanting to rule the Kingdom of Graces as well as his own, and he ordered the captain of his guard, a black knight named Desmond Destry, to prepare...for war." Saphyre was barely able to keep from giggling as she saw Marcellus's and Thaddeus's eyes widen. "There would be no warning, King Gregory explained to Desmond. The Kingdom of Graces would not expect an attack, and therefore he ordered Desmond to take only a fraction of his army to conquer King Jordan and his beautiful kingdom.

"Yet Desmond was fearful...for he knew King Jordan had a valiant and powerful, able and alert captain of his own guard...a great knight by the name of Sebastian Ottokar." Saphyre paused for striking effect and then continued, "Sebastian Ottokar was handsome and strong. He owned many titles bestowed of the king, had won much wealth in tournament, warriored well in battle. He stood nearly six feet and four and had the deepest blue eyes. Some say he was, in truth, born of a king and queen in a far-off land...a land destroyed by corruption and greed, forcing him to flee. But

Sebastian was good, and he owned the heart of a good and beautiful young woman…one of the queen's ladies-in-waiting. Her name was Augustynia, and she was as beautiful as Sebastian was handsome. They wished to wed, but Sebastian paused, thinking himself beneath the beautiful lady-in-waiting…he only a knight and she such a fair and graceful creature."

"But…but knights are the greatest of men!" Marcellus argued.

Again Thaddeus's elbow met with Marcellus's ribs.

"That is true," Saphyre said. "But Sebastian was as humble as he was great, and he was troubled, doubting his worthiness as a match for Augustynia…for Augustynia had proven royal ancestry herself, her mother having been a princess in a far kingdom. Oh, and Augustynia was so very beautiful!"

"How beautiful was she?" Marcellus asked.

Saphyre smiled and whispered, "As beautiful as any angel! Her hair was the color of the sun and her eyes as—"

"As deep a green as any emerald ever mined," No-Nose mumbled, sitting down next to Thaddeus.

Saphyre glanced up to No-Nose, delighted at his knowledge of the story. "Yes," she said. "Her eyes were as deep a green as any emerald ever mined, and her heart belonged to the captain of the guard—"

"Sebastian Ottokar," Marcellus finished.

"Yes, but I lose my path," Saphyre said. She cleared her throat and began again. "Sebastian was indeed King Jordan's captain of the guard, and he was able…with his own troops more ready than the small army of King Gregory's was prepared for. And so it was when King Gregory's army attacked the Kingdom of Graces, they found stiff and impenetrable troops led by the great captain of the guard, Sebastian Ottokar. Desmond Destry was forced to retreat, but Sebastian and his king knew this first attack was as a droplet of rain…a whisper of the storm about to descend upon the kingdom."

Marcellus rubbed his hands together with delight and, nodding, said, "Go on!"

Saphyre smiled. "Sebastian told King Jordan all precautions

must be taken, lest the kingdom be in danger of being lost. He told the king all able-bodied men must be armed, and all the knights… the best warriors of the Kingdom of Graces must be gathered in preparation for the battle to come. 'And we must certainly send for Roar,' Sebastian told the king."

"Roar?" Belmiro asked, sitting down next to Thaddeus.

Saphyre smiled, delighted she had been able to capture the attention of Belmiro. He was oft so uninterested in anything, let alone stories.

"Have you not heard of Roar?" Marcellus asked in disbelief.

"No. Should I have?" Belmiro replied.

Marcellus and Thaddeus both rolled their eyes with irritation at his ignorance.

"Roar is only the greatest knight, the greatest warrior, to ever ride over the face of this land!" Thaddeus explained, full exasperated.

"Is that so?" Belmiro asked, smiling with mirth. "Then why have I never heard of him…this…this Roar?"

"Because you never listen," Salomonè grumbled, sitting down next to Belmiro.

Saphyre glanced up to where Rogan sat across the room with Edmund. Her heart warmed as he smiled, obviously amused by his brothers' interest in her story.

"Shhh! Quiet now! I want to hear more," Marcellus said. "Go on, please. Saphyre, go on."

"Roar was the greatest knight in the Kingdom of Graces," Saphyre continued, "and in all the kingdoms surrounding. He was large in stature, the breadth of his shoulders unmatched. He was strangely powerful…unusually strong. It was said the chain mail he wore beneath his armor, when he bothered to wear his armor, weighed as much as any man. He had bested every other knight in the joust and in swords—even Sebastian—and it was said he was as invincible as Achilles himself and that he had no weakness…not even the smallest the like in the tender heel of the great god Achilles. It was further said, in particular among the ladies in spinning circles, that Roar was ever as handsome…if not more so than Adonis!"

"More handsome even than Adonis?" Marcellus exclaimed.

Saphyre smiled and answered, "Yes. More handsome even than Adonis. And so it was Sebastian sent word for Roar to return to the Kingdom of Graces...and to make haste in doing so.

"But even the great warrior Roar...even Sebastian, the king's captain, could not have foreseen the depth of King Gregory's cowardice in treachery. No!" Saphyre said. "For as word went out for the knights of the kingdom to return, a traitor was able to penetrate the kingdom. And what he took...what the coward and thief sent from Gregoria took...I tell you, no one could have guessed."

Saphyre paused, but Marcellus could stand no silence and said, "What did he take?"

Saphyre glanced around the room. Lowering her voice to a whisper, she watched Marcellus's eyes widen as she said, "The innocent young daughter of a nobleman...the king's trusted friend and counselor. The only daughter of the king's most trusted familiar...was taken."

"No!" Marcellus and Thaddeus exclaimed together.

Saphyre nodded and said, "'Tis true. The thief seized the young girl and made for Gregoria."

"What an evil king was Gregory," Marcellus said, shaking his head. "To prey on such innocence as a pawn in trying to take hold of what was not his."

Saphyre nodded and said, "Word was sent out to the gathering knights of the girl taken by a thief in Desmond Destry's employ. The knights were told the girl was the daughter of the king's friend, and being the king's friend...well, the nobleman was friend to all the knights as well."

"Abduction! And of an innocent!" Marcellus breathed.

Saphyre smiled, delighted with Marcellus's enchantment. Her smile faded, however, when she looked up to see Rogan frowning as he listened. It was all too apparent he did not find the story as captivating as did Marcellus. Still, the story was a gift for Marcellus—not for Rogan—and Saphyre continued.

"Word first reached the great warrior-knight Roar, and he set out to rescue the girl. It was said nothing infuriated Roar more than a coward who would use a woman or a child to try to best his enemy.

"In the interim, the young woman was bound and gagged. Her captor changed her fine clothing for rags. Cloth was wound about her head to conceal her hair and cover her eyes so she would not be recognized. She, being only twelve, was more frightened than she had ever imagined she could be…even in her worst of nightmares. She was never more terrified as the thief put her into a weathered carriage and set out for Gregoria.

"Oh, how terrified the young girl was when she heard the thief talking to a man who soon joined them. They spoke of her impending murder…and…and what they meant to do to her before killing her." Saphyre's voice broke, and she swallowed hard.

"Are you well? Did you know her then?" Marcellus asked.

Saphyre nodded and continued, "But fear not…for it was not long before the great knight Roar came upon the two roughened men," she said. "The girl heard the thunderous pounding of his horse's gallop as he approached! Her heart leapt with hope as she felt the carriage stop…heard a strong voice shout, 'What are you men about?'"

"It was Roar?" Marcellus asked.

"It was!" Saphyre whispered, smiling. "It was Roar…the greatest warrior-knight in any kingdom!" Saphyre giggled when Marcellus clapped his hands together with excitement.

"One knight and two thieves," Marcellus chuckled. "Not a fair match…for the thieves."

"Indeed," Saphyre said. "But there were not just two thieves," she said.

Marcellus's eyes widened. "No?" he asked.

"No. There were not two," Saphyre continued, "but thirteen! For the thieves' counterparts had been escorting the girl's captors all along…in secret…skulking through the woods and keeping watch over the carriage with the girl in it."

"Thirteen!" Marcellus exclaimed.

"A good many…even for one great knight!" Thaddeus said, nodding at his brother.

"The fighting began…the noise of swords clashing…blade against blade," Saphyre said. "There was shouting and the sound of metal meeting metal and of metal meeting flesh!" Saphyre smiled when Marcellus wrinkled his nose in delighted disgust. "And then… of a sudden…all was quiet. And the young girl…sitting still bound, still gagged, her eyes still covered…waited. She waited to meet her fate. Had she been rescued? Had Roar championed her? Or had he fallen…murdered at the hands of Desmond Destry's villains?"

Saphyre paused again, and Marcellus, impatient, asked, "Well? What happened?"

Saphyre smiled and nodded, "The young girl was…was…"

"Was what?" Marcellus demanded an answer.

"She was rescued! Roar himself broke into the carriage and pulled her out of it. He sat her on the ground…pulled the cloth from her eyes. 'Are you unharmed?' he asked the girl. She could only nod, tears streaming down her face as she looked up at him…a crimson feather adorning his helmet…his helmet shield drawn down over his face. 'You are safe now, little one,' Roar said. 'You are safe.' His voice was calm, soothing, and the girl knew she was secure in his care.

"It was in that moment Sebastian Ottokar rode to them. Sebastian looked about at the thirteen dead men slain by Roar, shaking his head in disbelief. 'I must away,' Roar told the girl. 'But fear not, Sebastian is here! You have heard of Sebastian, no doubt…the great warrior-knight and captain of the king's guard.' Roar said. The girl nodded, trembling in the presence of the man she knew to be Roar… the greatest of knights and warriors. 'Sebastian will see you to your father safely, for I must away to meet with the king at once,' Roar told the girl.

"The young girl, still terribly frightened, knowing Roar would champion her against any odds, shook her head. Still gagged, she could utter not a word in begging him not to leave her…but he soothed her with his handsome smile and whispered, 'Shhh. Hush, girl. Sebastian will keep you.' Then Roar took a chain from around his neck. An emblem it held, and he offered it out to her, saying, 'There, now. You keep this 'round your throat, and no one would dare to harm you. Very well?' The emblem was a precious treasure, presented to Roar by the king himself. It was fashioned in gold and in the shape and image of a roaring lion, its kingly mane flaming 'round its face. Roar placed the chain and its precious emblem around the girl's neck and kissed the top of her head before mounting his horse. A few words he said to Sebastian, and then he rode away…a mad gallop carrying him toward King Jordan's castle.

"Sebastian safely returned the girl to her father…and no one was told of the incident. No one, save the royal family, the captain of the guard, and the great knight Roar, ever knew what had happened concerning the nobleman's daughter."

Saphyre was silent, pensive for a moment before continuing. "There are those who say the beloved queen, the first wife of King Jordan, Queen Penelope—there are those who say her untimely death so soon after the attempt at taking the nobleman's daughter to Gregoria…was also the work of Desmond Destry. For the queen died only a few days after the nobleman's daughter was returned. The kingdom was still in deep mourning, and all thought it very peculiar when King Jordan married one of Queen Penelope's young ladies-in-waiting only a few weeks after the queen's death. It was then the king began to change, they say."

"He did not marry Augustynia, did he?" Marcellus exclaimed. "He did not take Sebastian's lover to wife, did he?"

Saphyre smiled, amused by Marcellus's concern.

"No," No-Nose answered. "He married Lady Carmen…and some say her wicked manner was what changed the king."

"Ah, yes," Marcellus mumbled. "I was not thinking. The old queen is named Carmen…not Augustynia."

"Yes, that is as it was," Saphyre confirmed. "King Jordan married Carmen only a few weeks after the queen's death, and he soon began to behave strangely. Some say it was his grief, mourning over the loss of his beloved wife, that changed him. Some say had it not been for Roar and Sebastian…the Kingdom of Graces would have been lost to King Gregory when his army attacked in force some two months later."

Saphyre sighed as she said, "And now...now for the stirring of the story."

"The *stirring*?" Marcellus exclaimed. "What wasn't stirring about the story so far?"

Saphyre smiled. Her brow puckered next, and she asked, "Do you want to hear the rest, Marcellus? Even...even if it does not end just as we all wish it would?"

"Even if it is the saddest, most miserable story ever told...I want to hear it through to the end," he said.

"Very well then." Saphyre inhaled and continued, "King Jordan married Lady Carmen, she became queen, and the king began to change. Quiet whispers abounded throughout the kingdom that Carmen was to blame for the king's strange behavior...that she had bewitched him somehow, learned to beguile him. And as King Jordan indeed became quick and bad-tempered, dispassionate, even seeming not to care about the welfare of his kingdom...Sebastian remained loyal to the king *and* his subjects...and, with Roar's help, King Jordan's legions were prepared when King Gregory's army attacked.

"The warring was, however, marked with terrible battles. Many men were lost, killed in fighting. The wheat fields to the west of the Kingdom of Graces were marred...marred with fire, dead and dying men...the soil soaked in blood." Saphyre nearly giggled when Marcellus and Thaddeus each wrinkled their noses—aghast. "Oh, so many valiant and brave men fell in battle...many knights too... knights of Gregoria and knights of the Kingdom of Graces. The evil Desmond Destry was slain by Roar himself...his throat slit from ear to ear, his belly run through. It was said, by those who survived the great battles, that often Roar and Sebastian could be seen fighting together in the fields, back to back, the glint of their swords radiant in the sun as they fought, slaying hundreds of the enemy between the mere two of them. And finally...the battles were won."

"The Kingdom of Graces was not taken by King Gregory?" Marcellus asked.

Saphyre shook her head. "But...there are those who say it might have been better had it been taken...for King Jordan began to fail.

His mind, his health, and in the end…he was a cruel king, entirely changed from the man he had once been. In the end he…he even sent his great captain, Sebastian, to his death…and the great warrior, Roar."

"What?" Marcellus exclaimed, leaping to his feet. "How? What of them? I have never heard this part of the legend of Roar! And Sebastian? Did Sebastian never marry Augustynia?"

"No," Saphyre whispered, tears filling her eyes. "He did not."

"But…but why?" Marcellus asked, sinking to his knees once more.

Saphyre forced a smile as she looked at his expectant face. "Sometime before his own death, the king demanded Roar and Sebastian leave on a charge. He gave them this charge…to bring King Gregory to justice. King Jordan, in his madness or whatever it was that overcame him, had taken on the greed that once plagued his enemy. He wanted the Kingdom of Gregoria as payment for all King Gregory had done…and so he ordered the great warrior-knight Roar and the great captain of the guard Sebastian…to bring King Gregory to him. And if they could not strip him from his castle, they were to…to kill him and bring him anyway.

"Roar and Sebastian refused, of course, being men of honor as they were. Though they still loved the king…they could not serve what he had become. The king was furious! He accused both men of treason and banished them from the Kingdom of Graces, telling them never to return. And when Roar and Sebastian had left the kingdom, hearts broken and bodies sickened for the king's treachery—the traitorous behavior of the king they loved and had served so well—even for it all they obeyed him and left the kingdom…striking hands and parting to their own paths. But the king, in his state of unrest and sick-mindedness, was proud and angry…furious at his two great warriors refusing to do his bidding, and he sent out assassins."

"No!" Marcellus gasped.

"Yes," Saphyre said, nodding. "He sent assassins, one to Roar's path and one to Sebastian's, and being that great warriors the like of Roar and Sebastian are not accustomed to fighting as cowards, the assassins were finally able to use their dishonest and snaking ways to…to murder them both. The great knight-warrior Roar and the great captain of the guard Sebastian…the heroes of the Kingdom of Graces were lost to it and to all who loved them…lost to all who they had safeguarded and protected for so very, very long."

Marcellus and Thaddeus shook their heads in disbelieving disappointment. "I cannot believe it," Marcellus whispered. "They were slain? Were…were they buried with honor or the lack of it?"

"Sebastian was never buried, for his body was never found. The assassins murdered him, leaving his flesh to the wolves…for the pestilence of the earth to slowly devour," Saphyre said. "As for Roar, his body was found, but not his head…and the king had him stripped of his armor and buried, headless in a traitor's tomb."

"Headless?" Marcellus gasped.

Saphyre nodded, continuing, "Word of their murders came swift to the grieving people of the once great Kingdom of Graces…and the people's hearts were further tarnished."

"And…and what of the poor Lady Augustynia?" Thaddeus asked. "Did she die of a broken heart?"

Saphyre shook her head and smiled a sad smile. "No. She lived."

"Did…did she marry another?" Marcellus asked.

"No," Saphyre answered. "Never did she marry. She continued to love only Sebastian…and she continued to wait. 'After all,' she would say, 'I have not seen his body dead, and until I do…I will wait for him. Until I see his bones laid out before me…I will ever wait,' were her words." Saphyre smiled at Marcellus as she saw moisture gathering in his eyes.

"She would say just that to whomever asked her about her Sebastian?" Marcellus asked.

Saphyre lowered her voice and leaned toward Marcellus, saying, "She would say that to *me*, Marcellus."

"To you?" he exclaimed.

"Yes. For after my own mother's untimely death, Augustynia befriended me ever so lovingly," Saphyre explained.

"But what of the girl who was taken?" Thaddeus asked. "The

nobleman's daughter? Did she ever tell of her adventure? Of being championed by Roar?"

Saphyre gazed at the kind little man and smiled. "No...she never did. And her greatest regret was that she never had the chance to thank him. He had saved her life, and she loved him for it. For that, she loves him still. The knowledge her own grandfather had sent him to his death...remains as painful to her as if someone had plunged a dagger through her own heart."

"Her grandfather?" No-Nose mumbled. "I...I thought you said it was the *king* who had Roar and Sebastian murdered. Not the nobleman whose daughter had been taken."

"The girl has simply misspoken, No-Nose," Rogan said.

"But I have not misspoken, sir," Saphyre said, irritated he would doubt her story. She glared at him—hurt he would try to find fault with her gift to Marcellus. His eyes met hers, burning with challenge she defy him.

"But...but you said it was a nobleman's daughter captured," Marcellus reminded her, arresting her attention once more. "How then could it have been the king who..."

Marcellus paused as Saphyre smiled and reached into the front of her frock. Slowly she withdrew a long gold chain. Held by the chain was a gold lion's head, its mane flaming around its face as it roared.

Saphyre's smile broadened as she held the emblem toward Marcellus—watched as Marcellus, Thaddeus, No-Nose, Salomonè, and Belmiro leaned forward, their mouths dropping open in astonishment.

"You see here, engravened on the back of this emblem," she said, turning the treasure over for their inspection.

"Roar!" Marcellus breathed. Then he looked up at Saphyre, eyes wide with delighted awe, and said, "It was *you!* *You* were the girl taken!"

"I was," Saphyre said, reaching out and cupping his cheek with fondness. "It was I...the girl taken by King Gregory and Desmond Destry's men. The king did not wish to distress the kingdom, and so it was sent out it was a nobleman's daughter who had been taken."

Saphyre smiled, for it seemed Edmund and Rogan could pretend indifference no longer. Both men, who had sat away from Saphyre as she told the story, now rose and came to her. Both took a turn looking at the lion's head emblem, studying it and reading aloud the name engravened on the back.

"Roar," Rogan whispered. His eyes narrowed as he gazed at Saphyre for a long moment and then said, "Forgive me. I admit I doubted your true knowledge of the story."

Saphyre smiled at him, her entire being erupting into pleasurable shivers as Rogan laid his hand against her throat, letting the emblem and chain fall into its hiding place beneath her frock.

"It is a fantastic story. Perhaps hard to believe for some," she stammered as Rogan continued to stare at her.

"It was the most wonderful story I have ever heard told!" Marcellus exclaimed, leaping to his feet. Unexpectedly he threw his arms around Saphyre's neck, saying, "Thank you, thank you, thank you! I will never be the same man after such a tale told to me by a princess herself!"

Saphyre returned his embrace, delighted at having given him something to treasure. It was in that moment her mind came alive with thoughts and schemes of how she too might give to the spirit of the keep—a treasure for each man, something unique and personal to each. She smiled, overjoyed at having finally thought of what to offer as small recompense—how she may better their lives in some small way, as they had on such a grand measure bettered hers.

"I am off to bed!" Marcellus announced, quite of a sudden.

"So soon?" his brother asked.

"Ah, but yes! While the story is still fresh in me so I may dream of it all through the night," Marcellus said. "Good night then, Princess...the princess Saphyre Snow," he added.

"Good night then, Marcellus," Saphyre said.

"It is a good tale to take to bed," Belmiro said. "A very good tale." Saphyre smiled.

"Indeed," No-Nose said. "Good night, Saphyre."

"And good night to you, No-Nose," Saphyre said.

Saphyre's heart warmed as every man in turn nodded his approval of her tale before leaving the room. Every man save Rogan, who lingered once the others had retired.

"I am sorry I was in doubt of your story," he said, moving to stand near to her.

Of a sudden, Saphyre's heart began to hammer within her bosom, her mouth watering for want of the taste of his kiss.

"I wish you would trust that I am a good person, Rogan," she whispered. "I wish you would believe me when I say I—"

"Sshhhh," he said, pressing his fingers to her lips. "I know you to be a good person, Saphyre," he said. "The best of persons. And I enjoyed your story."

"Did you?" she asked, her gaze enthralled by the movement of his lips as he spoke.

"I did," he whispered, smiling. "Still, I have one question."

"What is that?" Saphyre asked.

"Is it true...what Marcellus says...that a man has but one head to lose? Or may a man be hanged twice?" he asked. "Can the executioner's blade rob me of my head more than once?"

Saphyre was perplexed by his question. "No. No, of course not," she said.

"I thought not," he whispered a moment before his head descended—his lips gently pressing her own.

Saphyre melted breathless against him as he drew her into the strength of his arms. His mouth mingled with her own—moist, warm, and driven.

He did not extend their exchange—rather ended it abruptly, saying, "And I would hang a third time...but this night I am weak. It would be dangerous to linger in baiting the executioner this night." He turned then, vanishing into the shadows as the others had only moments before, leaving Saphyre weak, elated—and very much alive.

THE GIFT OF TRUST AND FRIENDSHIP

"I would beg you a favor, Salomonè," Saphyre whispered to Salomonè.

The men of the keep and their princess sat around the fire pit in the keep. Their labors had been hard previous in the day, for the weather had been wet and cool.

"Beg a favor of me?" Salomonè asked, in evident surprised.

"Yes," she whispered.

Saphyre had spent a restless night. After having told to Marcellus the story of the great warrior-knight Roar and Sebastian, captain of the guard—after having seen the joy it brought him—Saphyre had lain awake all the night long and into the wee hours of morning. Her mind had been thorough taxed and alive with what she could do—in contemplation of what service she might provide to each of the other men. Gripped with the desire to serve them all—each and every one—she had been somewhat relieved to awaken with at least two thoughts of two men—Salomonè and Belmiro. True, her mind yet labored in thinking of the others—in consideration of what may be offered as kind recompense. Still, she was glad of what she had been able to grasp for her long pondering.

So it was—as Salomonè continued to gaze at her, consider her with much perplexity—Saphyre reached beneath the sleeve of her frock and unclasped and removed from her forearm a bracelet—a thick band of gold. The bracelet had been a gift from Kornelius. It was not engravened in any manner to lend to its identity, nor was it precious in any regard of sentiment to Saphyre.

Slipping it into Salomonè's hand, she whispered, "It is all I can give you to take to the village. Any other thing may be recognized."

Salomonè frowned and stammered, "I-I do not understand. I—"

"I would ask you to sell it for me, Salomonè," she said quietly. "And I would ask you to purchase several items with the price."

Saphyre watched as Salomonè's eyes widened with astonishment, and she well understood his wonder. Further, it was just why she had chosen Salomonè to go to the village for her instead of one of the other able men. She desired to offer confidence in him—to assure him she knew he could be trusted.

"You would entrust this task to...to *me*?" he asked, his voice barely more than a breath. "To...to a thief?"

"You are a thief no more, Salomonè," she whispered, smiling and placing a reassuring hand on his arm. "You are one of the brothers of the keep...and my friend. I have entrusted you with my life in a manner. Why would I not trust you with such favor and errand as this?"

Saphyre's eyes began to brim with tears as she saw Salomonè's lower lip quiver in slight—witnessed the excess moisture in his own eyes. She had offered the greatest trust she could to a once thief, and in the depths of her heart her trust was sincere. She full did trust Salomonè and desired he believe in her trust.

"What would you have me purchase with the price, Princess?" he humble asked.

"Saphyre," she said, smiling at him.

Salomonè smiled and nodded, saying, "What would you have me purchase with the price, Saphyre?"

Saphyre's smile broadened. Salomonè had accepted her trust. His acceptance of her trust was as true a gift to her as her trust was to him.

"I am in need of several lengths of cloth...perhaps four lengths of green cloth—a regal weave," she explained. "You are a man of great care in his appearance…and it is thus I trust your judgment in choosing the cloth for me. I require thread and needles as well."

"You mean to make a new dress for yourself? A lovely green frock will most certainly become you," Salomonè said.

Saphyre smiled and shook her head. "No. This what I own and wear will serve me," she told him. "But there is another in the keep… one who might make good use of a better-fitting garment than the one he owns."

Salomonè quick glanced to Belmiro. He smiled as he looked back to Saphyre, nodding his approval. "You have the heart of an angel," Salomonè whispered.

"No," Saphyre told him. "But let us hope my fingers are as nimble as a tailor's might be. Shall we?"

Salomonè smiled at her. The joy in his eyes was bright and hopeful—filled with happiness and pride. "Is there more you desire me to acquire for you?" he asked.

"Yes," she told him. "Is there, in the village to which you will travel…is there a craftsman of instruments? Someone who may provide us with new strings and a new bow for Belmiro's viol?"

Saphyre had often witnessed Belmiro's frustration with the rather ragged viol bow he possessed. Likewise, she had often overheard him whispering to the beloved instrument—begging the strings to hold their strength a bit longer, that he may continue to play his dearly loved music. Saphyre knew Belmiro's only comfort was his beloved viol and the music they made together. A musician and his instrument were of one soul.

"There is a village…further from us to which I must travel," Salomonè told her. "But for Belmiro's happiness, I will most joyously go."

"Thank you, Salomonè," Saphyre said, covering his hand with her own and smiling at him. "It is well you know I could do nothing to ease Belmiro's mind and discomfort of clothing without your help. If there is any sum remaining after these purchases are made…I would beg you keep it as remuneration for the efforts for my sake."

"Your smile is the only sum I would ever long for, Saphyre," he began. "To know I pleased you will be fair payment enough for me. And it is glad I am to help. Further, any sum remaining will go into your pocket...or toward another set of strings for Belmiro's viol when next they are so worn as now."

Saphyre smiled at the man. The light in his eyes spoke to her soul: he was pleased with her gift of trust. She was, however, rendered discomfited as she glanced up to see Rogan watching her from across the room. He did not wear a frown, nor any expression of anger, but rather that of suspicion, and it great unsettled Saphyre to see him looking at her so.

His eyes narrowed. He gave a nod and gestured with one forefinger that she should come to him. She did not pause, and as she rose and began to walk to him, she wondered at the incredible power he had—the power to will a princess to do his bidding.

"You are in secret with Salomonè," Rogan said quietly as she sat next to him. "Is all well?"

For a moment, Saphyre fancied Rogan was jealous of her seemingly intimate moments with Salomonè. Yet when she looked at him to see an expression of only concern full on his handsome countenance—no hint of envy—she silent scolded herself for her own foolishness.

"He has agreed to travel to the village and gather several particulars for me...items I am in need of in order that I may—" she began.

"He is a good man," Rogan interrupted. "It is wisdom to place your trust in him for such tasks. He is well-liked in the villages."

Saphyre only nodded. She had been in hopes Rogan had been envious of her time with Salomonè. It seemed he was simply concerned for the goings-on in the keep—as ever protective of each therein.

"I would ask you a thing, Saphyre," he said then.

Saphyre's heart began to race. Would he ask her if he could once more risk the hangman's noose—the executioner's blade—to kiss her again?

"Yes?" she breathed. She tried to steady her breath—tried to appear tranquil.

Yet her heart slowed and a crimson blush of humiliation rose to her cheeks as he asked, "Do you remember your grandfather's change from a good and wise man to a...to a..."

"To a lunatic?" she finished for him. She was somewhat angry with him—angry he would inquire of her grandfather when her hopes had been toward somehow knowing his kiss.

"Yes," he mumbled, seeming rather regretful of having presented the inquiry.

Saphyre glanced away, her hands wringing the folds of her frock. "I do," she said. She was silent a moment, remembering the terror she had known in watching her grandfather so alter in countenance and person. "He had been the most magnificent of men...ever loving to me...doting on me and feeling no indignity at doing so. And he loved my grandmother..."

"Queen Penelope," Rogan said.

Saphyre nodded. "He loved her with all his heart," she told him. "And...and I do remember when he began to change. It was soon after I was returned to my father and mother...soon after King Gregory's men had taken me. My grandmother fell ill...a strange illness that rendered her senseless. She slipped into what seemed to be a deep sleep...but one from which no one could awaken her. My mother used to tell me it was her feeling that grandmother simply starved to death...or died of not being able to take water. She died just four days after the strange sleep overcame her. There was no explanation." Saphyre felt a tear trickle down her cheek. Oh, how she had loved her grandmother! How devastating the loss had been for her.

"You do not have to continue," Rogan said, obviously feeling guilty at having brought such a painful memory to her.

"I have been told of...of your father's murder, Rogan," she whispered. "Please do not be angry with the one who told me."

"No-Nose," Rogan grumbled.

"Yes," Saphyre said. "But...but I think that is why you are asking me about my grandfather's madness. I would like to tell you of it...if you still desire to know of what I witnessed."

Rogan breathed a heavy, weary sort of sigh. "I could no more be angry with No-Nose than I could with…" He paused, sighing once more and saying, "I would beg you to tell me of what you witnessed in your grandfather."

Saphyre nodded and began again. "After my grandmother's death, he began to change."

"How?" Rogan asked.

"Small things at first…near trivial," she told him. "A sort of distant look about his eyes. He spoke very little and would often recluse to solitude. Even my father seemed unable to breach his mind or thoughts. It was as if he did not even hear us speaking to him at times. I remember once taking his hand, squeezing it as I had done as a small child…a gesture of affection."

"And?" Rogan prodded.

"And…and he did not even seem to know I was there…that I was touching him," Saphyre explained. "It was as if he saw no one… even if he were looking straight at them. He only saw Lady Carmen."

"And he very quick married her," Rogan mumbled.

"Too quick," Saphyre agreed. "In his right mind, he could not so easily have forgotten my grandmother."

"And Lady Carmen," Rogan began, "was your grandfather as indifferent to her as he seemed to everyone else?"

Saphyre shook her head, frowning. "No. And in fact it was as if she were the only person he saw…recognized in any manner. There are many who say Carmen bewitched him—that it was she who wanted to war with King Gregory, who wanted my grandfather to turn against his own kingdom…and that somehow she willed it."

"And what do *you* think?" Rogan asked.

Saphyre looked into the fire of his violet and crimson-brown eyes. He was so strong—so handsome! Yet not only was he far pleasing to her eyes; she felt entirely safe in his presence, as if nothing could ever bring harm to her.

"I believe the whispers," Saphyre answered. "I believe what happened to my grandfather…even perhaps my grandmother…is in some way Queen Carmen's doing." There! She'd spoken it. Never had she spoken her suspicions aloud. "Perhaps…even what happened to…to your father. Though it was ashamedly at my grandfather's hand…perhaps Carmen's hand was in it as much as it was in the murder she designed for me."

"My father was beloved of your grandfather," Rogan said, his voice low—angry. "My father was King Jordan's friend and confidant for many years. And as angry as I am, as much bitterness as I carry in my heart…it was many the time I sat at my father's knee and heard of his admiration, respect, and love for King Jordan. I know my father would have held no evil man in such high regard. No man my father was loyal to would be capable of such evil…at his own and lone hand." He grinned at Saphyre rather wistfully. "You have made me remember that. In you I see what your grandfather once was…and I too am led to wonder what possessed him in the end."

"You have forgiven me then?" Saphyre breathed with hope. Her heart continued to increase its pace within her bosom as she looked at him, hoping he would now see *her* when he looked at her—not merely a mad king's granddaughter.

His brow puckered, and he asked, "What is there in you to forgive?"

"Much, I am certain," Saphyre told him, smiling. She felt lifted—refreshed in the knowledge Rogan no longer seemed to place blame on her for her heritage.

Of a sudden, however, Rogan's smile faded. "Saphyre," he began, "what manner of illness took your mother?"

Saphyre's joy was saddened—tarnished by the memory of her mother's death. "I know only that Michael, king of the Kingdom of Graces, lost his queen a year past. Yet as I consider it, I find I know nothing of the circumstance of the queen's death."

Saphyre felt the raw stab of pain pierce her heart at the thought of her mother's sudden death. She knew then—as she had from the moment her mother had slipped away—she would never complete recover from it.

"The same strange illness that killed my grandmother," Saphyre said. "At least, it is what I know it to be."

"It is too painful to mention," Rogan said, shaking his head. "Let us speak of other—"

"She was overcome with fever," Saphyre continued, however. "She was so warm...fiery to the touch. I remember she tried to speak to me just as it—whatever it was—was overtaking her. 'Saphyre, my angel,' she said. 'Love. It will keep you,' she whispered to me. And... and then she fainted...never to fully awaken or speak again. She... she was feverish and unconscious for three days...and then...and then her fever heightened, and Lord Death took her from us."

"Did not the manner of your mother's death breed suspicion in the court? To your father?" Rogan asked.

Saphyre nodded, answering, "Yes. Until a poisonous spider was found in the shoe she had been wearing the day the illness overcame her."

"A spider?" Rogan seemed doubtful of the spider being the purpose of the queen's death.

"The viol spider," Saphyre explained. "Do you know of it?"

"I do," Rogan said, nodding. "The shape of a viol about its head."

"Yes," Saphyre said. "The physicians all agreed...the spider was the cause."

"And you. Do you agree? Was it the spider's bite that killed your mother?" Rogan asked.

Saphyre shrugged. She was beginning to feel fearful—nervous. The deaths of her grandmother and mother were too similar. Most in the kingdom suspected something evil—or someone evil—had, in the least, contributed to their deaths. With her own knowledge of Queen Carmen's murderous resentment toward herself, fear was once more in Saphyre's mind.

"I do not know," Saphyre said. "I only know I am terrified of any spider. I wasn't as a child...but now I am." She looked to Rogan, unable to discern whether it was the fire's light reflected in his beautiful eyes or their own color and glow that so enchanted her. "And I fear Carmen," she whispered, tears filling her eyes. "I fear that either the spider or Carmen may find me and bring harm to me... and I am ashamed at my cowardice."

"It is not cowardice to endeavor to preserve one's life, Saphyre," Rogan said, his voice low and alluring, "or to endeavor to preserve one's virtue…as you do now."

"What?" Saphyre asked. His words perplexed her—at once comforting, at once perplexing.

"To preserve your life you linger here at the keep…out of harm's way," he said. "You are no coward for that. To preserve your virtue… you will now away to your own bed alone…instead of to mine with me."

"What?" Saphyre exclaimed, somehow pure delighted by his improper insinuation. She knew he would never violate her in any manner. Still, his teasing threat to do so thrilled her far beyond what it should have.

"It is late, and the men have retired, leaving thee and me to our own devices, Saphyre," he whispered. "You would not see me more than hanged for stealing more than your kiss…would you?"

"You are not so formidable as to make me believe you are in earnest, Rogan," she giggled. She rose to her feet and made ready to leave him.

"Yet you flee like the lamb from the wolf," he chuckled.

"For the sake I have much work to perform on the morrow and need rest," she told him, "not because I am a lamb who fears being eaten by the wolf. Besides, Marcellus and Thaddeus both tell me… you have never eaten anyone once you have been given their name. Therefore…I am safe."

She gasped when Rogan reached out, taking hold of her hand. With a sly and mischievous grin spread across his face, he drew her wrist to his mouth—nipping at the tender flesh of it just below her palm. A moment next, he placed a moist, lingering kiss there.

Saphyre's full body broke into gooseflesh—her greatest desire being to throw herself into Rogan's arms, to take his mouth with her own. Yet she stood straight and strong, and he released her hand, smiling with knowing he had so affected her.

"Are you so certain of your safety in my care, Saphyre?" he asked.

"Yes," she answered plain.

"Then…away with you," he said, still smiling. "To your own bed…alone. For now."

Saphyre attempted to appear calm as she walked away from him—tried not to clutch at her arm, the place where he had kissed her wrist, for it was numb with the pleasure of his touch.

Lying in her bed sometime later, she thought of what it might be like to lie next to Rogan there—his arms about her—the warmth of his body so close. Surely it would be the safest, most blissful sense in the world. Saphyre imagined that with Rogan so near to her, nothing could harm her—nothing. So long as Rogan was in her sight—she would be safe.

She lay in her bed, gazing out through her tiny keep window at the stars twinkling so brightly in the night sky. Soon Belmiro would have a new tunic fit for the nobleman's heart he owned—a new tunic and fresh, steadfast strings for his beloved viol. Soon Belmiro would know a better comfort in these things, as Salomonè knew comfort in the gift of trust Saphyre had offered him. Yet as Saphyre thought of her gifts to Salomonè and Belmiro, she knew not what gift she could ever give the others—in particular Rogan. Thus, she drifted off to sleep—dreaming of a night—a night spent in the blissful console given of Rogan's embrace.

❧

The cloth Salomonè procured was of the finest quality and of such a color of wondrous green as to put Saphyre's mind to thinking on the handsome peacocks roaming the gardens of the castle.

"It is pure perfect, Salomonè!" Saphyre exclaimed, drawing the cloth across her arm to better admire it. "I knew I was wise to beg you to choose it! Oh, look at the way it catches the sunlight. The weave and weight are faultless…perfect for Belmiro's tunic!" Saphyre giggled with delight and threw her cloth-draped arms about Salomonè's neck. "Thank you, my friend! Oh, thank you, Salomonè!"

Saphyre sighed as she felt Salomonè embrace her, returning her affection.

"I have a new bow and fresh strings for Belmiro's viol, as well," he said. He released Saphyre and turned to his horse, opening a leather sack hanging from his saddle pommel and withdrawing a finely crafted viol bow and set of strings.

Saphyre gasped, delighted with the particulars Salomonè had gathered from the village.

"Surely he will be pleased...will he not, Salomonè?" Saphyre said. She was of a sudden fearful Belmiro might somehow know offense at her offerings. "He will not be angry with me for endeavoring to gift him comfort, will he?"

"Belmiro? Angry?" Salomonè chuckled, returning the bow and strings to the leather sack, setting them aside on the ground. "I do not think Belmiro has the spirit for anger, Saphyre. He is far too kindhearted...and humble. He will treasure your gifts of comfort."

Saphyre smiled, reassured by Salomonè words. She thought then of the price of the bracelet—of the sum of its worth.

"The bracelet...did it bring a great enough sum as to leave something for your trouble?" she asked.

Drawing the sleeve of his tunic up from his wrist, Salomonè smiled—and Saphyre saw he wore the gold-banded bracelet at his wrist.

"Forgive me, Saphyre," he began, "but I could not part with it." He began to unclasp the gold bracelet, and Saphyre marveled at how well it fit his wrist. Always it had been too large for her to don in comfort—even she was ever pushing it up to her forearm. She liked the manner in which it shackled Salomonè. It was handsome next to his bronzed skin.

Saphyre placed a hand at his wrist, over the bracelet, that he should not release the clasp.

"It is yours, Salomonè," she began, "my gift of thanks to you... for your assistance...and because we are friends." She frowned as she wondered then how Salomonè had afforded the particulars for Belmiro. "But how came you by the cloth...the bow and strings? Certainly you did not expend your own hard-earned coin for my needs. Oh, tell me you did not empty your own purse, Salomonè! I should not rest in thinking I had stripped you of its contents."

Salomonè smiled and chuckled, his bright eyes merry with

amusement. "Perhaps I stole the bow and strings...the cloth," he said.

Saphyre knew there was no thief lingering in her friend, and she playful pushed at his broad shoulders. "I will not have you teasing of thievery. I know you emptied your purse...did you not? And now you will have not coin for your own needs."

He laughed, studying the gold bracelet at his wrist. "You have seen that I take care in my appearance. You have told me you have seen this in me...and I admit to a slight sinful vanity. Thus, I am happy to keep about me your bracelet, for it is comely on my wrist... and a token of your goodness and friendship to me."

"But the particulars for Belmiro," Saphyre said.

"My purse is not emptied for the sake of these things," he said. "It is simply I have traded one token of a bright memory in favor of another."

Saphyre felt her brow pucker in wondering at his words. "What do you mean?" she asked. Yet as her gaze again fell to her bracelet at his wrist, she gasped, "Diana's ring!" Taking his hand, she studied the smallest finger of his right hand—the ring of flesh, scarred from so many years of donning the ring, lighter than the bronze skin of his hand. "Tell me you did not sacrifice your great treasure, Salomonè! I am sick of heart in knowing you sacrificed Diana's ring for senseless things of my desiring!"

Saphyre felt tears brimming in her eyes as Salomonè shook his head.

"Your desires are not senseless. They are benevolent and good," he said. "Further, I have not sacrificed my memory of sweet Diana and her kiss...only the ring she gifted me. The bracelet is of far more value to my soul, Saphyre. Do not begrudge me of keeping a token of the true gift you have gifted me...the gift of your trust and friendship. Your gift is far more to me than even Diana's was."

"But I knew you with this ring," Saphyre said, letting her fingers trace the light scar at his smallest finger.

"And now you know me with this," he said, turning his wrist to allow the bracelet to glint in the sunlight, "a token of your trust in me."

"But your ring, Salomonè," Saphyre said, tears slipping from her eyes.

Again he chuckled. "That you would weep for sake of my ring," he began, "it is only further evidence of your rare goodness and beauty of spirit, Saphyre. Now take your particulars and be off," he said, retrieving the leather sack from the ground and handing it to her. "I would not have Rogan to happen upon us in such intimate conversation. I do not wish to see him run me through with his blade. I much prefer to keep my heart beating in my breast as it now does."

"It would far more be he would run me through for keeping you from your labors than he would ever harm you," she said, smiling, for she delighted in Salomonè's implication Rogan should be jealous were he to come upon them.

"Only a fool would risk his life on that assumption, Saphyre Snow," he chuckled. "And now, I will take my leave." He raised his arm, studying the glinting gold bracelet in the sunlight. "I feel quite regal with this about my wrist," he said. He smiled, turned, and strode away.

Saphyre gathered the lovely peacock cloth in her arms, the leather sack carrying the new bow and strings for Belmiro's viol swaying this way and that as she walked back toward the keep.

Salomonè of the keep knew a princess trusted him. Salomonè of the keep knew Saphyre Snow called him friend. Saphyre smiled, pleased she had been able to offer gratitude to another brother of the keep. She hoped now Belmiro would be as pleased with her humble offering of comfort—and true friendship.

COMFORT

It took near a week for Saphyre to complete the tunic for Belmiro. Each night she would sit in her diminutive room in the keep—sit near the small hearth, working her stitches by fire and moonlight. There had been several hours one day she was able to stitch during full sunlight. Yet Belmiro had taken upon himself a rather constant cough and been forced to remain at the keep for several days in resting. Thus Saphyre—desiring that the tunic be an unexpected gift to her friend and unable to stitch with Belmiro so near in lingering in the keep—stitched in diligence in whatever hour of the day or night presented itself as convenience.

Still, whether stitching by the bright sun or veiled in the silver moonbeams of night, Saphyre delighted in fashioning the tunic for sweet Belmiro. As she labored, she would often smile, imagining dear Belmiro dressed in the beautiful green cloth. Certainly, a tunic fashioned in full awareness of his need of easement where clothing was concerned would offer far more comfort. Yet Saphyre delighted in knowing the fabric Salomonè had chosen would drape poor Belmiro in a tunic fit for a great knight or nobleman as well. To Saphyre, Belmiro was noble—humble, kind, and noble.

Salomonè was most helpful in another regard. It was true he had made the trip to the far village to gather the particulars that Saphyre might construct the tunic for Belmiro and procured the new viol bow and strings. Yet it was also true that Salomonè served as the form by which Saphyre fit the tunic. By filling a leather sack with straw and having Salomonè hang it over his shoulder to his back, Saphyre was better able to alter the cut of the tunic to allow for Belmiro's particular shape.

It was during one of these secreted fittings, in a clearing near the stream—Salomonè with the leather sack of straw at his back, Saphyre working to better fit the tunic—that Rogan happened upon them.

"There," Saphyre said, stepping back from Salomonè to better study the drape of the tunic. "I think it will suffice."

"It will more than suffice, Saphyre," Salomonè replied, raising his arm to admire the tunic sleeve. "It has the look of nobility and strength. It will serve well for Belmiro's comfort...as well as his vanity."

Saphyre giggled. "I cannot see where Belmiro owns one thread of vanity, Salomonè."

Salomonè smiled. "True...but he will own, I hope, a measure more assurance in his fine appearance. He is a good man...a kind and compassionate soul. He deserves far more than the world has ever given him...respect and admiration in the very least. This tunic will lend him joy...and not simply in comfort."

"And what are you two about?" Rogan asked.

Saphrye gasped as she turned to see Rogan leaning against a nearby tree. She wondered how long he had been in study of them— she and Salomonè.

"Rogan," Salomonè greeted, "what think you of Saphyre's secret gift for Belmiro? Will not it give him more comfort and pride in appearance?"

Rogan strode to them—studied Salomonè before looking to Saphyre. His gaze unsettled her. The strange violet and crimson-brown of his eyes caused gooseflesh to ripple over her arms. Of a sudden, her mouth began to thirst for the memory of his kiss. It was ever Rogan affected Saphyre so. With all she was—all the will in her—she ever tried to keep such sensibilities from overwhelming her, but to no avail.

"So this is what you have been about in the dark hours of night," he said. "This is what has kept you from your bed."

"Yes," Saphyre confessed. "But how knew you I have been kept from—"

"Nothing goes about in the keep without Rogan's knowledge," Salomonè said. "Surely you know this by now, Saphyre."

"It is a very fine garment," Rogan said, looking to Salomonè once more. "Proper and perfect fashioned for Belmiro. Yet how came you by such fine cloth?"

Salomonè smiled, pulling one sleeve of the tunic up, displaying his wrist and the gold band bracelet there.

"She sent a thief to the far village to sell her jewels and procure it," Salomonè explained.

"You are not thief, Salomonè," Saphyre scolded.

Rogan glanced to Saphyre, then back to the bracelet at Salomonè's wrist.

"Yet if you still possess the bracelet…" Rogan began. He sighed then—smiled—taking hold of the smallest finger of Salomonè's hand. "Ah…the ring of the nobleman's daughter who granted you her kiss," he said. "So you kept the bracelet and traded the ring for the sum."

"I did," Salomonè said, "for I much prefer the golden band. I find it quite handsome. Do you not think it well befits me, Rogan?"

Rogan chuckled, and the sound of his merriment caused Saphyre's heart to swell within her bosom.

"Yes, my brother," Rogan said, "near as well as this tunic will befit our friend Belmiro."

He turned then to Saphyre, seeming to study her thorough for a time. "I did not know the Kingdom of Graces owned such a benevolent princess," he said.

"I am not benevolent," Saphyre said, a blush rising to her cheeks. "I only wish to serve in whatever manner I may. Belmiro owns little comfort and joy in life. I only wish to offer him what small comfort I may."

"She has fresh strings and a strong new bow for Belmiro's viol… as well as the tunic," Salomonè said.

"Our Saphyre seems uncanny aware of each of we brothers—our pain, our needs…our desires," Rogan said.

Saphyre began to tremble beneath his gaze. She knew he toyed with her—meant to unsettle her.

Salomonè must have noted her discomfort, for he chuckled and said, "Uncanny aware indeed." Salomonè removed the noble tunic meant for Belmiro. "It is finished then?" he asked as Saphyre carefully folded the garment.

"Yes…as well as it can be finished by one so little skilled with a needle as I," she said.

"When will you gift it to Belmiro?" he asked. "Tonight? At the fire circle?"

"Do think it would befit?" she asked.

"Most assuredly," Salomonè smiled. "Do you not agree, Rogan?"

"I do," Rogan said.

His smoldering gaze lingered on Saphyre. She sensed he could somehow see through her flesh—to the deepest desires of her heart. She could not fathom why Rogan of the keep should have such power over her—such a grip on her mind. He was the leader of the men, yes— strong, wise, and handsome. Yet many men Saphyre had known— knights, soldiers, and kings—many men of her acquaintance were wise and strong. Even some were handsome. None had ever known the comeliness of Rogan, yet handsome men there were in the world. Still, Rogan possessed a near bewitching quality, a powerful aura of allure that Saphyre could not strive against—nor resist. Something of this man Rogan had pure captured not only her mind and heart but her very soul.

"Very well," Salomonè said. "Then I shall take my leave…for the daylight fast wanes, and I have yet much to accomplish before sun's set."

Salomonè nodded to Saphyre and then strode away, leaving her to linger in solitude with Rogan.

"It is a kind and good thing you have done for Belmiro," Rogan said. His eyes narrowed as he studied her, adding, "And for Salomonè."

"Salomonè?" Saphyre asked, glancing from Rogan and to the tunic she yet held in her arms. She would feign ignorance, for in truth, she was not certain Rogan knew of her gift to Salomonè—her gift of trust.

Rogan chuckled. "Did not you hear Salomonè himself, only moments ago, when he informed you that nothing goes about in the keep without my knowing? You have gifted Salomonè your confidence...your trust. No greater thing could you have offered him. He is a better man for it...for owning knowledge a princess would trust him with her jewels, her errands of need, even her life."

"Then...have I earned your esteem in some regard?" Saphyre ventured. Oh, how desperately she desired to own Rogan's good favor!

He moved closer to her, his head descending toward her own. Saphyre did not draw breath, for the nearness of his body to hers warmed her to the very core of her being.

"Yes, Saphyre Snow," he began, his voice low, his mouth so near to her own she could taste the sweet flavor of his breath, "you own my esteem."

He did not kiss her—though she was near certain he had meant to. Simply he straightened, his smoldering gaze still caressing her face.

"You well own my esteem...for your gifts to my brothers Belmiro and Salomonè...and to Marcellus, for he yet babbles endless over your tale of having been taken by King Gregory...of the great Sebastian Ottokar and his sad lady Augusta."

"Au-Augustynia," Saphyre whispered.

Rogan chuckled. "Ah, yes, that was it...Augustynia. Marcellus is ravenous to know more of this great captain and his sad lady. He will, no doubt, beg you once again this night for another tale the like you offered before. Will you oblige him?" he asked, reaching out to brush a strand of hair from her cheek.

Rogan's touch caused Saphyre to tremble in slight, and she hoped he did not take note of it. "Of course," she answered.

"Then I will anticipate the gathering at the keep fire with interest," he said, "for I will delight in witnessing Belmiro's heart warmed by your kind stitching…see Marcellus's eyes bright with merriment as you give him a tale…watch your pretty mouth move as you tell it to him."

"You are a flatterer, Rogan," Saphyre said. "A scoundrel." He was, once more, toying with her. She fancied he was well aware of the effect his seducing manner bore down upon her. He was a rascaling rogue—yet she loved him still.

"A flatterer? Conceivably," he said. "A scoundrel? Perhaps." He paused, smiling with mischief as he looked at her. "A supreme and proficient lover? Absolutely."

Saphyre gasped—blushed at his insinuative manner of speech.

"I leave you then, Saphyre," he said, "to your stitching…your contemplation of tales to tell."

He turned and strode away through the woods, toward the keep.

Saphyre clutched Belmiro's tunic close to her bosom, willing the gooseflesh caused of Rogan's alluring trifling to lessen on her arms. She wondered at such a man lingering at the keep. Rogan was so very dissimilar from the others. Marcellus and Thaddeus were at the keep for purposes of cruel prejudice. Salomonè sought redemption from his past. Edmund required solitude—a healing from long-carried heartbreak. Belmiro—Belmiro had ever been outcast, desiring fellowship of some who would not loathe him for his imperfections. Even Saphyre could reason at No-Nose's lingering. Such thorough mutilation—such as he bore upon his face—was endurable by few, and No-Nose had found the few who would endure it. Yet Rogan— Rogan's reasoning for existing at the keep—a murdered father and loathing of the monarchy of the Kingdom of Graces? No, there must be more—some crime, misdeed, or transgression that forced him into hiding. But what?

Saphyre sighed—of a sudden well worn from so many nights of lost slumber. The sun would set soon, and Marcellus would beg the telling of a tale. Though the thought of reciting a yarn only served to give rise to further weariness in her, Saphyre smiled, for tonight Belmiro would have his noble tunic, fresh strings, and viol bow. This night Belmiro of the keep would know a measure of comfort—a small measure, perhaps—but comfort all the same.

❧

"This great captain of the guard," Marcellus began, "Sebastian Ottokar and his lady Augustynia...I wish to know more of them."

"What more can I offer, dear Marcellus?" Saphyre asked. "I have already told you of their love...of Sebastian's death at the hand of assassins...of Augustynia's faithful heart. What more do you wish to know of them?"

She glanced to Rogan, leaning against the inner keep wall. He smiled at her, pure understanding the depth of Marcellus's determination, Saphyre's perplexity at how she might quench his insatiable thirst for stories.

"Everything!" Marcellus exclaimed. "And tell me more of Roar... the kingdom's greatest knight. Did he too own a lover in secret? And what of your grandfather...the lunatic?"

"Pray draw breath, Marcellus," Edmund grumbled, "before you are rendered to pure senselessness."

Marcellus sighed, smiled at Saphyre, and said, "Tell me of Lady Augustynia first...another story of her. I have dreamt of her in the night...of her beauty and faithful love for the captain of the guard."

"Very well," Saphyre said. "A tale of Augustynia...and how she came to love the great knight, Sebastian Ottokar."

Marcellus chuckled, smiled, and rubbed his hands together with delight in anticipation. "Yes! Yes, that's the story I want to hear," he said.

"Augustynia Dacianatis came to the Kingdom of Graces as a lady-in-waiting to the once Princess Felice of Avaron...now princess of the Kingdom of Graces."

"Augustynia Dacianatis?" Edmund asked.

Saphyre smiled, delighted in Edmund's recognition of the name.

"Yes, Edmund," Saphyre said. "A name you would recognize from Rothbain's royal history."

"King Dacian Dacianatis…once great ruler of Karvana," Edmund said.

"Karvana?" Marcellus exclaimed. "The Kingdom of Karvana from whence came the legendary sword, the Crimson Frost?"

Saphyre giggled. "Yes, Marcellus. The lady Augustynia was born of Karvana. A far-distant cousin to my mother, Augustynia traveled to this kingdom to offer her company. Grandmother thought Augustynia—born of remote royal lineage and being of the same bloodline as my mother—might offer comfortable companionship for my mother. It is true, my mother was older than Augustynia. Still they became fast friends."

"But when did she meet Sebastian? When did she first love the captain of the guard?" Marcellus demanded.

"Hush, brother!" Thaddeus scolded. "Saphyre will tell the tale as it needs be told."

Marcellus nodded. "Forgive me, Saphyre. I will hold my tongue."

Saphyre glanced up when she heard Rogan chuckle. He still leaned against the keep wall, shaking his head with amusement at his friend.

"There was a tournament," Saphyre began once more. "Sir Sebastian Ottokar was entered. He was Sir Sebastian then, a knight of my grandfather's table round of conferring…not yet captain of the guard. It was Sebastian took triumph in swords in the tournament… and maces. And at last, it stood there was but one knight left to face Sebastian Ottokar in the joust. Yet Sebastian had been injured… brutal wounded in the joust previous. Bloodied and bruised, with also broken bones at his ribs, yet Sebastian made ready to meet his final challenger…Sir Rance Mortimer of Alvar."

"Sir Rance?" Edmund exclaimed. "The villainous, traitorous Sir Rance?"

"Do you know him, Edmund?" Marcellus asked.

"I have heard of him…of his dishonorable deeds," Edmund

answered. Edmund shook his head and gestured to Saphyre, saying, "Forgive me, Saphyre. Forgive me. Please, continue."

"Yes, Saphyre," Marcellus prodded. "Please...go on."

"Very well," Saphyre said. "Augustynia had witnessed the full tournament...seen the great Sebastian battle. And her heart had swelled with compassion and admiration, for Sebastian was honorable, even when other knights—knights such as Sir Rance—were not. And it was she worried for him...was somehow drawn to watch him...worry over him.

"For his injured state, Sebastian was given half the hour of respite, a small measure of time to prepare before facing Sir Rance. His squire begged him to forfeit the joust, knowing his knight-lord was great with pain and injury. 'I will not forfeit!' Sebastian told his squire. 'Not before my king, my queen...and not for the sake of the beautiful Lady Augustynia who attends her.' Sebastian had seen Lady Augustynia before in court, learned of her all he could, and he knew she lingered in the seats surrounding the jousting arena. And his heart had beat faster in knowing she looked on. Therefore, Sebastian's squire did no longer beg his master to forfeit."

"He did not?" Marcellus asked.

"No," Saphyre said, "for Sebastian's squire was strong and valiant too. Sir Sebastian's squire in those days would soon thereafter be knighted...knighted and one day known as Roar."

"No!" Marcellus gasped. "Roar? The very one who saved you from the grip of villains?"

"Yes," Saphyre said. "Thus, in service to the great Sir Sebastian, the squire who would one day be the knight Roar did not further press his master to forfeit. No...he did not. Rather, the squire prepared Sebastian for the joust...for Sir Sebastian told his squire then..."

"Told him what?" Marcellus asked.

"Told him there was far more than honor and prize in his mind to keep him from forfeit...for Sir Rance Mortimer had, in secret, entered into conferring with Augustynia's father...asking for his daughter's hand. Sir Rance meant to wed Augustynia."

"Oh! Not Sir Rance!" Thaddeus growled.

"Yes," Saphyre assured him. "And Sir Rance's performance in the tournament was to determine whether Sir Rance would wed Augustynia. Augustynia's father would grant her hand to Sir Rance only if Sir Rance were named tournament champion. Sebastian had bested Sir Rance at maces and swords...yet Sir Rance had bested Sebastian as archer and in wrestling. Therefore, they stood even... and the joust between them would determine the champion."

"And Sebastian knew of this. He knew of Augustynia's father's agreement with Sir Rance?" Belmiro inquired.

Saphyre nodded. "Yes. The information had come to him by way of an acquaintance in Alvar...a servant in the house of Augustynia's father. Therefore, Sebastian could not forfeit the joust. He could not sacrifice the beautiful lady who had won his heart to the will of a dishonorable knight the like of Sir Rance. And Sebastian's squire agreed.

"Yet as they were preparing, Sebastian and his squire...just as the squire was securing Sebastian's armor...who should appear at the pavilion of the great Sebastian Ottokar but Lady Augustynia herself!"

"The beautiful lady herself?" Marcellus and Thaddeus gasped.

Saphyre giggled and continued, "Yes! For Augustynia had been drawn to Sebastian Ottokar...had sensed of his spirit yearning to know hers. Thus, she had come to the pavilion to inquire after his health. As their eyes met—as Lady Augustynia gazed into Sebastian's eyes, eyes as blue as the sea, as clear as a cloudless sky—her heart melted with his. Augustynia ever said to me, 'Sebastian owned me in that moment...as a master owns a slave...as only true love can own the soul of another.'"

Marcellus sighed, and the other men of the keep chuckled at his rapt emotion.

"And did she keep him from the joust?" Salomonè asked.

"No," Saphyre said, "for even though she did not know of her father's accord with Sir Rance, something whispered to her soul that she should not discourage Sir Sebastian...that she should instead offer her favour, that he might find renewed strength in knowing she cared for his well-being. Thus, she offered Sebastian a token—

an emerald ribbon from her hair. Sebastian accepted the ribbon…accepted Lady Augustynia's favour."

"What then?" Marcellus asked in a whisper. "Did he triumph?"

"He did!" Saphyre said. "He unhorsed Sir Rance with one lance, thus saving Augustynia from a sentence of marriage to a dishonorable man…whom she did not love."

Marcellus and Thaddeus both cheered—clapped their hands together with delight.

"And that is how Sebastian Ottokar won the heart of the beautiful lady Augustynia?" Marcellus asked.

Saphyre smiled. "In part…yet Augustynia ever told me Sebastian owned her heart long before he championed her against Sir Rance."

"Thus, Sebastian was named captain of the guard, his squire was knighted…and he and Lady Augustynia loved long."

"Loved forever," Saphyre said, "for she loves him still."

Marcellus frowned. "When last did she speak to you of loving him?" he asked.

Saphyre sighed, remembered fear causing her to tremble of slight. "The day before Queen Carmen's huntsman bid I flee," she said. "We were in the gardens. Augustynia is so fond of the late summer flowers there. As we walked, we came upon a gazing pool. It is a gazing pool embellished with rare blue crystals…crystals that look as bright and as blue as the sky. 'This is my favored beauty of the gardens,' Augustynia told me. I asked her why a gazing pool of blue crystals and clear water should be her favorite garden thing. 'It reminds me of Sebastian,' she said. 'His eyes were pure as beautiful a blue as the crystals and water in this pool.' She told me then, as she had many times before, that she did not believe Lord Death had triumphed over Sebastian. 'I feel him…in my heart,' she said. 'Not as one feels a memory but as a lover knows the one she loves yet lives. I can hear his breath at night…as I lay on my pillow. Sometimes I hear his voice in the first moments of my waking at sunrise.'"

"Perhaps she is mad," Thaddeus suggested. "It would not be the first madness to haunt the castle of your father."

"No. It would not," Saphyre said.

"Thaddeus!" Marcellus scolded, driving an elbow of reprimand against his brother's ribs. "Don't go on so about the madness of Saphyre's family!"

Thaddeus then nudged Marcellus. "You're the one who named her father a lunatic not moments ago!"

Saphyre giggled and did not take offense. "Augustynia is not mad," she said. "She is only faithful and true in her love for Sebastian. She will never love another. I know she will not. She cannot…for it is not in her to love any man but Sebastian."

"Augustynia and Sebastian," Marcellus sighed. "It is a tragic tale…yet somehow…it leaves my heart happy."

"How so, Marcellus?" Edmund asked. "For it does not leave one feeling cheerful…knowing a beautiful and kind woman lingers in loving a man who is dead and cannot return to her."

Saphyre smiled as she saw Rogan's eyebrows arch. Edmund? Owning compassion toward a woman?

"I do not care if it saddens. It was a wonderful story, Saphyre," Marcellus sighed.

Thaddeus looked to Belmiro then. "You should fashion a ballad, Belmiro," he said. "You are gifted with sad, mournful-sounding tunes. Why not compose…'The Ballad of Sebastian and His Lady.' What say you, Belmiro?"

"I say I am worn through this night," Belmiro said, smiling. "My bed calls to me. It wishes to offer me respite from the pain my back knows."

"May I offer something first, Belmiro?" Saphyre asked.

"What is that, Saphyre?" Belmiro asked.

"Just a thing I have fashioned," she said. She reached behind her—to the place where she had hidden the tunic. She drew the tunic from its hiding place and held a hand toward Belmiro. "Here," she said, taking his hand as he stood. "It is this I have stitched for you. Though I do not claim the stitches are lovely…they are strong."

Belmiro's eyes filled with tears as Saphyre endeavored to fasten the tunic at his chest. The green cloth from which Saphyre had fashioned the tunic shimmered by the firelight. Further, the tunic fit flawlessly—as perfectly as a tunic could, considering the physical ailment owning Belmiro's posture.

"There now," Saphyre said, fastening the last of the loops and buttons, standing back to study him. "It quite becomes you...the green," she said. "And I have two others nearly finished, Belmiro. I hope you do not mind their being of the same cloth."

"Thaddeus and I are the same," Marcellus interjected. "And Belmiro is glad of us that way."

Thaddeus nodded his agreement.

"You...you cannot possibly know of the depth of my gratitude, Princess," Belmiro stammered, his voice breaking with emotion.

"I am only Saphyre to you, dear Belmiro," Saphyre said. "And you cannot possibly know of my gratitude to you...for your music... for playing as you do." She reached into the leather sack at the back of her seat, withdrawing the viol strings and bow. She offered them to him, and as he accepted the gifts, tears spilled from his eyes.

"I-I cannot believe it," he whispered.

Saphyre was delighted with Belmiro's joy. It was plain he was happy. It was plain he would be more comfortable in the tunic she had fashioned—and it caused Saphyre's heart to soar.

She glanced around at the other men of the keep, wondering if they were drawing as much joy from Belmiro's happy countenance as was she. Yet as she looked at each man in turn, it was to find their eyes lingered on her and not their friend. Each man wore a smile of admiration; each man held excess moisture in his eyes, in particular Salomonè. Saphyre understood then—with her simple gifts to Belmiro, she had given comfort to all the men of the keep. In trusting Salomonè, she had trusted them all. It was the same as when she had given Marcellus the gift of a tale; in giving to him, she had given to them all. Saphyre began to feel a sense joy and hope—relief in offering recompense to the men of the keep. In small measures, Saphyre had begun to repay them their kindnesses, and it caused her bosom to burn with contentment.

Saphyre's gaze lingered on Rogan even as Belmiro said to her, "The new strings must be worked soon, Saphyre, but the old ones must know their final melody first…and you may choose it for them. What do you choose?"

Saphyre's heart thrilled as Rogan smiled at her with full approval. Thinking of the rather sad, melancholy music Belmiro always played in the past, she said, "I think…'The Thatcher's Weave.' Do you know it?"

"It is well I know it!" Belmiro chuckled. Instantly the viol gave voice to the happy tune.

"Stop stomping about, Thaddeus," Marcellus said. "You have the look of a great bumbling drunkard."

"Hush, Marcellus!" Thaddeus scolded. "It is I love the dance… and well you know it."

"Love it you may, brother…but in performing it…you have the look of a drunken toad," Marcellus chuckled.

"I care not what you say, Marcellus," Thaddeus said. "My heart was made to dance!"

"In that he is correct," Marcellus whispered to Saphyre. "Always he has wanted to learn the dances—not the ridiculous ones we performed as jesters…but the bransle, the almain. The dances performed in court…the dances a man performs with a lady."

"Is that so?" Saphyre asked.

Of a sudden, a thought of what she might gift Thaddeus entered her mind. She looked up to see Rogan nod at her, as if he had gazed through her flesh to discern her thoughts and was offering his blessing. Saphyre could think of no greater gift to be given *her* at that moment than that of Rogan's favor. Winning his heart would be far too great a hope to wish for, this she knew. Thus, knowing he esteemed her, she would find bliss in such knowledge.

TO THADDEUS, THE DANCE

"They are saying the old queen had him killed for his disobedience," Salomonè whispered in a lowered voice.

"The fool," Rogan said. "He should have kept to his silence. Did he tell the others who the queen had sent him to slaughter?"

"No. Not that I could discern," Salomonè said, "simply that he could not slaughter an innocent. He did also speak of his mind being overcome with a fever...and that he well would have killed the innocent the queen had charged him to had not the fever broken quick previous to his setting out to the task."

"It is surely the princess the man was speaking of," No-Nose said. "And now...now the old queen suspects the girl lives."

"She will undoubted send out searchers," Edmund grumbled.

"Searchers to find either Saphyre's remains..." Marcellus began.

"Or her living self," Thaddeus finished.

"Yes," Rogan agreed. "We must be on our guard."

"And Saphyre must be told," Belmiro added. "You know she must be told, Rogan."

The beauty of the evening before—Belmiro's joy and Salomonè's—was quick fleeing as Saphyre listened at the door just outside the keep kitchen. The sun shone bright enough; the autumn breeze was warm, but the beauty of the day had diminished.

"What must I be told?" Saphyre asked, stepping into the room.

All sets of eyes glanced away guiltily—all save Rogan's.

Rogan did not pause. Simply he began, "When Salomonè was in the village this morning, there was some disturbing talk…a tale of a castle huntsman, murdered under suspicious circumstance. Previous to the huntsman having being found—found with his heart torn from his chest—he had been sitting in the inn telling a tale of Queen Carmen ordering him to murder, as he spoke it, 'an innocent.'"

Saphyre began to tremble. "Go on," she encouraged, however.

"The huntsman said he was taken with a strange fever, which broke only quick before he was to murder this innocent," Rogan continued. "Had the fever not broken, he would have surely followed through with his charge."

"You believe this is the huntsman who…who did not kill me?" Saphyre asked, though her knowledge was already certain.

Rogan simply nodded.

"You must be wary, Saphyre," No-Nose said. "As must we all be lest strangers approach…for any man strange to us may be about the old queen's errand."

"I have put you all in danger," Saphyre whispered. Her heart began to race with fear. Her step-grandmother would surely seek her out—surely kill her—and perhaps her friends as well.

Rogan rose from his chair. Striding to her, he took her hand in his. "We are all in danger every day that we yet draw breath, Saphyre," he said. "No-Nose might be out about cutting wood, become distracted, and swing his ax carelessly, mortally wounding himself. Salomonè might be riding to the village, his mount may bolt…throw him… and he could break his neck and perish. A stone from the mountain where we quarry may fall and crush me without warning."

"I am certain Saphyre is much soothed with these thoughts, Rogan," Edmund grumbled.

"I do not mean to frighten you, Saphyre…simply to tell you that life in and of itself may be dangerous. We must each be watchful. That is all."

Saphyre's hand tingled with delight as he held it—the blissful sense of his touch traveling over her arm to fill her bosom. She believed these men could and would keep her safe. They had become her friends, and as she stood looking at them, each in turn—even Edmund nodding his assurance in keeping her safe—she wondered that she would ever be able to leave them. In the weeks that had passed since she too settled at the keep, she had come to cherish these men. Though each haunted in some regard, yet they were good men—happy in their companionship. She was akin to them, owning her own fears and secrets. She loved each one as a brother—save Rogan. Her love for Rogan greatly differed from her love for each of the others, and she would save the knowledge in silence—for of all the men in the keep, it was Rogan who seemed most content with his life there. If she should return to her kingdom—if she should seek to help her father and his subjects, to vindicate herself of her step-grandmother's evil—she knew Rogan would remain at the keep. What man would sacrifice such a peaceful existence, in favor of the life she would know? Further, Saphyre knew her feelings to be unlike his own. In that moment, she silent admitted she was lost in love with Rogan—and ever would be. For her, there would never be one to capture her heart the way he had. Rogan of the keep would own her heart forever.

"We will each stay watchful then," she said finally.

"Yes," Rogan said. "And now, my brothers, I will be about my bath."

All the men in the room chuckled, and Saphyre's brow wrinkled with perplexity. It was his way. Rogan always announced his intentions at bathing, and Saphyre could never fathom why he did so. Always he would say, "I will be bathing," or "I will be about my bath," thus informing everyone of his intent.

Rogan left the keep, and Saphyre sat down at the table, next to Edmund.

"It is strange the manner in which he ever tells us he will be about his bath," she said to the brooding man next to her. "Does he not bathe in the same manner as the rest of us?"

Edmund actually chuckled, and the sound of his laughter both pleased and surprised Saphyre as ever it did.

"In truth…no, Saphyre. He does not," Edmund said.

"What do you mean?" she asked.

Smiling, Edmund told her, "We…all of us men and you…we walk to the warm spring at the foot of the mountain, yes?"

"Yes," Saphyre said.

"Preferring the privacy of the walk and the warm spring there, the soothing, temperate water…all of us choose to bathe in more private, more comfortable surroundings. But Rogan is impatient. He finds little joy in a meandering walk or the warmer water. Rarely at peace in any regard, Rogan chooses to bathe in the stream…just outside the keep."

"What?" Saphyre exclaimed in astonishment. "Just outside… here? Why…why, anyone could happen upon him!"

No-Nose chuckled, and Marcellus and Thaddeus nodded their like thinking.

"It is true," Edmund said. "And since your coming, it is why he announces his intention to bathe…so that we may keep you close to us and far from his stubborn nakedness."

Saphyre felt her cheeks go crimson at the thought of Rogan's indiscreet behavior so close at hand. "It is against all propriety," she mumbled, putting her hands to her cheeks to cool her blush.

Edmund chuckled again, obviously amused at her discomfort. "It is his way," he said. "It is his way just as hard labor and little respite are likewise his way. But perhaps he would change his ways… were you to happen upon him in the act of bathing so rebellious."

Saphyre gasped—blushed more deeply.

"Yes, Saphyre!" Marcellus exclaimed. "Perhaps if you were to happen upon him, perhaps Rogan would learn to find peace in bathing in the warm mountain spring."

Saphyre shook her head, her blush near painful upon her cheeks. "Certainly not! I am more inclined to avoid the stream altogether!"

Every man in the room laughed, delighted with her distress. Saphyre could not help but smile at the thought of what expression would find Rogan's face were she to intrude upon him—catch him as vulnerable as a newborn babe.

"Perhaps I shall happen upon him one day," she said. "Simply to witness the expression of dismay on his face."

All the men laughed once more, and Saphyre laughed with them. Yet she was still oddly unsettled in thinking of Rogan bathing so near. Further, she could not understand why anyone would prefer the frigid water of the stream to the soothing temperature of the warm spring at the foot of the mountain.

"The sun will be setting soon," No-Nose said, rising from his seat. "I will be about the fire in the pit." He took his leave of the kitchen, Marcellus and Thaddeus close at his heels. Salomonè also followed, as did Edmund. Yet as Belmiro rose, Saphyre placed her hand on his arm to stay him.

"I would beg a favor of you, Belmiro," she said quietly.

Belmiro smiled, the green of his noble tunic reflected in the light of his eyes. In truth, Belmiro was a comely man. Saphyre had always known it, and her heart ached for him—knowing few women would ever consider him. At least, few women of Saphyre's acquaintance.

"Anything for you, Saphyre," he said, smiling at her.

"You play so well the viol, Belmiro, that I am certain you indeed may play any piece of music…including any bransle…the almain. Is this so?" she asked.

Belmiro smiled and nodded. "Yes. Most anything you would ask of me, I am able to play."

Saphyre clapped her hands together with delight. "Would you… for Thaddeus's sake, would you be agreeable to play for us this evening…the music of any dance performed in the courts?" she asked.

Of a sudden, Belmiro's smile broadened, and he nodded with understanding. "I will. Most assuredly, I will," he told her.

"Oh, thank you, kind friend," Saphyre said, rising quick to her feet and throwing her arms about Belmiro's shoulders in a warm embrace.

"You mean to teach Thaddeus the dances of the court," he chuckled.

"I do," she admitted.

"Then he will love you all the more, Saphyre Snow."

"I wish only to make him smile."

"The way you have made me smile," Belmiro said.

"The way you have made yourself smile, Belmiro…with your comfort in your music."

Belmiro nodded. "I will be about preparing my viol," he said as he left the room.

Saphyre sighed with pleasure—smiled at the realization that Belmiro too would benefit from Thaddeus's gift, the gift of dance. She would not linger in thoughts of Queen Carmen or fear. She would think only of the men of the keep—of gifting them joy as best she may.

❦

The sun had set, and the fire burned warm in the pit. So eager was Saphyre in anticipation of giving Thaddeus's gift, she could not sit calm.

"You twitch about fair as much as Marcellus this evening, Saphyre," Rogan observed.

Saphyre looked to him, attempting to fix her gaze to his face—at his still-damp hair instead of to his bare chest. He had returned from his bath and, as was his habit, had only dressed in his breeches, leaving his upper body bare. The strength of his body was far too visible when he appeared in such a state, and it oft unsettled Saphyre. Yet he sat next to her as if his bareness were of no consequence.

"Do I?" she asked, discomfited at his nearness. "Then…then perhaps it is activity I require."

"Activity?" Rogan said. "Of what sort?"

Saphyre rose to her feet and nodded to Belmiro. "I believe a lively dance may calm my need for activity," she said.

"A lively dance?" Edmund grumbled. "Indeed."

"A lively dance? Delightful!" Thaddeus exclaimed, hopping to his feet. "What dance, Saphyre?"

"Sit down, Thaddeus," Marcellus told him. "Saphyre does not speak of the dances you and I perform."

"Perhaps not," Saphyre said, "and it is why, Thaddeus, I think it is time I taught you the court dances."

"The court dances?" Thaddeus breathed in awe. "You...you mean to teach me the dances of the court?"

"I do," Saphyre said, smiling. She glanced at Rogan to see his eyebrows arched in astonishment. "And where would you like to begin, Thaddeus? For Belmiro has granted he will play the dances for us."

"I-I...I do not know," Thaddeus stammered, overcome with delight.

"May I suggest a simple 'Black Almain'? Or perhaps the 'Bransle Charlotte'?" No-Nose said.

Saphyre studied No-Nose for a long moment. Once again she was surprised at his knowledge of the court.

"A wise suggestion," Saphyre said. "Thank you, No-Nose."

Thaddeus approached Saphyre, so gleeful he near trembled. "Then what am I to do, Saphyre?" he asked.

Saphyre giggled, delighted with his enthusiasm. "The almain is perhaps easiest...considering we are the only couple and it usually requires a trio of couples," she explained. "Still, we can form it...so take my hands."

Thaddeus did as he was instructed, fairly bouncing with joy, and Saphyre began to instruct him in the steps of the dance.

He learned quickly. His steps were, at first, awkward, yet Belmiro played his viol to mirror the slow pace of Saphyre's tutoring.

"You see, Thaddeus," she said, giggling again as he stepped on her toe. "It is not as difficult as it may appear."

Thaddeus's face was resplendent with joy as he nodded, glancing down at his feet. "But I am quite awkward yet," he said.

"Then we shall practice often," Saphyre said, smiling at him.

Of a sudden, however, Thaddeus dropped Saphyre's hands, saying, "No-Nose, will you demonstrate the entire dance with

Saphyre so that I may see it done properly? Perhaps then I may be a better pupil."

Saphyre's heart ached when she saw No-Nose drop his gaze from her, his smile fading. "I may be a rather fearsome partner, Thaddeus," he said. "Perhaps Salomonè or one of the others would better serve as—"

"You will not dance with me, No-Nose?" Saphyre asked, assuring her disappointment was evident in her voice.

"I am not the handsome rogue Rogan or Salomonè is, Saphyre," No-Nose told her.

"My darling friend," Saphyre said, holding her hand toward him, "a man uses his feet to dance with…not his nose."

"That is true," Thaddeus said aside to Marcellus. "A man has not need of a nose when he is about the dance."

No-Nose chuckled, a smile returning to his face. He stepped forward and took Saphyre's hands in his own.

"Musician," he said—and Belmiro began to play.

Saphyre smiled, delighted at No-Nose's talent of the dance. It was obvious he was pure experienced. As Saphyre performed the dance with him, she was again struck with an overwhelming sense of awareness. She had a sense of having met No-Nose before, and it rather haunted her in that moment. Certainly, it had been No-Nose's face she had first set eyes upon when she had awoken in the keep upon her arrival; it had been No-Nose's face before her. She knew this was the familiarity of him, for he had been the first brother of the keep her heart had known.

"Perfect!" Thaddeus said, clapping his hands with pure enjoyment. "That is how I want to dance! As wonderfully as does No-Nose! Can you make it so, Saphyre?" he asked.

"Only with your help, my friend," she said, "for you must be willing to practice often to become so accomplished as is No-Nose."

"I will do anything to learn it so," Thaddeus said, "even though I may never have the opportunity to dance it in court…for what woman would ever dance with me?"

Saphyre's heart was pierced with pain, even though Thaddeus's enthusiasm remained undaunted. "I will ever dance with you," Saphyre told him, "and wherever you may wish."

Though she thought it impossible, Thaddeus's smile broadened, his face radiant with even deeper delight. "Then I may always say, 'I may dance, and have danced, with the princess of the Kingdom of Graces…and she chooses me as partner,' can I not?"

"Yes," Saphyre said, giggling. "Yes. You may always say it."

"Then let us dance!" Thaddeus exclaimed. "Marcellus! Take No-Nose as partner! Salomonè…take Edmund or Rogan, and we shall form the necessary trio of couples."

"I will assist Belmiro," Edmund grumbled.

Saphyre smiled and nodded to him with understanding. One with a broken heart such as Edmund's should not be pressed. She smiled then, amused and delighted when the other four men did just as Thaddeus asked, standing to join her and Thaddeus in position.

"Am I to be the man or the woman?" No-Nose inquired of Marcellus.

"The woman, of course!" Marcellus said, taking No-Nose's hand. "How else am I to learn the man's place…and you know it already."

No-Nose chuckled as he looked at his tiny friend, saying, "You have the point of it, my friend."

"Do you choose man or woman, Salomonè?" Rogan asked.

Saphyre bit her lip to keep from bursting into laughter as both men stood looking awkward at one another.

"We…we should take the part each in turn," Salomonè said. "I will begin in the woman's place…for I am the more heroic herein."

Rogan nodded and took Salomonè's hands, wrinkling his nose. "I find myself quite discomfited," he mumbled.

"But we are all friends here!" Saphyre exclaimed. "Further you are each confident in your thorough masculinity." Saphyre giggled as Rogan again wrinkled his nose. It was a rather boyish gesture, and she adored it. "Belmiro…at your ready," she said.

Belmiro began to play, and the trio of strange couples began the dance.

Thaddeus's joy was magnificent! Laughing with delight and

excitement, he learned each dance with the enthusiasm of a child receiving gift after gift. Saphyre's feet were sorely trodden upon, but she cared not—for Thaddeus was happy.

Even Edmund smiled. A broad smile of delight and amusement gave a light to his countenance, which Saphyre had not before witnessed—and she was warmed by it. Still, she had no gift for Edmund, and the fact began to tax her mind as she danced.

"Are you growing weary, Saphyre?" Thaddeus asked of a sudden.

Saphyre turned her thoughts to Thaddeus once more, smiling down into his happy face. "Never!" she giggled. "And there is so much more to learn."

"Let us have the 'Knight's Lady,'" No-Nose suggested, "for I am worn and in need of respite in sitting."

"The Knight's Lady?" Saphyre asked. "It is...it is a rather questionable dance, No-Nose."

"In the courts perhaps, but not in the inns surrounding the kingdom," he chuckled. "Do you know it, Saphyre?" he asked.

"I do," she admitted.

"What is 'The Knight's Lady'?" Thaddeus asked.

"It is one of the more...intimate of dances," Saphyre explained, "for our hands are never separated."

"Ohhhh! I like the sound of that!" Thaddeus exclaimed. "Do teach it to me."

Saphyre smiled, delighted once more with his excitement. "Very well. Do you know the tune, Belmiro?" she asked.

"Quite well," Belmiro admitted.

"Then Rogan shall exhibit it for me...with you, Saphyre," Thaddeus said. "You take Saphyre's hands, Rogan...and I shall watch closely your example."

"My pleasure," Rogan said. A mischievous smile spread across his handsome face.

Saphyre immediate began to perspire—and not from the labor of the previous dance. "Perhaps you wish to...acquire your tunic," Saphyre suggested. "Surely the air is growing chill, and you would not want to catch your death."

But Rogan chuckled, as did the other men of the keep, all too aware of Saphyre's discomfort. "I require no tunic to perform this dance," Rogan said, taking Saphyre's hands in his own, and she began to tremble—to quiver with the pleasure of his touch. "It might be I may even perform it more apt without."

"The Knight's Lady" was indeed the most intimate of dances. Although it was Lady Augustynia herself who taught the dance to Saphyre, Saphyre had never revealed to anyone—before the moment Thaddeus had asked her of it—that she did indeed own knowledge of it. It was a dance known to be beloved of knights, a dance they cherished with their ladies, whether performed in public—or in secret.

"Belmiro...if you please," Rogan said. "Understand, Thaddeus, this is a dance most common performed by those not of the upper courts...and it begins with the interlacing of fingers...thus." Rogan raised his hands in unison with Saphyre's—their palms meet. Slowly he interlaced his fingers with hers and then led her through the first steps of the dance.

"Ohhh! I like this dance best of all!" Thaddeus said.

"As do I," No-Nose agreed with a chuckle.

"And then to the palms again," Rogan said as his and Saphyre's fingers parted—palms meet once more. "And now...she will move into me...and we will link the tips of our fingers, thus."

Saphyre moved closer to Rogan. She was certain she could feel the heat of his bare flesh as she danced. She could most sure feel the warmth of it against the sleeves of her frock as she moved.

"And this, Thaddeus," Rogan continued as he guided Saphyre to turn, her back to his broad chest, his arms encircling her without losing hold of her fingers, "will be your favorite moment of the dance."

Saphyre trembled as Rogan placed a lingering kiss to one side of her neck. He turned her out then, and she faced him once more. She was certain the blush on her face was profound a crimson.

"I like this dance!" Marcellus said.

"As do I," No-Nose agreed once more—still smiling.

"Rogan embellishes 'The Knight's Lady,' Thaddeus," Saphyre breathed. "The kiss is not commonly a measurement of it."

"Still," Thaddeus said, "I prefer it this way, I am sure."

"Further," Edmund added, "he is already as good as hanged. What is one more, eh, Rogan?"

"Precisely," Rogan chuckled, continuing to lead Saphyre in the dance.

By the time all the steps had been performed, Saphyre was hard trembling and weak. Rogan had performed the dance perfectly, and she had near swooned from the pleasure of being in his arms.

"And now," Rogan said, releasing a blushing and breathless Saphyre, "it is to your turn, Thaddeus."

Smiling with delight, Thaddeus said, "Another time, Rogan. If you do not mind it, Saphyre…for I am weary to the bone from the labor of dancing. It is a strange activity to my body, and I find I now yearn for rest…if it is agreeable to you, Saphyre."

"Oh, of…of course, Thaddeus," Saphyre stammered, still thoroughly undone by Rogan's attentions. "Rest is indeed required if we are to continue with your lessons another day."

"Rest is *far* from what I am yearning for," Rogan whispered into Saphyre's ear.

"You are an incorrigible trifler," Saphyre said, stepping away from him. His nearness was far too unsettling—as was his teasing manner.

"I mean to retire as well," Belmiro said, "for I too am weary."

"Thank you for your music, Belmiro," Saphyre said as he turned to leave.

"You are welcome, Saphyre," Belmiro said with a smile.

The other men all followed Belmiro and Thaddeus into the shadows of the keep—all save Rogan. He remained. As was his habit in the evenings after the others had retired, he went to the fire pit and sat before it, gazing into the dying embers therein.

Saphyre moved to stand near to where he sat. "You are quite skilled in the dance," she said.

Rogan shrugged broad shoulders, saying, "I used to watch my

father and mother. My mother was a lover of dancing, and my father danced to please her. Therefore, I learned easily."

"By example," Saphyre said.

"Yes," he mumbled, still gazing into the glowing cinders before him.

"I will leave you to your thoughts then. Good night, Rogan," Saphyre said.

She made her way through the shadowy keep. She smiled when she saw one of the men had already laid and lit a fire in her hearth—for she could see its glow as she approached her chamber. She thought of the magnificent joy on Thaddeus's face as he had danced, and it warmed her heart. She thought of the resplendent bliss she had experienced at Rogan's touch during their dance. This thought heated her so thorough, she placed a hand to her cheek to cool her blush.

Saphyre gasped and startled, however, when she felt someone take hold of her arm from behind.

"I cannot present such a dance with you and not be driven to crave the taste of your mouth," Rogan said as he quick turned her to face him. Placing his powerful hands at her waist, he commanded her kiss with his own. His mouth was moist and hot against hers, first taunting—then coaxing—until she could resist him no longer. Letting her arms slide beneath his—her palms caressing the warm flesh and muscles of his back—Saphyre surrendered to Rogan, and he acquired her surrender with fervor.

In Rogan's arms, Saphyre imagined she was not an exiled princess but merely a happy, common woman—lost in the ecstasy of her lover's embrace. Her heart swelled with each tender press of his lips to hers—with each impassioned exchange of their mingling mouths.

She knew Rogan's measures were perhaps the result of careless lust, but her own responses were borne of love—of dreams of a life spent together—of finding passion and safety in each other's arms—always.

He took her face in his hands, gazing at her wantonly.

"I should not behave thus toward you, Saphyre," he whispered, his breath heavy and labored. "You are princess to the kingdom, a royal treasure…to be championed, protected…to remain innocent, not tainted."

Saphyre was troubled by the shame in his countenance. He was a rogue and a scoundrel. Why ever should he worry over her innocence so?

"My innocence was lost long ago, Rogan," she began—feeling, of a sudden, very shy. "When first I was taken by King Gregory's men… it was then I began to see the evil and ugliness in the world. It was then my innocence was lost. It was then I first knew fear, hatred… anger…the brutality of war."

Rogan's eyes narrowed as he looked at her. For a moment, Saphyre was overcome—astonished to disbelief—astonished at being in the presence of such a magnificent man. Being held in his arms was even more difficult to fathom. It seemed a dream—for what man as this would find reason to linger with her?

"Further," she continued then, weaving her fingers through his dark hair, "you have kept me safe…protected me…and championed me by doing so. As for remaining 'not tainted,' as you name it…you have never moved to threaten my virtue. Teased, perhaps…but never acted upon such a threat. And it is well I know you would not…for even if I were the woman to tempt you to do so…even if I were such a woman as to bewitch you into dishonorable behavior…I know—"

"Sshhh," Rogan whispered, pressing his whiskered cheek to her soft one. "Only hush, my beauty…and let me taste you once more before you drift from my arms into the warm embrace of sleep." He started to kiss her but paused—smiling. A quiet chuckle escaped his throat, and he said, "Of all the dangers of life endured…it is amusing to think it would be a young woman's kiss that may find me hanged."

"You would not hang for my sake," Saphyre told him.

"Would I not?" he mumbled an instant before taking her mouth with his own again.

Oh, how Rogan smothered her with passion! How he caused Saphyre's heart to beat so brutal within her chest, she feared she may drop dead from the hammer of it. Wrapped in his arms—his mouth melted to her own—Saphyre thought again of her first night in the keep. She thought of Rogan's asking her of whether she had sorted out the men of the keep—sorted them into who would serve as her footman and who would serve as her lover. She remembered also how rapid the answer had sprung to her mind. *You, Rogan, would most certainly be sorted in as my lover*, had her mind cried. And now she stood, her body held tightly against his—his kiss weaving a spell of enchantment about her.

She thought, *I can endure whatever my father's fate, whatever my kingdom's fate, whatever my own fate. I can even endure Kornelius's attention, for I have lived a dream...been receiver of such affection from such a man as Rogan of the keep.*

"To bed with you now, my princess," Rogan said, breaking the seal of their lips at last. She smiled at him as he held her hands, keeping her near him a moment longer. "I see the true breadth of what you are about, you know," he said.

"What do you mean?" she asked, still too blissfully dizzied from his kiss to think with clarity.

"It began with Marcellus," he said. "You gave to him the gift of a story...a story to be matched by no other. Then to Salomonè you gave trust...that which had been so lacking in his miserable life...in particular before he came to us in the keep."

"It was a good enough gift to him? Do you truly think it was?" she could not help but ask.

Rogan smiled, weariness heavy in his eyes. "As I told you before...it is the greatest gift ever given him, I think. And then," he continued, "to poor Belmiro, such gifts of comfort I could never have fathomed...in his clothing and care for his instrument. And tonight to Thaddeus you gave the dance. It was all he ever dreamed."

Saphyre smiled, pleased in his esteem.

"Still, how you will win Edmund I do not know."

"The way will come to me," Saphyre told him. "It will. Perhaps even tomorrow. I have an inkling of it already."

"Do you?" he chuckled. Then, releasing her hands, he smiled once more before saying, "Good night, Saphyre."

"Good night, Rogan," she said as he vanished into the shadows. "Keep safe my heart," she whispered once she was certain he was gone. "Keep safe my heart as you have kept me safe." In a more silent whisper, she added, "For my heart is in your keeping…forever."

THE _Hero's Price_

Days passed, days in which Saphyre's heart and mind were filled with little else save thoughts of Rogan—and his attentions. Each time she closed her eyes, visions of his handsome face would appear in her mind. Each day as he disappeared into the forest to cut wood or to travel to the quarry, Saphyre's heart ached to go with him—simply to be near him—to linger in his company. Each night as she lay in her small bed, she thought of Rogan—of his strength, of his smile, of his wit, of his kiss—and she longed for the sun to rise so she might linger in his presence again.

One morning Saphyre found herself wandering about the keep. The brothers of the keep had gone some moments previous—gone in pursuit of their daily labors. Alone and rather blithe concerning her intended tasks, Saphyre wandered from chamber to chamber, seeking further knowledge of what once had been the purpose of each chamber of the keep.

There were the stores—chambers meant to store supplies for the warriors who had long ago defended the once great edifice. There were chambers meant for respite, several of which had been since occupied by the brothers of the keep now dwelling in its bosom.

It was while thus wandering Saphyre came upon a narrow stone stairway. Curious as to its leading, she climbed the worn stone steps, mindful the narrow nature of the passage allowed only one person to easy access it. Up she climbed, until she reached the top of the stairway. She found herself stepping into a small turret—a tower room. There hung above her a large bell of iron and a rope. No doubt the keep bell once warned warriors of impending danger, and she wondered that the rope still appeared so strong and void of weathering.

"The warning bell of the keep."

Saphyre startled at the sound of Rogan's voice behind her, whirling about to find herself facing her heart's desire.

"You caused my heart near to leap from my breast, Rogan!" she told him. Instantly she felt her face warm crimson, the hot blush filling her to her toes as a mischievous smile spread across his face.

"Am I that handsome then?" he inquired, still smiling.

Saphyre reined her unsettled nerves and turned her attention to the bell once more. "The rope looks fresh…not ancient and rotted as one might expect."

"Yes," Rogan said, moving to stand just behind her.

She gasped as she felt his hands at her waist.

"We attached it ourselves, for it is now our signal bell…as it was a warning for the warriors who once defended this keep."

"Oh, I see," Saphyre breathed, trembling as she felt his breath on her neck.

"It has been too many sunrises and sunsets since last I was alone with you thus, Saphyre," he whispered.

"You mock me without mercy, sir," Saphyre whispered.

"Mock you?" he said, taking her shoulders and turning her to face him. His frown was that of concern. "I would not mock you, Saphyre. I may toy with you…in other matters…but I would not mock you in this."

"No?" Saphyre asked, the fire of his eyes burning into the gemmy blue of her own.

"No," he said. "Though I would steal a taste of you…a sweet sampling of the taste of you…for I crave it, as I crave nourishment when hunger twists my empty stomach."

"Truly, Rogan?" Saphyre breathed as his head began to descend to hers.

Rogan smiled, a quiet chuckle escaping him as he whispered, "Truly, Saphyre." He took her face in his hands and whispered, "Nourish me then, my beauty. Do not let me hunger longer."

Saphyre drew a deep breath as first his lips pressed her own. Each time he took her thus—kissed her—held her to the strength of his body—with each playful taunting kiss he administered, she was further astonished at his aptitude to lift her soul to the heavens. With each moist melt of his mouth to her own, she felt herself drawn further from her fears—further from her kingdom—further from any desire to be the princess Saphyre Snow. With each soft caress of his fingers to her face, with each strong embrace, she wanted only to be his, to stay in his arms, to belong to him—wholly.

Saphyre stumbled backward, the strength of Rogan's body pressed to hers too heavy, her knees too weak to support it. Seeking to regain her footing, she reached out, her hand finding support on the bellrope of the keep bell. Yet she gasped a moment later—for the bell sounded. Lost in the passion of Rogan's kiss, her weight had been too heavy on the rope, and she had, without intention, sounded the keep signal.

Rogan broke the seal of their lips. Reaching up, he took hold the rope, staying the bell as he chuckled.

"Are you so afraid of the weakening of your resolve to resist me... afraid of finding yourself in my bed, as well as my arms...that you endeavor to signal the others to come to your aid?" he asked, still smiling at her.

Saphyre blushed—gasped, drawing her hands to her mouth. "They will come?" she asked, horrified at having been so lost in passion as to have careless sounded the keep bell.

"Indeed, they will," Rogan laughed. "And what shall we tell them then? Shall we say, 'We were lost in each others' arms...so lost in the sense of our mouths mingled in passion that we—'"

"No!" Saphyre exclaimed, placing her fingers to his mouth to stay his words.

Rogan chuckled and took hold of her wrist, kissing the tips of her fingers. "Then I would champion your pride and reputation, Princess," he said. "I shall meet my brothers of the keep in the wood and explain my own clumsiness. I shall tell them I was testing the rope, assuring its strength, and accidental sounded it."

"It…it would be a falsehood," Saphyre said, ashamed at her own blundering.

"It would save your pretty face from burning to ash from the blush now blazon upon it," he chuckled.

Rogan stooped, pressing a firm kiss to her mouth before saying, "I am off then…to champion your reputation. We would not want the world knowing of your dalliance with a rogue in the keep bell tower."

Saphyre smiled, delighted by his laughter echoing through the stone steps passageway. Her heart still beat brutal within her bosom, her lips still tingling with the delicious sense of his kiss. Oh, how complete he owned her heart! How complete he owned her! Saphyre knew then, no other man would own her. Kornelius may one day lay claim to her hand, but no man would ever own her. Only Rogan of the keep—only ever Rogan.

Of a sudden, however, Saphyre frowned, for in the shadowed corners of her mind something murmured—the knowledge Salomonè had gathered in the village, the story of the dead huntsman. A foreboding lessening of light seemed to linger over her, and she feared what would become of her if, of a sudden, it cloaked her.

❧

Edmund was quiet. Ever he seemed to shrink to the shadows. He was broken and bitter, and although Saphyre knew this sense of him must be the meat of whatever gift she chose to give him, still his thick skin and hardened heart were difficult to penetrate.

Edmund had been betrayed, heartbroken, and even imprisoned for doing good. It would be a difficult thing to mend his heart and free his soul. It was an unfathomable task. Yet Saphyre, though somewhat discouraged, was not conquered. As she observed Edmund during the passing days, she was further determined to bring the smallest spark of hope and joy to him.

As for the other concern plaguing her mind, she tried to imagine the murdered huntsman had not been speaking of her when he had spoken to others of "an innocent" he was charged to murder. She tried to imagine even that, if she were the innocent, perhaps someone else was responsible for the huntsman's grueling death—someone other than her step-grandmother, Queen Carmen. Yet try as she may to convince herself of safety and no need of worry, she did worry still.

One morning as her mind was occupied with thoughts of Edmund's gift—scattered among bountiful thoughts and dreams of Rogan—Saphyre found herself about the streambed. She wandered there near without awareness—so lost in pondering had she been—when, of a sudden, there came a rustling among the bushes nearby.

Saphyre stood quite unmoving as the hair on the back of her neck prickled a warning. She sensed a menacing presence, though her mind endeavored to convince it was only a fox or a large squirrel rummaging for food. Still, slowly, as to appear unaffected, she turned and began walking back toward the keep.

The sense of foreboding—of ominous danger—began to heighten in her blood as she quickened her step, wishing one of the men of the keep would return early from his labors. She stumbled once and gasped as she felt a hand reach out to take hold of her arm. Turning, she cried out, having found herself facing the most rough-looking of men. Four men—one still holding her arm—stood with her now, all dressed in the vermilion tunics of the old queen's guard.

"You...you will release me, at once," Saphyre commanded, of a sudden remembering she was a princess—heir to the throne of the Kingdom of Graces. "How dare you startle me so! How dare you lay hands upon me!"

The man held fast to her arm, however, shaking his head and saying, "Tsk tsk, Princess. It is well you know we are the queen's guard and not your own."

"You will unhand me still," Saphyre said. "And further...in the chance you have been without the kingdom for this past year…the queen is dead."

"It is well you know we speak of Queen Carmen, Princess…for we bear her colors," another man said, stepping forward and taking hold of Saphyre's free arm. "And our mistress, Queen Carmen, wishes an audience with her beloved granddaughter…for she has been greatly concerned over your welfare these past weeks."

Saphyre's eyes narrowed as she glared at the second man. "I know you," she said. "You are Flavian…once captain of my mother's guardsmen."

"I serve Queen Carmen," was all the man said.

Saphyre was perplexed by the glassy appearance of Flavian's eyes. There seemed no emotion present in him, his countenance bearing only complete indifference. "You have traded your angel's sapphire-blue tunic—the tunic of my mother's guard—for the murderous blood-red of Carmen's?" Saphyre asked him.

She gasped when the first man struck her sound across the cheek with the back of his hand.

"You may well hang for such an act against me, guardsman."

The man seemed unmoved by Saphyre's threat. Simply he said, "You will return with us to the castle, Princess. At once."

"I will not!" Saphyre shouted as she began to struggle. "Return to be murdered? I will not!"

Instantly the other two men bent, taking hold one each of her ankles. With the assistance of the two guardsmen at her arms, they lifted her.

Saphyre began to struggle, frantic and screaming, "Help! Help me!"

"Hush, Princess," Flavian said, "for there is no one to come to your aid…and no need for you to struggle. We mean only to return you to your rightful place."

"You will unhand the princess at once or die for your deeds!"

"Edmund!" she called to Edmund as he stepped from the shadow of the forest. "Edmund! Help me!"

She heard Flavian laugh, saying, "What? A woodsman come to fight four of the queen's guard?"

"I am Edmund Englehardt," Edmund said, "Edmund the Strong, first knight of the Kingdom of Rothbain…and it would go better for you were you to show wisdom and unhand the girl before I am forced to bid you do it a second time."

The queen's guardsmen chuckled, though they did drop Saphyre rather rough to the ground. Quickly she stood and tried to run, but Flavian took hold of her arm, staying her.

"Edmund Englehardt of Rothbain, say you?" one of the men—the ugliest—asked.

"The same am I," Edmund confirmed.

"Nay," the man said. "You are not he…for I was in Rothbain when he was thrown in the castle dungeons for murder. A great knight was he…tricked to murder by a peasant girl." The man studied Edmund brow to boot and shook his head. "You are no knight. You are nothing akin to Edmund Englehardt."

"If I am no knight in your eyes," Edmund said, "then why lay you your hand at the hilt of your sword? I have no sword here…only this dagger. Surely you would not fear fighting a woodsman with only a dagger to wield."

The ugly man laughed and said, "I have no fear of fighting any man…let alone a dirty woodsman who claims to be an imprisoned knight."

"Edmund!" Saphyre called to her friend. "No! They are four, and you are but one!"

"This is true, Saphyre," Edmund told her with a nod and a raised brow. "Still, I am easy to best them…even if there are only four."

The smile on the ugly man's face faded, his thick brow puckering into an insulted frown. "It is I will cut out your tongue in the first of it," the ugly man said, drawing his sword, handing it to one of his comrades. "When you find my dagger through your liar's heart… then we will see who knows best Edmund of Rothbain."

"Edmund! No!" Saphyre sobbed, tears spilling over her cheeks. She would not see poor Edmund murdered for her sake.

The ugly man chuckled and affirmed the grasp of his dagger. Edmund stood still—dagger in hand—but as yet not wielded.

"Do you mean to kill me, man?" Edmund asked the ugly villain.

The ugly man chuckled again and said, "Most assuredly so, woodsman."

"Then I warn you…I will drop you dead before you strike to harm me," Edmund calm told him.

The ugly man shook his head and smiled, saying, "No. It is you who will die…as miserable as an old wolf."

The man thrust his weapon at Edmund then—his dagger intent on Edmund's heart. Saphyre cried out, certain Edmund was to be killed. She gasped, however—rendered breathless when she saw Edmund's hand and dagger swift slice the air. Edmund stepped aside, and the ugly man fell to the ground—hands drawn to his throat as blood flowed from a wound at the right of his neck.

"Your comrade has chosen death over wisdom," Edmund said, wiping the man's blood on the leg of his breeches. Instantly the three remaining men drew their swords, mouths yet gaping at what had so quick transpired. Flavian released Saphyre in order that he may grasp his sword firm with both hands as he stared with astonishment at Edmund.

Saphyre stood, her hands covering her mouth—tears still streaming over her cheeks as she looked from Edmund to the now dead man.

"You will go now, Saphyre," Edmund said. "You will go and seek out the others. I will keep these filthy wolves at bay until you return."

Saphyre shook her head, stammering, "I-I cannot leave you, Edmund!"

"Go!" Edmund shouted as one of the villains raised his sword to strike him.

Saphyre turned to run, but Flavian grabbed hold of her skirt, causing her to stumble to the ground. She tried to raise herself, but Flavian pounced on her as a hungry lion.

"Help!" Saphyre cried. Managing to raise her knee, she hard planted it firm below Flavian's stomach—where Rogan had once told her men are most vulnerable. She dragged herself from beneath him when he doubled over in pain. Yet the ground was wet and slick—her frock cumbersome—and she was pulled back down as Flavian quick regained his wits and took hold of her ankle.

"Leave me!" she screamed, kicking at him with her free foot. "Unhand me!"

Then she felt strong hands under each of her arms—felt herself being lifted. Marcellus appeared from somewhere at her back. A torch in hand, he set it to Flavian's tunic, and Saphyre struggled to her feet as Flavian shouted and began madly beating at the flaming cloth he wore.

"They have beset Edmund!" Saphyre sobbed as she turned to find herself in the safety of Rogan's powerful embrace.

Yet she knew comfort only for a moment—for, releasing her, Rogan said, "Attend her, Marcellus!" He then drew a dagger from its sheath at his waist and shouted, "Edmund!"

The battle was swift, the victors sure. One man turned to face Rogan and found himself quick absent of his sword—Rogan having kicked it from his hands.

The man fighting Edmund had likewise been rid of his sword and now wielded only a dagger. He glared at Edmund, who raised a brow and said, "You are too thick in it now, man."

The man thrust at Edmund, only to find himself quick upon the ground—his fate the same as the first man who had challenged Edmund.

"If I let you live...would you remain about the queen's charge?" Rogan asked the man he faced—now without sword and only a dagger in his hand.

The man smiled, saying, "I am to bring the princess home. It matters not whether she is harmed...nor even if she is alive."

"Then I bid you...when you meet him, tell the devil he owes me thanks for sending another soul to boil in hell," Rogan growled.

The man was vexed and thrust forth his dagger at Rogan. The villain's weapon was well-aimed, but Rogan simply caught his wielding wrist—raising the man's hand and plunging his own dagger deep into the man's belly.

"Do not forget to tell the devil who sent you," Rogan said, twisting the dagger twice before letting go of the man and pushing him to the ground.

Saphyre could not believe the scene before her! Her knees went weak, a sudden dizziness overtaking her. Marcellus placed an arm around her waist, however, and Saphyre clung to him—for her limbs were numb with astonishment.

"Th-thank you, Marcellus," Saphyre breathed. When she heard no response, she glanced down to see Marcellus's mouth gaping as he looked on in awe.

Flavian had dropped to his knees—managed to snuff out his fiery tunic. He knelt, stunned, drawing heavy breath, as if he meant to cough up the contents of his stomach.

Rogan and Edmund were instant upon him—Rogan's hand at Flavian's throat, his dagger leveled with one of Flavian's eyes.

"You are the old queen's guardsman?" Rogan growled.

"I...I...what am I about here?" Flavian stammered.

Rogan's grip at the man's throat tightened, and Flavian said, "Pray release me. I am once guardsman to Queen Felice...now in King Michael's guard."

"Liar!" Edmund shouted, leveling his own dagger at Flavian's other eye.

"No! No! I speak the truth!" Flavian begged. "I am about some business of a curious nature...yet I cannot fathom it now."

Saphyre followed Marcellus to stand nearer Rogan. There was fear apparent in Flavian's eyes—also perplexity.

"You are about killing the Princess Saphyre!" Rogan growled, kicking the man in the belly.

"No! No!" Flavian coughed. "I am...I am sent to return her to the old queen, it is true. But...but I cannot fathom it all."

"You did not refer to her as the 'old queen' before," Saphyre said, wiping tears from her cheeks, trying to ignore the bloody mess of death so close at her side.

"My…my mind is in a fever," Flavian stammered. "I cannot…I cannot make sense of it."

"A moment ago," Edmund began, "you were at the ready to harm the princess. Do you endeavor now to have us believe you have forgotten this so quick?"

"No," Flavian breathed, "only that…that my mind cannot fathom myself before. Such intentions toward the princess…I should die for them. Yet I swear to you, they are gone from me. As instant as my comrades fell…I know my mind was in a fever…my intentions not of my will."

"I will bleed you dry for laying hands on her," Rogan growled.

Saphyre watched Flavian wince as Rogan's grip tightened once more, the tip of his dagger moving to the man's throat just below his right ear.

"And it is well I should die for it," Flavian said, "but stay your strike that I may tell you of the old queen's instruction."

Rogan pressed the tip of his dagger against Flavian's neck. Saphyre was astonished by the fury on Rogan's face—awed at the prominence and strength of the muscles in his arms.

Edmund placed a hand at Rogan's forearm, however, saying, "Let us inquire of him first. Perhaps we will glean something of importance."

Rogan's body was trembling with anger, yet he released Flavian, standing and attempting to calm his labored breathing. "Are you… are you unharmed, Saphyre?" Rogan asked. His furious gaze fell to her and lingered as she nodded her assurance she was well—as she brushed tears from her cheeks.

"Speak then, villain," Edmund commanded. "Tell us of the old queen and her instruction to you."

"I will," Flavian said, rubbing at the flesh of his neck, still red from Rogan's grip. "I will tell you…as well as I can remember…for it is fast leaving me as is the feeling of fever."

"Speak then!" Rogan demanded.

"The old queen," Flavian began, "is want of the princess to be harmed, I think."

"This we know, idiot," Edmund shouted. "What else of it?"

"I know not much…only she sent us to find the princess, saying she had run away and was in danger. Yet in the same breath, the old queen instructed that we return the princess to the castle…even if we need cut her heart out in performance of the charge."

Saphyre's fearful trembling increased, tears spilling from her eyes anew. It was true—the old queen had learned Saphyre was not dead and now endeavored to make certain Lord Death did find her.

"Fear not, Saphyre," Marcellus said.

Saphyre looked to him to see only kindness and encouragement in his eyes—a loving smile upon his face.

"With two such champions as these…you have nothing ever to fear."

"Three such champions," Saphyre said, tenderly pressing her palm to Marcellus's cheek.

"Three," Marcellus said, taking her hand between his with kind adoration.

"This information I gleaned for myself!" Rogan shouted to Flavian, tightening his grip on his dagger.

"You obeyed this order without thought or question?" Edmund asked. "You…who once served the mother of your princess?"

"I…I did," Flavian did confess. "Still…my will was not my own, nor my mind. It was as if an odd bewitchment had befallen me and I could not deny the old queen the tasks demanded of me. Surely I would have denied her before three days past…for I loathe her for ill-treating her guardsmen…for her ill-treatment of anyone in her company."

"Three days past?" Rogan said. "What happened three days past?"

Flavian shook his head and said, "I cannot fathom it. I cannot even remember it…only that for three days I have been with these same guardsmen on the old queen's errand."

"We cannot let you live," Edmund said, "for you will return to the old queen and tell her of the princess dwelling safe here."

"She holds no power over me now," Flavian said. "I will not

return to the castle. I will keep the princess's station as unknown as it was before we came."

"Traitor!" a hoarse voice shouted.

As Rogan and Edmund turned to see which of the guardsmen yet lived, the third guardsman to drop threw his dagger straight and sure. It found its rest in Flavian's own heart. Instantly Rogan let go his own dagger, and it plunged into the forehead of the already dying villain's—rendering him, at last, most assuredly expired.

Saphyre screamed—dropped to her knees—overcome by the terrifying and ghastly ordeal.

"You must not return to the castle, Princess," Flavian choked. "The old queen would see you in the arms of Lord Death." With one final deep and futile gasp, Flavian fell dead.

Saphyre stared at him for long moments. She looked about at the scattered and bloodied bodies of the other men who had been sent by the queen to bring her to harm—to bring her to her death. She looked to Rogan and Edmund as they stood in quiet conversing.

She then looked to Marcellus, who said, "They meant to harm you, Saphyre. Had Edmund and Rogan not killed them…they surely would have killed you."

There was only darkness in the next moment—the mindless peace of senselessness.

⁂

"Saphyre?" It was No-Nose's voice she heard, drifting into the darkness of her oblivion. "Princess? All is well," he said to her.

Saphyre felt her eyes open—felt relief and joy flood her being as she looked into the weathered and beloved face of No-Nose. "They could have been killed!" she exclaimed in a whisper.

"Who?" No-Nose asked. "Do you mean Rogan and Edmund? Marcellus?"

"Yes," Saphyre said.

"Never," No-Nose told her, smiling. "Never."

Instantly tears began to well in Saphyre's eyes. Throwing her arms about No-Nose's neck, she bitter sobbed onto his shoulder—moistening the fabric of his tunic with her tears.

"All is well, Saphyre," No-Nose said, soft embracing her. His voice was deep and soothing, his intonation comforting, warm with assurance of safety. "You are safe…as are your friends…though I cannot say the same for the queen's guardsmen."

At No-Nose's mention of the guardsmen, Saphyre clung more desperately to her friend. It had been a ghastly scene, and she knew it would appear in her nightmares again and again and again.

"I knew him," Saphyre whispered.

"Who?" No-Nose asked, holding her away from him in order to study her face.

"Flavian," she said.

"The last killed?" Rogan said, crouching down beside No-Nose.

"Yes," Saphyre told him. "He is…he was Flavian…once captain of my mother's guardsmen," she explained. "He…he was ever kind to me…protected me."

"He spoke and behaved most strange," Rogan said to No-Nose. "As if…as if…"

"As if he had not known what he was about when first he arrived," Marcellus said, coming to stand near them. "It was as if he were perplexed…unaware of why he was here."

"It was perhaps only pretense," No-Nose suggested.

Rogan shook his head and said, "No…for he was intent upon taking Saphyre in the least, when first Edmund arrived. So says Edmund."

"It is true," Saphyre said. "At first seeing me, he looked at me as if his mind…as if his soul were empty of emotion. And yet after Marcellus set him aflame…after he saw his comrades dead before him, he seemed to…to…"

"He spoke of a fever," Rogan said. "He said a fever had overtaken him…and since three days past he was perplexed."

"A fever?" No-Nose mumbled.

"Where is Edmund?" Saphyre asked, realizing Edmund had not joined them. "Is he well?"

"He is well," Rogan said. "He was insistent he be the one to bury the bodies of the men. Still, Salomonè and Belmiro watch over him…as does Thaddeus."

"What would have become of me had you three not come?" Saphyre whispered, tears moistening her cheeks once more.

"We did come," Rogan said, cupping her face with one hand, smiling. His eyes were warm as sunset, his touch more comforting than soft down. "And you are well…as are we."

"Other guardsmen will—" Saphyre began.

"A walk will do you good, Saphyre," No-Nose interrupted, standing and pulling Saphyre to her feet. "A bit of activity…a breath of evening air."

"You are kind to endeavor to distract me, No-Nose," Saphyre said, smiling at her friend. "But…I would like to return to the keep, to sit near the fire…if you would permit me." She knew No-Nose was simply attempting to distract her from speaking of the danger they all were aware now loomed before them. Four of the old queen's guardsmen would be missed. One may have been less considered than four; four would raise suspicion. The keep was no longer the safe haven it had been, and it was Saphyre's doing—however unforeseen.

Saphyre was frightened, hopeless, and sickened. The men of the keep were in danger. As she walked toward the keep in the safe company of Rogan, Marcellus, and No-Nose, she winced when she thought of how easy the earlier events could have found Edmund, Marcellus, and Rogan bled out on the ground—instead of the queen's guardsmen. She again began to tremble at the thought, and Rogan— misunderstanding her visible shivering—put his arm around her shoulders in an effort to warm her.

Of a sudden, Saphyre stopped, turned, and took hold of Rogan's tunic—fisting her hands, desperately grasping at the cloth as she pleaded, "Promise me…promise me you will never again put yourself in harm's way on my account!" Rogan's eyes narrowed as he looked at her. "All of you," Saphyre said, looking to No-Nose and Marcellus— then back to Rogan. "All of you…promise me I will never be the cause of harm come to you."

"No," Rogan said, his eyes burning into hers. "I will not promise it."

"Nor I," added No-Nose.

"Nor I," Marcellus said, yet donning an understanding smile.

Saphyre gazed up into Rogan's handsome face, whispering, "I would die if you were to—"

"You will not die, Saphyre," Rogan said. "And neither will I. None of us will die."

"Seal it with a kiss now, Rogan," Marcellus whispered. "She will believe it of your kiss."

Rogan chuckled, and Saphyre smiled through her tears. Sweet Marcellus—ever the bright-hearted jester. Saphyre glanced down to Marcellus. She pressed her warm palm on his cheek. Marcellus placed his hand over Saphyre's for a moment before drawing it to his lips and kissing her palm. No-Nose then took hold of her other hand, raising it to his lips and kissing the back of it.

"All is well, Saphyre," No-Nose said.

"Yes," said Marcellus. "All is well."

Saphyre smiled at them both—then looked back to Rogan.

"All *is* well, Princess," he whispered, taking her face between his hands. "And a kiss to seal it," he whispered as his lips met her own in a firm kiss of comfort and reassurance.

"Oh, he is a fine rogue. Is he not?" Marcellus said with admiration.

"A fine rogue indeed," No-Nose chuckled.

❧

The hours grew late, finding Marcellus and No-Nose retired first. As Saphyre sat at the fire pit restless in the events of the day—further restless in Edmund's delayed return—the men of the keep undertook to reassure her. Still, night had fallen fast and long, and at last, Rogan escorted her to her bower.

"He is well, Saphyre," he told her of Edmund, his own worries apparent in the great weariness of his eyes. "No doubt quite...quite unsettled with the transpirings of the day...but he is safe and will return to us by morning. I am certain." He brushed a strand of hair from her cheek and added, "And you are safe."

"I am awkward in thanking you for my life, Rogan," she stammered, tears filling her eyes. "I cannot believe that for my sake you...you..." Saphyre could not speak it—Rogan had killed to save her. Without pause he had faced and conquered evil. Still, Edmund had done the same. She knew Edmund held no more sentiment for her than that of perhaps a friend—perhaps less—and it caused her to wonder—did Rogan truly care any more for her than did Edmund?

"Shhh," Rogan soothed. "You are weary...beyond weary. Retire now, and I will await Edmund's return."

Saphyre was disenchanted when he did not move to kiss her as he had done on the occasion several nights before. Still, she nodded and watched him disappear into the shadows of the keep.

Saphyre retired to the little bed in her keep chamber. The fire burned warm and comforting in the hearth, yet nothing served to soothe her. Visions of the battle between the queen's guardsmen and her friends of the keep kept appearing as she closed her eyes. She felt startled by the threat that had come so unexpected at the stream's bank. She felt guilt—responsible for the deaths of the men who had endeavored to take her. She was frightened for the safety of all in the keep—for her father's—for that of her kingdom. She was fearful of her own fate at the hand of the queen, and she was anxious over Edmund's absence.

In the wee hours of the morning, however, she was awakened by a noise—the sound of footsteps on the stairs outside her chamber. Instantly her heart began to hammer with fear as she thought of the queen's guardsmen. She watched the entrance to her chamber—watched a broad-shouldered figure step out of the shadows and into the moonlight beaming in from the window.

"Oh, Edmund!" she exclaimed, leaping from her bed and rushing to him. "Edmund!" she cried, sliding her arms around his waist to embrace him. "I was fearful of your welfare," she said.

"I am well, Saphyre," he said. His voice was low—calm, but very weary. "And you?"

"I am well now you are returned," she told him. Of a sudden, realizing how bold she had been in her greeting, she stepped back from him. Yet she took his hands in hers and raised each, in turn, to her lips. "I thank you for my life, Edmund," she said. "For my life... and for...and for whatever else may have been lost to me had you not championed me."

"It is as any man would have done," he mumbled, but Saphyre shook her head.

"No," she said. "It is not. And for you to have done this for me... you...who has been so wronged." Edmund dropped his gaze to the floor as Saphyre continued, "May I beg a moment of your time, Edmund? To speak with you in earnest?"

Edmund nodded, and Saphyre led him to sit with her on the floor before the warm, glowing embers in the hearth.

"Do you remember Marcellus's story?" she asked him. "The one I told not so many nights past?"

"I do," Edmund said. "It was a wonderful story for our friend."

Saphyre nodded and continued, "When the great knight Sebastian was returning me to my mother and father...to the castle and my safe protection...he tried to soothe me with stories of great ladies of honor and virtue...stories of knights defending such worthy women," she told him. "When he had finished telling me these tales—when we were in sight of my home and I began to thank him for caring for me—he said something I have never forgotten. It has remained with me always...for it became my greatest wish to be such a woman as to deserve the attentions of such a man as the great Sebastian Ottokar. 'A woman with kindness in her countenance and action,' Sebastian said to me, 'a woman of humility and virtue, of loving nature...these attributes in a woman are worth the greatest sacrifice. Such a woman is worth a man's life in defense of all that she is,' he said. I asked him then if his lady, Augustynia, were indeed the sort of woman he spoke of...and he told me without hesitation, 'I would defend her to my death...lay down my life...see my heart torn from my breast before I would see her spoiled or harmed in any manner.' Do you know what I thought then, my dearest friend, Edmund?" Saphyre asked.

"You wished to be such a woman worthy of such a man," he mumbled, the emotion of great pain in betrayal on his face.

"I thought, 'And is Augustynia such a woman to lay down her life for Sebastian's sake? Is she such a woman as to see her heart torn from her breast in defense of her great knight? For he is surely deserving as such.'"

Saphyre paused—gathered her courage—then asked, "What price was paid you, Edmund...for your great sacrifice in defending virtue... in defending your maiden? What was shown you but betrayal? What was absent unto you but loyalty, faithfulness, and love?" Saphyre tried to keep the tears from escaping her eyes as she saw the excess moisture gathering in Edmund's. No doubt the memories she had evoked in him were profound painful, but she must continue. To begin the healing of his carefully guarded, carefully masked tender heart, she must continue.

"What you have lost, Edmund, I am admitted unable to return to you. Yet I can offer you what I may...my astonished admiration as I stand in wonder of your heroic deeds...my respect and gratitude as I see you are yet, after all the evil that has befallen you for doing good...you are yet the champion of virtue and honor. It is well I know my paltry gratitude and admiration are of little consequence... but with all my heart I give them. I give them to you, Edmund...a hero's price...worth not that of gold or jeweled treasure...but worth far more.

"Oh, how I esteem a man who would give his life to defend virtue! And you are such a man. Oh, how I stand in awe of a man... strong, determined, seeming...who would give his heart so fully to a woman as to defend her with his life...as to slay evil in her way... and you are such a man."

Saphyre paused, unable to restrain her tears as moisture spilled from Edmund's eyes. After a moment, she continued, "And oh, Edmund...how I loathe a woman who does not see such a man for the rare prize that he is. A loathsome woman who would betray such a champion...who would rob such a hero of the simple price due him...gratitude, admiration, love. Please know I am none such as she you knew…for I recognize the great sacrifice of self given in killing one to save another. I recognized the sacrifice of it…the strength in character in protecting any woman of virtue. In you I find safety, for I know you are noble and strong and would protect me against any threat. What better awareness can there be to give comfort to a woman?" Again Saphyre paused.

Edmund's breath was labored as his burden of the past began to lift.

"And I would beg you, Edmund," Saphyre told him then. "I would beg you to leave the pain given you, forsake the memory of wrongdoing done you. I would beg you leave the past…release it and look to the path before you. I beg you value my sincerity in this too—Sebastian's lady, Augustynia…I have witnessed her faithfulness, her loyalty, and her love. I have watched her endure…for, and only for, Sebastian…beyond even his life. I have seen the hero's price paid by such a woman worthy to pay it. Therefore, believe me in this, Edmund—that all you fought for, all you defended in your king's kingdom, was of profound merit. And you, Edmund…you are of immeasurable worth."

Edmund brushed a tear from his chin and looked to Saphyre, his voice breaking as he said, "You are such a jewel as I have never seen before, Saphyre."

"And you are such a friend as I have never known before," Saphyre whispered, taking his hands in hers and kissing the back of them again. "Thank you for my life, Edmund." Smiling, she added, "I have grown quite fond of it."

Edmund chuckled, saying, "So have I, Saphyre. So have I."

Saphyre threw her arms about Edmund's neck. "Swear to me you will find such a woman as Sebastian's lady. Promise me you will find love and happiness in a life with her. Swear to me your hero's price, once lost, will no longer haunt you nor harden your heart."

"I swear it," Edmund said.

"Then I am well enough to let you go to your bed to rest," Saphyre said. "I am well enough to rest myself."

"Rest then, tender friend," Edmund said, standing and helping

Saphyre to her feet. "And dream of he who likewise earned the hero's price this day." Edmund smiled and bent toward Saphyre, whispering in her ear, "Dream of Rogan, Princess. For I know he has won your heart...and there is none more deserving." He was gone then—swallowed in shadow as had been Rogan hours earlier.

Saphyre returned to her bed, her heart lightened at witnessing the beginning—the beginning of the end of bitterness in Edmund's countenance—and soul.

THE MASK OF CONFIDENCE

The air grew crisp and chill. Fallen leaves of crimson, gold, and orange covered the forest floor. The days since the queen's guardsmen endeavored to spirit Saphyre back to the castle found the men of the keep, and their princess, unsettled—far less certain of the safety in solitude of the keep. It had been determined by all that either Saphyre was to accompany one or two of the men as they went about their day labors or that one of the men, each in turn, would ever remain at the keep with her.

At first—once all had been affirmed—Saphyre felt she had brought yet another burden to the brothers of the keep. Still, she soon realized the men of the keep were indeed her friends. Thus, she accepted their friendship and increased protection with gratitude.

One morning in particular, Saphyre was to accompany No-Nose. Rogan and Salomonè were riding to the village for supplies. As Saphyre dared not be seen and No-Nose chose not to be seen—as often he did—she smiled as she walked beside No-Nose and into the wood. It was No-Nose unknowing offered some tranquil sense of calm. Ever did Saphyre enjoy his company, and this day did not differ.

"Have I ever told you, No-Nose," Saphyre began, shivering just a little at the coolness of the morning, "that you put me in mind of someone? Of whom I cannot be certain…but there has always been a thing about you that I feel is…somehow…near familiar."

"Truly?" No-Nose said, smiling. "What is it makes me seem familiar?"

Saphyre smiled and shrugged. "You will think me silly, but it is your eyes, your posture…even your voice. I often feel that if you still had your…" Saphyre abrupt stopped speaking—mortified at having nearly mentioned No-Nose's ghastly and painful wound.

Yet he broke into amused laughter. Smiling at her, he said, "You mean to say that, were it I still owned the entirety of my nose…you would know me?"

Saphyre nodded, still blushing with embarrassment at having referred to No-Nose's lack of nose. "Perhaps if you were clean-shaven," she said then. She stopped, gazing up at him. As always she felt as if recognition were a breath away, but she could not inhale it. "There is something so familiar about you," she said. "Have you any brothers in the Kingdom of Graces?"

"None," No-Nose said. "None in any kingdom."

"Have you no family? No fair maiden who owns your heart?" Saphyre pressed.

No-Nose sighed and shook his head. "No," he said. "My family…all are dead—father, mother, sister. And as fair maidens are concerned…what fair maiden would look beyond this?" he added with a disgusted gesture at his face.

It was in that moment that Saphyre's mind thought of a gift befitting No-Nose. Her heart swelled with eagerness; her smile broadened. She would not make to argue with him. Though she knew a woman could love a man with a nose as well as without, she remembered her own response at first setting eyes on him as he was. She understood then—No-Nose had no hope of meeting any new acquaintance and not being greeted with a surprised or horrified expression, no hope of finding a woman to love him. Still, Saphyre loved him—not as she did Rogan, of course. But she did love him, and in her mind a woman could love No-Nose the way she loved Rogan.

"Many a fair maiden would," Saphyre told him. She would hold her secret until she had time to work her ways.

No-Nose smiled at Saphyre, saying, "You are such a woman of hope, Saphyre."

"Was there, in your heart, a fair maiden before...before...your misfortune?" she asked.

She watched as No-Nose's beautiful blue eyes seemed to glaze over—as if he were looking to the past. "In truth...there was," he mumbled. "But it was long ago."

"Did...did she abandon you because of your...your..."

"Because my nose was cut off?" he finished, smiling at her.

"Yes," Saphyre admitted.

"No," he said. "She thinks I am dead...and for all that is good and well for her sake...I remain dead."

Saphyre's brow puckered in a concerned frown. "You mean to say...you never gave her the chance to accept or refuse you? You never gave her the choice of having you without your nose...or not at all?" She saw guilt wash through his countenance.

"No," he told her. "I...I...could not bear to think of her being repulsed by the sight of me. In truth, the injury was even more disturbing when it was fresh, so many years ago...more ghastly even than it is now."

"It does not matter, No-Nose," Saphyre gently scolded. "You should have given her the choice...the chance to prove to you that you were more to her than just a nose."

Again No-Nose laughed, this time reaching out and gathering Saphyre into his arms in a tender, friendly embrace. "Oh, how you delight us all, Saphyre," he said. "What manner of men were we before you came?"

"Great men," Saphyre told him. "And it is why I endeavor to thank you...failing miserably day by day."

No-Nose released her, still smiling. He studied her, saying, "Yet do you not see your meekness? See how completely you forget yourself and think of others? Even giving hope to a maimed, noseless woodsman."

Saphyre smiled at him. She again thought of how familiar the man seemed to her. Even his soothing embrace had seemed familiar—and the truth of it haunted her. "I have a thought about me," Saphyre said. "If you are so concerned that no woman would love you upon seeing your noselessness...then indeed I must simply find a sightless woman for you to love!"

"A blind woman to love a noseless man?" No-Nose asked. "A very strange...yet clever notion," he laughed.

"Many stranger and more clever notions have there been in the world, No-Nose, my friend," Saphyre said.

"Indeed there have been," No-Nose said, wielding his ax at a large tree trunk. "Indeed there have."

❦

"It would be helpful if you would tell me what you are about, Saphyre," Rogan said, working the thin piece of wood in his hands.

"I cannot," she told him. "You would...you would think the reason ridiculous...the entire notion far too feminine in nature."

Rogan ceased in his labor over the wood to look at her, frowning. "I would think nothing of the sort," he said. "Further, if you tell me what you are about, I would more able be in crafting this...this whatever it is for you."

Saphyre searched his eyes—their depth and fire. Dare she tell him of her intent, of her gift for No-Nose? After all, Rogan held No-Nose in high esteem, valued his advice and knowledge, protected him without wavering.

"If I confide in you, Rogan," she began, "will you promise...will you promise not to laugh at me...at my simple endeavor? Will you promise not to—"

"What reason would I own for laughing?" he interrupted. His frown showed concern and hurt at her not trusting him.

"It is...it is a gift," she told him. Reaching into the front of her frock, she retrieved a length of sapphire cloth. "For No-Nose," she said.

Rogan continued to frown. "A scrap of cloth? Torn from your frock?" he asked, perplexed. "I do not understand."

164

"I-I have fashioned it in a certain manner," she stammered in explaining, "stitched it as to a certain fitted shape…and to allow this tiny pocket to hold a carved piece of wood or bone." She turned the length of cloth over, displaying the tiny pocket to Rogan. "The crafted wood or bone fits in here, thus," she said, taking the small piece of wood from his hand and pressing it into the tiny pocket of the soft blue velvet. "And the cloth would fit just under his eyes…above his mouth…with two openings beneath his nose so he may breathe… fastening at the back of his head…thus." Saphyre held the cloth up to her own face. She saw Rogan's eyes widen with understanding as he looked at her.

"A mask," he whispered. "A mask to hide his nose."

"Yes," Saphyre told him. "You see how the wood—"

"Raises the cloth…causing it to appear as if there is a nose beneath it," Rogan mumbled, thoughtful.

"He is so terribly lonely, Rogan," Saphyre began, "only ever leaving the keep to labor…near never traveling to the village. Perhaps he could grow accustomed to strangers wondering at what is beneath the mask…instead of staring at him in stunned horror."

Rogan's eyes narrowed, and she feared he would scold her— reprimand her for prompting No-Nose to further awareness of his maimed feature. Therefore, she burst into desperate explanation.

"Do you not think it would go easier for him? For I do. Having first set eyes on him when I came here…I would certain have been less disturbed by a man with a mask than I was by a man without a nose." She watched as Rogan closed his eyes, the frown at his brow deepening. "Please do not be angry with me, Rogan!" she pleaded. "I only mean to—"

"Who could ever be angry with such as you, Saphyre Snow?" he mumbled. He opened his eyes then, and she saw the excess moisture gathered in them. "Who could ever be angry with such a heart as yours?"

"You will carve the piece for me?" she asked, of a sudden enchanted by the manner in which he moistened his lips with his tongue as he gazed at her.

"I will," he said, his voice alluring and low. "But...but I do wonder...why did you tear your frock? You have cloth enough remaining from Belmiro's tunics."

Saphyre smiled, sensing her own blush, as she said, "The blue of my frock will complement the blue of his eyes."

Rogan tossed his head back, a joyous and hearty laugh escaping him. His eyes fairly twinkled with pleasure as he looked back to her, taking her face in his hands.

"When first I saw you," he began, "when first I heard you tell of who you are...I thought to evade your presence completely, thinking no good could come from the royal house of the kingdom...thinking no strength could be borne of a princess kept so innocent, so protected from the hardships of life."

Saphyre shivered with delight as his thumb slowly caressed her lower lip. His touch was wonderful—his face before her magnificent!

"Have you altered your thinking...where I am in question?" she ventured in a whisper, her eyes entranced by his own.

"Some thoughts of you I have indeed altered," he did admit. Then smiling, he said, "Yet there are other thoughts I owned when first I saw you...other thoughts that remain steadfast."

Mistaking his inference entirely, Saphyre frowned, her heart hard hammering with disappointment. "But...but I have endeavored to show my gratitude to you and the others," she stammered pleadingly. "I have worked in the keep to earn my—"

"Shhhh," Rogan chuckled. "You misunderstand me, pretty princess. The other thoughts of which I speak are admittedly...dare I say...carnal in nature...for you are a beautiful woman. And although a measure of my reasoning may have altered...I yet entertain thoughts of you and I—"

Saphyre quickly pressed her fingers to his lips, silencing his words. "You dare not speak of it, lest someone intrudes to hear you!"

He chuckled and took hold of her hand, pressing her fingers firm to his lips as he kissed them. "You asked me if my thoughts of you have altered, and I confess only the truth," he said. "Some thoughts indeed have altered...as others have not."

Saphyre glanced away from him, bashful under his smoldering gaze. Mustering her courage, she asked then, "Do you…do you have these thoughts of me mere for the sake I am a woman and you have been in solitude with only men as companions for so long? Or do you have these thoughts—the unaltered ones of which you speak—do you have them because…because I am…me?"

He kissed her soft on the mouth. "Do you let me kiss you… indeed, do you kiss me for the sake I am a man…or for the sake I am Rogan?" he asked. His voice was deep, syruped in seduction—Saphyre's seduction. "Therein lies your answer, sweet Saphyre."

Saphyre melted to him—welcomed and accepted the impassioned affections given from his mouth to her own. Such a flame of desire was in her—such bliss and rapt wonder! Rogan's mouth was warm and moist—demanding—laced with such a flavor of heated ambrosia as to cause Saphyre's entire being to quiver with an insatiable thirst—a thirst for his kiss she feared would never know quench! His hands held her face a moment longer before his fingers wove through her hair as he kissed her. Careful, he eased her back—until she lay on the leafy bed of the forest floor—all the while kissing her, mingling the moisture of his mouth with her own. He hovered over her, supporting his strength of body with his arms as he kissed her. Yet Saphyre could not deny her own desire to embrace him. Allowing her arms to go around him—endeavoring to pull him closer to her—she was rendered breathless as his massive chest of a sudden crushed to her own, the rest of his heavy body settling on the ground next to her.

Saphyre gasped, breathless as his lips traveled over her neck—lingered at the hollow of her throat—his hands caressing her arms—her shoulders—his fingers weaving through her hair. She thought she might cry out for want of his mouth to hers once more! When, at last, his attentions did return to her mouth, she was rendered powerless in his arms—lost to time and reason.

As the breeze played among the near leafless branches of the trees, Rogan wove an enchantment of passion and desire over Saphyre. She reveled in the feel of his strong jaw beneath her palm, the movement of it a further indication she was true owning of his affection—not mere dreaming. She allowed her own fingers to seek pleasure in his hair—the softness of it a sense of purest pleasure. Letting her hands travel over his shoulders to his arms, she delighted in the feel of leather bands at his forearms stretching up from his wrists—reveled in the sense of his faultlessly carved muscles.

So long did they remain so entwined—lost in the bliss of their shared affection—Saphyre's lips and the flesh surrounding her mouth began to pleasant ache. Rogan's three-day growth of beard scratched her tender cheeks, but she cared not—for the ecstasy of his attentions was worth any discomfort.

In time, however, Rogan broke from her—sitting up of a sudden and running his fingers through his hair. "You are princess to the kingdom," he growled.

Saphyre frowned, for it was as if he had in the first come to such realization. "No," she said. Sitting then, she studied him. He appeared, of a sudden, concerned—awash with guilt. "Here...with you...I am only..."

"You are princess to the kingdom and would I should be your champion...not your corruptor," he said. He stood, offering a hand to her, in order he may assist her in standing.

Saphyre stood and, looking at him, said, "Many are the moments in which you have been my champion. You did not throw me out of the keep...rather let me stay, knowing well what danger you may be in. You have taught me, protected me...even you have killed in my defense. Even you did champion me in the Executioner's Kiss...full knowing the consequence. Never would I have known such...such passion otherwise."

"I would have you, Saphyre...here...this moment!" he growled. "Were I not the man I am...were you not the woman you are...I would indeed have you. And yet it comes to me full lucid somehow— for near the first time it comes to me you *are* princess to the kingdom. You *are* Saphyre Snow...and no one may own you. No one should own you."

"You regret me," Saphyre whispered. She felt as if her heart were being torn in two. Something had changed in Rogan. In that instant, he had changed from the leader of the men of the keep to the champion of the kingdom's princess.

He took hold of her shoulders, frowning at her as he spoke. "I would take you, Saphyre," he said. "Understand…were I a scoundrel and you easy prey…I would take you. These thoughts I must not entertain longer…for I am Rogan, and you are the princess, Saphyre…heir to the throne of the Kingdom of Graces. And we, both of us, are made better and stronger for who we are and what we have endured. Yet you tempt me near beyond my aptitude to resist."

Saphyre tried to still her hammering heart—for something in his words delighted her, as well as frightened her. Yet his words spoke of putting her away from him—of never touching her—of never kissing her again.

"What then…what then do you mean to do with me?" she asked, tears welling in her eyes.

Rogan closed his smoldering eyes for a moment, frowning. "I mean to champion you," he said. "I mean to champion my princess." He released his hold on her shoulders.

"And…and what of me?" she whispered.

He opened his eyes and looked at her, a sad sort of smile tugging at the corners of his mouth. "For you I shall carve a nose to fit in the pocket of your mask for our friend," he said. "And for myself," he whispered, "one last sip of the sweet nectar that is your mouth." He leaned to her, tasting her trembling lips once more.

❧

"Rogan has vowed then?" No-Nose asked. "Vowed to champion you rather than to corrupt you?"

"Yes," Saphyre said. Her heart yet ached from thoughts of nevermore being in Rogan's arms. Thus, her heart broken, her mind taxed, she had chosen to confide in No-Nose—spoken of Rogan to he who ever seemed yet familiar in her mind.

No-Nose chuckled. "Fear not, Saphyre," he said. "He will realize soon enough he can serve as both lover and champion to you."

"Lover?" Saphyre exclaimed, blushing to her toes.

No-Nose's smile broadened. "Yes. He is your lover, Saphyre. You being such an innocent have not yet begun to understand…it is a lover you own in Rogan. Oh, I know what sort of talk abounds in the courts. I know what terms a lover to less moral men and women. Still, your lover he is, and he is now enduring a manner of…awakening. His heart has been hardened for many years, and it is right he should endeavor to know himself now. But fear not…he will not keep himself from your berry-sweet lips for long."

Saphyre smiled again in admiration of No-Nose's wisdom and goodness. She reached into the front of her frock and withdrew the mask—perfect stitched, finished, and folded.

"I have a thing for you, No-Nose," she said. Oh, how her hands trembled; how her mind endeavored to stop her from revealing her gift to him.

"A thing for me?" No-Nose asked. Propping his ax against a nearby stump, he wiped his hands on his breeches.

"I confess, I am fearful in giving it to you," Saphyre told him. "It may seem a childish gift. It may even bring you to anger." Slowly, Saphyre held the mask up to her own face—pressing it over her nose and against her cheeks. She saw then No-Nose's smile fade, his eyes fill with moisture. Thus, she quick endeavored to explain her purpose to him.

"Might it not be more endurable to be looked upon with curious eyes…for the sake of wearing a mask of mystery, No-Nose," she hastened to ask, "rather than for the sake of your…your injury?"

When he said nothing—only continued to stare at her with tears in his eyes—she removed the mask from her own face, offering it to him. "See here…Rogan has fashioned a piece of wood—shaped as much like your nose as he can imagine—with tender crafted sides, as to set against your face in support of the mask." When still he made no response, she asked, "Are you indeed very angry with me, my friend? For I only meant to—"

Saphyre's words were lost as No-Nose reached out, taking the mask from her. Slowly, he held it to his face, and she said, "Let me assist you, for it fastens with ease enough at the back of your head."

Careful, she fastened the button to the thread loop she had

sewn at the back of the mask. When No-Nose raised his head and looked at her, Saphyre gasped. The sapphire of the cloth indeed gave resplendence to No-Nose's eyes, causing his gaze to pierce her very soul with its brilliance—enhanced by only just restrained tears.

The mask made of velvet, joined with the skillfully crafted piece of wood there inserted, gifted No-Nose the look of some handsome nobleman dressed for a masque. With his eyes such a brilliant blue, the shape of a nose added to his features—refined and finished his appearance—and Saphyre was further convinced she had been in his company before. It was well the mask fit too, covering little of his cheeks, leaving the space between his nose and upper lip free.

"And my appearance now, Saphyre?" No-Nose asked. "Is it...is it endurable?"

"It is a great, great deal more than endurable, No-Nose," she said. "Further, I know we have met before...and I see you are still the handsomest of men. Yet, pray, No-Nose...are you indeed my familiar?"

No-Nose closed his eyes a moment. "In this mask I can near find the courage to look at myself in the mirror of the stream," he said. He then opened his eyes, smiling at her. "Yes, Princess...you know me."

At last! At last Saphyre knew of certain—she had not dreamed the familiarity of No-Nose to her mind and heart. "Yet how do I know you?" Saphyre asked.

"You knew my soul, Saphyre," No-Nose near whispered. "You have seen beyond my hideous appearance. You have looked into my eyes to see my soul. You...so beautiful of body and face...you...so beautiful of heart, word, and deed. You...finding beauty in anything, no matter how ugly it may appear to others. You knew me. Perhaps heaven itself sent you, an angel, to recognize me. Could this be the reason you seem to know me?"

Saphyre smiled, though her heart owned an odd discontent. Certain she was that she knew him before, but his words did not confirm it. Yet she felt joy too, for No-Nose's very spirit had changed. For a simple piece of cloth and a chip of wood, she saw the man straighten his posture, broaden his shoulders, and freely smile—a true and happy smile. It was a smile of confidence the mask had given his face. Near more than the false shape of a nose beneath the mask, it was his confident smile that changed his appearance—his very countenance.

"If you say this is the reason you seem to have been in my mind before I came to the keep...then I will accept it. Still, I know you were in my mind long before. Somehow I know it," Saphyre told him.

"That is the blessing of heaven given angels who pretend at being princesses," No-Nose said, gathering her into his embrace. "I shall go to the village with Rogan when next he travels there," No-Nose said. "Yes! I shall go with him. And perhaps, my little mask-stitching angel," he chuckled, "perhaps I shall talk to the women who are sighted...as well as the ones who are not."

Saphyre smiled. Her heart warmed with joy in her friend's newborn confidence.

❧

"It is a comely mask indeed," Thaddeus said as he stared at No-Nose.

No-Nose and Saphyre had returned to the keep before the others. Now Saphyre reveled in observing the response of each man as he entered to see No-Nose's altered appearance.

Marcellus had clapped his hands and danced about with delight at seeing No-Nose so altered. Now Thaddeus smiled and nodded, saying, "It gives you something, No-Nose. Yet I cannot discern if it is the mask that has changed you or if there has been something else altered."

Belmiro, Salomonè, and Edmund likewise noted the alteration in their friend's countenance. Thus, all were sitting around the fire mingling in cheerful conversation when Rogan returned.

No-Nose stood to greet his friend, embracing him firm and sound patting his back saying, "My thanks, good friend...for your efforts on my behalf."

Rogan smiled at his friend, reached up, and straightened the mask a bit. "She is right," he said. "The blue does become your eyes."

No-Nose laughed, as did the others. Saphyre closed her eyes, offering a silent prayer of thanks—for another member of the keep had found a morsel of himself.

Rogan's gaze met hers then, and he nodded his approval. Saphyre forced a smile, though her heart ached. He had made his resolution where she was concerned. No matter what words of encouragement No-Nose had offered her, Saphyre knew Rogan had begun to see her as princess to the kingdom and not merely as Saphyre.

Yet as she later passed him in the keep hallway, he reached out, taking several tresses of her hair between his fingers.

"Good night, Saphyre," he whispered. Closing his eyes, he drew the tresses to his nostrils—drawing a deep breath of their scent before releasing them to fall to her shoulder once more.

"Good night, Rogan," she whispered as he mingled with the shadows in leaving her.

As Saphyre lay in her bed in her keep chamber, she thought of No-Nose—of his jewel-blue, familiar eyes—of his smile—of his returning assurance. Certainly the mask was far from anything to replace what had been lost to him at the tip of an enemy's sword. Yet it had given him hope, a renewed love of self—restored a confidence Saphyre sensed he had once possessed and lost.

Saphyre thought of Rogan then—her lover, as No-Nose had termed him. Would he return to her, take her in his arms, and rain kisses upon her wanting mouth? Her mind began taxing—worrying—wondering of what she might give Rogan as thanks for his championing her. She realized then how complete he had championed her. From the moment she had entered the keep, even when he had threatened to put her from shelter, growled and grumbled at her, always he had been protecting her. Rogan's gift would be the most difficult to discern, she knew—had always known.

The gift of imagination through story given Marcellus—of trust to Salomonè—of comfort to Belmiro—of joyous dance to Thaddeus—of gratitude in the hero's price to Edmund—and, to No-Nose, confidence restored. Yet to Rogan—what gift was there worthy of offering to one such as he?

ROGAN'S RESPITE

"We are ignorant to not have thought of it before," Salomonè said.

"Perhaps," No-Nose said. "Yet Saphyre has inspired me now." He paused and smiled at Saphyre, and she was warmed by the look of confidence in his eyes.

"The silversmith in the east village is quite skilled," Salomonè explained to the others as all, save Rogan, sat at the table in the keep kitchen. The evening shadows were fast falling, the air cool and crisp, announcing autumn was deep and winter around the bend.

No-Nose and Salomonè had taken wood to the village in the east that morning. Upon passing a certain establishment, a man had stopped them, having noted No-Nose's mask and guessing at its purpose. The man was a craftsman of silver and had suggested No-Nose's mask of cloth and wood could be replaced with a crafted mask of silver, silver being more durable. It would not quick wear as the cloth mask and would therefore be simpler to sustain. The silversmith explained his talent for working silver, further assuring No-Nose such a mask could be crafted as to imitate the entire shape of a nose.

Saphyre had been delighted at the suggestion. How much more comfortable would No-Nose live with a mask of silver to include the actual shape of his nose?

175

"Is the sum of the cost very great?" Marcellus asked.

"Not so great considering the prize," No-Nose said. "At least, not to my mind."

"How will the silver mask fit and fasten?" Saphyre asked.

"Fashioned to curve upward just before my ears at each side of my face, it will be made to fit just over the top of my ears," No-Nose explained. "This will make for ease of removal, and support as well, while I wear it."

Saphyre smiled at her friend. The enthusiasm, hope, and confidence in his eyes were astonishing! How glad she was her simple cloth mask had given him the strength to press forward in his own interest.

"When will you ask him to craft it?" Belmiro asked.

"He has begun already," Salomonè answered, "for he measured No-Nose's face this very morning and will meet us on the morrow to deliver it."

"It is glad I am to see you thus," Edmund said, smiling. "You are well deserving of such happiness, my friend."

Saphyre's heart swelled at the sight of Edmund's smile. He had grown increasing calm and more pleasant, and it caused Saphyre to feel greater joy.

"Are we to practice our dance this night, Saphyre?" Thaddeus asked then. "For it has been three nights since we danced."

"We are," Saphyre giggled.

Although Thaddeus's demands for dancing were near too taxing, Saphyre was pleased in the manner in which all the men of the keep involved themselves in it. The evenings spent in the merriment of dance were some of the happiest Saphyre had known at the keep.

"Good evening, all," Rogan greeted as he entered then.

As every time Rogan entered a room or stood near to her, the rapidity of Saphyre's heartbeat increased. She felt flushed—weak and strong in the same moment. He had indeed kept a distance from her since his pledge to do so. Still the truth of it—though frustrating—only served to increase Saphyre's love for him. How chivalrous he was to attempt to treat her as a princess when he indeed had no great care for the royal family in rule of the kingdom.

"Good evening, Rogan," Edmund greeted. "What have you been about till this late hour?"

Saphyre noted how particular weary Rogan appeared—more so even than was common.

"Labor, my friend," Rogan said, sliding weary into a chair next to No-Nose. "I want to be certain the keep woodpiles are as healthy as possible...for I have no desire to freeze in the coming winter."

"Our woodpiles are plenty in health," Marcellus said. "You work too hard, Rogan."

Saphyre watched as Rogan clenched his hands into fists and then opened them, wincing at their soreness. He turned his head to one side and pressed a sore hand to the back of his neck, again wincing.

"You will put yourself to an early grave with such overlaboring, Rogan," No-Nose told him.

"Indeed," Rogan said, frowning as he squeezed the muscle of his shoulder.

"You take no time for repossession of strength...no time for peace of mind," Belmiro offered. "Both will wear too greatly if you do not learn to take respite, Rogan."

Rogan frowned and looked about the room, studying each face. "Have I entered into a nest of grandmothers?" he asked, smiling with wearied amusement. "You coddle me as an infant."

"And you have worn yourself too tired to dance with us tonight," Thaddeus said, his expression akin to that of a pouting child.

"I fear that I have, Thaddeus," Rogan confessed. "I will be about my dinner and then retire."

Saphyre frowned, concerned for Rogan's deep weariness of body and mind. With all she had endeavored to offer as gifts for the others—great or small—was there not any manner in which she might gift Rogan respite? She watched as he made his sore hands into fists, wincing at the pain caused by doing so. She thought of his inconceivable perseverance to hard labor—to his incapability to sit tranquil as the others did around the fire at night. In truth, the only moments she could fancy of Rogan having been at ease in some manner were the moments he had spent in wooing her with his affectionate attentions. Even then she was suspect he was not at peace—simply distracted for a measure of time.

It was often—nearly each and every evening—Saphyre would witness Rogan pressing his thumb into the palm of each sore hand as he did this night. Sometimes he winced at turning his head too quick or groaned when sitting still for long intervals found him stiff and awkward to rise. Likewise, his mind seemed in constant taxed. Ever he appeared deep in thought—even during moments of mirth and humor. Even when he smiled or laughed, it seemed Rogan's mind was elsewhere occupied.

As Saphyre sat watching Rogan as the others rose to adjourn to the fire, she realized how wholly he was worn—body and mind. It came to her then. As her thoughts lingered over her study of him, she was in certain that Rogan was never at peace—never, neither his mind nor body. She wondered then what it was that kept him so stirred—so ill at ease. She thought of the brutal murder of his father, the bitterness in him over tragedy. She thought of the burden weighing heavy on his shoulders, the charge of every soul in the keep being dependent upon him for command and care. What great heavy-laden yoke should ever be put to any beast—let alone a mortal man?

Respite—one moment of peace—this would be Saphyre's gift to Rogan of the keep. She rose to follow the others to the fire pit. First she would dance—enjoy merriment with the other men. Then, when Rogan had finished nourishing himself, when he had retired to his keep chamber, she would offer her gift. She would offer a moment— however fleeting—of peaceful respite.

❦

Rogan startled when Saphyre entered his keep chamber. He had removed his shirt and stood before the hearth, his countenance that of the weariest of men.

"Saphyre?" he said. "You near put my heart to quitting."

Saphyre smiled at him, his tousled hair and drowsy appearance all the more endearing. His eyes flashed like jewels in the low firelight, and she wary approached him.

"Forgive me," she said as she drew nearer him. Her heart beat as a blacksmith's hammer on an anvil. Her hands began to tremble, and she felt as if summer moths had taken flight in her stomach. Never before that moment had she considered Rogan's denying her gift. What if he should turn her out of his chamber—refuse to let her help him? It was obvious he somewhat deliberate avoided respite. Perhaps he was happy in his own great weariness.

Yet Saphyre was determined. She would help him, and surely he would not reject her offer of it. "I-I have come to gift you a thing," she stammered.

Rogan smiled the smile of a weary man and said, "Pray…have not you given me sufficient already?"

Saphyre was of a sudden delighted at his teasing manner. For since the day he had sworn to champion her as princess, he had little smiled at her, let alone jested. "Come and sit before the fire," she told him, taking his hand and leading him to the hearth.

"Is the dancing then ended?" he asked, wearily following her lead.

She smiled, for his great weariness had made him as easy to influence as a small child. How she did adore the sense of his hand in hers—the manner in which his eyes studied her from face to foot as he allowed her to guide him to sitting on the floor before the fire.

"It is," she told him. "And you missed the best of it."

"I regret it, but I am near full spent this night," he told her.

It was time to weave her spell of respite, and so she asked, "Do you dream, Rogan? Or as you sleep each night in your bed…are you too overweary to dream?"

Rogan shrugged, answering, "At times I dream…even for my desire not to do so." He frowned as Saphyre tossed several sprigs of dry lavender into the fire.

"You find no respite, Rogan," she told him as she knelt down beside him and took his hand in hers. "All of us worry for you in that."

"I find respite enough," he said, frowning at her as she pressed her thumb into his palm. He winced as she began rubbing his hand between her fingers and thumb.

"Your hands ache from your labors. Do they not?" she asked him.

"They do," he confessed. "But such is the result of hard labor."

Saphyre could sense the faint perfume of lavender beginning to fill the room. She was silent for some time as she sat, taking each of his hands in turn and pressing his palms and fingers—first gently then more firmly.

"What are you about, Saphyre?" Rogan asked, pulling his hand from her grasp. He smiled at her and asked, "Are you about seducing me, Princess? For it is well you may indeed accomplish such a task for sake of my weariness and weakness of mind and strength this night."

Saphyre blushed and, reaching, took his other hand in hers, pressing the palm with her fingers. Though she was pleased—delighted in his teasing her, in his implication—she was not swayed. Her gift must be given, for Rogan was weary of body and mind—and, no doubt, spirit.

"Once there came to the castle a beautiful and enchanting woman from the east," she told him, moving to kneel behind him, combing his hair with her fingers. Tenderly she pressed his scalp with her fingertips, pausing on occasion to allow her hands to gently rake his dark hair. She heard him sigh, knowing herself how full soothing the manner was. "She taught me to soothe and calm another in a method most strange to our kingdom," she explained.

"Your touch far from settles me, Saphyre," Rogan said. "It is little you know of men if you imagine this will find me settled." Still, he did not move. In truth, his eyes closed as she reached up, tender pressing her fingers to his temples a moment—then moving her fingers to travel in a firm arch over his brows and back again. Rogan ever displayed perfect posture. Never had Saphyre seen his shoulders round as he sat or stood. Yet as another sigh escaped him, she smiled—for his broad shoulders drooped forward in slight at last.

"You have, no doubt, forgotten how to enjoy moments of comfort and respite," she said, repeating the attention to his temples and forehead several times in succession. "It is important to let your mind find quiet…to let your body rest." Again she combed his hair with her fingers, kneading the back of his neck gently with her small hands. "This beautiful visitor who came to us from the east often spoke of cherry blossoms in spring…the way the scented breezes pluck them from the trees, sprinkling them like flowered snow over the new grass."

"I am wise to your ways, Saphyre. You endeavor to mend me," he said as she firm kneaded the tight strength of his neck and shoulders. "But I am not a man to be mended. In particular by the soft touch of a beautiful young woman who I…"

"You have heard the story of the night I was born then?" she asked him, seeing his smoldering eyes grew heavy. She knew he was too tired—too completely worn even to aggress upon her, no matter what teasing threats he may make.

"I have heard of it, yes," he confessed. "The night of the legendary sapphire snow."

She smiled when he yawned, and firm, yet tender squeezing his upper arms, she said, "My mother always said it was the most beautiful sapphire snow to ever have fallen on the Kingdom of Graces. The night was still, she told me. The sky clear, save the blue frost floating through the air."

The woman from the east had taught Saphyre to speak in a soothing voice—to describe restful moments of nature's wonder as she worked to calm a body and mind in need of soothing. Thus, Saphyre continued, "The moonlight shone warm and blue on the falling frost…and I was born." Saphyre used her small hands to rub Rogan's right arm—then his left. She smiled when she saw his eyes close for a long moment, his body sway in slight.

"I remember seeing such a snow when I was but a little girl," she continued. "One winter my father and I had taken an evening walk. Growing tired of the gardens close to the castle, we wandered out to the edge of the woods. There, we stood gazing up into the night sky as the sapphire snow fell." She took his right hand in her own, rubbing his palm with her thumb, gently squeezing and caressing each of his fingers. She could see he was growing more weary, and so she stood, gently tugging at his arm until he stood as well. Slowly she led him to his bed and bade him sit upon it.

"I love to think of the beautiful blue frost of the sapphire snow," she said, her voice softening even more as she turned her attention to his left arm. "And of the cherry blossoms dancing on the breezes in spring." She caressed and rubbed his left arm and hand, saying, "Even I love the falling leaves of autumn. They are near spent this season, are they not?" He nodded, and she noted he could near no longer keep his eyes open.

Taking hold of his wrist, she ran her hand up and down his arm—rubbing away the tautness in his muscles there. She repeated the measure on his other arm. He frowned as he looked at her, scarce able to keep his eyes from closing.

"You endeavor to bewitch me," he mumbled.

"I hope so," she said, smiling at him.

"I fear if I close my eyes, I may sleep far too—" he whispered.

"Yes, the lovely leaves of autumn," she interrupted, attempting to keep him from entering into any conversation that might stimulate his mind. "Light as down feathers they float through the air, covering the forest ground as a warm blanket…a tapestry of beauty meant to enfold the earth as it begins its winter respite."

Saphyre's hands miserable ached—for working the firm muscles and flesh of such a powerful man was laborious indeed. Still, she persisted, for she could see Rogan's countenance softening—see his eyes growing heavy—feel the muscles in his body beginning to take their rest.

"I…I…" he stammered, full weary. "I should make to seduce you at such intimate handling as this," he said. "Yet I am so wholly somnolent. What weak man am I…rendered complete unable to…"

"Winter's breath will soon be upon us," Saphyre said, again attempting to keep Rogan's mind and body at rest. "It is winter that brings the best and deepest of sleeps. It is when the cold and snow lay heavy in the air and on the ground, when the fire burns most warm in the hearth, that sleep and peace are found with the sweetest ease." Saphyre feared she could work Rogan's muscles and flesh no longer.

It was as if the pain and soreness once stiffening Rogan's hands had somehow transferred to her own. Still, she endeavored to relax him— to work an enchantment of such weariness and peace as to render him unable to deny accepting his respite, at last.

Thus, soon, he surrendered. Rogan's eyes closed, his body swaying, and Saphyre bid him lay down upon his bed. Continuing to gently rub his hands and arms, Saphyre watched as even the slight pucker in his brow softened.

"Saphyre," Rogan whispered, "I can no longer resist. I must…I must…" His breathing slowed, the tranquil expression of senselessness softened his features, and he slept.

Saphyre winced as she squeezed her small hands into fists. Oh, how they ached for the labor of manipulating the powerful muscles and strong hands of such a man as Rogan. Her arms ached, as did her shoulders—but Rogan slept. She had seen him sleep before. Many mornings she would find him asleep by the fire pit, having never retired to his keep chamber. Always he was restless, frowning, tossing and turning with uneasiness. At first, Saphyre had assumed his broken sleep by the fire pit was due to lack of physical comfort. Yet she soon came to realize Rogan's restless sleep was caused by something else— something unspoken—secreted deep in his own soul.

Not this night, however. As Saphyre lingered in watching Rogan sleep—in listening to his rhythmic breathing—she smiled, for Rogan had at last found respite. Perhaps only for a time, yet it was her doing, and she owned a small measure of contentment in the knowledge. Perhaps it was not the greatest gift she had given to a member of the keep, but it was something—something Rogan desperate needed, even should he be unaware of his need for it.

She took one of his powerful hands in her own, studying it at her leisure. She tried to memorize every part of it—from his calloused fingertips to the rather large scar in the palm. Rogan did not stir at her touch, nor did he stir when she laid her head against the strength of his chest—drawing comfort, security, and delight from the strong sound of his beating heart. To stay as such forever—what bliss would it be? Saphyre tried to imagine the depth of comfort, the perfect sense of safety she would know, were she able to herself sleep in Rogan's arms. She smiled at the thought, running her hand caressively over the broad expanse of his chest. Even then he did not stir. Even when she bent, kissing him softly on the mouth.

She meant to leave him—to let the night enfold him in its peace—but she found she could not. The scent of lavender was yet discernable in the room as Saphyre stood at Rogan's bedside. Longingly she gazed at him, trying to forget she was a princess—a princess in peril. She entertained thoughts of never returning to her father—of never again setting eyes on the castle of the Kingdom of Graces.

Saphyre cared for nothing in that moment, save Rogan. Further, she knew she would do anything to keep him ever her own. Could she win him? If she endeavored to make it so, could she make him love her as she loved him? Could she own him as lover—as husband—as father to the children she often dreamt of having? She doubted the man could ever know the depth of feeling she secreted for him—her consuming love.

She drew the woolen blanket lying on the bed at his feet, covering him so he may slumber warm through the night. Even this did nothing to stir him. The scent of lavender was fading, and Saphyre kissed him once more before leaving him—leaving him to his sleep, his peace, his gift of rare respite.

❧

Though his hand on her cheek woke her, she did not startle. Saphyre knew at once the feel of Rogan's hand to her face, and she opened her eyes to see him standing over her. The blue of the moonlight still shone through her bower window, for night was still thick.

"Rogan?" she whispered, yet somnolent. Surely she was dreaming. She had left Rogan in his chamber—the deep sleep of surrender about him. Still, he stood next to her bed now, gazing down at her through yet weary eyes.

"You wish to give me respite, Saphyre?" he asked. His voice was low and coarse. She knew he had stirred only of recent.

"I-I do," she told him.

"Then take me to your bed," he said, "for there is no complete respite in me save I know you are safe."

"Do...do you mean to..." she began. She most certain misunderstood him. Most certain he did not mean to...

"I mean only to sleep in your company...know that I allow myself to sleep...know you are close at hand should danger come, should you need protection," he explained. "I confess I will sleep restless otherwise...even for your bewitching spell of peace about me."

"Do you mean *I* am the cause of your unrest these many weeks?" she asked. Her heart ached at the thought. She had brought this misery upon him.

"Shhh," he said, gentle pushing her as to make a place for himself in her bed. "I am weary and still under your spell. I mean to have a peaceful night's sleep, and I can only attain it," he continued as he lay down on the bed next to her, "with you close at hand...that I may know of your welfare."

"It...it would mock propriety...to say the least," Saphyre told him. "Termed scandalous in the least."

"Shhh," he whispered, taking her chin in his hand and pressing his parted lips to her own in a single, yet moist and delicious kiss of intimacy. "I must rest now. But on the morrow I shall make amends, and you will find comfort in my arms...taste the sweet ambrosia of our mouths mingled in the kiss. Tomorrow there is much to be said between us, Saphyre. But for your own endeavors this night, I am too weary to seduce you. Thus rest peaceful in my arms that I may rest peaceful in yours."

Rogan lay on his back, slipping one arm beneath Saphyre's shoulders, pulling her against his warm and powerful body. As she lay on her side—warmed by his flesh and very existence—he reached across his body and took her hand, lacing his fingers with hers. As her hand lay laced with his—both resting at his stomach—she watched as his chest rose and fell with weary breathing. It was not long before she sensed he slept once more, and she closed her own eyes, allowing the sound of Rogan's breath—the quiet beat of his heart in his bosom—to soothe her better than any quiet hummed lullaby.

Saphyre woke to find she had moved but little during the night. Rogan as well remained just as he had lain down. She smiled at realizing the sun had risen some time before. Rogan never slept to sunrise. Always he was awake and about any task before the moonlight had waned or the sun beamed.

Carefully she rose from her bed, astonished he did not stir yet. She studied him for a moment before quiet leaving him to his rest in her keep chamber. Fearful the sound of her disturbing the water in the pitcher and bowl in her chamber would rouse him, she determined she would wash her face in the stream—refresh her appearance before he woke.

It was six sets of smiling, knowing eyes that met Saphyre as she entered the keep kitchen. Instant she began to blush vermilion—for she knew all the men must well be aware of Rogan's lingering in her bower chamber.

"We could not find Rogan this morning," Marcellus said, smiling.

"No, indeed, we could not," Thaddeus answered.

"We sought him here and there," Marcellus began, "until we thought he had left for the woods already."

"And so we were coming to tell you which of us would be your protector today. Thus, can you guess just where we found Rogan?" Thaddeus asked.

"I-I…it is not what you might suppose," Saphyre stammered.

All the men chuckled, amused by her discomfort. It was No-Nose who said, "Fear not, Saphyre. We know Rogan to be the most honorable of men and you to be the most virtuous of women."

"How indeed did you coax him to such a deep slumber?" Edmund asked. "He is fair dead asleep."

"I-I…the method was taught to me by a…a visitor from the east…some years ago," Saphyre explained, still well aware of the heated blush on her cheek.

"What strange magic it would have to be…to find Rogan so asleep," Belmiro offered.

"Magic indeed," Salomonè agreed.

"Thus, we have decided—without Rogan's permission, mind you,

Saphyre—that it should be Rogan who stays at the keep with you today," No-Nose said, still smiling—even yet amused at Saphyre's discomfort. "Venture no farther than the stream without him. Yes?"

"Of course," Saphyre said, disheartened as she was reminded of her need for protection at the hands of her friends.

"We are off then," No-Nose said, rising from his chair. The others followed, each man in turn smiling at Saphyre as he left the room.

As No-Nose brushed past, he whispered, "Did I not assure you… he could not keep himself from you long?"

Saphyre smiled and nodded.

Once they had gone, Saphyre crept to her keep chamber once more. Rogan still slept sound, and she smiled, shaking her head in awe. Never had she seen him slumber so deep. She would leave him to it. She would go to the stream and wash her face before taking her breakfast.

Her heart swelled with joyous anticipation as she left the keep, meandering toward the stream—for she lingered on the memory of Rogan's words whispered in the night.

I must rest now. But on the morrow I shall make amends, and you will find comfort in my arms…taste the sweet ambrosia of our mouths mingled in the kiss. Tomorrow there is much to be said between us, Saphyre, he had said. His beloved voice echoed through her mind, his words thrilling her to her very core. He had promised her such things as only were woven in dreams, and she wondered if he would remember his promises.

As Saphyre knelt at the stream bank, she thought of nothing but Rogan. In her mind there was nothing but the vision of his face—the sense of being held in his arms—the remembered taste of his kiss. In all this, Saphyre knew: in those moments the princess Saphyre Snow knew she would never leave Rogan of the keep—never.

FEVER

It was a beautiful autumn morning. The sun shone bright, the breeze allowing the cool air to refresh, not uncomfortably chill. Sunlight glistened over the stream's surface, and Saphyre smiled as she gazed into the water, to the tiny fish darting about in its shimmering course.

Cupping her hands, Saphyre drew the cold water to her face, thinking she may need to begin to heat a sum of stream water for use in the morning, for it was indeed far too cold to feel sweet upon her face. Still, it exhilarated her, and she smiled, cheerful in the day—resplendent in her thoughts of Rogan—in the ecstasy of his being.

So lost in her loving thoughts was Saphyre, she did not hear the old woman approach.

Saphyre startled as an unfamiliar voice greeted, "Good morning to you, girl."

Saphyre fair leapt to her feet, turning to see an elderly, withered woman—bent with age and weakness. The woman was dressed in a dark and worn woolen cloak, her gray hair bound tight into a knot at the back of her head. She carried on her arm a basket of red and green apples. Saphyre surmised the woman had been about the neglected and overgrown orchard near the foothills.

"Good morning," Saphyre said. Her heart was hammering with fear. Still, what harm could an old woman mean her? She thought once of calling out for Rogan, yet she was loath to wake him when he slept in such rare serenity.

The old woman smiled, displaying the five yellowed teeth remaining in her mouth. Instantly Saphyre's heart pricked, her sympathy for the old woman kindled. No doubt her back was bent from many, many years of hard labor, her aged and weathered appearance the result of a long life lived.

"Indeed it is a good morning, for I have been about the old orchard. Do you know it?" the old woman asked.

Saphyre nodded and said, "Yes. The apples are near gone for the season."

"Still there are many about on the ground yet good enough. See here?" the old woman said, taking an apple from her basket and holding it out to Saphyre. "Not a brown spot upon it."

"Yes," Saphyre said, yet uneasy. "A fine piece of fruit is that one."

"You must take it for your breakfast," the old woman said. "I have plenty here."

"Oh, no. I could not," Saphyre said. She could not accept an apple gathered by a woman so obvious in need of the nourishment it would give.

"Oh, you must have it. I have many," the old woman said, gesturing to the basket on her arm. "I shall have one for my breakfast, and you shall have one for yours."

Still Saphyre did not accept the offered fruit, and the old woman's smile faded.

"Is…is it unworthy of you then, girl…the simple gift of a gathered apple from an old woman?" The old woman's eyes grew veiled; her shoulders seemed of a sudden more stooped, her back more bent.

Saphyre frowned, both for the woman's pitiful condition and countenance and for her own apprehensive suspicions. Again she thought of calling out for Rogan; again she did not.

Tentative, she reached out, accepting the apple from the woman's knotty fingers. "I thank you, sweet mother," Saphyre said. She smiled as a twinkle seemed to leap to the old woman's eyes, her toothless smile displaying her pleasure in Saphyre's acceptance of the gift.

"Thank you, miss," the old woman said, "for you have received my humble gift, and I am glad." The old woman drew an apple from her basket, rubbing it on her worn sleeve a moment before biting into it. The crunch of the crisp apple and the smile of delight on the woman's face caused Saphyre to warm toward her even further. "I am thankful to the heavens each time I am able still to manage a bite... for my teeth are near gone altogether."

Saphyre smiled, drawing the apple to her lips as the old woman nodded a gesture she should do so.

"Crisp and sweet they are," the old woman said.

Saphyre smiled and bit into the piece of fruit. Crisp and sweet it was indeed, but there was something else about it—a strange, almost bitter flavor to the skin—and it caused her to frown.

"There now," the old woman said. "A good, crisp, sweet apple for your breakfast."

Almost at once, Saphyre felt strangely weak, overcome by a wild dizziness. She tried to remain standing but could not, her knees giving way beneath her. She fell to her knees in the grass beside the stream—watching as the apple fell from her hand.

"You...you have poisoned me, old woman," she breathed as the dizziness worsened.

"No, indeed," the old woman said. "Not I."

Fear rained upon Saphyre as she saw the old queen, Carmen, step from behind a nearby tree. She was dressed in the clothing of a common woman, but there was no mistaking her. Her beauty was unfathomable still—her grace, her posture, her hair as golden as it was when first Saphyre had seen her come into her grandmother's court—her eyes as emerald green.

"Dearest Saphyre," Queen Carmen said, smiling down at Saphyre. "Whatever have you been about these past months? Your father has been beside himself with worry."

Saphyre was sickened by growing dizziness. "I-I...I have been about...preserving my...my life," Saphyre stammered in a whisper.

"I will be gone now," the old woman said. "My coin, your majesty."

"Of course," Carmen said, pressing three gold coins into the old woman's knurled hand. "Now off with you. Go about your pitiful existence."

The old woman ventured a final glance at Saphyre—but there was no remorse in her countenance or manner, and she hobbled into the forest.

"I-I have friends. They will protect me…" Saphyre breathed.

"Friends? Do you mean the pestilence I saw in the forest only moments ago?" Carmen asked. "They cannot hear you. Further, I have ridden out myself…ridden alone in search of my darling granddaughter. What a beloved grandmother am I?"

"You have killed me," Saphyre said—struggled to keep from lying down in the grass. "Poison…a coward's device."

Carmen's triumphant smile faded as she said, "You are not poisoned unto death. It is simply an invisible varnish of my special herbs, and an hour would find you well enough once more." The old queen brushed a leaf from her sleeve and continued, "Yet…you do understand that you cannot exist, do you not, Saphyre? You cannot exist in my kingdom. I cannot allow you to turn a head away from me, nor will I chance you may cause good judgment to again rise to your father. Pray, look a moment at this," she said then, withdrawing from her frock bodice a gold chain hung around her neck.

Saphyre blinked several times, attempting to fix her gaze on the old queen's hand.

"This is my golden, jeweled apple, Saphyre," she said. She held the gold chain in her hand—a golden apple bejeweled with rubies dangling from it. "Look at it, Saphyre. It is my greatest treasure… next to my beauty. Is it not full enthralling?"

Saphyre gazed at the ruby-jeweled apple pendant, unable somehow to tear her gaze from it as the old queen caused it should begin swaying to and fro.

"Do you know from whence I gathered this apple?" asked the old queen. "Do you?"

Saphyre could not answer, her voice having been lost to her, her attention still bewitching fixed on the apple.

"A visitor to the castle whom you may remember…a beautiful woman from the east, eyes as deep as the night and hair just as thick. She came to the castle on several occasions to teach me…teach me the art of maintaining my perfect beauty. Do you remember her, Saphyre?"

Saphyre's mind could think clear enough, yet it seemed she had lost the will to move or in any other way command her body. She did remember the woman from the east—the same who had taught Saphyre the calming arts, the manner by which she had soothed Rogan the night before.

"Gaze at the apple, Saphyre, and listen to me," Carmen said, her voice soft and calm, "for I shall tell you now of the fates of your grandparents…of your own mother…and soon…your father. Most important, however, I shall in the last tell you of your fate. Blame your mother if you will…for it was she who gave birth to your beauty, and although your beauty is profound in its essence, it cannot measure to my own. Still, you are young, and I cannot have attention falling to you instead of me…in any regard. So it is you who must die, Saphyre…your beauty with you."

Saphyre wanted to scream—to shriek for Rogan—for help—but she could not. She found she could not move—not her lips, not her arms, nor hands, nor legs. She found herself complete still—complete helpless. Her mind, though dizzy, was alive—frantic—but she could not move. At the old queen's mercy she knew no choice but to listen—listen to the wicked woman's insanity and murderous plans.

"Where shall I begin?" Carmen sighed. "With your grandmother, I suppose…for it was she who allowed me to become lady-in-waiting to her. What brave woman would choose one so beautiful as I to wait in her court…so close to her king husband? Still, it was soon I discovered King Jordan loved Queen Penelope…truly loved her and would not be swayed by another…even one as beautiful as I. Yet I was meant to be queen, Saphyre. I have always known I was meant to be queen."

Saphyre's gaze remained transfixed on the swinging pendant, her body unable to shift. At least she would know the truth before her death. She sensed the old queen knew all concerning her grandparents' wretched ends—and her mother's.

"And so I took him from your grandmother," Carmen continued. "I had heard tell of a woman from the east and her power to manage the minds of men. She received an invitation to the castle—my invitation, for I was allowed to introduce to court one visitor each year. And thus I invited the woman from the east. She gifted me this apple pendant…taught me the arts of managing minds…of sinking one's mind into the depths of fever. And so I sank your grandmother there…into a fever's depths, where she failed on the third day."

Saphyre wanted to cry—to weep for her grandmother's murder. All the legends, the tales of Queen Penelope's untimely death, all the suspicion heaped to Carmen—all was justified. Still, her tears would not come. Saphyre could only endure the torment of the truth in still silence.

"Now understand, Saphyre," Carmen continued, "for each fever, two cures must be planted…else the management will not hold fast. I drove your grandmother into the mind fever, wherein she would die—as her body starved, as her thirst increased—but there were two cures planted in her mind. Had anyone set fire to her in any manner…she would be cured. Still, who would set fire to the queen? At least, who would set fire to her whilst she was still breathing? A safe and secure cure the fire was. The second cure was the most plain I could fathom. Would your grandfather simply kiss her lips thrice in succession…she would have awakened. But men rarely kiss twice, let alone thrice…and so she died." Carmen shrugged with indifference. "So you see, in truth, your grandmother's death was your grandfather's doing."

Pain and rage the like Saphyre had never known flamed in her bosom. She thought her very being might fly apart with the forced restraint of her anger and pain. She thought of the long years she had spent in the castle, her grandmother's murderer so close at hand. It caused her stomach to churn, her very flesh to burn with disgust.

"Your grandfather, however," Carmen sighed, "I could not

immediate sink him into the fever...for I was meant to be queen and could not rise to queen without first wedding the king. Still, with my precious apple, I managed his mind well enough to become his wife and rule beside him as queen of the Kingdom of Graces." Carmen frowned a moment. "Yet he was strong-minded, and it grew increasing difficult for me to manage him. And so the fever found him as well...and he too died. His mind was given two cures as well," she added. "The first was the flame, and who would burn a king whilst he was yet breathing? The second cure...simple. Had his son—your father, Saphyre—had Prince Michael simply spoken to his father, saying, 'I love you, Father, I do,' your grandfather might have been saved. But Prince Michael did not speak these words and therefore caused your grandfather's death."

Saphyre felt the dizziness in her mind dwindling, but she was yet unable to move—unable to tear her gaze from the jeweled apple pendant. She feared most what Carmen might reveal next—feared hearing of her mother's end at Carmen's treacherous hand.

"And then came Felice," Carmen said. Her delight diminished somewhat as she spoke again. "Upon first sight of your mother, I knew she was mine enemy," Carmen near growled. "Her beauty was near as great as my own. I gathered she was descended of a great line of beauty and legend...a line reaching back for generation upon generation, a line rich with tales of a dark knight and a beautiful princess of Karvana. Your mother's beauty...I could not allow it to survive. Though allow it I did...for a time. For I was queen... Queen Carmen, the widowed queen of the Kingdom of Graces." She paused for a moment, frowning. "Your grandfather bested me there, I will admit...by abdicating the throne to your father only moments before he slipped into the fever. I knew not of it until he was already dead. Still, I let your father rule for a time...until Felice grew too beautiful. Even then I waited...waited until I could no longer tolerate her presence. Do you remember when your mother fell ill, Saphyre?" she asked. Saphyre could not yet speak, and so the old queen answered, "It was the very day following something I overheard. One of your mother's ladies-in-waiting referred to me as 'the old queen.' I could not endure it, Saphyre! You understand, do you not? For I am yet young and very beautiful. I knew without your mother at your father's side, all attention would again return to me as 'queen'…my deserved title. And so I cast the fever upon your mother. Yet she was strong. Her strength was particular strong where you were concerned, Saphyre. It was more than once I heard the servants bold telling one another of your mother's managing to speak to you, and that I could not have, Saphyre. And so I planted the cures deep in her mind—the flame…and who would set a young queen aflame whilst yet she breathed? And there was another, of course… another cure that might have saved her…save for your ignorance."

Saphyre braced her mind—for she sensed what was to come. She sensed the evil woman's madness—her path of thought. She was not astonished when Carmen told her of the supposed cure to her mother's fever.

"It was you, Saphyre," Carmen said. "Her untimely death was indeed your fault…for had you simply spit upon your mother's beauty of face, slapped her sound on the right cheek, and told her of your disdain for her…she might have been saved. Instead you tender kissed her fevered cheeks and brow, caressing her hands and speaking of your abiding love for her." Carmen smiled a wicked, evil smile and added, "So you see, dear…had it not been for your ignorance, your mother might have lived."

Carmen then clapped her hands together in a gesture of exhilaration. "And that brings us to you…does it not?" she asked. "I know you will understand my dismay—my utter astonishment— when Prince Kornelius visited the castle six months past to inquire of the king concerning his intentions of granting your hand. Your father was easy enough to control…so grievous over your mother's death that I have been his master for nearly a year. But Kornelius spoke to your father, King Michael…*King* Michael," Carmen paused, laughing. "How ridiculous! King Michael…when it is I who manage his mind and his affairs! But I lose myself. Your father indeed promised your hand to Kornelius, and it was Kornelius himself who has sent you to your demise, Saphyre. Kornelius…and it is Kornelius who you truly must blame for your own death. For it was thus Kornelius spoke to your father, in my presence…in the presence of my beauty he spoke only months ago, 'Your daughter, King Michael,' he said. 'Your daughter is the most beautiful woman I have ever been blessed to set eyes upon. The most beautiful in all the kingdoms of all the earth.' And, Saphyre…I cannot have it."

As Saphyre's gaze followed the swinging apple pendant, Carmen whispered, "Close your eyes now, Saphyre. Close your eyes."

Saphyre felt further panic rise within her as her eyes did as Carmen commanded. Without being able to see the old queen—what harm was next meant for her?

"I feared sinking you into the fever, Saphyre," Carmen explained, "for suspicion had already befallen me. Thus, I set one of my huntsmen about the task of cutting out your heart. But he was stronger in mind than I supposed and deceived me. Yet his deception was discovered, and he has paid for such wrong disobedience," she growled. Softening her voice once more, she continued, "I had, for a time, lost hope of finding you…until four of my guardsmen disappeared several days past…four guardsmen who were sent to this section of the woods to search. Soon the old woman—the one who gave you the apple—soon she, having heard of my desire to find my step-granddaughter safe returned and the reward promised to any who helped me, sent word to me of a girl she had seen bathing in the warm spring near the foot of the mountain…a girl of tender youth and great beauty. I had the old woman brought to me, and she agreed to help me…understanding you had run away from your father…your father who is growing mad, as did his own father. I explained to her my desire to bring you back, and she agreed to help me…for a price. In the courts I might have triumphed in finding another manner in which to rid myself of you. Yet I find I have changed my plans, Saphyre…for Kornelius is meant to set out this very morning, in search of the four missing guardsmen…and you. Think how heartbroken he will be to find you overcome with fever. A fever no doubt contracted from the beasts with which you have been keeping company. Perhaps he will think these filthy men captured you…and he will kill them all in the name of being ever your champion.'

Saphyre heard the old queen sigh with impatience. "I grow weary of this chatter, Saphyre. Lie down. Lie down in the grass."

Saphyre was silent astonished as her body obeyed the old queen's command.

"I will tell you of what you may know before Lord Death finds you, Saphyre. You will be awake and aware…as awake and aware as you are now. Your mind will sleep and waken as it does each day…but your body will only sleep. No manner of shaking you, no manner of physician will be able to stir you. You will hunger and thirst, you will feel pain and discomfort…but you will not open your eyes, nor speak, nor move. And within three, perhaps four days—for you are young and healthy—you will feel your body fail, and you will die. It is quite simple, Saphyre. You will die. And neither Kornelius nor your father nor this rabble with which you have kept company will be able to draw you from it."

Saphyre's mind was screaming with terror, the agony over the knowledge of the miserable deaths of her grandparents and mother nearly unendurable!

"Still, the cures must be planted else the fever will not hold," Carmen said. Saphyre heard her delighted laughter as she said, "Yes! I have just the cure, Saphyre! Just the cure to give you hope! Of course there will be the flame…but who would set a princess aflame whilst she still breathes? Still…it must be planted, and therefore I tell you, Saphyre—should any flame touch your person, you will awaken from the fever at once…your mind and body restored, whole and unharmed."

Even cloaked in fear—even frantic—Saphyre's thoughts of a sudden turned to Flavian, the old queen's guardsman. Had not Flavian been rendered more lucid once Marcellus had set his tunic aflame? Had not Flavian then spoken of a strange fever? Of his will not being his own?

"As for the second cure," Carmen said. "Hmmm. Let me think on it a moment. Ah! Yes! Yes!" she laughed. "The second cure shall be dependent upon the Executioner's Kiss! Yes! The Executioner's Kiss and the very breath of love. But who is to love you, Saphyre? Who? For you are acquainted with no man…no man save Kornelius. And being acquainted with no man save Kornelius, who then? Who but Kornelius is to love you, Saphyre? Certainly Kornelius is to be your betrothed, but does Kornelius love you, Saphyre? Do you think he does? For I think he does not. I think he loves the throne of the Kingdom of Graces. Would he risk the Executioner's Kiss to try and save you? When he arrives to find you waning with fever, will he dare to kiss the princess of the Kingdom of Graces? Asleep or awake…a kiss is still a kiss, Saphyre. Will he risk it, do you think? And if he does—pray, if he is the bravest of men, willing to die for your kiss—does he love you? For the kiss is only half of the cure. In order that the cure may awaken you from the fever, he who kisses you must love you…love you so complete that it is in his very breath. Would Kornelius give his breath to you, Saphyre? Even his last breath? Would any man? And again, what men might you know, other than these vagabonds here, Saphyre? None save Kornelius…and Kornelius does not love you. What hope is left you then?"

Saphyre felt the old queen kneel beside her—felt Carmen place a wicked kiss on her forehead. Still, she could not move nor speak. She would die—as her mother had died, as her grandmother and grandfather had died. Even she suspected her father would soon die. Yet a vision of Rogan lingered in her mind, and she knew Rogan would live. This gave her an odd comfort—to know he would now be safe, as would all his brothers of the keep.

"I am weary, Saphyre," Carmen sighed with mad indifference. "And so I leave you to your fever…to your pain and to your fear and death. Do not worry. I will comfort your father when Kornelius brings you back to us to die. Farewell, Saphyre Snow…once beauty… once princess of the Kingdom of Graces."

Saphyre heard the dry autumn leaves crush beneath the old queen's feet as she took her leave. Moments later, she heard the drumming of horse's hooves. No doubt the old queen's mount would carry her back to the castle, where she would feign surprise and grief upon the return of Saphyre's dying, or dead, body.

As Saphyre lay in the grass and leaves near the stream bank, she listened—listened to the breeze—to the water tumbling over smoothed rocks in the stream bed. Her sense of smell, taste, sound, even all feeling seemed stronger as she silent screamed for help. Her mind called out for Rogan—for No-Nose—for Marcellus and Thaddeus, Edmund, Salomonè, and Belmiro. But no sound escaped her throat; no movement could she make. Thus, she lay in the grass and leaves near the stream's bank waiting—waiting—waiting to die.

REATH

Saphyre knew not how long she lay in the grass and leaves of the forest floor—awash in terror—alone—and still. Her head hammered for the pain of withheld screaming; her body ached from the stiffness of her limbs, her eyes dry from the tears that would not come. She felt the cool grass beneath her, tickling her arms—felt an insect creep across her nose, down one cheek, and onto her neck. She thought of her mother—the fear and misery she had endured for three days before terror and lack of water killed her. She thought of Rogan, asleep in the keep, of the other brothers of the keep—all innocent of the evil that had befallen her.

As the minutes passed, Saphyre wondered at what true madness had owned her grandmother, grandfather, and mother as they lay unable to move, yet understanding all too well what was to become of them. She would go mad too. Indeed she would, and she wondered how long it would be—how long before madness would overtake her.

Of a sudden—in the air of the morning breeze—she heard him call her name.

"Saphyre!"

Rogan! His voice, though strong, seemed distant, as if it drifted from a hilltop to the stream below.

"Saphyre!" he shouted again. Her heart leapt when she heard the old keep bell. It sounded thrice and thrice only—yet she knew the meaning of the chime. Rogan had sounded it—sounded the bell that the others might come. Had he awakened and looked out Saphyre's chamber window to the stream below? Had he seen her near the stream's bank, unmoving, her body lying in an unnatural, contorted manner as she felt it most certain did? He must surely have looked down upon her from the window.

It seemed mere moments, and Rogan was there beside her, cradling her in the strength of his arms, taking her chin in hand and shouting, "Saphyre! Saphyre!" She felt him turn her over, no doubt inspecting her for an injury. When he found none, he again took her face in one powerful hand. "Saphyre!" he shouted again, and she heard the fear in his voice—for it broke with emotion. "Heaven, oh, heaven," he mumbled as he pressed one ear against her bosom. "Oh, merciful God…let her yet breathe." Saphyre sensed Rogan held his own breath for a moment as his ear yet pressed her bosom. "She breathes," he whispered to himself. "Strong still beats her heart."

Saphyre's hope glimmered. At least he did not think her dead. At least she would not be buried alive.

He took her chin in hand again, turning her head from side to side. He lifted the lid of her eye, and for one glorious moment she caught a glimpse of him—ever handsome, ever powerful. Tears filled his worried eyes, and her mind cried out to him—cried out for his help—cried out for her life. As he released her face, her lid closing over her eye once more, her soul begged for the strength to see him again—to speak—to feel his lips press hers in a reassuring kiss.

Saphyre felt Rogan pull her body against his own, his voice breaking as he mumbled into her hair, "I weakened…weakened toward sleep and now wake to find my punishment before me. What harm has overtaken you, my Saphyre? What illness or evil finds you as silent and as still as death?"

She tried to open her eyes—tried to raise her hand to his face. Oh, how desperate she wanted to feel the strength of his jaw beneath her palm! Still, her body would not obey her mind's commands, and panic rose in her anew.

"Saphyre?" Rogan whispered. "Saphyre?" She felt moisture on her cheeks and knew it sprung from Rogan eyes. "What has happened? What am I to do? Never have I felt so powerless as I do now!"

Saphyre heard the beat of heavy footsteps. She heard No-Nose shout, "Rogan! Why rang you the bell? What has—"

"She is near to death!" Rogan shouted. "I-I know not how, only that I have failed her. It was late into this morning I slept, and now my weakness finds her thus," he explained. "Why did you not wake me before leaving?" Anger mingled with the fear in his voice.

Saphyre felt No-Nose's hand take her own—heard Marcellus cry out, "Saphyre!" She heard and felt every other man—her friends of the keep—speaking to her—speaking to one another as they each in turn took hold of her hands, caressed her face.

"Awaken, Saphyre!" Rogan pleaded, his voice weak with emotion. "Pray awaken and gaze at me once more. Let me drown in the beauty of your eyes, see your smile, hear your voice." He paused and then growled, "Saphyre!"

"Shouting at her will not serve to help her," Thaddeus said.

"Silence!" Rogan shouted. "You know not what is in my heart this moment! All is lost to me if she dies! All is lost to me!"

"We, all of us, are desperate to heal her, Rogan," Edmund said. "Madness will not assist us."

"Silence!" Rogan shouted once more, and Saphyre felt him draw her away from the others, wrapping her body firm in his powerful embrace. "This is my doing!" he said. "I-I have failed in protecting her. I have failed."

"She may yet be well," Salomonè said. "Let us all think of this... try to discern what has happened here."

"There are two paths of tracks leading into the wood," Edmund said. "Both appear to be the size and look of women—two different women—and one looks to have mounted a horse in the woods there."

"The old queen," Belmiro mumbled.

Saphyre felt a rough, callused hand press to her forehead, then to her cheek. "She is over warm with fever," Rogan said. "She does not open her eyes, nor does she make any sound, save that of her shallow breath. Yet her heart beats strong and fast."

"It was the same with her mother," No-Nose said, "and her grandmother before her."

"Yet she has been with us these past months," Marcellus said. "How could she have taken the illness borne of the castle?"

"The tracks tell the tale," Rogan said. "Belmiro has spoken it. The old queen has found Saphyre. It was said a spider was found in the queen's shoe…short after she fell," Rogan mumbled. "But I see no bite here."

"It was no spider killed Queen Felice," No-Nose stated. "Rather it was the strange fever. A strange fever from which she never awoke…a fever of Carmen's doing as I have ever maintained. And Carmen has found Saphyre this day. I fear the same fever will take our beloved—"

"Look!" Salomonè exclaimed. "Look here…this apple. It lies here in the grass, and there is a bite from it."

"Let me look at it," Rogan said. Saphyre felt one of Rogan's hands leave her body—felt him jolt and heard the sound of the apple hitting his palm.

"Perhaps she has only but choked upon a bit of it," Thaddeus suggested.

"Doubtful," Rogan said. "I know this taste. Taste the skin of this apple, Edmund…No-Nose. What do you detect?"

There was silence for a moment, and then Edmund said, "Brown's Plant."

"Yes. It is not easy mistaken," No-Nose agreed.

"Indeed it is Brown's Plant," Rogan said. "Used to render Saphyre dizzy…helpless."

"Still, would Brown's Plant raise a fever?" Belmiro asked.

"No," Rogan said. "The old queen has done this. I am certain of it. But I am not certain by what means."

"Hold!" Edmund demanded. For a moment no one spoke. There was only the sound of the stream—of Rogan's heart beating where Saphyre's head lay against his chest. "Riders approach. Perhaps the old queen has returned to claim her victim."

"We must hide her!" Rogan said. Saphyre felt herself lifted into his powerful arms.

"There is no time," No-Nose said. "For they are sure upon us."

Saphyre heard the heavy thunder of approaching riders on horseback. "I will die before I let them take her," Rogan growled.

"We are all dead men, no doubt," Edmund said.

Saphyre silently begged Rogan not to release her as she felt him lay her down on the ground once more.

"Even for this wicked fever, even if Lord Death stands before you...I defend you, Saphyre," he whispered into her ear. "She shall not have you. I will see my own heart torn from my chest before she touches you. My life she will have before she has yours. To my death I love you, Saphyre," he whispered. "And yet beyond."

Hope welled within Saphyre's still and silent body. Rogan—her beloved champion—had spoken to her of his love—full confessed loving her! Would he not kiss her once more before turning to face the riders? Would he not—after all the times before—would he not risk the Executioner's Kiss once more? Would he not unknowing save her from the terror of death at the hand of Carmen's evil fever?

"It is a royal guard!" Marcellus exclaimed.

"But not of this kingdom—green tunics and weaker chain mail," No-Nose said.

Saphyre heard the riders rein in, their horses snorting and stomping their hooves with impatience.

"What seek ye here?" Edmund asked, his voice strong and demanding.

"We seek four of Queen Carmen's guardsmen who have gone missing in these parts." Saphyre recognized Kornelius's voice at once. "And we seek likewise the princess of the Kingdom of Graces, Saphyre Snow."

"We know nothing of guardsmen or princesses," No-Nose said. "We are but woodsmen and stonecutters here. Ride on."

But the riders did not ride on. In truth, it was Kornelius who asked, "What are you men about there? Is someone injured?"

Rogan's body bent over Saphyre's must have at first hindered

Kornelius's vision of her. Still, her heart raced with hope and hopelessness entwined, for Carmen had set two cures for Saphyre's mind—flame and the Executioner's Kiss given with the breath of love. Saphyre's despair grew in Kornelius's arrival, for he would undoubted return her to the castle were the men of the keep bested—allowing him to take her. In doing so he would seal her death—by taking her from Rogan. Rogan was her only hope.

"I love you, Saphyre," Rogan whispered. She felt his tears moisten her cheek. "I love you more than living, and should you, by some miracle of heaven…should you awaken to find me dead at the hand of evil…know that I died for loving you."

"Saphyre!" she heard Kornelius shout. "It is the princess!"

"Saphyre…you have been my heart's only ambition," Rogan whispered. She knew his lips trembled as he kissed her, for she could feel the tremor in them. Still the touch of his lips to hers was stimulating to her body. She fancied her toes began to move when she commanded them to. Rogan took her chin in hand, slight pressing it down so that her lips indeed parted. "And I give my last breath to you, that you may breathe. Breathe me as long as there is breath left in you." And then—ever so light—Saphyre felt Rogan breathe soft into her mouth as he kissed her once more.

"He has violated the princess!" Kornelius shouted. "Slay him!"

Saphyre heard swords being drawn from their sheaths—saw Rogan draw his dagger and stand to face the guardsman and Kornelius as they commanded their mounts to charge. Her limbs felt stiff, and it took her several moments to draw herself into a sitting position.

Yet as Rogan stood at the ready to unhorse Kornelius, Saphyre found her voice and screamed, "No! Stop!"

The sound of her voice, however, so startled the men of the keep they each turned to look back at her, leaving them full vulnerable to Kornelius and his guardsmen.

"Kornelius! I am well! Stop!" she cried out. Rogan spared no time in turning to face Kornelius again, pulling him from his mount as he aggressed. Yet Marcellus and Thaddeus were easily overtaken, having been stunned into immobility at the sound of Saphyre's voice. Two of Kornelius's guardsmen—armor ready, helmet shields drawn over their faces—held their swords at Marcellus's and Thaddeus's necks.

"Cease in defending yourself or the small men die!" Kornelius shouted. Rogan looked to Edmund and No-Nose, standing at the ready. "They will die, I swear it!" Kornelius added.

"Kornelius!" Saphyre shouted. "You misunderstand! Leave them be!"

"Your weapon, man!" Kornelius shouted to Rogan. "Drop it...or I will order their throats cut ear to ear."

Rogan looked to Saphyre—his rage at Kornelius and his astonishment at her awakening apparent in his full countenance.

"Harm one of them, Kornelius," Saphyre said, struggling to her feet, "and I will behead you myself!"

Rogan started toward Saphyre, his hand outstretched, tears fresh on his cheeks. "Saphyre," he breathed, but Kornelius was quick—drew his sword to Rogan's throat.

"No! Leave him!" Saphyre screamed. "Harm him not!"

"He has violated you, Saphyre!" Kornelius growled. "He must die! It is the law."

"No! He has this moment saved me from death!" Saphyre cried. "For Carmen was here only just...and she...she put a fever upon me as she did my mother! This man has saved me...and all these men with him have protected me. You will not harm them. Not one."

"Queen Carmen? Here?" Kornelius asked. It was obvious he did not believe Saphyre. "Men...at the ready...swords at their throats."

Saphyre began to weep as she watched other guardsmen advance on Edmund, No-Nose, Salomonè, and even poor Belmiro. Each brother of the keep stood, a guardsman's sword at his neck.

"Yes!" Saphyre explained, desperate to save Rogan—desperate to spare the others. Saphyre stared in pleading at Rogan as she spoke. "The old queen has a wicked manner of managing minds," Saphyre said. "She told me of my grandmother's death, my grandfather's madness, brought on by her own wicked ways...her woven fever of mystery. She spoke of my mother's death, and she worked the mind-managing on me…for I was weak-minded and did not suspect her methods."

"You are no doubt sore weary, Saphyre," Kornelius said, attempting to soothe her. "Let us away to the castle. There you will be safe," he told her.

"There she will be dead," Rogan growled.

Saphyre winced as Kornelius's sword pressed into the flesh of Rogan's neck, drawing blood.

"Silence, woodsman!" Kornelius demanded. "Else you find your head on the ground next to your feet."

"It is of my own choosing…the fact you are yet living, man," Rogan said.

Kornelius pressed the sword further into Rogan's neck, causing the blood to quicken.

"Stop this, Kornelius!" Saphyre exclaimed. "Stop and only listen to what I am telling you. The old queen has done this! She means to see me dead as she has murdered thrice before. A fever she put upon me and only two manners of cure…flame being one." She nodded to Rogan and said, "Remember…the guardsman, Flavian? The flame cooled his fever and—"

"You are ill, Saphyre," Kornelius said. "It is obvious you need rest and…and, no doubt, a physician."

"Pray, only listen, Kornelius," Saphyre continued. "She wears a pendant…a golden and ruby jeweled apple. With the pendant she… she works some bewitchment or spell of the mind."

"I have seen this pendent," Kornelius said. "The queen wears it always. I have seen it often, and I am well enough. Am I not?"

Saphyre was silent then. Rogan's eyes burned into her own, and she knew he believed her. Further she knew he was suspect of Kornelius. Was his mind also being managed by Carmen?

"You will return with us to the castle, Saphyre," Kornelius said. "You will return, or these men will die for you…as I suspect Flavian and the others died for you."

"Your queen's guardsmen died for want of harming her," Rogan growled. Again the blade of Kornelius's sword drew blood from Rogan's neck.

"You would deliver me into the hands of a murderess, Kornelius?" Saphyre asked, weeping as she saw the crimson blood begin to saturate Rogan's tunic. "You would take me back to find my death?"

"There will be no death there for you, Saphyre," Kornelius said, his voice softening. "Only respite, rest, and comfort. I promise."

Saphyre was silent. She looked to Rogan, certain his eyes were telling her he would rather die than to see her returned to the castle. She looked to Marcellus, Thaddeus, Belmiro, Salomonè, and Edmund—all shaking their heads in turn that she should not return. Last she looked to No-Nose.

"Rogan," No-Nose said, "there is an evil infesting the castle in the Kingdom of Graces…and it will only spread if its heart is not stilled."

"She will not live to see the castle," Rogan growled. "I am certain of it." Again Kornelius's blade pressed hard against Rogan's throat.

"You will not live to see the morrow," Kornelius said, "for what you have taken is cause for execution in this land. And I speak not of the lives of the queen's guard."

"He took nothing, Kornelius!" Saphyre cried, rushing forward. "Take your sword from him, or it will be you who knows the blade of the ax!" Saphyre stood before Rogan, wanting desperate to throw herself into his arms. Yet she dared not for the sake of his life. "Take your sword from him…and vow you will leave him and the others to their peace…and…and I will go with you," Saphyre said.

"No!" Rogan shouted, reaching up and taking hold of the blade at his neck with his hands. He began to struggle, and Saphyre watched as his hands too began to bleed.

"Halt! Rogan!" No-Nose shouted. "Your mind is not clear. It has been too greatly taxed this day."

Saphyre watched as Rogan looked to No-Nose.

"The princess will be safe returned to the castle," No-Nose said, "for she will have the best guardsmen to accompany her. Is that not so, Prince Kornelius?"

Saphyre watched as Rogan's eyes narrowed. Again he looked

to his friend, who said, "The best guardsmen to guard her…and we…we shall remain behind and go about our planning…for the winter. We have protected the princess as well we were able. It falls to Kornelius now." Rogan deep inhaled and looked back to Saphyre as No-Nose continued, "You are renowned as a great and honorable prince, Prince Kornelius. A man of your word as well. Therefore, give to us your word we will be left in peace…and we seven will let you leave with your princess. We have much work to be about in preparation for…for winter."

Kornelius's brow puckered. "My men are ten and me," he said. "We would well best you with ease and take the princess."

"Why fight when simple men have admitted defeat?" Edmund asked.

"Yet this one has touched the princess," Kornelius reminded them.

"I commanded him to do so," Saphyre stammered. "I wished to see if there was a man on this earth courageous enough to brave the executioner on my behalf."

"She is lying to you, Prince," Rogan growled.

"Stupidity and bravery are often misunderstood," Kornelius said.

"Still, it was my doing. These men protected me during these past months. Would that one kiss was payment enough for all they have done…sacrificed," Saphyre explained.

"You would have me leave them with no price paid by this one who has defiled you?" Kornelius asked.

"I am well," Saphyre said. "The only moments I have been unwell were in the presence of Queen Carmen. They deserve no less than the honor given heroes. Your word, Kornelius…and I will go with you."

"Saphyre," Rogan growled through clenched teeth.

"She is the princess of the Kingdom of Graces, fool!" Kornelius shouted, releasing Rogan at last and pushing him to his knees. "And she has saved you your life."

Rogan looked up to Saphyre, and she knew he meant to turn and attack Kornelius. Therefore, she instantly dropped to her knees before him.

"I will be well," she told him, weeping. "Indeed, I know the tricks of my enemy now. She…she can no longer harm me." Carefully she reached out, placing her palm on his whiskery cheek. Her touch seemed to complete drive all measured thought from Rogan's mind, for he reached out, gathering the front of her frock in his fist and pulling her toward him. Their mouths met in such a kiss—a kiss drenched with delicious passion—and Saphyre's heart broke for her immeasurable love of Rogan.

"Enough!" Kornelius shouted, taking Saphyre's arm and pulling her to her feet. "I give you my word I will not harm these men…even for such a loathsome creature who would dare to touch you thus. You then will return with us to the castle at once."

As Kornelius led Saphyre to his mount, Rogan, still kneeling, put a hand to his bleeding throat and turned. "You lead her to Lord Death, you arrogant idiot," he growled.

"Rogan," No-Nose said, "our plans must be set…for the winter. Let her go now…for she belongs to the castle."

"You there," Kornelius said, pointing to one of the men who held a blade to Marcellus's throat. "And you," he added, pointing to Thaddeus's captor. "You will stay behind until we are on our way to ensure they do not follow. In particular, this one," he said, pointing to Rogan. "When they have settled, join us on the return path."

"Yes, your highness," one of the men said.

With his assistance, Saphyre mounted Kornelius's horse—her tears so profound she could but barely see Rogan's face clear. She knew it spent every ounce of control he could muster not to advance toward her—not to attack Kornelius and his men. He stood, teeth clenched, fists clenched, a deep frown furrowing his handsome brow.

Quick she looked to Marcellus and Thaddeus, grateful as Kornelius's guardsmen lowered their swords. She looked to Belmiro, Salomonè, and Edmund—breathing easier as they were then left unguarded. Her eyes next fell to No-Nose, who nodded at her, his piercing blue eyes flashing with determination. He smiled, holding his palm upturned toward his own face and slowly nodding, once. Saphyre's breath was stilled a moment—her eyes widened—for she well knew the gesture: the secret greeting of King Jordan's knights. The upturned palm and single nod was the manner in which her grandfather's knights had greeted the king in the brighter days of the Kingdom of Graces. Her recognition of No-Nose heightened at once, though she still could not name him. Quick she tried to see beyond the mask, beyond the thick beard of his face and unkempt hair that framed it—but she could not. Still, No-Nose's familiar gesture gave her hope—as did Rogan's rising to his feet.

As Kornelius mounted behind her, Saphyre watched Rogan straighten to his full posture, broaden his shoulders, and lift his chin in defiance of defeat. As she knew No-Nose to be one of her grandfather's knights, she like knew the expression of determination on Rogan's face. Her tears increased as he stretched one powerful arm toward her, making a fist and slamming it to his bosom just over his heart. She understood this at once—a signal of hope—a manner of telling her he would not let her go so easy. He ran one hand across his neck then, careless wiping the blood on his tunic as he watched her go.

"You owe them no debt," Kornelius said, urging his horse to a trot. "Their profound treachery in keeping you from your father and your kingdom should not have gone unpunished."

"And well you know it is my father's choice...not yours," Saphyre said.

"Indeed," Kornelius said. "It is why I will tell your father of this and leave the choice to him. Yet be mindful, Saphyre...I could have as well run the one through as shown him my mercy. He should not have touched you. I have proven myself worthy of you, have I not? By reigning my pride and allowing him to live...simply because you asked it of me?"

"He saved my life, Kornelius," she told him. "And more than once. Tell me now...tell me now as you deliver me into the hands of a murderess...what less did he deserve than you?"

Kornelius said nothing—simply urged his horse on at a faster pace. Saphyre closed her eyes, breathing at her will, moving at her will—all too aware it might be lost lest she fathom to be wary of Carmen's poisoned pendant.

Rogan had indeed saved her life and drawn her from the fever—from the torturous death she might have known. For this, she owed him her strength, her faith, her endurance. Strength to withstand Carmen's mind charms—faith in knowing he would not let her go had he not intended to retrieve her—endurance in waiting till he did. And he would—she knew it. Rogan had given her life, his very breath, and with every breath she took—every scent of autumn on the breeze—she knew he would come for her.

$\mathcal{T}$HUS, $\mathcal{D}$ELIVERED

They rode through the wood, Saphyre with Kornelius and eight of his men. With each stride Saphyre's heart despaired. Though she longed to see her father—to see the expression on Carmen's face as she entered the castle alive and awakened, no doubt thinking it was Kornelius's kiss that roused the fevered princess—she despaired over Rogan. With every stride carrying her toward the castle and away from her lover, Saphyre's heart ached—felt as if it bled for worry and want of him. Still she hoped, as she had promised herself she would hope.

Closing her eyes, she could see the brothers of the keep—see them as she had last seen them more than two hours before. There in her memory they lingered, standing before the keep, near the stream, Rogan's eyes burning with anger, determination, and love. She could see too No-Nose's familiar blue eyes, his nod of reassurance. It was in like manner she saw the faces of all the brothers of the keep. Still, it was Rogan's face—Rogan's powerful presence—that flamed her hope, kept her from the purest panic.

Saphyre's heartbeat increased as she heard the approach of more riders. She turned to see the approach of the two guardsmen Kornelius had commanded to stay behind. As did the other guardsmen, these two yet wore their helmets, helmet shields drawn down.

215

"What news?" Kornelius said, reining in.

"None," one of the men said.

"As it should be," Kornelius said. "Let us slow our pace. The princess is not conditioned for such uncomfortable riding."

Saphyre said nothing—simply sighed with relief at the knowledge the men of the keep were safe. She had heard her father's guardsmen respond in the same manner when he had asked, *What news?* She knew the response meant there had been no alteration in what had been anticipated. The men of the keep were well, and Saphyre thanked the heavens for it.

The company rode on in silence for some time. Saphyre's mind was alive with worry and fear. Yet she tried to fathom measures in avoiding the old queen's mind-managing—endeavored to prepare herself to see her father so fast bound in them. She must be strong. She thought then of her desires—her musings only the night before as she had lain in Rogan's arms. She had wished then never to return to the castle, to shirk her duty as the king's daughter, to cleave only to Rogan—live only for Rogan. She sighed, astonished at what had transpired in such a short space of time. Only hours before, she had witnessed Rogan's respite—endeavored to hope he could belong to her—dreamed of belonging to him. Instead, she was returning to the castle—and danger. Returning to a life of royalty, where love was not considered and simple policy ruled the choice of a companion.

"This must be a merry man indeed," Kornelius said.

"I beg your pardon?" Saphyre asked, pulled from her thoughts.

"The guardsman," Kornelius explained. "Do you not hear him whistling? And such the merriest of tunes."

Saphyre turned and looked back at the guardsmen, in particular to the two guardsmen who had only just returned. Indeed one of them was whistling, his head bobbing to and fro in apparent delight and individual amusement. Saphyre gasped, her mouth gaping when she saw the whistling guardsman nod to his companion, his companion then joining in the whistle. "The Knight's Lady"! She recognized near at once as the melody of Thaddeus's favorite dance, "The Knight's Lady." Upon seeing her looking at them, each of the two whistling guardsmen began bobbing his head side to side in the very same fashion as did Thaddeus whilst he was about his dance.

Saphyre's eyes widened as one of the guardsmen lifted his helmet shield only brief, revealing the familiar and beloved face of Salomonè! His companion then followed suit. Edmund!

"Enough," Kornelius chuckled. "I too am happy to see the princess returned. Yet we are to be wary yet, lest man or beast be lurking who mean us harm."

"Of course, your highness," Edmund mumbled.

Saphyre glanced to the other guardsmen. They seemed unaware of any change having come over their counterparts.

"We ride on then, men," Kornelius ordered. "We must return the princess to her father. He has been lost without her."

Saphyre smiled, breathed relief, and thanked the heavens for her friends. Her hope renewed in knowing that, were Edmund and Salomonè so near, Rogan could not be far.

❦

Late into night's darkness, Kornelius summoned the king. Saphyre saw the tears of joy in her father's eyes as he beheld her, yet she sensed a fever about him. Not quite as hers had been, for he owned wakefulness and full movement. He appeared very lucid. However, the light in King Michael's once bright eyes had dulled; he appeared as if to have aged somewhat quick, acting only when prompted of Carmen or his counselors.

As for Carmen, the old queen, Saphyre thought—and indeed secret hoped—Carmen might drop dead at her feet with pure astonishment upon seeing her step-granddaughter not only returned but full awake and well. Carmen's face had run pale, her mouth gaping as she looked upon Saphyre.

"I am healed," Saphyre had told her, "as will my father be."

Carmen's eyes glowed red with fury. Saphyre knew she would not stay unsettled long. Still, love and pity for her father spurred her courage, and she vowed to help him.

Kornelius commanded two of his own guardsmen should stand watch outside Saphyre's bower. Salomonè and Edmund volunteered, and Saphyre knew a measure of feeling respite from distress in knowing they were thus near. Still, she worried, for though Edmund and Salomonè knew of Carmen's power, Saphyre knew its full strength.

As she readied for bed—yet certain she would not find rest—there came a knock upon her door.

Pressing a hand against the door, Saphyre asked, "Who is there?"

"It is Lady Augustynia, Princess," Edmund answered.

Saphyre opened the door, near falling into the tender embrace of Lady Augustynia. "Augustynia!" Saphyre cried.

"Hush now, Princess," Edmund said, his face still shielded, "lest you wake the curious that do roam this night."

Saphyre nodded and drew Augustynia into her bower room, bolting the door behind them. What joy filled Saphyre's soul at the sight of her dear friend!

"Saphyre! Oh, Saphyre!" Augustynia cried. She brushed the tears from her eyes and took Saphyre's hands in her own. "I heard of Kornelius's arrival and prayed you were with him! Are you well? Are you untouched?"

Saphyre smiled and brushed tears from her own cheeks. "I am well. However, I know I am not untouched," Saphyre answered.

"Where have you been, Saphyre?" Augustynia asked. "I have been so worried as to find myself ill! You can never know what dreadful fates my imagination brought you to."

"And a dreadful fate it near was," Saphyre said. "Will you be missed?" she asked. "Will the queen know you are here with me?"

"Never," Augustynia said. "I have kept myself outward calm, Saphyre. I have been pretending these past months, pretending I do not notice the changes overcoming your father…for something is amiss here in the castle, Saphyre. And since your vanishing, I am convinced it is all of it Carmen's doing. Somehow."

"All the evil ever brought to us is of Carmen's doing," Saphyre whispered. "Pray, sit and hear my story, Augustynia. And though you may think I have run mad…indeed, I have not. What I will tell you is as true as you and I are in this room."

Saphyre told Augustynia then—told her of the huntsman—of the keep and the men therein. Saphyre told Augustynia of Rogan— of their love—of Rogan's braving the Executioner's Kiss. She told her of Flavian and the other dead guardsman—of the old woman and the poisoned apple—of Queen Carmen and her powers of tricking the mind. She told her of Rogan's love—his breath breathed—his kiss given—the cure for Saphyre's fever. Saphyre told Augustynia of Kornelius's coming—of the true identity of the two guardsmen keeping watch outside her chamber door. And when it had all been told—when an hour had passed and then two—Augustynia shook her head and dried her tears on her sleeve.

"Thus, I am delivered to my father…and to she who endeavors to murder me," Saphyre whispered.

"Are you certain your Rogan will come, Saphyre?" Augustynia asked. "Are you certain? For I was once as certain as you are now."

Of a sudden, Saphyre felt fear anew creep further into her heart. "He will come, Augustynia," Saphyre said. "I know he will come for me. He would well have died in protecting me at the keep. Would such a man not champion me here?"

Augustynia brushed a tear from her cheek and nodded, smiling. "He will come, and he will save us all…just as my Sebastian saved us from Gregoria."

Saphyre noted the manner in which Augustynia's hand went to the ornate pendent at her throat. Lovingly she pressed it between her thumb and fingers.

"Was this a gift from Sebastian?" Saphyre asked, reaching out to touch the pendant.

Augustynia nodded, her tears refreshed. "Yes," she whispered. "And I admit I have kept it to myself these many years…afraid any other eyes, save mine, might set it aflame…cause it lost to me forever."

"I understand, Augustynia," Saphyre said, wishing she had such a token of Rogan.

"No," Augustynia said. "I do not think you understand…at least, not fully." Saphyre watched then as Augustynia pressed the small emerald adorning the pendant's center. A quiet click—and the pendant opened. A locket it was, revealing a likeness within. "There," Augustynia said, holding the locket and its hidden likeness toward Saphyre. "It is his image…Sebastian's. I have worn it every moment since he first gifted it to me so long ago."

Saphyre gasped—gasped not for astonishment at Augustynia's hidden likeness of the great knight and captain of the guard, Sebastian Ottokar—no. Saphyre's gasp—her own tears upon her cheeks—all for the recognition at last gifted her. The image in Augustynia's locket was handsome, clean-shaven, the tunic and chain mail of a great knight about his shoulders. Yet it was his eyes—the perfect blue of his piercing eyes—that robbed her of her breath.

"He is Sebastian!" Saphyre breathed.

"Yes," Augustynia said. "And you recognize him? I was not certain that you would. He has been away so very long, and you were so young when last…"

Saphyre felt her own face run pale. She closed her eyes a moment as a vision appeared in her mind. His nose whole, his chin void of his heavy beard, his hair well kept, posture straight and strong. In her vision, No-Nose became familiar, and in her memory, Saphyre heard the kingdom calling his name. "Hail, Sebastian!" In that moment, in the depths of her mind and heart, she saw him as she had witnessed him in her youth—the gallant knight astride his magnificent white horse, his chain mail and armor glinting in the sunlight. In those moments, Saphyre saw Sebastian—saw his lady Augustynia tying her favour at his arm as he made ready to joust.

She knew not how Sebastian had bested her grandfather's assassins. Perhaps he had lost his nose there, the result of doing battle with the would-be assassins—assassins who had succeeded in beheading even the great warrior-knight Roar. How he had come to find his brothers of the keep she knew not. Still, she knew him then—the piercing blue of his eyes, the manner of his carriage, even his gesture, the manner of greeting given only to King Jordan. Yes—No-Nose was Sebastian Ottokar!

"Are you well, Saphyre?" Augustynia asked. "What a ridiculous question I have spoken. Of course you are not well. You need rest."

Saphyre's first notion was to tell Augustynia of No-Nose—to tell the great lady Sebastian yet lived. Still, she paused, for what reason she knew not. Yet she did pause.

"Y-yes," Saphyre said. "I am so very, very weary." Her mind was indeed worn in fathoming the truth. Sebastian! It could not be! Nevertheless, it was, and Saphyre knew the truth of it.

"Shall I stay with you?" Augustynia asked.

"You would stay with me?" Saphyre whispered. "Though any who venture near to me may find themselves taken with a strange fever...dead within days?"

"You are my greatest friend, Saphyre," Augustynia said. Her smile was warm and gave comfort. "How could you think I would not stay? And I will stay until your Rogan comes for you. I promise."

Saphyre smiled, tears again escaping her eyes. "You are deserving of the greatest happiness life can bring, Augustynia. Thank you," Saphyre whispered.

Yet even with Augustynia at her side, Saphyre found sleep restless. She awoke often to find herself glancing at the door, searching the shadows for any evil lurking there. In her heart, she knew Edmund and Salomonè were near. In her heart, she knew Rogan would come for her—and that he would somehow vanquish the evil threatening her, her father, and all in the Kingdom of Graces.

Thus, Saphyre slept little. Yet in moments of rest, she did dream dreams of wonderment. She dreamt of Rogan—of his strength, his handsome face, his powerful form. In her dreams, she relived their moments together—from first when he had asked if she had determined which of the brothers of the keep would serve as her lover—to the moment he breathed life into her with his passion's kiss. Oh, how she loved him! How she desired to have him near—to touch him—to know he was well and safe.

In her dreams of Rogan, the others smiled also—the other brothers of the keep. Kind Marcellus, who so loved a fine story— sweet Thaddeus, who delighted in the dance. No-Nose, who was truly Sebastian, the great and vanished captain of the guard of the Kingdom of Graces. Salomonè smiled in her dreams, as did Belmiro.

Even Edmund nodded his approval in her memory. And in her beautiful dreams of Rogan—of his kiss, his smile, his strength, and his love—Saphyre found moments of peace, of comfort, of happiness, and of hope. Rogan would come for her. Rogan would come for her. Rogan would come for her!

THE LEGEND'S CAUSE

"Our princess is returned to us!" King Michael announced to the court. The throne room erupted with applause and well-wishes.

Saphyre sat upon her throne, the throne to the left of her father's. Queen Carmen sat in the throne at his right, and a great fury rose within Saphyre's bosom at the sight.

Saphyre dared a glance at Edmund and Salomonè, standing guard to her left near Kornelius. Augustynia stood with the other ladies-in-waiting and nodded to her with encouragement.

"Yes," Carmen said, withdrawing the apple pendant from its hiding place beneath her frock bodice. "And we are glad."

Saphyre noted the manner in which her father's eyes rested on the pendant.

"Pray, do not leave us again, daughter," Saphyre heard Carmen whisper.

"Pray, do not leave us again, daughter," her father repeated. It was as Saphyre feared. Her father was full victim of Carmen's twisting of minds. "Further, Saphyre, I would ask—"

"Hush, Michael," Carmen scolded. "You speak too much." Carmen cleared her throat and announced, "This is a day to be celebrated! Therefore, bring in the musicians! The jesters! Let us find joy in mirth and laughter."

Saphyre glared at Carmen—every muscle in her body begging to attack the villainess with her own hands. How Saphyre loathed the woman for the poison of mind she had heaped upon her father—the humiliation, to so hush him as a dog before all the court. However, Edmund and Salomonè had told Saphyre in confidence the night before that she must remain seeming unsettled. There was no way of knowing who was under Carmen's control—nor how many. Carmen must suspect nothing of Edmund's and Salomonè's presence. She must not suspect Saphyre had any ally. More they could not say, for they were interrupted by another guardsman summoning them to the throne room.

"Here ye! Here ye!" the herald announced. "Your majesty," he said, nodding to the queen first. "Your majesty," he said, nodding then at Saphyre's father. "And your highness," he said, nodding to Saphyre. "I give you the two merry jesters and the viol minstrel Belmiro!"

Saphyre startled at the sound of Belmiro's name, quick glancing to the queen—fearful she had given summons to suspicion. Yet the queen was intent, applauding as two small men appeared, dressed in the vibrant purple, green, and gold attire of jesters. In a whirl of tumbling and cartwheels, Marcellus and Thaddeus entered the throne room. Belmiro entered with them, a lively tune aflame on the strings of his viol.

Tears sprang to Saphyre's eyes at the sight of her three friends. She found it near impossible to keep from calling out to them—to keep from sobbing for the joy of seeing them again. She feigned laughter as she watched Marcellus and Thaddeus dance about, performing all nature of tricks and trades.

Marcellus approached, dropping to one knee before the queen and saying, "Oh, but you are as beautiful as we have heard, your majesty."

"You have heard of my beauty?" Carmen asked, obvious delighted.

"That I have, oh, loveliest queen," he said. "And it is why we brought these to you." From behind his back, as if by magic, Marcellus produced a bouquet of wild daisies. The queen gasped, amazed, and he said, "For you, my beautiful queen."

Was this distraction? Saphyre thought. It surely seemed distraction, for Belmiro continued to play the lively tune, and Thaddeus continued to captivate the occupants of the throne room.

"And what say you, King Michael?" Marcellus asked, kneeling before Saphyre's father.

"You say nothing, Michael," Carmen whispered.

"I say nothing," Saphyre heard her father repeat.

"Nothing?" Marcellus said. "Not when spoken to?"

"No," the king said.

Marcellus made a dramatic face of perplexity and said, "Nor when pinched?" He reached out and pinched the king.

The king did not move, saying only, "No."

"Do not waste your effort, jester," Carmen said. "The king is not amused at your silly ways."

"Is he not?" Marcellus asked. Then from behind his back Marcellus indeed produced a tiny flaming torch, quick setting the king's tunic aflame and shouting, "Will he even say nothing now?"

Saphyre screamed as her father's tunic erupted into flames!

"Father!" Saphyre cried.

"You fool!" Carmen screeched. "You fool!"

At once, Edmund and Salomonè rushed to the king's aid, throwing him to the floor and smothering the flame.

"Fools! All of you!" Carmen shouted. "Hang them! Hang them both! The minstrel as well! Hang them all!" She reached forth, slapping Edmund hard on the helmet. "And gag the king, you idiot…lest he speak without my permission!"

Edmund, seeing the king was well enough, stood facing the queen—raised his helmet shield. "I am no man you have mind-twisted, witch," he growled.

Then aware Edmund was not under her mind spell, Carmen shouted, "Guards! Guards!"

Saphyre glanced to Kornelius, who merely stood still, a perplexed expression upon his face.

"Kornelius!" Saphyre cried. "Help him!" Yet Kornelius stood unmoving. Salomonè released the king and stood as well. He shook his head at Saphyre, an indication she should not look to him for aid. However, Carmen, having found one traitorous guard in her midst, instantly set her guardsmen on Salomonè as well.

"Fools!" Carmen growled. "Did you truly think you could outwit me? Best me?"

"Saphyre?" King Michael mumbled.

"Father!" Saphyre cried at the sound of her father's voice. Dropping to her knees, she cradled his head in her lap. "Father! Are you…are you here?" she asked.

King Michael grimaced, the searing of his flesh having no doubt been very painful—his full awareness slow in returning after lingering so long under Carmen's control.

"I-I am returned, my darling," he said.

"No! No!" Carmen shouted. "Kill him! Kill the king!"

Saphyre looked up to see indeed all of Carmen's guardsmen—twenty to count—advancing toward her, toward her father. From the screams bursting from the others in the throne room, she surmised that most were as Augustynia—untouched by Carmen's spell, yet frightened and perplexed.

Augustynia rushed to Saphyre, throwing herself across the king and shouting, "Stop! Stop this advancement upon the king!"

"I command you, halt!" Saphyre shouted. But her words had held no power to them.

Edmund and Salomonè had broken free of their captors and now drew swords, causing the guardsmen to pause in their aggression. Even Marcellus and Thaddeus now stood facing the line of soldiers, daggers drawn, Belmiro at their side.

"Hear us!" Edmund shouted. "You have been wooed by a witch… the witch Carmen, there!" He turned and pointed to the queen. "She endeavors to own your minds, to have you murder your king!"

"Hear me, guardsmen," Carmen interrupted. "Kill them all. Slaughter your king and his daughter…for I have commanded it!"

The guardsmen again began their advance, but there arose such a commotion without the room—such an uproar of shouting and cheering from beyond—that they again paused. Every person in the throne room—every guardsman, every lady, every nobleman—paused at the noise.

The doors of the throne room burst open to reveal such a sight—an armored knight on horseback.

The knight sat tall upon his mount, donning a tunic of sapphire blue. His chain mail, armor, and helmet shone radiant in the sun streaming through the windows. His helmet shield was down, covering his face, yet the shield he carried, engraved with the oak and ax, was familiar to all—and there rose among those in the throne room an awed silence as the great knight rode forth. His mount was white, pristine, unblemished, and its hooves echoed in the awed silence as it pranced across the floor.

"Sebastian!" Augustynia breathed, rising to her feet.

"Sebastian?" Carmen laughed. "Sebastian is dead these six years past, Augustynia."

The whispering began then—the astonished whispering of noble and peasant alike as curious observers poured into the throne room.

"Sebastian!" Augustynia cried out. She started toward him, but Edmund stayed her.

"Please hold, milady," Edmund said. "There is much wickedness at work here, and it will take all good to overcome it."

No one in the room breathed as Sebastian reached up, pushing back his helmet shield. Saphyre felt tears flood her cheeks as she saw his face then, clean-shaven, a silver mask with the shape of his nose pressed to his face.

"Step down, old queen!" Sebastian ordered. "Step down and face your fate."

Carmen tossed her head and laughed. "I have fifty and more guardsmen awaiting my command, Sebastian. Think you that you can vanquish me? One to fifty?"

"We are eight in number, witch," Sebastian said. "Step down or die."

"Guardsmen! Kill the princess!" Carmen quick ordered.

"No!" King Michael shouted.

Saphyre gasped as she saw the guardsmen begin an advance in her direction. Edmund fought, as did Salomonè—Marcellus and Thaddeus—Belmiro. Saphyre reached down, taking her father's dagger from its sheath at his waist. But where was Rogan? She could not fathom how Sebastian had come but Rogan had not.

"Your guardsmen at the gate have seen their throats slit, witch!" Sebastian shouted as he ran his sword through a guardsman. "Only now does your true terror advance!" Sebastian dismounted, running his sword through another guardsman's belly.

"Hold! What is that I hear?" Carmen said, raising a hand in command of silence. The guardsmen stepped back from their battle, swords at the ready yet. "What do my ears hear? I am deceived! It must be I am deceived!"

"You are not deceived, witch," Sebastian growled. "Listen…for the hour of your meeting with Lord Death is at hand."

Saphyre's heart began to pound brutal within her bosom—for the sound ringing in her ears had not been heard in the Kingdom of Graces for years. It was the sound stirred by one person—the roar— the roar of the crowd—the foretelling of his coming.

"Roar! Roar! Roar!" the crowd chanted.

"It…it cannot be," Saphyre whispered. "It cannot be."

"Roar! Roar! Roar!" The chanting grew louder until it drowned out even the queen's shouts and screams.

He rode in without pause—without caution—the great warrior-knight, Roar, mounted upon a magnificent black steed. His blood-red tunic, dark helmet adorned with a crimson feather, and dark chain mail appeared dark ominous in contrast to Sebastian. Further, he made no graceful entrance the like of the once great captain of the guard. Rather the warrior-knight Roar rode straight away to rein in just before the old queen. His horse circled once, snorting and rearing, stomping at the queen's feet.

"Release them all, witch," he demanded, and Saphyre thought she might never draw breath again at the sound of the voice from beneath his helmet shield, "lest there be more blood on your hands this day…for I have vanquished your fifteen guardsmen at the gate." As the warrior-knight Roar raised his helmet shield, revealing the handsome and beloved face of Rogan, Saphyre stumbled forward— astonished near to fainting.

Rogan had come for her! Indeed, he had—as she knew he would! She understood in that moment the reason for his delay. No doubt there were many of the queen's men to be bested in order that Edmund, Salomonè, Saphyre, and the others could easy escape.

"And I six more at the throne room door. As well as these two within," Sebastian said, nodding to the two dead men on the ground.

"Imposters! They are imposters, I say!" Carmen shouted. "Sebastian is dead. Likewise Roar! For I sent them who did the killing! Sebastian is dead…fed to the wolves. And the bones and burnt skull of Roar lie at the bottom of a traitor's tomb."

Rogan reached to his side and removed his shield from its place at his horse's flank. He tossed it to the ground before the queen, the crashing noise it made deafening as it hit the floor. Emblazoned on the shield was the image of a roaring lion, its kingly mane flaming about its face. Likewise, Rogan took from about his neck a gold chain held to an emblem of the same image—a roaring lion, its kingly mane flaming about its face. Saphyre's hand instant went to the emblem about her own neck—the emblem in exact similitude to the one Rogan had tossed at the queen's feet.

"One of your assassins lies headless in a traitor's tomb, witch," Rogan growled, "for I am Roar, and I slit his throat before he could think to slit mine."

The queen was silent for a moment. She looked from Rogan to Sebastian to Saphyre.

"The rabble in the woods," Carmen said. "Woodsman or warriors…they cannot save you now. All within the sound of my voice…listen and obey. Kill them all! The king, his daughter, and any who make to champion them! Kill them!"

At once the guardsmen advanced upon Rogan and Sebastian, others upon Edmund, Salomonè, Belmiro, Thaddeus, and Marcellus. Likewise, the expression of perplexed weakness disappeared from

Kornelius's face, and he drew his sword, his eyes fixed on Saphyre.

"No!" Saphyre screamed. "Kornelius! No!"

"Saphyre!" she heard Rogan shout, drawing his sword. He instant dismounted, throwing off his helmet. Plunging his sword through an aggressing guardsman's throat, he withdrew it and stepped over the dead man.

Saphyre stepped backward, unable to fathom Kornelius leveling his sword at her. "Kornelius?" she pleaded. "Do not—"

"You are bewitched, man!" Rogan shouted, stepping between Saphyre and Kornelius. "Hear me now—you would not kill this girl!" As Rogan leveled his sword at Kornelius, he reached back, shoving Saphyre hard and causing her to stumble backward.

"Out of his way, Saphyre," the king said, raising himself at last. "Augustynia! Out of his way!" The king took hold of Augustynia's arm, pulling her back as Kornelius charged at Rogan.

"The torches, Marcellus!" Rogan shouted. "Thaddeus! The torches!"

Saphyre screamed as more guardsmen and even some nobles drew swords against her friends—against her love! "Father! They will be killed!" she screamed.

"No," the king said. "Not whilst I yet draw breath." King Michael drew his sword and shouted, "Find your wits about you, friends! Or perish!"

But the once mighty king was weak, both from the fever of his mind so long endured and the merciful flame set to him by Marcellus. He crumbled to the ground, too quick overcome.

"Sebastian!" Saphyre heard Augustynia scream.

Saphyre looked up to see a guardsman's blade only just miss Sebastian's throat.

"I do not want the blood of a good prince on my hands, Kornelius," Rogan spoke. "But I will slit your throat before I let harm come near to Saphyre."

Saphyre looked about frantic—terrified—horror-stricken at what was taking place around her! Everywhere there was shouting, battle, blood, and death! Even for those who Marcellus and Thaddeus were touching torches to, there seemed more who were not set aflame—more under the queen's power bent on murder. Saphyre looked to Carmen, who stood shrieking commands. She appeared overcome with madness—fearful and stricken with perplexity. No doubt she knew any of the men of the keep would slay her if they drew nearer.

"Here! Marcellus!" Rogan shouted. "The flame! Set it to the prince!"

A guardsman caught hold of Marcellus's belt, but the small man turned, setting the flame to the guard's tunic. The guard released Marcellus, and he made toward Rogan and the prince.

Distracted—for Marcellus did indeed hold the torch at Kornelius's leg—Rogan growled as Kornelius's blade grazed his thigh at the back.

"Awaken, man!" Rogan shouted at Kornelius. "You would not do this of your own will!"

Kornelius winced, crying out as Marcellus pressed the torch more firm against Kornelius's leg. Saphyre watched as he crumpled to the ground in agony, his countenance speaking his mind was restored once more.

Unexpected, Rogan took the torch from Marcellus, and with his sword in one hand, the flaming torch in the other, he set about battling with swords—setting fire to anyone who came near with murderous intent.

"Sebastian!" Rogan shouted. "Set fire to any who advance!"

"Aye!" Sebastian shouted, taking a torch from the wall and following Rogan's lead.

Edmund and Salomonè—both bleeding from wounds to their legs and arms—each took a torch from the wall as well, battling onward. Belmiro, Thaddeus, and Marcellus endeavored to assist those fallen men who were not yet dead but once again lucid.

Soon the battle and bloodshed began to lessen. Between them—the legend who was Roar, the legend of Sebastian Ottokar, the five remaining men of the keep—for sake of these, all who would murder for the old queen were vanquished or burned to their senses.

Rogan turned to look at Saphyre. His breathing was labored from the battle, his arm bleeding from a sword wound, as was his leg. His chain mail chimed as he fell to his knees before her, resting on his sword, the Crimson Frost—the great sword of legend, the sword of the heir to the throne of Graces.

"Saphyre," he breathed, "I am come to champion you."

Saphyre gasped, covering her mouth with trembling hands. Her tears ran unreserved over her cheeks as she looked to her Rogan—Rogan, who was her champion, her heart's great desire—Rogan—Rogan, who was the great warrior-knight Roar.

Slowly she walked to him, uncertain of a sudden as to what she might speak to him—uncertain as to what action to take.

"I am come to you, Saphyre," Rogan said. "I raised your own sword in your defense…wielded the Crimson Frost of legend to aid your kingdom. Is it enough? Is it enough to stay the executioner's ax or noose? Is it enough…enough to win your heart?"

"But…but you…you are Roar," she whispered. "How is it that I can hope to…how can I hope to keep you?"

Rogan breathed a chuckle—next threw his head back with a stronger chuckle. Rising to his feet, he held the sword to her—offered the legendary sword, the Crimson Frost, to its mistress. "Stay the executioner's hand, Saphyre," he said. "Pray, stay the executioner… and only love me with as much wild madness as I love you."

"Roar!" King Michael shouted.

Saphyre glanced from her Rogan to see Carmen, wielding a dagger and running at Saphyre's lover. Saphyre screamed as Rogan reached out, catching Carmen's hand in his own and staying the dagger.

"You!" Carmen shrieked. "You who were dead…you breathed love's breath in a kiss…did you not? Breathed life into her…and you have killed me!"

Rogan twisted Carmen's arm at her back—merciless bending her wrist to cause the dagger to slip from her hand.

"I breathed my love to her, yes. But it is only I can wish that I would see you die at my hand, witch," Rogan growled.

"You shall lose your head, stepmother," King Michael breathed, limping toward her. "You shall lose it this very day. For though I know not yet the true extent of your crimes…I feel in my soul you have bid Lord Death enter in this castle before."

The laughter of madness burst from Carmen's lungs as she said, "Indeed! Indeed! But I shall die yet beautiful. For three more days, my beauty will reign in this kingdom."

"She is mad," Augustynia said to Sebastian as he ventured near, but not too.

"It is the laughter of madness that unsettles me," Marcellus said to his brother, Thaddeus nodding in agreement.

"For you see, King Michael," Carmen began, "there is a price to pay for beauty. And with Saphyre's awakening at the hand…the very breath of love…for with her cure comes my demise. It is the price of the mind fever…the skill of the golden apple." She drew the pendant from around her neck, gazing upon it. "Healed from the fever by that other than flame, Saphyre," she mumbled. "And it is my payment for great beauty…for I must now take on the fever at sun's set this day… never to awaken. The woman from the east set forth my cures…two cures…the first, the flame. But who would set a beautiful queen such as I aflame? Who would set me aflame whilst yet I breathe?"

Saphyre trembled at the memory of the fever—of the helpless madness of the fever. "But there are planted two cures…as you said," Saphyre said.

Again Carmen laughed, "It is true, Saphyre. It is true. But you see, I know not the second cure. And so…I shall slip into the fever this very sun's set…and then…and then I shall die, and my great beauty will be dust."

"Take her away!" King Michael shouted. "I will not hear her voice again! Set guards about her now…and we will see what sun's set brings." Then, turning to Saphyre, her father drew her into his embrace, saying, "My precious Saphyre! How miserable I have been without you. How sorry I am for my weak-mindedness."

"Oh, Father," Saphyre breathed, tears streaming down her face as she returned his loving embrace. "How I have missed you."

Saphyre smiled as her father drew her away from him, having kissed her cheek full adoring.

"And what miracles travel in your wake," King Michael said. "Once heroic, once wrongly banished…our legends return to us."

"Your majesty," Rogan said, taking a knee before the king.

"Roar," the king breathed, "in flesh and bone and blood before me. I am near unable to believe it." The king then turned his attention to Sebastian, standing to one side. "And Sebastian, my friend. How I grieved at your death…at the deaths of my two greatest champions… and friends."

"Your majesty," Sebastian said, also taking a knee.

"Will you at last take your lady Augustynia to wife, Sebastian?" the king asked, smiling. "It is long she has had faith in your return. Rise and take her hand."

"I-I dare not, sire," Sebastian said, though he did stand at the king's first command. "For I…I am far more unworthy than ever I was before."

Saphyre looked to Rogan—saw the moisture and pain in his eyes, empathy for his friend. She wept further also, frightened when her father asked, "Is this mask you wear…is this what deems you unworthy?"

"This…and so much more," Sebastian mumbled.

"Augustynia," the king said. "Do you want Sebastian as your husband? For I will command him to marry you. Pray, tell me…do you wish it?"

Saphyre stilled her sobbing—did not breathe as she watched Augustynia go to Sebastian, as she saw the beautiful woman reach up and remove the silver mask from his face.

Augustynia inhaled a slow, quiet breath. Tears filled her eyes, her hands beginning to tremble as she looked upon Sebastian's maimed feature.

"Oh, my love," she whispered, placing loving hands to his cheeks. Tears spilled from her eyes as she caressed his brow with her fingertips—caressed his lips with her thumbs. "Is this what kept you from me so long, my own Sebastian?" Augustynia asked. "How could you endure such pain, such suffering, and not allow my love to help in the healing of it? How could you abandon me for such a trifle as this?"

"It...this is a ghastly wound, Augustynia," Sebastian said. "It is horrific to look upon. What man would subject his love to such a vision each morn...each day...each night?"

"Command him, sire. I beg of you," Augustynia said to the king as she gazed lovingly up at Sebastian. Augustynia wove gentle fingers though Sebastian's hair—and as she drew his head down toward her own, she said, "For I have ever only wanted him...this man as my husband." The beautiful lady pressed her lips to Sebastian's, kissing him full square on the mouth before the king and all else about him.

Tears fell from Sebastian's eyes as Augustynia kissed him once more. Awkward—unbelieving he yet owned her heart—Sebastian said, "But...but I have no...no nose, Augustynia."

Augustynia smiled, again running her fingers through his hair and saying, "It was not your nose I loved so long, Sebastian. It was you...my Sebastian. You are whom I loved. You are whom I have ever loved...whom I still love."

"Then have him, Augustynia," the king said. "Have him to wed. Own him forever...as you already own him."

Saphyre sighed through her tears as she saw Sebastian's smile— as she saw Augustynia's smile—as she heard Marcellus, Thaddeus, Edmund, Salomonè, and Belmiro cheer in unison.

Her gaze met Rogan's to find his fixed on her, moisture plentiful in his eyes. Standing before her dressed in the garments and chain mail of a hero, he unsettled her. He seemed too much a great man to hope for—too great a legend to have a heart that could be owned.

"I am come to you, Saphyre," Rogan said—as he had before.

"You are come to her...how, Roar?" the king asked. "How are you come to her? And why?"

Rogan kneeled before the king. Raising his gaze to he whom Roar the warrior-knight served, he spoke. "How I come to her...it will need a length of time to tell, sire," he said. "Why I come to her, however, I can speak."

"Then speak it, Roar," the king said. "For I owe you my life...

and hers. What would you have for your hero's price? Riches? Titles?"

"I would have the greatest price you could offer, sire. I would have Saphyre Snow," Rogan said. "I would have her for mine own…for I love her more than I love my own life…and I would hold her in my arms each night I yet live, taste of her sweet mouth each moment I breathe…hear her laughter, see her smile, know her wit and wisdom, feel her compassion and her soft caress."

Saphyre did not attempt to wipe the tears from her cheeks. Nor did she take her gaze from him—not for a moment—not even when she heard Marcellus clear his nose and brush his tears with his sleeve.

"I would have Saphyre as my price, King Michael," Rogan said. "I would have Saphyre as my wife."

At his request Saphyre felt her knees give way beneath her, and she crumpled to the floor, burying her sobs of joy in her hands.

"And what say you, Saphyre?" King Michael asked. "What say you of the hero's price requested?"

Saphyre looked again to Rogan. "Though…though I am no price worthy of such a man, Father," she stumbled, "I know I only ever loved he who kneels before you now. More than life…I love him."

"Then rise, Roar," King Michael said. "Rise and take your hero's price…the hand of the princess, Saphyre Snow." The subjects who had filled the throne room cheered, applauded, and tossed their wares into the air, joyous at their hero's price.

Rogan left his knees, standing proud and again offering the great sword, the Crimson Frost, to Saphyre as proof of his loyalty—and love.

Saphyre smiled. "I cannot wield such a weapon, sir knight," she said. "Therefore, I gift the sword to you. The Crimson Frost…forged for the great Crimson Knight of old—let it be known throughout all the Kingdom of Graces and beyond…that the Crimson Frost once wielded by he of legend now lies in the hand of another. The Crimson Frost, gifted me by my father, King Michael, knows a new master…the great warrior-knight Roar!"

The crowd cheered as Rogan nodded and sheathed the sword at his hip.

"But he...he is a traitor, your majesty," Kornelius shouted, limping to stand near Saphyre. "For I witnessed the Executioner's Kiss. In the wood, when I came upon the princess...I witnessed this very man defile her."

The crowd's cheers turned to breathless gasps as the king frowned at Kornelius—looked to Rogan, who without pause said, "It is true, your majesty. I braved the threat...challenged Lord Death by way of the Executioner's Kiss...for love of your daughter, sire. Would that I would die at the executioner's hand...than never to have tasted such as Saphyre Snow's sweet kiss."

"Then we are true brothers, Roar," the king said, smiling. "Brothers in besting a preposterous law...for I knew well her mother's kiss before we were betrothed...and here do decree the end of the Executioner's Kiss."

Rogan smiled, offering his hand to Saphyre. Her hand trembled as she tentative took his. A moment later she was in his arms—held firm against his body—safe in the power of his embrace.

"I will take my leave then, King Michael," Kornelius said.

"Take your leave then, Kornelius," the king said, "for my kingdom shall not be yours. My kingdom will pass to the great warrior-knight Roar, when one day Saphyre is queen."

Saphyre smiled as she felt Rogan loving kiss the top of her head. His arms were powerful about her; his heart beat strong and sure within his breast.

"I cannot believe you are truly wanting of me," she said.

She heard him chuckle. "I cannot believe your father did not run me through."

It was then the chant began—first with six voices beloved and familiar—quick joined by others. "The Kiss! The Kiss! The Kiss!" all chanted.

Rogan smiled at Saphyre—she still trembling in his arms.

"Sire?" he asked, looking to King Michael.

Saphyre turned and looked to her father to see him smile and nod.

"And so...the Executioner's Kiss," Rogan whispered as he took

Saphyre's face between his powerful hands—took her mouth with his own—caused the court and subjects of the kingdom to cheer. Long and loud they cheered—cheered for their freedom, for their king restored to them, for the return of their heroes of legend—their legends whose cause was good—their legends whose cause was love.

"I love you. You, Roar...and you, Rogan, hero of the keep," Saphyre whispered when their lips brief parted.

"And I love you. You, Saphyre Snow...and princess...princess of the keep. *My* princess of the keep," Rogan smiled. "Have you sorted us all out then?" he asked, pressing a lingering kiss to her mouth. "Have you sorted out who then is to serve as your lover and who is to serve as your footman? For I will gladly serve as either, my beauty."

Saphyre smiled at him, saying, "It is the same I chose the moment I first heard you speak the words the same. It is then I chose you as lover."

Rogan smiled, and Saphyre melted to him—for he was joy—he was love—he was Rogan—and Rogan was life.

THE *Keep—Epilogue*

It was the measure of legends—the legend of Saphyre Snow and the great warrior-knight Roar—the vanquishing of the wicked queen, Carmen. The wicked queen had indeed slipped into a mysterious fever only hours after having been bested by the great legends Roar and Sebastian—by the legendary Brothers of the Keep. As the court physicians attended the ailing king, Michael—endeavored to remove the seared flesh that was his saving—Carmen sank into fever. Three days later, her breath stilled forever.

Moments prior to her being buried deep in a traitor's tomb, those preparing her for burial came to King Michael—the apple pendant in their hands. "Look here," said one of the burial women as she handed the pendant to the king. "There reads an engraving on one side of the queen's poisoned apple."

King Michael accepted the pendant, reading the words engravened thereon before handing the golden apple to Saphyre, who was at his side, with Rogan Roar at hers.

"*The flame the cure, the cure the flame,*" Saphyre read.

Rogan frowned. "Blinded in her madness and vanity, she did not discern the simple answer. The simple cures for her death…were one in the same."

"The flame was both cures," Saphyre said.

"We knew the flame to be the first cure…and in that we would not see her cured by the flame, we would not put the flame to her," Rogan said.

Thus the wicked queen died and was buried, and the story of her vanquishing—the legend told of Rogan Roar and Saphyre Snow, of Sebastian and the Brothers of the Keep—thus passed legend from father to son—from mother to daughter—forever.

❧

The travelers stood in awed and reflective silence before the ruins of the ancient keep. Many there were, intimate in association. The once great king of the Kingdom of Graces, Michael, there stood. Weakened by injury and age, King Michael had of recent abdicated his crown to his daughter and her husband, the great warrior-knight Rogan Roar.

Thus, King Rogan stood at King Michael's side, one hand resting on the pommel of the legend sword, the Crimson Frost, as he studied the old keep—as Rogan's queen and Michael's daughter, Saphyre Snow, stood gazing upon ancient stone walls as well. The young prince Sebastian was there and also the small princess, Penelope— and the wee prince Jordan.

Unaware of the great worth of the crumbling edifice before which their grandfather and parents stood, Prince Bastian, Princess Penelope, and the young Prince Jordan played innocent on the banks of the nearby stream. Other children played with them— their friends, sons and daughters of the great Sebastian Ottokar and the remaining Brothers of the Keep. Two sons of Edmund and one son and one daughter of Salomonè played happily. There near the stream's bank laughed two daughters of Marcellus's—twin daughters were they—and two sons of Thaddeus, likewise twins. There near the stream's bank, laughing and tumbling with the others, was the son of Belmiro, there also the son and daughter of the great Sebastian and his lady Augustynia.

"It is changed," Sebastian said, Augustynia at his side.

"And yet not so much," said Edmund.

"Careful of the rocks, children," Lady Englehardt told the gaggle of children cheerful playing in the cool grasses.

"To imagine you here," Marcellus's wife whispered, smiling. "It makes me happy...to imagine you here with your brothers...a tortured princess in your care."

"She was in *my* care, generally," Thaddeus said, his wife pushing a playful elbow to his ribs.

"She was not," Marcellus argued.

"She was generally in Rogan's arms," Salomonè chuckled, his own wife taking his arm and smiling up at him.

"Indeed she was," Belmiro agreed, smiling at his own adored wife. "Indeed she was."

"I am humbled to think of you men...here in this keep, broken and bruised, several even victims of my own father's madness," King Michael said. "And to you—you who would have no cause...no cause save the honor and nobleness flowing thick in your blood—to you we owe the happiness and safety of the entire kingdom."

Saphyre stood gazing at the keep and lingered in the company of her beloved husband, in the company of her cherished father, and in company of the six most trusted counselors to the throne of the Kingdom of Graces. Tears filled her eyes, her heart smoldering with memory and love.

"I *was* generally in your arms," Saphyre said, taking Rogan's hand. "And in them...I was in the arms of heaven."

"You were fortunate not to be generally in my bed, woman," Rogan said, smiling.

"Hush, Rogan!" Saphyre scolded, blushing to her toes and glancing to her father for fear he may have heard her husband's teasing. "The others will hear you!"

"I am sure your husband is correct in his telling of your being fortunate, daughter," King Michael said, smiling.

"Come, grandfather! Come with us!" Princess Penelope giggled, taking hold of her grandfather's hand and merciless tugging at it. "Come and see what many fish are in the stream and how they tickle your hands!"

King Michael smiled at the child and said, "Very well, my darling. Very well. Show these tickling fish to me."

"Are we to go in then?" Augustynia asked.

"Yes! Oh, yes! Do let us go in," Marcellus's wife said, fairly bouncing with delighted anticipation.

"Yes," Sebastian said. "Perhaps the fire pit will be set that we may share many memories."

Saphyre looked to Rogan as he firm held her hand, staying her from following the others into the keep. Her brow puckered, for she was perplexed at his wanting to linger a moment without.

"It was here you healed me, Saphyre," he said. "It was here I first loved you. To think of it crumbling, abandoned…it heavy saddens me."

Saphyre smiled, her eyes filling with tears as she saw the concern on her husband's face.

"Then we shall come and visit it more often," she told him. "We shall away to the bell tower that you may endeavor to seduce me."

Rogan chuckled, his handsome smile displayed as he gazed lovingly at his wife—the young and beautiful queen of the Kingdom of Graces.

"Come then," he whispered. "There is another path to the bell tower."

Saphyre giggled as he bent and quick kissed her, leading her then to the east side of the keep. Saphyre delighted in the boyish expression owning Rogan's countenance as he led her through a small hole in a damaged wall of the keep. Soon they had climbed the ancient stone steps to stand in the bell tower. Saphyre looked through the tower window to her father playing with the children below.

Turning, she slipped her arms around Rogan's waist, smiling up at him.

"I am quite ready to be corrupted, your majesty," she said, kissing him as his head descended toward her own.

"Are you, then, Princess?" he chuckled. Rogan's mouth melted to Saphyre's—passion burning between them—happiness enfolding them. "Am I yet as able to please you as I was when you once knew me only as the rogue of the keep, Saphyre?" Rogan asked.

"Hush now, Rogan," Saphyre said, smiling. "For you please me more with each sunrise, and I would have your attentions about my mouth this moment."

Rogan smiled, saying, "Very well, Princess. Yet mind the rope, for there are far more than six other brothers of the keep who would hear the signal this day."

"Hush now, Rogan, and kiss your wife," Saphyre whispered, pulling her husband's head toward her own. Saphyre knew bliss in Rogan's arms; in his arms she knew life and all its promised happiness.

As the bell of the keep began to chime—the laughter of King Rogan and Queen Saphyre floating on the air—Sir Marcellus of the Kingdom of Graces chuckled and was heard to say, "In general she was...and is...in Rogan's arms."

AUTHOR'S NOTE

I really can't even tell you why exactly—just can't seem to put it into words—but for some reason I just love the story of *Saphyre Snow*! I'm certain that it does have a fair amount to do with the fact I adore fairy tales. I've always adored fairy tales, for as long as I can remember. Yet there's something much deeper in *Saphyre Snow* that I love—the rich tapestry of discerning the hearts and needs of others.

When I was six or seven, my mom started purchasing *Let's Pretend* story records for me. Each *Let's Pretend* album included two fairy tale "dramatizations," one on each side of the album. Oh, how I loved my *Let's Pretend* records! I would spend hours and hours and hours in my room, listening to my favorite fairy tales as I clipped photos of my favorite movie stars out of magazines, played dress-up, or just flittered about in a world of my own imagining. The dramatization of *Cinderella* was one of my favorites—being that the stepsisters in it were hilarious! *Let's Pretend* was also where I was first introduced to the tales of *Donkeyskin*, *The Goose Girl*, and *The Twelve Dancing Princesses* (which remains one of my very favorite fairy tales to this day).

In truth, the tale of *Snow White* has always been one of my very least, least, least favorite fairy tales. I'm not quite sure why, but I've never really liked it much. In truth, I own one Brothers Grimm version a little more true to the original tale—quite gruesome, actually—that is probably my favorite *Snow White* retelling. (In that version the wicked queen is forced to wear iron shoes, heated to red-hot in a fire, and then dance until she dies! Hello? Ouch!) Still, overall, I just never did enjoy *Snow White* (except for a movie I saw on TV as a kid a couple of times—a foreign version with dubbed-in voices, where a girl is actually chosen to reprise the role of *Snow White* in a school play and ends up getting to kiss the boy she has as crush on—now that one I liked!). Yet *Snow White* as a whole just isn't my favorite.

And that's why I myself think it's odd that I was inspired to write *Saphyre Snow*. Of course, maybe that's just it: I never really liked the story, so I wrote my own version, molding it into what I would want it to be. You see, in truth, I never went in much for the "handsome prince" hero theory in *Snow White*. I much prefer a handsome, smoldering-eyed rogue! I mean, let's face it—why would a princess want a lily-livered, rose-perfumed, lacy-collared prince when she could have a brave, strong, rugged, shirtless rogue with a great five-o'clock shadow, who smells like cedar, leather, and wood smoke? I mean, duh! Let's see—a prince defending your honor with his vast vocabulary and political competency—okay, maybe. But a rogue defending you with fists and bladed weaponry? No contest there! Thus, one aspect of *Saphyre Snow* that veers from the norm—forsake the prince and all his wealth and influence in favor of the handsome rogue and his powerful prowess of passion!

Yet the aspect of *Saphyre Snow* that most endears the book to me is the thread of "thinking of others" woven through it—of truly knowing a person's pain, sensing and seeing true countenances, and endeavoring to prove to each person his or her individual and infinite importance! I truly believe that every person we come in contact with—each and every one—should feel better about themselves because we passed through their life. Not for the sake of our own glory or ego but because each and every person is as precious as the next and should know it. Saphyre's gifts to the men of the keep—her empathetic ability to know what would help each man to heal, what would remind each man of his great worth—is one of my favorite things about the story.

Oddly enough, when *Saphyre Snow* was first released as an e-book three years ago, it was slow to gain favoritism. Personally, I think one reason is because it was initially viewed it as a "fairy tale," and this somehow didn't immediately resonate with readers the way it did later. However, over time, *Saphyre Snow* has become one of the stories readers mention to me most—telling me it is certainly a favorite now.

Of course, you know I had always wanted to lengthen the story of *Saphyre Snow*—always wanted to see it in print as a novel—for you must understand that, though I knew there was a bit more to

Saphyre's heritage than I had been able to include in the e-book, it bothered me that I hadn't told the whole tale to everyone! Thus, as I was completing *A Crimson Frost*—knowing that Channing Snow was Saphyre's great-grandfather, knowing that the Crimson Knight and Scarlet Princess were her great-great-grandparents—I knew I just had to tell the tale to the fullest extent my time might allow. Thus, *Saphyre Snow* joins its counterpart and another personal favorite, *A Crimson Frost*, on my bookshelf! Whew!

I know this "Author's Note" doesn't provide a plethora of insight into my secret sources of inspiration and reasons for writing *Saphyre Snow*. Still, I hope it offered a little glimpse into my heart and mind where the story is concerned. I do so love fairy tales, knights in armor, rascally rogues stealing kisses—and I know you do too. We're "kindred spirits," you and I—and in the end, I simply hope *Saphyre Snow* gifted you a smile—and perhaps a sigh—or two...

Marcia Lynn McClure

To my husband, Kevin…
"Mr. Perfectly Imperfect" Personified!

And now, enjoy the first chapter of
the prequel to **Saphyre Snow,**
A Crimson Frost
by Marcia Lynn McClure.

AN INQUIRY OF FAVOUR

"And yet no knight has ever carried Monet's favour," Anais began, "not even in one of her own father's tournaments."

"Perhaps she simply does not fancy any knight in particular and, in owning no partiality, does not wish to proffer her favour," Portia spoke in defense of Monet.

Hidden behind one of the heavy tapestries hanging in the Hall of Ancestors at Ivar Castle, Monet smiled, grateful for at least one ally in Portia. She stood motionless—continued to eavesdrop on the conversation taking place in the room beyond the great hanging drapery.

"Every living creature owns a partiality where knights are concerned. Some simply offer no declaration," Anais said. "I hold no fear of declaring my partiality. Thus, my favour has been carried in many a grand tournament."

Though she could not see her face for the tapestry, Monet noted the thick vanity in Anais's voice. It was true: many a renowned knight had carried Anais's favour of color in tournaments past. Greatly sought after was the favour, and hand, of Anais of Alvar. It seemed a familiar length of lavender silk or satin—her preferred color of ribbon, veil, or ornament—adorned some strong arm at each tournament—ever the arm of a celebrated or distinguished knight of a king's round table.

However, Monet's favour, a scarlet veil or length of silk worn as embellishment to her gowns, had never known the joust—never ridden into battle—for she did not hold favours with lighthearted dalliance the way Anais of Alvar did. Thus, Monet had never lent her scarlet favour to any knight, nor had she requested any knight carry it.

Nevertheless, on this day, the whispered gossip of the young royals beyond the tapestry vexed her exceedingly. She knew the speculation concerning her father and his kingdom—the hushed inferences regarding his only daughter and only heir. Many were they in whose opinion the widower King Dacian—reigning monarch of the Kingdom of Karvana—should again take a wife in attempt to produce a male heir. Many were they who worried King Dacian's daughter, Monet, would not prove a strong enough monarch to hold at bay King James of the neighboring Kingdom of Rothbain. James was Dacian's distant cousin, and it was truth James coveted Karvana to near madness. Many were they who whispered Monet—as one day queen—could not stay Karvana from falling to James.

Moreover—and further vexing to Monet—was the gossip concerning her troth. King Dacian refused to proclaim her intended—even to Monet herself. Her marriage would be arranged, there was no doubt. Still, Dacian would not name the man to whom he intended to wed his daughter—the man who would one day rule beside her. This caused a great unrest in Dacian's kingdom and to other kingdoms whose rulers sensed James of Rothbain's thirst for conquering—fearing one weak kingdom would find theirs also vulnerable.

"And who has asked to carry your favour in King Ivan's tournament, Anais?" It was Lenore's voice questioning now. "Who will you choose to bear it tomorrow?"

"Oh, many have begged a token of me…I assure you that," Anais answered. Monet's teeth clenched as Anais giggled with triumph.

"Nevertheless, I will not grant my favour to any of those brave knights who have thus far requested it."

"What?" went up the common exclamation among the young women beyond the tapestry.

"You are in jest…surely," Lenore offered.

"Nay," Anais said, giggling once again.

"Then your favour will not be represented in the tournament?" Portia inquired.

"Unquestionably it shall be!" There was a pause. In a lowered voice, Anais spoke, "For I intend to appeal to one knight in particular. I intend to ask the Crimson Knight to bear my favour in tomorrow's tournament."

As Monet's hand covered her mouth, she was grateful for the harmonious gasps of the young women in the Hall of Ancestors—a chorus of quickly inhaled breaths, which masked her own. Thus, she was not found to be hiding.

"You cannot be in earnest, Anais!" Portia exclaimed. "The Crimson Knight? Sir Broderick Dougray? He has never borne any woman's favour in tournament or battle."

"Perhaps merely for the fact no woman has ever mustered the courage to request it of him," Anais said.

"He is King Dacian's first knight," Lenore began, "celebrated beyond any other knight in the five kingdoms!"

"Yes," Anais said. "And he shall bear my favour in the tournament tomorrow."

"What if he declines, Anais?" Portia asked.

"He will not," Anais answered, her vanity secure. "I assure you, Sir Broderick will bear my favour…and I have no doubt he will be crowned champion."

"If only I had been born with a thread of your daring countenance, Anais," Lenore sighed. "Then I might have the courage to beg Sir Broderick to bear my favour in some future tournament…for he is the handsomest of any knight living!"

"Oh, but you are not daring, Lenore," Anais sighed, feigning compassion. "Still, take heart…for there are many good knights who would be honored to carry your favour tomorrow. Sir Terrence, for example."

"He is near as old as my father, Anais!" Lenore exclaimed.

"He is a valiant man," Portia said, "and my father's first knight."

"I meant no offense, Portia," Lenore said, "only that I wish to have a younger knight carry my favour tomorrow."

"A younger knight might not have such a superior chance of besting the others," Portia offered. "Sir Terrence, with his experience and tried strength, is the only knight entered tomorrow who may well best them all...including Sir Broderick Dougray."

"If it is a champion you seek to bear your favour, Lenore," Anais began, "you may as well not lend your favour to any knight...for Sir Broderick will be champion. And he will bear a length of my lavender ribbon."

"Perhaps he will bear Monet's favour," Portia suggested.

Monet frowned and clenched her teeth tightly as she heard Anais's amused laughter echo through the room.

"Monet? Now who is in jest, Portia?" Anais asked.

"He is her father's first knight, Anais," Portia reminded. "Further, it would serve King Dacian well to have his first knight crowned champion tomorrow...and it would serve the people of Karvana."

"Serve King Dacian and Karvana it may...but if the Crimson Knight is named champion, it will be my favour he bears when he is presented," Anais said.

Monet placed one dainty hand to her bosom. Her heart was mad with pounding—mad with angst and apprehension! She could not endure to see her father's first knight carry Anais of Alvar's favour in the tournament. She could not! If Sir Broderick Dougray did win the tournament, the glory should be showered over King Dacian, not over Anais of Alvar—nor her father, King Rudolph. The Crimson Knight's triumph would be the triumph of Karvana as well—Karvana's strength displayed before all, including King James. Nothing must distract from King Dacian's first knight—from Karvana's first knight. A lavender favour at Sir Broderick's arm would distract, drawing attention to Alvar and its king—and away from Karvana and her king.

Monet closed her eyes and silently prayed Sir Broderick would refuse Anais's request to bear her lavender favour. There was more, of course—more to Monet's sudden sense of desperation, her loathing of the thought of Sir Broderick bearing Anais's favour—more than merely her father's triumph and her kingdom's approval. Yet she would not whisper of it. She would endeavor even not to think of it—her jealousy—her own secreted partiality toward Sir Broderick Dougray. Shaking her head to dispel all thoughts other than those of her father and her kingdom, Monet held her breath and listened as the sound of hastening footsteps met her ears.

"When will you ask Sir Broderick, Anais?" Lenore asked.

"Eventide…after King Ivan's feast."

They were gone. Monet stepped from behind the tapestry into the now empty Hall of Ancestors. Her eyes were moist with emotion. Sir Broderick could not bear Anais's favour! She must find the courage to approach the Crimson Knight—the courage to ask him to refuse a princess, the daughter of one of the most powerful kings of the five kingdoms. She must!

f

The sun hung exactly overhead, round and bright as a golden coin resting against a swath of sky-blue silk. Monet pulled the hood of her cloak over her head as she made her way through the knight encampment. The black cloak well hid her gown and face. Nevertheless, she worried it was yet too fine a garment—that its black velvet sheen might lure attention. And Monet did not want to lure attention on such an errand.

Monet worried Sir Broderick would be away from his pavilion. Nevertheless, she would endeavor to find him—to ask for his loyalty to her father and Karvana. She already knew the profound depth of his loyalty to both. Yet she must be certain—and so she would solicit.

She saw it then—just ahead—the refuge of the Crimson Knight, the white pavilion with crimson flag unfurled atop its center. The crimson flag—its black dragon reared on hind legs, flaming eyes boring through her—threatened Monet with immediate intimidation. Monet paused, wary of being recognized, frightened of facing Sir Broderick Dougray. She clasped her hands together, attempting to steady their sudden trembling. She drew a calming breath, for she was Karvana's princess, and the royals of Karvana were known for their courage. Were they not?

The two front flaps of the pavilion were tied back, allowing Monet to see within. A lone man lay stretched out on the ground. His hands tucked beneath his head, he appeared to be resting. It was Sir Broderick—she knew it was. Even though he lay in repose facing away from her, his form was unmistakable. The Crimson Knight was known as a man satisfied in his isolation. Save for his squire and the men he commanded in battle, he squandered little of his time in casual mingling with others. Thus, Monet's emotions alternated between fear, uncertainty, and determination.

Straightening her posture in an effort to appear more courageous than she felt, Monet glanced about. Where was Sir Broderick's squire? She surely could not approach without some manner of chaperone, could she? Yet time was waning; Anais of Alvar was well known for her impatience. Monet knew Anais would not wait until after King Ivan's feast to approach the Crimson Knight. If she wished to ensure her father's first knight would compete only for his king and kingdom, Monet knew she must act without hesitation.

She approached the pavilion—looked within. Sir Broderick's eyes were closed. It seemed he slept. Still, time was too valuable to stand on propriety.

"May I beg audience with you, Sir Broderick?" Monet asked. She stood just without the pavilion and was pleased when the great knight did not startle—did not even open his eyes.

Simply he asked, "Who is begging audience, young woman?" The deep intonation of his voice sent gooseflesh prickling over Monet's arms.

"Monet, Sir Broderick," she answered. Lowering her voice, she added, "King Dacian's daughter."

At this, the Crimson Knight's eyes opened, his brow furrowing with an inquisitive scowl.

He looked up, and Monet was rendered breathless. Ever the appearance of Sir Broderick Dougray, the Crimson Knight, had flustered her. Even as a young girl, the acute blue of his eyes had discomposed her nature. There was such a manner of brooding in their remarkable blue, of daring, and of something akin to danger. The Crimson Knight was renowned for his steel gaze—his piercing, dominate gaze—a gaze to set fear into the hearts of men one moment, to infuse desire to the hearts of women the next.

"Princess?" he mumbled. He raised himself and stood. His bewitching gaze caused Monet to tremble further. Sir Broderick glanced beyond her a moment—to one side of the knight encampment and then to the other. "You are not escorted?" he asked.

The Crimson Knight was of great height, and Monet held her cloak hood near her cheek to ensure it would not slip from her head as she looked up at him.

"I am not," Monet answered.

Sir Broderick's scowl changed to a frown of inquisition. "Princess, you should not be here…without escort…without—" he began.

"I know, sir," Monet stammered. "However, I must beg audience with you, Sir Broderick…for I own a request…a request of a personal nature…a request I wish to remain unheard by any but you."

"Are you threatened in some way?" he asked, one powerful hand grasping the hilt of the sword sheathed at his hip. "Is your father well?"

"My father is well," Monet answered, "as am I." Monet swallowed, flustered by the odd warmth bathing her limbs as she looked at him.

Sir Broderick's raven hair gave prominence to the severe blue of his eyes, the perfect angles of his face. Her attention rested for a moment on the small cleft marking his squared chin. Indeed, his features of face were far beyond merely remarkable, as was the breadth of his chest and shoulders. The length of his muscular limbs also lent to his exceptional appearance.

"Then why came you here without escort, Princess?" Sir Broderick inquired.

"To beg your benevolence, sir," Monet answered.

She watched as the handsome knight's piercing eyes narrowed. "My benevolence?" he asked. "What benevolence could a princess beg of me?"

Monet glanced away, his striking appearance yet disturbing her. She fixed her gaze to his broad chest before her—to the white tunic with red shield and black dragon coat of arms emblazoned upon it.

"I would have your honor shared with my father…with our kingdom…with these and none other. This I would beg you, though temptation would endeavor to lead you otherwise," she confessed.

"My honor?" he asked. "My honor already belongs to your father…and our kingdom."

"It is tomorrow's honor I speak of," she began, venturing to raise her gaze to meet his once more. "It is said you will easily win King Ivan's tournament, and I would beg you…please share the honor with my father and all of Karvana."

Still he frowned; still the severe blue of his eyes lingered on her.

"Your appeal near confounds me, Princess," he said. "Do I not ever bring honor to my king and kingdom? Should I *live* through the trials of the tournament—let alone prevail as champion—what thing could possibly divert the honor from resting on my king and Karvana?"

Monet glanced away—cast her gaze to the ground. Oh, why did he disquiet her so? It seemed she was ever out of countenance in his presence.

"Anais intends to beg you bear her favour in the tournament," she explained.

"Anais?" he asked. "Who is Anais?"

Monet looked back to him, delighted to see the sincere, unknowing expression on his face.

"Anais of Alvar." Sir Broderick's frown deepened. Thus Monet offered, "Alvar's princess? King Rudolph's daughter?"

His frown softened, yet disdain seemed to flame in his eyes. "I never beg tokens or carry favour," he grumbled.

"Yes...I know," Monet said. "But how will you refuse without offending?"

"I will simply decline." The loathing in his eyes was growing, yet Monet knew the depth of consequence should her father's first knight provoke a wounded countenance in Anais of Alvar. Anais's father, King Rudolph, saw no fault in his daughter—no matter her behavior or another's testimony. King Rudolph would demand recompense for his daughter's spurned request.

"But you must not simply decline," Monet began, "not a request of Anais of Alvar. I am certain you have heard of King Rudolph's prejudicial concerns for his daughter's sake. Your refusal would not bode well for you or my father. No doubt King Rudolph would demand compensation...of some sort."

Sir Broderick inhaled a deep breath, his massive chest rising with indignation and near-spent patience.

"Again you confound me, Princess," he said. "You ask that I share the honor of triumph with only your father and our kingdom... yet inform me I may not refuse this princess her request. I beg you then, Princess Monet...offer me a path of safe conduct wherein I can remain honorable in your eyes, loyal to my king and kingdom, and yet avoid provoking King Rudolph."

Monet shook her head. "I-I know none. It is why I have sought you out. To refuse Anais's request would certainly bring discomfort to my father. But to accept it...for were King Dacian's first knight to wear—"

"Hush!" he interrupted. He closed his eyes a moment—seemed to strain his hearing. He looked to Monet then, demanding, "Step into the pavilion, Princess."

"What? I cannot!" Monet argued. She wondered why her voice had instantly dropped to a whisper.

"I hear an approach," he said. "A company...and not of knights. Therefore, unless you wish to be found out—"

Monet stepped into the pavilion as the Crimson Knight

demanded. He, however, immediately stepped without, quickly unleashing the ties of the two front flaps, concealing her within.

"Sir Broderick?"

It was Anais! Monet held her breath, fearful both of being found out and of the Crimson Knight's response to Anais's request.

"Yes?" Sir Broderick's deep voice boomed.

"I am Anais…Princess of Alvar," Anais said.

"I am your servant, Princess," Sir Broderick greeted.

Of a sudden, feelings of vexation leapt in Monet's bosom. She loathed Anais of Alvar! Ever she had loathed her—even as a child. She wondered what manner of assembly accompanied Anais. Ladies-in-waiting? Servants?

Curiosity triumphed, and Monet knelt, pressing a hand to the ground in the endeavor of peering through the small opening at the bottom of the pavilion. She could discern the hems of three gowns—ladies-in-waiting—and further the boots of two guards.

"I have come to offer a great honor to you, Sir Broderick," Anais said. "I believe you are one who is worthy of such an honor."

"I am worthy of nothing, your highness," Sir Broderick began, "let alone the honor of basking in your lovely presence."

Anais and her ladies giggled with vain delight.

"You are humble…as well as handsome, Sir Broderick!"

Monet frowned, jealousy, resentment, and anger coursing through her limbs. She watched as Anais's hem moved toward Sir Broderick—advanced upon the Crimson Knight.

"And I believe you are he—the only knight at King Ivan's tournament worthy of this honor," Anais said.

"Pray, Princess…may I ask what honor you intend to bestow?"

"I would have you bear my favour in this tournament, Sir Broderick," Anais stated. "I do wish you to know that it would be my honor as well as yours…for I have heard you have never carried favour into a tournament or battle."

"None visible, your highness," Sir Broderick said.

Monet frowned. None visible? Had Sir Broderick Dougray

carried a hidden favour? Again jealousy rose within her bosom—a diverse jealousy—a competitor to the jealousy Anais wrought.

"Do you accept my offer, Sir Broderick?" Anais asked. "Do you accept the honor I am willing to bestow upon you?"

Monet could not breathe! How would he answer? Would King Dacian's first knight prove himself wholly loyal? Furthermore, would he prove to be clever—clever enough to circumvent offense to Alvar, its princess, and its king?

"I fear it is with heavy heart that I must decline, Princess," Sir Broderick said. Monet still did not draw breath. Instead, she waited—waited for Anais's emotional eruption—the eruption of angry indignation Monet knew was forthcoming.

"You refuse?" Anais asked, anger rising in her voice.

"No, your highness," Sir Broderick answered. "Rather, I must decline…wretchedly decline."

"Decline? And why?" Anais demanded. "When I offer such an honor to you, Sir Broderick…what reason would you have of declination?"

Monet still did not breathe—waited for his response.

"I already carry favour, your highness," Sir Broderick said. "Only this morning I begged a token of another…and she has only just granted me the honor to bear *her* favour in King Ivan's tournament."

At last Monet drew breath, sighing reprieve. Sir Broderick Dougray had declined! The Crimson Knight had gallantly offered declination and without contributing malicious offense. He had proffered a lie, it was true, yet in protection of his king. Who would not allow it? For a moment, Monet frowned. *Had* Sir Broderick offered a lie to Anais? Or had he hidden the truth from Monet? Perhaps he had begged token from another—before she had entered his pavilion, before Anais had sought him out. She closed her eyes, shaking her head slightly to dispel the unhappy thought. No. The Crimson Knight was known for his loyalty. Monet was certain he would have informed her had he already begged a token or accepted favour.

There was silence for a moment. Monet knew Anais well; the

Princess of Alvar was reigning in her temper. Anais was infuriated—there could be no doubt of it. Nevertheless, even Anais, daughter of Alvar's King Rudolph, could not find fault with a knight who would honor his own word and previous commitment.

"Your loyalty and honor are praiseworthy, Sir Broderick." Anais began, "To keep your pledge and bear another's favour when Anais of Alvar has offered hers? Noble, indeed."

Monet clenched her teeth. It seemed Anais's vanity knew no bounds. Of what greater worth was Anais's favour than that of any other maiden upon the earth?

Monet rose from her knees, frowning with the familiar inflammation of temper provoked by Anais.

"I bid you good day, Sir Broderick," Anais said. "May you fare well in the tournament tomorrow."

"Thank you, your highness," Sir Broderick said.

Monet heard Anais's amused giggle. "Pray not as well as whichever knight bears my favour, however."

"Yes, your highness." Monet noted Sir Broderick's response sounded somewhat forced—thick with impatience.

The sound of retreating footsteps was soon followed by a low, angry growl.

Monet gasped as the pavilion flaps burst apart to reveal the infuriated countenance of the Crimson Knight. The enraged expression of indignation on Sir Broderick's face indeed caused Monet to step back and away from him.

"I have done your bidding, Princess, and declined Anais of Alvar's offer…and without striking great offense," he grumbled, his frown deepening still.

"I-I thank you, Sir Broderick," Monet stammered. As the Crimson Knight advanced into his pavilion and toward her, Monet took another step in retreat. "I am in your debt."

"You owe no debt to me, Princess," he said, glaring at her as if she were some threat or enemy he would at any moment strike from existence.

Monet shook her head as despair began to overtake her then. "Yet tomorrow, when Anais sees you bear no favour…what then?"

The Crimson Knight's frown softened from that of fury to one of inquisitiveness.

"Are you in earnest, Princess?" he asked.

"Concerning what, sir?" Monet asked in return.

"Do you truly think I would claim to bear a lady's favour and then appear in the tournament without one?" he asked.

Of a sudden, comprehension pierced Monet's awareness.

"Y-you would bear *my* favour, Sir Broderick?" she asked in an astonished whisper. "You would carry my scarlet into tournament?" Surely he was in jest! Yet the thought of the Crimson Knight entering the jousting arena, the scarlet veil of Princess Monet of Karvana knotted at his arm, sent gooseflesh rippling over Monet's limbs.

"Is not your father my king?" he asked. "Is not your kingdom the same I defend? And are not you also representative of Karvana and King Dacian?"

"Yes, sir," Monet answered.

"Then what more appropriate favour could I carry?"

"B-but the Crimson Knight of Karvana never carries favour…in tournament or battle."

"Then you have charged a maneuver against me no other foe ever has, Princess," he said, "and triumphed."

"I do not act against you, Sir Broderick," Monet defended. "I only sought to gain you as my ally."

He exhaled a heavy breath, shaking his head.

"I am your father's first knight, Princess," he said. The intenseness of his narrowed eyes increased. "I have ever been your ally…from the moment I pledged allegiance to Karvana and its king."

"And it is the reason I came to you," Monet said. "Imagine the people of Karvana—imagine their faces—had their first knight, their most beloved protector…imagine had he ridden into tournament with the Princess of Alvar's favour at his arm."

"I would not have accepted her favour, Princess," Sir Broderick nearly growled, his frown deep across his handsome brow.

"And King Rudolph's fury would have—"

"It is done, Princess," he interrupted, raking strong fingers through raven hair. "Whether or not you trusted my loyalty to my king and kingdom...I did decline, and I will bring honor to your father and all of Karvana...by carrying the favour of their princess into tournament."

"Please do not be angry with me, Sir Broderick," Monet ventured. She did not wish to own his vexation. In truth, she wished to own...

"I am not angry, Princess...not with you," he mumbled. "Believe what I tell you. I do understand the concerns that drove you to approach me...no matter my appearance of fickle temperament."

He did. She knew he did. For all his frowns and menacing glaring, Monet knew Sir Broderick Dougray understood why she had come.

His eyes narrowed as he studied her for a moment. "Do you know the prize King Ivan has named for the tournament champion, Princess?"

"Of course," Monet answered. In truth, she did not know precisely what prize King Ivan had named. Nevertheless, she did not wish to appear ignorant before one so seasoned in battle and tournament. Therefore, having attended many tournaments, Monet assumed the prize would be a golden statue, a finely crafted sword, a high-bred charger, or a thing of worth the like. No doubt a heavy purse would accompany whatever symbol of victory was bestowed as well.

Monet experienced a slight unsettling of her stomach as the Crimson Knight's frown vanished, something akin to a mischievous grin owning his lips.

"And do you still wish to grant me the honor of bearing your favour in the tournament?" he asked.

"Yes," she said, still attempting to appear to own knowledge she did not.

She forced herself to a facade of calm when Sir Broderick's dark brows arched with seeming slight surprise.

"Good. Then you further know the tournament will begin with the Ceremony of Colors...each lady presenting her chosen knight with her favour—a length of silk, a ribbon, or the like in the color significant to only her," he explained.

"Yes. An…an extraordinary beginning, indeed," Monet stammered. In truth, she had never witnessed such a ceremony. In all other tournaments to which she was in attendance, the competing knights were already in possession of their lady's color when they entered the arena. Monet felt her innards churn at having now twice misled the Crimson Knight concerning her knowledge of King Ivan's tournament.

"Indeed," Sir Broderick mumbled, his eyes narrowing with suspicion as he studied her face.

Monet sensed the heated blush of vermillion at her cheeks yet attempted to appear composed.

"And an unusual end, as well," he added.

"Indeed," she said, wondering if perhaps the champion's prize were something other than the customary honors presented.

"Then you will present me with your favour in the morning…at the Ceremony of Colors," he began, "and I will win this tournament for our kingdom, for your father—my king—and for you, your highness."

Monet could not stop a delighted smile from donning her lips. Her heart leapt within her bosom. The Crimson Knight would bear her favour! Sir Broderick Dougray would—for all common appearances—compete in King Ivan's tournament for Princess Monet of Karvana! In truth, Monet had dreamt of just such an occurrence many times. Still, she would not dwell on dreams.

"And you will *accept* my favour when I offer it on the morrow?" she asked, doubt suddenly besting her confidence.

"As eagerly as you will bestow my prize when I am named tournament champion," he said, his grin of mischief broadening. She returned his smile, basking in his pure masculinity, his ethereal comeliness. She wanted to touch him—simply know her hand had pressed to him—to know he was real and not some dream. She was a princess, was she not? Did not princesses own special allowances? Of course they did!

Reaching up, Monet gently placed a dainty hand against one broad shoulder belonging to Sir Broderick Dougray.

"I thank you, Sir Broderick," she said, "for your loyalty to your kingdom…and its king."

"I am—as ever—your servant, Princess," he said, lowering his head in a gesture of respect and compliance.

Monet smiled, her hand warmed by having touched him. She drew the hood of her cloak over her head once more. "I think I am not so afraid of you as I was before coming," she whispered.

Sir Broderick frowned. "What did you have to fear of me?" he asked.

Tilting her head to one side, Monet studied him for a moment—his powerful and handsome countenance causing her heart to flutter.

"Have you forgotten, Sir Broderick?" she asked, stepping from the pavilion. With a breath of light laughter, she pronounced, "There is reason Father christened you the Crimson Knight."

ABOUT THE AUTHOR

Marcia Lynn McClure's intoxicating succession of novels, novellas, and e-books—including *The Visions of Ransom Lake*, *A Crimson Frost*, *The Pirate Ruse*, and most recently *The Chimney Sweep Charm*—has established her as one of the most favored and engaging authors of true romance. Her unprecedented forte in weaving captivating stories of western, medieval, regency, and contemporary amour void of brusque intimacy has earned her the title "The Queen of Kissing."

Marcia, who was born in Albuquerque, New Mexico, has spent her life intrigued with people, history, love, and romance. A wife, mother, grandmother, family historian, poet, and author, Marcia Lynn McClure spins her tales of splendor for the sake of offering respite through the beauty, mirth, and delight of a worthwhile and wonderful story.

BIBLIOGRAPHY

Beneath the Honeysuckle Vine
A Better Reason to Fall in Love
Born for Thorton's Sake
The Chimney Sweep Charm
A Crimson Frost
Daydreams
Desert Fire
Divine Deception
Dusty Britches
The Fragrance of her Name
The Haunting of Autumn Lake
The Heavenly Surrender
The Highwayman of Tanglewood
Kiss in the Dark
Kissing Cousins
The Light of the Lovers' Moon
Love Me
An Old-Fashioned Romance
The Pirate Ruse
The Prairie Prince
The Rogue Knight
Romantic Vignettes—The Anthology of Premiere Novellas
Saphyre Snow
Shackles of Honor
Sudden Storms
Sweet Cherry Ray
Take a Walk with Me
The Tide of the Mermaid Tears
The Time of Aspen Falls
To Echo the Past
The Touch of Sage
The Trove of the Passion Room
The Visions of Ransom Lake

Weathered Too Young
The Whispered Kiss
The Windswept Flame

www.ingramcontent.com/pod-product-compliance
Lightning Source LLC
Chambersburg PA
CBHW060308260626
47160CB00007B/2535